T0368899

WHY DOES LOVE HURT SO GOOD?

WHY DOES LOVE HURT SO GOOD?

*The things we allow and put up with and
go through to have someone to love us*

Ondray Pearson

WHY DOES LOVE HURT SO GOOD?
THE THINGS WE ALLOW AND PUT UP WITH AND
GO THROUGH TO HAVE SOMEONE TO LOVE US

This is a work of fiction. All of the characters, names, incidents, organizations, and dialogue in this novel are either the products of the author's imagination or are used fictitiously.

KJV
Scripture quotations from the Holy Bible, King James Version (Authorized Version). First published in 1611. Quoted from the KJV Classic Reference Bible.

iUniverse books may be ordered through booksellers or by contacting:

iUniverse
1663 Liberty Drive
Bloomington, IN 47403
www.iuniverse.com
1-800-Authors (1-800-288-4677)

Because of the dynamic nature of the Internet, any web addresses or links contained in this book may have changed since publication and may no longer be valid. The views expressed in this work are solely those of the author and do not necessarily reflect the views of the publisher, and the publisher hereby disclaims any responsibility for them.

Any people depicted in stock imagery provided by Getty Images are models, and such images are being used for illustrative purposes only.
Certain stock imagery © Getty Images.

ISBN: 978-1-5320-8495-9 (sc)
ISBN: 978-1-5320-8496-6 (e)

Print information available on the last page.

iUniverse rev. date: 10/28/2019

Contents

Dedication

I am dedicating this book to my friend, Tonya. It is because of your inspiration and support through our reading sessions that I took this direction to present my thoughts and views on love, life and relationships for others to read. With your help, I have been able to reconnect and reacquaint myself with Christ and His teachings as taught to me as a child and young adult by my mother and grandmother.

I want you to know through your love and support the *pieces* of my learning *puzzle* have become a clear *picture*. With your loving spirit and willingness to listen, you have encouraged me to do what *I* felt God had directed me to do which is to share His *Word* with others in a way *I* felt comfortable. The time we spent together and the things we talked about (even though I did most of the talking) told me God felt I was ready and worthy of a friend like you. Through the good and the not so good times, I have cherished every moment with you. I wouldn't change a thing if it meant I'd lose you.

You have, through all our ups and downs, given and shown me love, even when I may not have deserved it at times, and for this, I thank you. So, when I say I love you, know that those are the first few words that come to mind to describe what I feel for you, but not the only ones, to express how you have made a difference in my life. Bottom line sweetheart, I feel blessed to have such a beautiful, smart, intelligent and Godly woman in my life. Thank you for being you, for loving me and allowing me to be me and giving me something I much needed in my life - balance!

Introduction

We all know and can agree that relationships are the cornerstone of human existence. Almost everything accomplished in our life comes from some form of social interaction, and love is no different. When it comes to *love,* it seems no matter how much our *love* experiences may hurt us, we continue to pursue, seek and want it in our lives. Loving someone as we all know, is tricky, and we also know when it's *good,* it is *good,* but when it is *bad,* it hurts. It is factual that hardly anyone finds their true love, gets it right or finds the *one* the first, second or third time they try. It usually takes us some time through dating someone through trial and error. We most certainly will all kiss many frogs before we find that *special ONE* we can call our own.

It's no secret and research shows that as we search for our *soulmate,* we date a lot hoping each time that person we have given our time and love to will be the *one. Relationship Boot Camp,* for lack of a better term, is an essential part of the process. It is here we find out some but not all of the things we are willing to do, go through and put up with in order to have someone love us. We learn a lot about ourselves during this process and sometimes, what we learn is that we are not as *good* as we thought we were. It is in these times that we realize how much being vulnerable can hurt if the person we love doesn't love us back the way we wanted or thought they should have.

We seem to forget sometimes that loving someone comes with both *pain and pleasure.* This is something that in all relationships is unavoidable and at some point, we all will experience them both. The *pleasure* we feel in our relationship is when things are going well or the way we may have hoped they would. It is the *pain* we experience or that suffering feeling we get where we feel *powerless* to stop the hurt that seems impossible. Although pain and suffering sometimes feel the same there is a difference. The difference is *pain* is inevitable. It is something that is going to happen regardless of who you are, but suffering, meaning allowing it to *be* your life going forward is optional. Don't panic. It's just something we all go through when loving someone.

The reason why this is so hard to avoid is that to experience *pain/ pleasure,* we must allow someone into our personal *space.* This kind of risk, meaning allowing someone into your *personal* space, trusting them and allowing them to see your sensitive side, especially when you're not sure if they like you the way you like them can sometimes be hard. However, if we want to experience love and loving someone, we must all do this. The one thing many of us forget and have no control over is that loving someone does not come with refunds or guarantees. I know for most this means nothing until we're the ones hurting at the end of the day.

Okay, before you say, "What's the point?" Why even put yourself out there if there is a chance you will get hurt? To understand the *point* of putting yourself *out* there, you must first understand *why* you even consider it in the first place. The answer is hard to understand, but the truth is you want to love and be loved by someone in your life. Knowing, believing and understanding first that "Loving someone isn't about getting. It's about giving." When you're able to share and come out of your comfort zone, be open to experiencing your mate's world, then you're saying to them, "I want to get to know your wants, needs and desires." You're hoping they reciprocate those feelings.

Many of us foolishly believe in our relationship that we're going to get our way 100% of the time. Believe me, this is not true at all. You must know that any *good* relationship involves and consists of two important things if they are to be successful. These are *compromisation* and *negotiation.* These are two words I suggest you learn and remember if you plan on having and maintaining a good relationship with someone. You will need to be able to give and take, not just take.

Here is a known fact many people consistently forget, "Not all love is good." Yes, in case you didn't know, most of us during our lifetime will waste our love and time on the wrong person in our quest to find, meet and fall in love with the right person. Some will figure this out sooner than later but for the most part, many won't. There will be those people who mistake "lust for love" and think they are the same when they aren't. When you're *in love* with someone, and sexually things are going well, it's hard to look past *good sex* to know if they are the right person for you. You tend to focus on how good *one* part of your relationship is and not the *whole* thing. It is because of your sex blindness that you do not see that you NEED both (love and intimacy) to *grow in love.*

You've heard people say "We fell in love" when what they meant to say was "We were sexually attracted to one another" because no one "falls in love." They are filled with infatuation more than anything else. Yes, there is a difference. All of this happens because many of us confuse *good sex* with being the same or equal to *love*. Don't get me wrong. Sex is a good part of the relationship, but a long-lasting, loving relationship has more components to it than just sex.

Sadly, though and I understand no one wants to be alone, but the fact is there are many people in relationships right now not because they are *in love* but more because they "don't want to be alone." Listen, it feels worse when you give 100% of yourself, and they hurt you anyway, not by accident but on purpose. When this happens we often ask ourselves, "Am I ready to be hurt like that again by someone else?" "Am I ready to handle another rejection from someone I care for?" It is okay to question if you're ready to try it again. Life hurts sometimes, but the good news is we often survive and live to do it again smarter (well, most of us). Let's face it, love is just like gambling, and just like playing the lotto, you can't win if you don't participate; and like the lotto, sometimes we win, and sometimes we don't. One thing is for sure, if we do not gamble, meaning, put ourselves out there or get ourselves in the game, for many of us, we've already lost.

It's true what they say... finding, meeting and falling in love these days is harder sometimes than finding a job. When you are single for a long time, you start to think and feel you're never going to meet anyone to love or to love you. It is during these times we must remember and believe, "There is someone out there for everyone." The question yet to be answered is "Where do we find them?" There is no way to know when we fall for someone if they are the right or wrong person for us. "Will they pick us up or drag us down?" "Are they going to hurt our heart?" It is hard to tell sometimes. I can say this though, *if* we want to be loved by someone, we must take a chance and hope the person we like likes us enough to care for us more so than they would hurt us.

I am not saying if you're single to get with just anyone. I am asking for you to choose wisely when choosing your next mate. Base your selection more on attributes and not solely on looks alone. The way to do this is to *know* before you meet someone what it is you want, and what it is you are willing to give to be with someone. Many will not admit it, but a lot of people looking for love will call someone and pay someone *per minute*. You know who I am talking to. They trust these people to tell them their future concerning love, life and money instead of trusting and asking for God's help. To some that's crazy. I know many people aren't religious, but for those who are, God can do anything you ask Him to do for you. He said so in the Bible.

Asking Him to help prepare you for the right person is an excellent place to start. If you're one of the ones relying on these people to tell you your future, you would have a better chance and odds by flipping a coin. I am not trying to knock someone's hustle, but the fact is there is no magic ball or spell anyone can give you that is going to help you (1) avoid pain in a relationship, (2) FIND the RIGHT one, (3) fall and stay in love, (4) make anyone stay with you no matter how good the sex is and (5) avoid anyone verbally, physically and mentally abusive in your relationship. Listen to me and get this in your head. Good sex is not *love*. A loving relationship involves a whole lot more components. Good sex with someone can get you into a relationship, but without love and a good friendship as your foundation to build and grow on, it will not last.

I am not saying you can't have both good sex and love at the same time because I found it with my wife. When my wife and I were dating, I set her mind at ease when I told her that I wanted more with her. I told her that I wanted both love and sex at the same time not separately. I didn't want a one night stand; I want her forever. I say this because people enter your life for one of four reasons: To *add, subtract, multiply* or *divide.*

Let me explain what I am saying. In a relationship situation, your potential mate is either going to *add* something to your life that's positive or *subtract,* meaning take away or bring you down. When I say *multiply,* I mean in a sense where you and your mate are taking steps in a direction that *grows* your relationship. Now, this could be by having kids, helping you start or grow your business, etc. When I say *divide*, I am saying *divide* in the way they cause problems in your life where there weren't any before, such as creating problems with friends and family you were close to *before* they came into your life. Now you find yourself at odds and you don't even know why. These kinds of people are dangerous in your life because their goal is to divide you from all that makes you happy, not add to your happiness. They are a self-centered, insecure and selfish person who is no good for you.

You, because you're *in love* with them, will not see this when you two are together. You will start to see there is a problem when you're with those who you've known and your mate notices that love seems to steal your attention from him/her. You will see then that they like *drama* for no other reason than to keep it going. If you find yourself arguing with your mate and you have no idea what point they are trying to make or why you are having this conversation, then you have someone in your life looking to *divide* you from all things and people that make you smile. In that sense, they are not the *one* for you.

It has been said that some people enter in your life for a *Season,* meaning just for a little while. During that time that they are there, their reason for being there will begin to show you why they are with you but not give you a clue for how long. An excellent example of this is my ex-girlfriend. We had known one another for a year and a half and as a couple for less than a year. During that period, and I wasn't aware of this until much later, her purpose for being there became clear. You see, I was turning 50 years old and she (and my mother) suggested I go to the doctor to get a full body checkup. Come to find out going to see the doctor was a damn good idea because I found out after the examination that I had Stage 2 Cancer.

It was because of her persistence that I found this out. It is one of the reasons I am here sharing this story with you. For whatever reason, I am not sure, we decided to part. We are still close friends to this day though. It wasn't until I met my future wife that I realized that my ex was brought into my life so that she would get me to go to the doctor. My wife would continue the process of getting me better because she was the one I was supposed to marry. My ex was a *stand-in* if you will for a *season.* She helped me, did her part and moved on. God had yet to present me with the *one* I would meet, fall in love with and marry. It is because of God, my lovely wife, the excellent doctors and my family that I was able to beat Cancer. I tell you this because even in a bad situation, my faith in God got me through. It was God who, when He thought I was ready to love and be loved presented her in my life.

Breakups are hard but contrary to what we want to believe, after a *break-up,* no matter how good or bad it may have been, if we're honest with ourselves, we learn something from it. A lot of soul searching is where this comes from. Self-evaluation and being honest about our role in the relationship good or bad, will help us to be able to move forward with our life or to re-enter a new relationship. It is then and only then that you will be able to understand what to do and not to do with a new person who trusts you with their heart. The reason I say this is because many of us have a hard time admitting we had anything to do with our break-up.

If we sincerely want to be better for someone else, we must take this time to correct our past mistakes, change our behavior, change our way of thinking on a few things, understand and listen before reacting to what we think we heard. I can tell you that lying to yourself will not help you change your behavior which is YOUR problem, but it will help and guarantee you repeat and get the same results as before. If you find yourself continually saying after every relationship encounter you have, "What's wrong with these people that they can't just accept me for who I am?" (**FYI:** You need to change YOUR behavior because 95% of the time it's you and not them.) The key to limiting mistakes starts with you!

You must put together in your head an *adjustable* plan. A plan that as you grow and learn more definitely what you feel you want and need from and with your mate, you'll be able to *adjust* it. Adjust it without losing most things you do want and desire in your mate and your relationship to be and feel happy with them. It is not uncommon to hear someone say they have no clue what they want in a person. On the contrary, it is a normal and sincere answer. The truth is hardly anyone really *knows* what they want from another person to be happy with them. Most people, when they do attempt to answer the question, often confine their responses to *surface* wants and needs rather than deeper needs. Our surface needs are those attributes we are attracted to when we first *see* someone we are interested in in the beginning. It is not because we know they are the right one for us. It's because we are naturally attracted to them.

I agree that *surface* wants need to play a role in our initial attraction because we see them first before we get to know them. If the relationship is going to last however, you need more than good looks. You need someone with whom you are compatible and have chemistry in order to grow. If you go off of looks alone, you will *be* alone shortly afterward. Al Green once wrote a song called *Love and Happiness*. To understand *how* love makes you do things you usually wouldn't do, the line in the song where it says, "Love will make you do wrong," and when you think about your past actions you will agree and laugh because you never thought you would "do wrong." It doesn't matter what I just said, many of you will continue to select your mates on their looks and figure after the fact that you wanted more from them.

Many people believe when they get with someone who *looks good* that they will *treat* them good and love them the way they deserve to be loved. Honestly, this is not always (if at all) true. I learned from an early age when I used to spend summers at my Aunt Sherry's house. As a young man, I would fall in love with every pretty face I saw and the women I met. Seeing me go through this, she pulled me aside one day and said, "Never fall in love only with a woman's body; fall in love with her soul. Once you're in love with her soul, everything else about her becomes much more beautiful and will last longer."

If you read your Bible, it tells you this in **Proverbs 17:24**, (KJV). It speaks to men choosing their mates wisely, "Wisdom is before him that hath understanding; but the eyes of a fool are in the ends of the earth." When we choose unwisely, we end up paying the price for it in various ways such as giving up half of your money and paying alimony for years to keep her in a lifestyle you helped create for her to mention a couple. Listen to what it says and understand you need to (as do women) look beyond the surface of someone when selecting a mate.

I am telling you that beauty and a beautiful body can fade, money can and will be made and spent (you can even go broke in the process) and if those are the only things you require to be happy, what would you be then once these things are gone? Unhappy most likely and the reason why is because *love* and *being in love* with someone must go much deeper than beauty and gadgets. Everyone likes the *new new* but once the *newness* of the attraction has worn off what do you have then? I will tell you, someone you don't want to be with anymore. However, since you've invested your time, love and money you have no idea what to do to get out of it without looking like a total a-hole. If you would have watched for more profound *qualities* from your *list* that you once claimed you wanted and needed in your mate in order to be happy with them, your relationship would have lasted longer. These are some of the things along with additional questions, you should be asking yourself to get a better picture of who you are possibly considering as a mate.

For women, the questions asked must be direct, and the answers given must satisfy you because it gives you a little better insight in who you are considering letting into your world. Questions such as:

(1) Does the guy have a job? (This tells you if he would be able to take care of a family.)

(2) How long has he been there? (This tells you about his work ethic and if he is stable or a job hopper.)

(3) How long was his last relationship, and when did it end? (This tells you about his commitment level if he is a long-term person or a one-night situation.)

(4) Are you looking for a long-term relationship that could lead to marriage? (This question helps you understand and know if long-term is something he is looking for because in most situations when a woman asks this question, she is considering and possibly wants to get married at some point.)

(5) Do you have kids and if not, do you want kids? (This question is because one or both of you want kids. Either you don't have any or you have kids and do not wish to have any more.)

Depending on your reasoning or preference you, (the woman), if you want to have children, you must be clear on this matter because if they don't want children, it doesn't make sense to continue seeking a relationship knowing you're not going to get what you want from them. If you sleep with them hoping that your sex will change their minds, don't be surprised if it doesn't and you feel used. Yes, I know many, if not all, men will see that you want children and think if they promise and agree with you, they can and will sleep with you. Here is the trick, if you stop, look, listen and realize they aren't telling you the truth, don't sleep with them thinking that is going to make them change their minds because most times it doesn't. Don't continue seeing them because all you're doing is setting yourself up for heartache.

At some point in your "getting to know you" conversation, you must have a "financial conversation," a discussion on where you both stand concerning the debt you are bringing into the relationship if you're planning to be a couple. I know it sounds risky, but you cannot be afraid to talk about money at some point. Maybe not on the first date, but if you're considering getting *seriously* involved, this has to happen. If you don't, you will find yourselves becoming a couple living and acting singly; meaning you are paying your bills and he/she is paying theirs. This doesn't help you grow in your relationship. It hurts your future here merely because some people, once they find out how much debt the other owes, they may or may not want to take it on. If you both cannot come to some agreement to work together on this matter, it will cause a division in your relationship.

I say this because this is something we all do and believe is right. A good-looking person doesn't translate to or mean that they will love you the way you deserve to be loved. It only says you are attracted to them and possibly them to you. Your search for love must be more in depth than a person's looks. Chemistry and compatibility are just a couple of *qualities* that help your relationship stand the test of time. They are the foundation on which you get through those "not so good times" we all will, at some point, have to deal with.

Don't be that person who "goes along with whatever" to be in a relationship with someone. If your relationship doesn't provide you with at least 80% percent of what you NEED and FEEL makes you happy, then why are you really in it? Stop foolishly thinking that good sex with someone is your (a woman's) gateway to *changing* your man because it hardly ever works. If this is where you are in your current friendship **STOP!** Realize you're not ready to be in a relationship with anyone unless you're thing is to be "following, wanting nothing in life, wanting always to be begging them for what you want and need to be happy."

I know what I am saying is harsh, but it is better to realize this now and stop the foolishness before it starts and consumes you. Stop before you reach a point where *YOU* start to think, act and feel that what you're doing is *NORMAL*. It is better to be rejected at this point in the friendship then down the road in the relationship. If you don't do this and you get hurt, blame yourself. The other person never knew, and very rarely will they ask you if they love you how you want to be *loved*. It's like the saying goes, "You don't know what you don't know." It is okay if you don't know but before you do something with someone, try and understand something because if not, *THEY* will tell you what you want.

I know this is hardly new news. Your *wants and needs* should never be based on what Hollywood, television or romantic novels say they should be. I am stressing this because if you have a clue of what it is you want, you would be able to dismiss the "flash, glitter and gold" that may have attracted you to that person in the first place. Can you see with clarity that the words they're speaking match their actions?

Just remember, "You can do badly by yourself." These skills are invaluable, especially when you are dating. You know we all *act* right when we first meet someone (well most of us), and many of us are on our *best* behavior. Our "representative" says the right things, does the right things, etc. because that is what "they" were hired to do for "us." They were hired to make us look good, seem desirable, and get us in! If our "representative" does their job well, the person you're trying to attract or get with will walk away from your first meeting saying to themselves, "Where has this person been all my life?" Many of us know about the "representative" and what they are there for, but still many of us (mostly women I am afraid to say) get drawn in.

Here is why this happens more often than any of us want to admit.

Because we are so attracted to them, and tired of being alone, we will believe almost any dream they tell us. Many of us know there is a good chance they are not telling us the truth, but we accept it all just as long as it sounds good and *could* be true at some point in a relationship. Why do you ask? Well, for those who are being honest with themselves, you're dying inside when you "think" you've found the right person to settle down with. You pray they take you off the "single market carousel" you've been on too long. Why? Because you're sick and tired of going home to an empty house. You're tired of people questioning why someone like you with the way you look is still single. When you do get in a relationship, hell, you LOOK for anyone who knew you were alone, to tell them you have someone EVEN if the person you're saying this to never asked nor seemed interested at all. You do this because you are happy. It feels good to be loved by someone who you *love*.

Think I am lying? Then answer this question, "How many times when you were interested in someone, and you SAW obvious signs that they weren't the *one* did you still get involved with them anyway?" You told yourself, "I got needs," as the reason why you did. Did it work out? Too often, we allow and convince ourselves to do things because we are lonely. A lot of single people will tell you if asked, "Why are you single?" that they like being alone. What they are saying because it is none of anyone's business is, "I haven't found anyone to put up with me yet. Don't feel bad. I don't, and the reason I don't is that I know I am not the only one who has played or been played by someone I cared for while trying to find true love and someone to truly love me for me, now am I?"

Listen, there is no reason to feel foolish for all you've done in your search for love. We've all been played and played someone. When that feeling of love hits you, there is NOTHING you wouldn't do to catch and keep it. It's why asking *valued* questions at the beginning of our friendship are so important. We need to stop relying on hope as a strategy and believing that a good relationship with someone is going to just happen by chance; we need to help ourselves by getting to know a person's mind before we get to know them in the bedroom. Not everyone wants to be someone's "one night stand" or "thot" but if you do, then you do. You need to understand, "You cannot change the way people see you most times, but what you can change is the way a person treats you ALL the time."

You cannot say after the fact that "they used me" or "played with your head or heart." If you accepted the lies and got involved with them anyway, that's on you. *"People can only do to you what you allow them to do."* You can't gamble and call foul when the results aren't in your favor, well, you can, but it will not help or change the fact that you chose to gamble without understanding what game you're playing. Think about it this way. You try new things in life because you want to *see* if you like them. If you do, there is a good chance you will do them again. But if you try it and you don't like it, and you repeat it knowing you didn't like it, who are you going to blame?

There is no *one size fits all* answer to prevent you from being hurt by someone you're interested in or love, but you can help yourself out by taking the time to get to know who you're dealing with.

Take things slow until you feel comfortable with them to share your personal space. Don't allow anyone to tell you what you *feel* for them or how you should react to them telling you they care for you; you control you, not them. How many people that you've dated or slept with turned out to be the opposite of who you thought they were? How did it feel learning this AFTER THE FACT? You felt tricked, foolish and used for *trying* and *believing* in the many lies they told you. I have often said to people, "Stop collecting red flags like they are valuable when they are not." Holding on to them means you don't mind being hurt by this person. How many times has a person told you, "When a person shows you who they are, you need to believe them?" Listen and believe me if your car or home is full of red flags that you have collected like souvenirs or collector items, then you need to accept the fact that you ignored the warnings. You choose to gamble, thinking you can beat the system; then you must also take the fault and not blame someone else for your foolish choices.

With so many looking for love, it is no surprise that we would use the latest technology to help us. With technology, online dating, texting, video chat, etc. we have numerous ways to find, meet and communicate with those we are trying to get to know better, date and be with in a relationship. Sure, many people use these methods to *hook up*. It is fair to say the various online dating services and social media sites are helpful at times for the most part, but it is still tough to know who is real and who is not, who is ready to settle down and get married and who is just playing games looking for a *hookup* only. It is okay to be skeptical because you don't know who you're talking to until you meet them at some point. Regardless of the risk, one thing that is crystal clear for us is *we* all want to *love* and *be loved*, and many times we are willing to gamble a few dollars on paid websites to try and meet someone.

Side note: If you paid to get on a website to meet people, you're hoping to find someone for real. Stop telling people you paid only to meet people because you're lying to yourself. Even though sometimes we find ourselves alone because we don't want to be a fool for someone knowingly, we prefer not to be alone. It is getting harder and harder to find *one* person to be with simply because many of us rather have *quantity* than *quality* meaning many instead of one. Some people say, "We are not meant to be with just one person." For some people, this is a true statement. With all the games people play today, it is no surprise that the phrase "single by choice" has become the "go-to" phrase when someone asks you the question, "Why are you still single?"

As we all know, there are many reasons why a person would be single, and it is not always because they aren't relationship material. A couple reasons that come to mind are someone who has just gotten out of a bad relationship or they realized what they thought they had just wasn't. Many people are single because they are tired of all the foolishness they've dealt with in a past relationship to a point where they need a break, some alone time to regenerate and start over again.

In many cities, there is a 5 to 1 ratio of women to men, meaning there are five women to every one man. Men in these cities know this and use this to their advantage to act up and disrespect the women they are dating. They feel that they can act out because they know there are four other women left to get with if this one doesn't work out. For most women, the fear of loneliness seems to be stronger than the *need* to be loved and respected by the person who claims to love them. It's not right for any man to disrespect any woman. No woman should ever be disrespected, degraded or physically or mentally abused to be with any man. Although it's not right, it is also not all their fault. Women have a say so in how they want their man to treat them. They don't have to be ruled by men to feel special or loved. Good men want to treat them respectfully if they would allow them to.

Merely sitting down, talking and, more importantly, listening to one another could help you learn a few things you both want in your mate (those seeking godly people). So, instead of doing this to avoid falling or feeling trapped in a relationship with a person you don't want to be with because you don't want to be alone, you go with the flow and end up being or allowing those people to treat you any old kind of way. Then you blame them when it isn't what YOU wanted or felt it should be.

Listen, if you're someone I am talking to, please understand that all the self-help books in the world cannot help you turn your life around but asking for His help *can* help you. Understand and know if you're in a difficult situation, "Where you are in your life now is not where you will stay." My grandmother often said to me, "People going through storms need to be still." She meant that sometimes we must be *still,* be patient and not rush. We need to believe and know that when God feels you're ready (meaning a relationship) He will present someone in your view to see. Think about it. If you've done things your way and you haven't gotten the results you were seeking, why are you still relying on yourself to figure out what you want and need? The Bible tells us this in **Proverbs 3:5,** (KJV), "Trust in the LORD with all thine heart; and lean not unto thine own understanding."

I suggest (if you believe in the Bible) that if you are genuinely ready to change the way you have been doing things, then ask through prayer for God's help. Be sincere, be specific and ask Him for what you want. He will hear you and give you what you need. Do your part; work on yourself and get ready. It doesn't matter if you have not spoken to Him in a while or been in His house. He still has His hands on you, and He hears you. We are His children, and He loves us. He said so, and He doesn't lie or break His promises. We need to remind ourselves daily that it is all because of Him that we can wake up and seek the things (such as love) we all feel we want and need in our lives. We need to stop only calling on Him when things are going badly. Also, we need to thank Him when things are not so good because it is ALL because of Him that we are among the living and can try over and over again to seek love.

Remember that your relationship is built on *trust*. Having this conversation in the beginning could do a few things, (1) you would have understood what you were facing as a couple and decided *IF* it was something you could handle together; (2) you would have been able to *know* how the two of you were going to make it work as a couple. In some cases, a person who gets involved with someone and learns "after the fact" of the other person's entire debt, it could and most likely will impact your relationship in a negative way. For some, it is a "deal-breaker."

When you do meet someone, and you both are feeling out one another, do not allow your friends or family to run them away because they think they are not your type. Your relationship isn't about what your friends want or what they believe. It is about what you (and your mate) think and want with one another. People comment all the time, so it isn't surprising. Friends and family often complain and try to make you choose to spend more of your time with them instead of your partner by saying things like, "You don't have time for us since you got your girlfriend/boyfriend, we don't matter anymore?"

It seems worse for those when they get married. God tells us *how* to live as a married couple and *Man* has shown us *his* views of how we should live which mostly are not Godly. The question is which one will you choose, His plan or Man's plan? God's plan is evident in **Ephesians 5:31**, (KJV), "For this cause shall a man leave his father and mother and shall be joined unto his wife, and they two shall be one flesh." In **Matthew 19:5**, (KJV), it says "And said, For this cause shall a man leave father and mother, and shall cleave to his wife: and they twain shall be one flesh?" In **Mark 10:7**, (KJV), "For this cause shall a man leave his father and mother, and cleave to his wife;" His plan for your relationship seems better than listening to outside people who have not invested anything in YOUR relationship.

Your friends are hoping you choose *Man's* way because following man's way could break up your relationship. Once you break it off, you hear them say, "They weren't your type anyway. You're better off without them." Making you feel foolish if you decide you want to fix or repair your relationship because you are thinking, "What would they think of me?" You're hesitant because you know when you two weren't in a *good* place you talked about him to another family member. Now since you have calmed down and talked things out, you realize you were wrong. Now if you did get back together, you're more concerned about what they'd think about you being with him/her again because you know they now are talking about him based on all you've told them. This process will continue to happen time and time again only because you will not draw the line between your friendships/ family and marriage. I know it sounds silly to say, but you know it's true.

Your so-called friends will spend their time and energy like it was their job (they are not getting paid to do) breaking down your relationship and searching for reasons as to why you should not be with the person who you're dating. The funny thing is people like this never realize they should put this effort into finding someone for them to love. If they did, they would have no time to mess with you. The bottom line is this. If you two have chemistry and are compatible, guess what? You are with someone who could be a good match for you. Living your relationship in God's way keeps you connected to Him and creates an atmosphere that yields success in most marriages.

Now perfect or not, the strength of your relationship is in the way you handle the rough patches, peaks and valleys when you agree to disagree. How you deal with these things will, in most cases, either strengthen or break down your relationship. The steps taken within that moment will outline and determine the future and direction of your relationship. "A good relationship is only as good as the foundation it stands on." There is no better feeling than to know the person you love loves you the same way. So, if you have an excellent foundation very few outsiders will be able to hurt it; the more positive things you add, the stronger it gets.

Many of us have a hard time dealing with and handling "ripples in the water" (problems in their relationship). Many people tend to panic when they are not sure how to fix or address issues in their relationship. The unknown sometimes makes us act a little crazy, scared, upset, unsure and unknowing of what to do next. It's in this moment that we question and wonder, "What have I gotten myself into?" By now it is too late; you're in it. The question is what are you going to do next?

Depending on what is going on with your life/relationship, you might find yourself asking out loud during this period of uneasiness and unsureness, "How can the very feeling that has made me feel so good inside turn around and hurt me so badly?" It is a common question that is asked and has no real answer. It is no secret, though. We often, with very little success, try and understand the complexities of the emotions we go through when loving someone. The one thing that is crystal clear and will *never change* however, is the fact that we will never fully understand why with the pleasures that love brings also comes pain, but we do know that "Love unexpressed is meaningless."

"Why does love hurt so good?" It's a question that has many answers with very little understanding. We've been told that *love* and *loving* someone isn't supposed to hurt if it's true love. Unfortunately and realistically it can and sometimes does. Only those who have experienced love before or are currently experiencing it can understand *ALL* the craziness, the ups and downs, the emotional ride and unexplained things many of us are willing to do to have someone in our lives to love us.

It's hard to explain to someone on the outside looking in "why" a person would stay with someone who isn't treating or loving them the way they should. Many would say that staying is foolish, not healthy or normal and many of them would be right. But for you to understand the "why," you must experience *loving* someone first. Until you do, you have no idea the power that *love* has over many of us and all the countless *adjustments* we are willing to make, the *bad behaviors* we will allow and the *sacrifices* we will go through to feel loved by someone.

Within these stories, you will read, experience, understand and learn what all those seeking love would do, allow and put up with to have someone to love them. For those involved, "right and wrong" were known and understood but served a minimal purpose in *their* quest for happiness. Sex, lies, deception, betrayal, abuse and infidelity were just a few traits used to obtain what they *thought* would make them happy in their relationship. As you read, you will at some point have to "rethink what you thought you knew" about love because contrary to what many people think and believe "Not all love is good love that we receive from those 'we' love."

Session One

I Never Knew Love Like This

It's Monday morning, July 01, 2019, my youngest daughter's birthday. It's around 8:30 a.m. and I am on my way to work, and like most mornings here in Atlanta, Georgia, I find myself stuck in heavy traffic on Highway 285. You would think after living here for over 15 years, I would have gotten used to the amount of traffic by now, but I haven't. As I make my way downtown to radio station K103 to do my daily talk show, *Why Does Love Hurt So Good?* I am still amazed after ten years of doing my show all that we, as people are willing to do, put up with and go through to be loved.

It's hard sometimes, but I find both my private practice and hosting my show satisfying. I feel it is because I enjoy helping people with their relationship issues and concerns. The not knowing every day what questions I will be asked or what will be said is exciting and fun. Being on the radio five days a week, two hours a day and running my practice would seem to most to be a lot, but to me, it is relaxing at best. My private practice allows me one-on-one time with people and time to get to know them without rushing. The big difference between the two is the radio show requires instant answers whereas my private clients allow me days, sometimes weeks to solve their issues.

For those who call in, I try to provide advice to them based on their question, and not to stray too far from what they are asking. I do my best to answer the listener's questions without judging or preaching to them. I am sharing advice on a real issue that is important to them. If I feel the caller's issues or concerns need a little more attention, I will ask them between commercial breaks if they would like to make an appointment so that we could talk more. Understanding the caller's questions and taking their concerns seriously, I try to be as courteous and respectful as I can while listening. By doing so, they are more willing to listen to all I want to say to help their situation.

I know that as individuals, we react differently. So to better answer and advise callers or my clients, I must listen to them individually and assess their concerns. I cannot group their issues into a category as if one answer fits all when it doesn't. Yes, there are moments when callers or listeners disagree with the advice, and I am okay with it. Everyone has their own opinion and right to agree or disagree. It is something I expect. I am not offended. It's part of my profession.

Overall, I use my experiences and insight to help those listening and those I work with to find alternative ways of handling and understanding their pain, issues, concerns and feelings in their situation. If my advice can help others move past their past pains and hurts in their relationships, then I feel I have done my job.

I remember at lunch one day a staff member told me she felt men lie too much. She was single because it was hard for her to trust them. I said to her that I understood and to some degree, I agree with her, but she should not blame all men. I told her I didn't feel most people go into a relationship planning to lie, cheat or hurt their mate, but situations change and things happen for whatever reason. Sometimes people get to a point in their relationship where they feel "the grass is greener on the other side," and they stray, only later to find out they were wrong. Not all people are the same, though; many stay with and are faithful to their mates.

The people who feel this way are getting attention from someone who sees an opportunity when you're having issues in your relationship. These "listeners" sometimes play on the information you tell them and flip it by giving you or promising you they would behave differently if they were with a person like you. You don't see this because you are stuck on the fact your mate isn't acting right. You do not have a clue that they are playing you to get with you.

Sometimes your friend of the opposite sex can sound very caring about your problems but at the same time be working at convincing you to leave what you have and try something new... meaning them! In this situation, when you are having issues with your mate, I suggest caution when you're telling someone about your problems. If you are a woman talking to a man and he is feeling you out but has never made a move because he knew you had a man, he will use this as HIS opportunity to get you with him. He will sympathize with you, claim he understands what you're going through all while trying to get you to leave your man and get with him.

If it is a girlfriend you're talking to and she is interested in your man, she will do the same– sympathize with you while at the same time plot on how to take your man. I know you don't want to tell your family because (1) you don't want them all in your business, (2) you don't want to hear, "I told you so" and (3) you don' need them to tell you "how" to run your relationship. I know what you're thinking, "Not everyone is like that, right?" I agree, but this kind of thing happens more often than many people will admit. So, you are asking who you can trust?

When I found myself at a crossroads in my relationship like this, and I felt I was unable to handle it alone, I remember something my mother told me growing up, "When you feel what you are going through is too much to bear, handle or carry, ask God to help you." For those who believe in Him, I suggest you seek Him. Usually, many of us only call or praise Him when things aren't going well in our lives. We all need to call on Him, thank Him and acknowledge Him daily regardless, in order to let Him know we appreciate the fact that He loves us unconditionally and watches over us. Thank Him for allowing us the opportunity to experience life itself. I promise you, if you ask for His help, He will help you.

3

After my show, I usually return to my office. Sometimes I have a session or two scheduled in the afternoon. But today, I get out early, so I am taking my family to my wife's favorite restaurant for dinner. It's only a few weeks until our fourth anniversary, which is on August 2nd. I've already gotten her anniversary gifts. My wife told me one thing she wanted, but she has no idea of all I ended up getting her. She hasn't asked me straight out if I have gotten her a gift, but she has been hinting and taking me to Kay Jewelers in Lenox Mall to "window shop." When she goes in, she goes straight to this diamond necklace and tells me how good it would look on her (*wink, wink*).

Okay, people, even Ray Charles could see what she was doing; but I went along. What she didn't know was that I had gotten it for her already weeks ago. I had some particular work done to it. I had them put three beautiful stones placed in a design very similar to the style she currently has to represent the number of years we have been together. I know she is not big on jewelry, but I feel she will like this one (I hope). What she doesn't know, and I can hardly wait to see the look on her face is when I surprise her with a honeymoon in Hawaii for two weeks as the fourth anniversary present to renew our wedding vows.

I invited her best friend and her husband and asked them to not say a word to her, which will be hard for those two. I felt this would be great because early in our marriage in our situation, we were unable financially to take a real honeymoon the way I thought we should have. I feel she will positively be surprised, and she deserves this. She has not spoken about not going anywhere special, so this is long overdue. She is the reason I work so hard (and will continue to work even harder) just to put a smile on her face and to show and express how much I love and appreciate her agreeing to marry and be my wife three years earlier.

On our way to dinner, I remembered a conversation I had with a caller the week prior on the subject of gift-giving for your spouse. I said to him that some foolishly believe the more money they spend on their wife, the more she will love them. Many feel the more expensive it is, the better it is, and this isn't always true. He's surprised when he doesn't get the reaction he thought he would from what they got. He thought he had hit a home run. He reacts bewildered and confused. It makes you ask, "Was he shopping for her or him?" I mentioned to the caller that gifts should be thoughtful and from the heart not something given to get a reaction out of someone. I told him, if you pay attention, your woman will provide you with "cues and clues" as to what she wants, where it is and in some cases the cost. Too many men think, "The more expensive the gift, the better." This is not always the case. It could be expensive and the wrong gift; how is that better? The best way to get this somewhat right most times is to listen to your woman. I am not saying you cannot surprise her because she would appreciate the effort every time. Men who know this will purposely do the opposite.

Here is why he called in to begin with:

It was his wife's birthday, and she had mentioned that she wanted a ring she had had her eye on for a while. He knew what kind of ring it was she was talking about, and he was prepared to get it until he talked to his friends at the sports bar one night. He mentioned to them the ring and even showed them a picture of it to see what they thought. When the guys saw it, they messed with him because of the price; it was under $500. They told him he should get her a big expensive ring instead of that cheap one, so he did. Remember he knew what she wanted, but his friends convinced him to get something else. He said when he gave her an expensive ring on her birthday in front of his friends and family, she looked happy, but it wasn't the reaction he was hoping for since the ring was much more expensive than the one she picked out. He said she acted like she was happy, but he could see she wasn't, and he didn't understand why.

It wasn't until after everyone was gone that he asked her if she liked her ring. She said to him, "I appreciate it and it looks good, but I had my heart set on the ring I had shown you." Without thinking, he said he told her, "This one is bigger and more expensive," but it made no difference to her. He then realized that he got the ring because his friends laughed at the cheaper one. It was the cheaper one that she wanted however and even though it wasn't as expensive or as big, it was the one she wanted. The next day without her knowing, he returned the expensive ring to the store and got her the ring she wanted. When he gave it to her, he got the reaction he thought he was going to get. Getting something he wanted her to have and not what she wanted was not the way to go.

He said he wasn't clear why the more expensive gift wasn't received well. Since we spoke, he understood the reason he needed to give her what she wanted and why it made her happy. He says she wears it like it is the other ring proudly.

I explained to him that as a man, you must understand when you are buying your mate a gift, it's not about what you think she will like, it's about what she wants that matters. At this time in your relationship, you're past the stage where you can get her something you think is cute and will make her smile. During that time of your dating, she accepted whatever you got as a small gesture because you were trying to impress her and at that moment it was the "thought" that counted not the actual gift.

Now that you two have been together for a while she expects, demands and deserves more than an afterthought gift with very little consideration put into it. She expects you to be more attentive and know something about her, her likes and dislikes in shoes, clothes, restaurants, etc. In other words, put forth the kind of effort you did when you were *trying* to get with her *AFTER* you have gotten her if you want her to know you genuinely care for her. Not all meaningful gifts have to be overly expensive to be the right gift.

All men need to understand this if they want to get this right. If you are a guy reading this right now, I can almost bet you are scratching your head, disagreeing and thinking you know what your lady wants already, right? You probably think I have done okay so far, and this information is for those who don't know how to please their woman. For those who are doing okay, keep it up, but all men need to know and understand that women will not always want the same thing. If you think this way, you may not keep your woman too much longer. Being creative can help you sometimes in your relationship. Many women I asked confirmed and said this phrase, "It's the little things a man does that makes them happy most of the time."

I am not suggesting women can't help a brother out from time to time. Listen ladies, men are not psychics, palm or mind readers. They need your help! Very few men will pick up on or even care about what it is you want or need without you telling them a few times. Women often say that they want their man just to know what they want, what to do, how to act and to act right. So, my question to those women thinking this way would be, "How can they know these things or do these things you want if you have never told them what you want?" For women, if you do not tell your man how you want to be loved or what you want, he will not figure it out. What they will do without your help is spend the time you two are together "guessing" by trial and error to see what makes you smile, happy, sad or mad in hopes of getting it right.

I ended our conversation by saying, "If you want to understand your wife better as it relates to gifts (or anything else), start by communicating with her when you are unclear about what she wants and needs. After a while, you will see and know a few things yourself. You will start thinking about her that way and pleasing her and keeping a smile on her face will become second nature for you. If you do this consistently, it will let her know emotionally that you are in tune with her wants and needs, which will make her happy. In most cases, we all must have the woman *define* "happy" so that we

7

can get it right. They must also do things to keep us happy as well because we're in the relationship to please one another. Remember what they say, "A happy wife makes a happy life."

Well, here I am. I parked and headed to the elevator upstairs. During my ride, I had a quick thought about a new client, Ms. Clark. She was someone who had called in on the show, but I felt, based on what we spoke about, that she could use a personal one-on-one. After we ended our call, I gave her the number to make an appointment to talk more. I am not sure why that popped in my head.

(Dink)

As I walk in the lobby, Wendy, the intern greets me.

Wendy is speaking: Hello, Mr. Pearson, how are you doing this morning?

Mr. Pearson is speaking: I am doing okay. I take it everything is going well with you? I heard you had been asked to come on permanently?

Wendy is speaking: Yes, starting next month. I've been here for six months as an intern, and I am happy to be put on staff and that I will be working with your crew. Come on in, and I will get you ready because you go on shortly, do you need anything?

Mr. Pearson speaking: No, I am okay.

As I enter the booth, I can see and hear that my show was coming up next.

K Rock is speaking: We're back. It's time to close out the show, but up next on K103 is our Relationship Consultant, Mr. Ondray Pearson, with his segment on **Why does love hurt so Good?** For those who do not know, his new book is out now and titled, <u>Why Does Love Hurt So Good</u>? I got an advance copy, and it is a page-turner. I enjoyed it. It's very well written, insightful and on point. This book is very different from his last project, <u>*Wrong Turn (Diary of a Good Man)*</u>. This book explores and shows the many sides of love as well as various points of view from very different perspectives. You need to make sure you get your copy when it comes out. Anyway, I enjoyed it. Up next, after the commercial, is Mr. Ondray Pearson. I've got to go. My time is up. I will talk to you tomorrow. Have a great rest of your day.

During the commercial break, my producer, Karen, gives me a few last minute thoughts. (Cue music intro)

Mr. Pearson is speaking: Good morning, everyone. I want to welcome our listeners to our show, ***Why does love hurt so good?*** I am Ondray Pearson, and for the next two hours, I will be taking your calls and answering your relationship questions, issues and concerns. If you are unable to get your questions on the air today, you can email me directly, and I will read and answer it, I promise.

We will give you additional information on how to do so during the show, but for now, the lines are open, and the number here is 1-800-877-K103. After the break, we will take our first caller of the day. I'm Ondray Pearson here on K103 we will be right back.

We are back. Karen who's on the line?

Karen is speaking: We have Debra from East Point, Georgia, on the line.

Mr. Pearson is speaking: Hi Debra, how are you doing today? What is your question?

Debra is speaking: First, let me say I just ordered a copy of your book online. I can hardly wait to read it. I have two questions for you. The first one is, what made you decide to title your current book, <u>*Why Does Love Hurt So Good?*</u> and the second question is, can you *define* in both your own opinion, biblically and worldly, the definition of what love is?

Mr. Pearson is speaking: Well, Debra, I titled this book, <u>*Why Does Love Hurt So Good*</u>? because I wanted those who read it to understand what it means and the consequences that come with telling someone you love them. The word *love* is said and used so loosely today that it is hard to differentiate the *value* put on it as it relates to our feelings for the one we call our mate. This is why most people, when it is said to them in their relationship, find it hard to believe and even harder to accept.

Not because the person saying it is lying but more because the person hearing it may have heard it so often. They find it difficult to believe or accept until they *see* in their mate that their actions match up with their words. In other words, they need to *see* more before they can believe what their mate is telling them. For some, love is just a four letter word. However, it is the word we use as a connection to how and what to describe how we're feeling at that moment for that person.

Many people have no clue or understanding of what they are committing to when they say the words, "I love you" to someone. It is this lack of understanding that diminishes the value of the phrase when said because we say we *love* so many things. For those hearing the words said to them as a form of our affection, a value must be attached to it for those hearing it to understand that they are being told that we care about them a lot. We must be careful when we use such powerful words because contrary to what we may or may not know, the words "I love you" are more than just eight letters in the alphabet. People today will say to one another "I love you" then move in together, shack up, play house, play husband and wife and be sexually active because they believe this is the best way to see if getting married is a good idea. Most agree this way doesn't guarantee that this way will lead to marriage but many will do it anyway.

Many who claim to believe in God and the Bible will omit the part that says, "He prefers couples being sexually active to be married first" thinking and telling themselves, "He understands their hearts and will forgive them for doing things in reverse." For those who believe in Him and claim to know His Word who are doing and living this, know if they read the Bible, it doesn't show or talk about *dating* but it does talk about *living in sin.* Those living their life this way today will gladly defend their decision, justify their choice and behavior by saying something like, "We've chosen to live our life the way we feel is best for us. We believe in the Bible, but we don't necessarily believe we have to get or be married to *be* in a relationship. We are exploring as well as observing the chemistry we share between one another both in and out of the bedroom."

Our way allows us to see how we are at sharing space, sharing a checkbook and dealing with financial issues and concerns before getting married. Right or wrong, we do not want to say, "I do" and later realize we were not sexually or mentally compatible or that we had no real chemistry between us to sustain a long-term loving relationship. Sure, some couples have children without being married, and yes, some couples live this way and never get married, but at the end of the day, we have to live our lives and pray that God will understand. Too many marriages are just a legal document that says you're legally married. It doesn't guarantee you're going to stay married forever. It only lets the *world* know as it pertains to the *law* you're married, that's all.

Don't get me wrong. Even if we both believe in God, go to church and all that, doing things the way we're doing them doesn't mean God will love us less or more. Many believe in God, go to church and look at what we're doing now as being wrong, but many of them forget they were young once, and they didn't follow all the commandments. Many feel this way because now they are in the Word of God. Many have no idea that there are over 613 commandments in the Bible, and I know not everyone is keeping them all.

11

So, tell me how many laws did they break before they started following Christ? The 613 commandments mentioned in the Bible don't apply to everyone; there are some for men, women and children. We're not perfect and very few, if any, will follow ALL of them. Now I am not saying since we aren't following some that we should abandon all. I am just saying there are many of us in our dating lives and in trying to find that perfect person for us, will do things differently. I believe we all are *trying* to do and be right with God at the end of the day. For those who are living their life the right way, sooner than most, I have much respect for them.

The way I see it, living together and having children before getting married is no different than those who test drive cars. *BEFORE* they sign the legal paperwork, the person tries it first to see if they like what they have selected. They contemplate if they can see themselves with their selection for the long term, and have to determine and know they can handle the financial responsibilities that come with having it. All of this is done because there are "consequences" when you do not honor the contract once it is signed. They know it is harder to get out of the agreement (but possible) than it was getting into it. Because of this, many like to take their time before making such a significant commitment.

Let's be honest. Who wants to be stuck with someone they DON'T want? No one! My lady and I are living together. For us, it helps us measure and see if we are ready for marriage. We are just preparing for it in a different way. To be real with you, it is cheaper than getting married only to find out that the person you've married isn't the person you thought they were. Divorce isn't something people who get married in the first place expect once they have said, "I do." For this reason, I feel this is why the divorce rate is so high today. People today would rather live together and play house to *see* if marriage is the next step in their relationship.

Debra is speaking: I didn't know myself that there were that many laws in the Bible or marriage, but it makes sense. I can understand why a person would think and respond that way; it's the world we live in. Living together and playing house as you mentioned is the way this generation does it, but I'm not sure how many end up getting married. Shouldn't there be, if they choose to live this way, a date and timeline on *seeing* if it works out?

Mr. Pearson is speaking: Yes, it should. If they choose to live their life this way, although it isn't biblical, they should have a date and timeline on breaking it off or to go on and make it legal and biblical *if* they believe or are trying to follow the Bible. Do you also remember where in the text or have heard where it says concerning this world "traditions" in **Romans 12:2**, (KJV), "And be not conformed to this world: but be ye transformed by the renewing of your mind, that ye may prove what is that is good and acceptable and the perfect will of God." In other words, we may live in this, but we don't have to do all that those in this world do. Taking these kinds of actions is called *worldly* thinking. Meaning they may believe in the Bible but have chosen to do what they feel is right concerning marriage not what the text says (God's rules as explained in **Ephesians 5:19-33**, (KJV).

As many of us know the Bible doesn't talk about *dating* or suggest it is acceptable to be sexually active before marriage. I know people are. Regardless of what they may know, they will do what they feel is best for them good or bad, right or wrong. I am not saying our choice is the reason why there are so many broken families, so many fatherless children or so many single women with multiple children by multiple men. However, I can say that those doing this vicious cycle are not building a healthy family unit nor are they sending the right message to those young children growing up hoping to have a family one day. It is sending a message that sleeping around is *normal.* It tells those looking to have a family that getting married, waiting to have sex after you get married or having children as the Bible instructs is not something they should even look to try and do.

Now before you think or get me wrong, thinking I believe everyone who reads and claims to follow the Bible is going to wait to have sex, wait to have kids or seek marriage as the scripture says, know that I am not that crazy because I know they are not going to do it at all. I will tell you like my sex education teacher told us, "If you're not going to be safe, be careful," meaning if you're going to make your own decision concerning sex and sleep around make it a safe one.

Men contributing to this "broken family" structure don't understand the effect of them not being there does to their children. **FYI:** Men paying child support doesn't make you "special", so stop saying as if you should get a medal, "I take care of my kids." Hell, you should, didn't you help make them? Who do you think should take care of them? No other man wants to take care of your children while you "play" father and come around every blue moon to remind them you are their biological daddy. You may be their biological father, but the man who is taking care of them, raising them, the one at their sporting events, school plays, feeding them, the one who medically takes care of them, that's who their dad is not you. Dropping a few dollars off to them when it's convenient for you, doesn't make you a dad. It just makes you the man who gives their mother money every so often.

The effect of the "drive-by dads" is enormous on the kids. The girls are affected because it deprives them of the love of their first love, their father. It affects the boys by not having that man in their lives to teach them how to be men. Not being there at that time in their lives to guide them and to be that person they can look up to leads them to seek what they feel they are missing from the streets and other people.

Don't get me wrong there are situations where some women will not allow the man to see or spend time with their children, and this is unfortunately not right even though it happens often, but this is another story altogether. No man, unless he is abusive toward the woman or the children should not be able to see his children, regardless of the woman's feelings toward him. He should be a part of their life in some way. For young men who are deprived of this growing up, it affects them in a way that they spill over into their adulthood. Not having their father in their life to show them *how* to treat a woman and them knowing that you left their mother to raise them alone sends them down a road that doesn't always end well.

Men need to ask themselves, "If my child emulated my life, would he be better or worse? Do you want them to mistreat women in their lives, have multiple kids with multiple women as I did, and leave a woman to perform your role and hers? Act as if it was the woman's fault for having so many kids, lies to them or cheats on them?"

A man's absence makes them turn to their surroundings, society, the media and those other men (and women) they follow (celebrities) as their role models. They learn from them "how" to live their lives and treat women, and that's never a good thing. I know what I am saying is not going to fix the world, but here's the thing for those men struggling to understand their role in "this" world. The Most High created you first and expected you as a father and the man of the house to step up and stop acting like the woman in your relationship and lead your family somewhere.

Debra is speaking: Amen!

Mr. Pearson is speaking: I am a firm believer that "Our past is not what our future holds." I know there are both good men and good women in this world. I am hoping those men who are out here perpetuating this broken family cycle will stop it.

Debra is speaking: What are your views on divorce?

Mr. Pearson is speaking: My views on divorce, the reason I feel it is so high is that many get married for many of the wrong reasons.

Debra is speaking: What would you consider some of the "wrong reasons"?

Mr. Pearson is speaking: In **Proverbs 13:11**, (KJV) "Wealth gotten by vanity shall be diminished: but he that gathereth by labor shall increase." In other words, if you do things just for monetary gain most times, you may be suitable for a while, but in time you will lose more than you have gained.

Debra is speaking: How so?

Mr. Pearson is speaking: Well this is a whole other discussion, and I don't want to stray too far from the questions you ask, but I will say this, our world moves so fast these days, and very few people take time to "get to know" each other before sleeping with one another. Both men and women sometimes jump into a relationship with their own *ulterior motives*, and most times it's not for love.

This generation for some, sees and views marriage and the commitment it requires as the end of a loving relationship and all that it could be. In fact, it is the beginning of a loving relationship if they allow it to be. 69% of people dating today see nothing wrong with a little bump and grind. Marriage is thought of, treated and viewed the same way as a leasing agreement for a car. They get all excited when they first get it and ride it until the wheels fall off. Later, they decide it is not working out for them, say, I can return it, it is the American way, and then they break the agreement and try out another one.

Don't get me wrong. I know many people don't believe in the Bible or marriage and I can respect that but for those who do believe in God and are having troubles in their relationship, maybe they need to review His Word. He told the Israelites in **Deuteronomy 28:1-2**, (KJV), "And it shall come to pass, if thou shalt hearken diligently unto the voice of the Lord thy God, to observe and do all his commandment which I command thee this day, that the Lord thy

God will set thee on high above all nations of the earth." "And all these blessings shall come on thee, and overtake thee if thou shalt hearken unto the voice of the Lord thy God."

In other words, God is telling us if we try our way, and our results are always the same, maybe it is time to try something else, like His way. Once again, I am not saying people have to be married to be happy; all I am assuming is many of our issues, concerns and problems that we have in our relationships come from us doing things "our way" and not His way. At some point, you will have to decide whose directions you will follow, those of "man" or God. You read this in **Luke 16:13**, (KJV), "No servant can serve two masters: for either he will hate the one, and love the other; or else he will hold to the one, and despise the other. Ye cannot serve God and mammon." So, the question then must be, "Are you going to live your life politically correct or biblically correct?"

Debra is speaking: I know what you mean, I have Christian friends who live together and are sexually active and have been "engaged" for over five years. I don't judge them because like you said, they know right from wrong, and they are going to do what they want to do, but it is hard to take them seriously when it comes to following Christ living and doing the opposite. My dad told me many years ago a man will never change your title from "girlfriend" to "wife" if he is getting the benefits of a married man. Why would he?

Mr. Pearson is speaking: This is correct. Men would hardly ever change their woman's title because as the saying goes, "Why buy the cow when you're getting the milk for free." In other words, what benefit would it be to them to marry when they're getting the benefits of a husband? I am not saying all women want to get married because many women are okay with not being married. A man living with a woman and getting the full benefits of a married man is telling the woman this "I am here with you now, but if things don't work out, I am out." Women in situations like this never understand what they are sharing with this man is just "A temporary convenience to fulfill a momentary need." Or better yet, we know it to be a 100% mental contract only."

Debra is speaking: What does that mean "mental" contract?

Mr. Pearson is speaking: It means they're not ready to commit to anything other than what they are going through at that moment. With this kind of agreement, he is saying without saying to you, "I am not ready to commit to marriage yet. I want to see how well you take care of me first before I commit fully to you." In other words, he is telling you that he doesn't want to sacrifice too much, nor give up his option to leave if things don't pan out right. He doesn't want to be responsible for too much meaning *you*! Relationships with these kinds of conditions and restrictions will not last long. This form of commitment is simply an escape plan that will be put to use sooner or later.

Debra is speaking: I agree with you.

Mr. Pearson is speaking: People who love one another for real don't rely on options or ways out of the marriage. It is a fact of life in any relationship that if you go in thinking of a way out, "as long as you know you have options, you will always doubt your relationship." If most people were to remove sex from a relationship, they would discover they never had that much in common. Thus, all they shared for one another was lust. When you take money out of your relationship, you will realize that 95% of most women will create / find ways to leave. Most feel if the man isn't "spending" on them or "giving" it to them, there is no reason to remain with them. What happens when the sex isn't as good as it once was, do you then break up? Do you break up and start looking for *good sex* thinking it is *love* again?

Debra is speaking: Why do you think some people think this way?

Mr. Pearson is speaking: You often hear people say, "God knows my heart" or "we're all sinners," and this is true. He does know your heart, and yes, we are all sinners, but it doesn't give us a free pass to continue committing sins. Repent doesn't mean repeat. You can't continue to do what you want, backslide, dishonor Him and expect a free pass. Thinking He is going to keep letting them slide as they continue to dishonor His Word must think He is a fool and stupid. Those doing this cannot believe, and I am not speaking for Him. Do they think that He is going to hear their prayers and answer them when they are repeatedly disrespecting Him at every turn they get? I can unequivocally say those who believe this and continue to act this way are the fools.

Debra is speaking: What about cheating, being married isn't going to stop either of them from happening?

Mr. Pearson is speaking: I agree, but married people should have no reason to feel, think or believe they are missing anything or that there is someone else better just around the corner if they have truly understood what they have. Those looking to cheat have already made up their minds to cheat, whether they are married or not. If they get married "thinking" they will need sex from other people when they have a willing sexual partner in their wife, they don't need to get married. The Bible tells you that your wife's body belongs to you and yours belongs to her, so unless either of them refuses to honor their marriage commitment to one another, what's the problem? I am not saying that people who are married don't cheat on one another, but for those taking this shortcut, I believe they are saying they do not know God, His Word or His plan for them nor do they fully understand or respect what being married and committed to someone means.

Debra is speaking: As you know, those people in their 20s or 30s are not thinking about settling down right away. Most are trying to find themselves and exploring life BEFORE they settle down with someone. Seriously, what's wrong with that?

Mr. Pearson is speaking: If by "exploring" you mean experience life that includes being sexually active among other things, I would say that according to the Bible it is wrong, but I am not here to judge anyone's lifestyle choices. I, before getting into the Word, thought and acted the same way, so I understand how and why this would be something they wanted to experience before settling down. These are the "choices" that concern me.

Debra is speaking: How so?

Mr. Pearson is speaking: As you know, our society views and judges men and women "differently" for doing the same thing. The world sees men who do this behavior as acceptable and applaud them for doing so. Women, on the other hand, doing the same thing, are viewed as "damaged" goods. I am not saying they are not able to find true love or sustain a relationship with someone. I am saying, and it is not right, but it's our reality, men will find women much more comfortable in accepting HIS situation of having multiple children by other women before she finds a man to take her with children by other men.

Debra is speaking: Why do you think that is so? Men sleep around, and they are looked at as players. Women who do the same are called harlots.

Mr. Pearson is speaking: You're right, and I agree it is not fair for a man to sleep with a woman, leave the relationship and leave the woman to raise "their" children on her own while they go out freely and create a new family repeatedly with someone else. Unfortunately, this has become the "norm" in our society with no change in sight. Men doing this are the reason we have broken families and fatherless children. They're acting like and being "drive-by dads," thinking if they drop off the money, it is the same as spending time with them. They leave the woman to be the "Mother and Dad," only stepping in when things are going good with the children. They're nowhere to be found when they're needed the most.

Women, on the other hand, are not blameless because they allow this cycle to continue to happen. Sure, the men should take the lead in breaking this cycle, but until they do (if they do), women need to stop allowing this to happen. This "double standard" hurts the woman and children more than it does the man. Now, I am not saying that being married means that people will not cheat on one another. However, people who continuously have unprotected sex before marriage have contributed to the issue of broken homes and fatherless children.

Debra is speaking: So why do men look side-eye at women with three-plus kids? They expect us to accept them if they have more than one child when we meet and date them. Many of my friends will not date a man with kids or more than two if they're not seventeen or above.

Mr. Pearson is speaking: When I surveyed over a thousand men on this very subject, the first thing most started out saying was, "The views of men and women back in the 60s and 70s were different. For most relationships, marriage back then meant something. It had value that it doesn't have today." The consensus of the room felt couples during that time stayed married for some 30 plus years. Yes, there were a few cheating men with outside families but nothing like today. Back then, it was a neighborhood secret known by few, but today fathering children outside of marriage is typical and seen as usual. Most men took pride and worked long and hard (using a job or hustling) to support their families. Women took care of the home and men brought in the money – creating a level of trust, love and respect that lasted for many years.

Today, couples hardly stay married for five years if they are lucky and see divorce as their "get out of jail" card waiting to be used at the slightest notion. Now they were all quick to point out that not every man back in the day thought or acted this way in their relationship. Some did cheat, lie, abuse and mistreat their women and a few had multiple families which contributed to the broken family cycle.

So, when I asked them, "Why do you find it hard to date women with multiple children? And why do you feel it's hard for both men and women to be faithful to each other?" Steve said he felt the roles of men and women in their relationship during that time were clear, defined and respected. They committed to one another, loved one another, were faithful to each other, respected, recognized one another and played "their" role which was that the woman take care of the home while the man made money for her to do so, for the most part. The woman saw, felt and knew her man would give them all the love they required, stay loyal, protect and honor them, kiss the ground she walked on and support her as she got older rather than leaving her for a younger woman. She would make him feel good and often tell him how she appreciated all he did for his family.

Debra is speaking: So, are you saying many men don't feel women could be faithful or loyal to them?

Mr. Pearson is speaking: No because many can. What I am saying is that there are a lot of women today who have never seen what loyalty or faithfulness looks like, as well as for some men. So, when a person expects their mate to understand and be loyal and faithful, it confuses them because they have no idea what it looks like because they have never had it for themselves. They overlook and ignore most good men because they do not fit their purpose yet. See, the guy working his way up, they pass on him. Women like this prefer getting with a guy who already got it going on (or so it seems) rather than invest in a guy with potential. Being loyal and believing in a man BEFORE he's accomplished, this is seen as crazy to many women.

Debra is speaking: Why is this, you think?

Mr. Pearson is speaking: It is because they are the kind of woman who thinks because they are young and beautiful, they should be with someone who can shower them with all things good today not tomorrow. These are the same ones who will waste their youth sleeping with Tom, Dick, Harry, Chad and Tyrone, having kids with different men, accelerating their age by drinking and smoking excessively, and showing in their actions and behavior that they are not loyal to any man but expect men to be faithful to them. All the while, they are thinking they have found a "good man" until they get into their late 30s.

Debra is speaking: Well, let's be honest. Most men are not reliable or loyal and very few can be faithful, so why would they expect a woman to be committed to them if they are not committed to the woman?

Mr. Pearson is speaking: I agree, and it is unfair for men who cheat to expect a woman to be faithful to them. The thing is that a lot of men have problems in these areas even when they get a good woman. Many of them will mess up their relationship because of their insecurities, lack of trust and ability to communicate what it is they want. Many of them don't know how to be faithful or committed these days because they cannot see the value of it. Many never had anyone, (meaning a man) in their lives growing up in the home to show them the value of this in a relationship.

Debra is speaking: What do you mean?

Mr. Pearson is speaking: Well, most men stated when they do try and take on the whole package, their authority is limited, challenged and ignored in the relationship when applying discipline to the kids. They felt if they are the head of the house, then everyone under his roof is under his authority. They expressed that they would have limits imposed on how they discipline the children, what they can and cannot say to the children. Also, the mother would not explain to the ex of the kids that her current man will have some authority to discipline their kids since he is the one taking care of them and her. Very few men want to deal with this kind of relationship, and many felt the love of that woman, under those circumstances, was not worth it.

Debra is speaking: Well, it is the same for women who date men with kids, so what is the difference? Why should we accept it if they won't?

Mr. Pearson is speaking: Good question. The reason why most men (but not all) will avoid dating women with young kids or kids at all is that they don't feel comfortable or that it is right that they should use all their resources to raise another man's children. They feel like fools when the woman allows the kid's biological dad to run things going on in their own home. They think their woman should stand with them when it comes to disciplining the children. Instead, she allows the kids to disrespect the man who is providing for them all by saying, "Those aren't your kids, and they have a dad who will discipline them." It serves to remind him every time it happens that he was a fool for taking on this situation; finally he comes to the point where he leaves and takes his "resources" with him. After all that, when he leaves the woman says, "He wasn't a real man." but what she meant to say was, "He wasn't a pure fool. He wouldn't allow me and my ex to use him to support us, so my ex doesn't have to pay child support."

Many women in these kinds of relationships came in expecting him to fix their brokenness, low self-esteem and all their emotional issues but cling to their self-righteousness of what they want and feel because they are who they are and they deserve it. They want to control the relationship and try to convince him that he is lucky to be in this position.

Not all men hearing this will feel this is the "best deal in town" or that they cannot find anyone else. In all fairness, who wants to walk into debt, foolishness and additional responsibilities knowing this woman has wasted her youth on others who got what she is offering you for free?

Debra is speaking: I understand what you're saying, but it is not fair that those men with kids expect women to accept their situation. If a man gets involved with a woman with kids, he needs to deal with it if he loves her.

Mr. Pearson is speaking: I agree. Years ago, I dealt with this same situation with my ex, Zonnique. When we first met, she was 37, and I was 42 years old. She had two boys, 17 and 15 years old and both were in high school. I knew if she and I clicked, if I wanted her, the kids came with the package, and I was cool with that. At that time, I had two kids around the same age in high school that lived with their mother. Neither of us saw any issues with blending families.

But to make a long story short, and the reason I am telling you this, is that when she came into the relationship, she mentioned she had been cheated on, hurt, lied to and taken advantage of by the kid's father. She felt damaged in so many areas for so long. It took two years before she would trust me. I knew I wasn't the problem, and I thought I could be a solution if she allowed me to be. Don't get me wrong. We had a great relationship, but it was draining to daily hear her trash talk and defend herself thinking I was going to do to her what her ex did. She always would tell me that she knew how men thought, and she wasn't going to be "played" again. As you can imagine, I had to work overtime to "have" a relationship with her. I hung in there because I felt she could be a great woman for me, but it took a toll on me after a while.

Debra is speaking: What happened? Why aren't you with her now?

Mr. Pearson is speaking: My job relocated me to the east coast, and she didn't want to relocate with me since she was in her hometown and all her family was there. It was hard to turn down the offer, so I took it. I asked her and the kids to move with me after I got there and got settled, but she said no. She said she wouldn't consider moving until her kids graduated high school. Don't get me wrong. We tried a long-distance relationship, but she convinced herself that the less she saw me, that probably I was seeing someone else on the side or that I was going to cheat on her or leave her eventually. All of this became just too much for me to handle and work out, so we just decided to be friends. I say this to point out how people, sometimes people in these kinds of situations, reflect on their past issues and allow them to sabotage their current relationship to avoid being hurt again before it even begins.

Debra is speaking: I see your point.

Mr. Pearson is speaking: Now, I am not here to judge nor am I trying to judge anyone's lifestyle choices in my book, nor am I telling anyone how to live their life. I am simply sharing relationship experiences of those who have, like most of us, been unsuccessful in finding true love. In sharing this information through different views and situations that others have gone through, I am trying to show the level of understanding along with the consequences that come with loving someone and them loving you. We all know there are always three sides to every story, yours, theirs and the truth. I try to provide different perspectives on what people refer to or think of as *love*.

I know people say love shouldn't hurt if it's real. Well, guess what? It does. Contrary to what most people believe, *loving someone hurts sometimes*. It does, and it shows how much we care for someone. We only get heartbroken over people we care for, not for those we don't. Even though it hurts sometimes, it should never prevent, deny or keep you from enjoying all the joys that loving someone brings.

It is in the tough times that we need to remember that our mate is trying their hardest to stay with us regardless of how difficult we are. We need to keep them at all costs because finding someone who cares enough to look past your flaws isn't something that happens every day. Finding someone who loves you the way you want and deserve is someone you need to keep. Knowing how much they love you helps ease the days when you may not feel very loved. Does that make sense?

Debra is speaking: Yes, and it makes sense.

Mr. Pearson is speaking: Now, your other question was, "Could I define, in my own opinion, what the biblical and worldly definition of love is" right? Well, let me tell you what the Webster's Dictionary says Love is. They define love as: "A feeling of strong or constant affection for a person." Now, as far as the Bible's view on love there are many scriptures that describe love in various contexts, but two scriptures that come to mind and that I found interesting are: **Galatians 5:22**, (KJV), that reads "But fruit of the spirit is love, joy, peace, longsuffering, gentleness, goodness and faith." And **1 John 4:8** (KJV), "He that loveth not knoweth not God; For God is love." The Bible speaks a lot of love, and it considers it a Law. It says love is an act of the will (meaning we choose to love someone).

Debra is speaking: What do you mean?

Mr. Pearson is speaking: Well, I believe what we feel for someone we are attracted to is more of a chemical reaction than an emotion. Many people tend to call what they're feeling for someone "love" because they are unable to explain it. As I have stated many times, "love" is a word; it is the connection we place on it that gives it meaning. I am not saying anyone is wrong for their definition of the word, but in reality, it is just a word. With that said, I feel that love is not an emotion because it does not have feelings. The way I see it is "we choose" to care and explore these so called feelings with someone, and this makes it a choice.

Debra is speaking: So, you're saying love is not a feeling but a choice?

Mr. Pearson is speaking: Yes and no. Let me explain what I mean. Love, in my opinion, is an "act of the will." It is a choice. We choose to explore, love those who hurt us, persecute us, use us and lie to us. The "choice" we make and the "emotions" we feel for that person help us better explain our interest in someone. The more time we spend with that person, the more we develop and feel our choice is a good one.

The emotion part of what you're feeling is like when you feel and realize the person you've chosen is someone you want to spend the rest of your life with, and you want the rest of your life to start as soon as possible. However, our first "action" when we are attracted to someone is a choice, a decision and an act of our will and this is called Agape love. Then, we develop those actions into feelings to explain our actions.

*A quick **side note** if you didn't know.*

In the Greek language, there are levels of love, and here are four of them. The first is *Storge,* which is an affectionate love. This is the kind of love you have for your parents or your children. Next, there is *Eros,* from which we get the English word, erotic. This is often the word we use to express the sexual love or the feelings of arousal for those we are physically attracted to. It is something we cannot control; some would even say it is a selfish love. It's because of the action we show when we're attracted to someone. We want those to whom we are drawn to want us at the same time at the same moment. Next, there is *Phileo or Philia* which refers to brotherly love. It is the kind of feeling you have for your best friend. Lastly, we have *Agape*; the essence of agape love is goodwill, benevolence and willful delight in the object of desire. Agape love involves faithfulness, commitment and an "act of the will." It is distinguished from the other types of love by its high moral nature and strong character.

An example of this can be found in **1 Corinthians Chapter 13**. Knowing this information helps classify the love you're feeling with who you're with currently. Does this make sense?

Debra is speaking: Yes! I never knew that.

Mr. Pearson is speaking: Let's continue. Love is, as I see it, the response and understanding of someone we care for in our life. Love is not just a choice; it is also an act of our will. We build our friendships and develop what we feel for a person through our understanding of that person, their ways, the way they interact with us, the way they treat us, etc. We often are afraid of being vulnerable in our relationship because we fear getting hurt or taken advantage of by that person.

It is that *fear* that keeps us from being who we are and who we can and would be with that person. The Bible says in **1 John 4:18**, (KJV) - "There is no fear in love; but perfect love casteth out fear: because of fear hath torment. He that feareth is not made perfect in love." In other words, we cannot allow the fear of being hurt again dictate if we have love in our lives or not. We must be smarter about our choices and choose wisely. As you can see, a lot of factors go into our decision to care for someone, the more we know and like about them, the more we care for them.

No matter what we say love is, "love" will forever be a word misunderstood and a mystery with a multitude of definitions of what it is. Those who experience it will define for themselves what it is and means to them. With that said, let me add how much you value what it is you feel for someone. What it is you are willing to do and give to show them you care for them will determine what kind of love you both have. When couples no longer "feel" the same about one another, they say they have "fallen out of love."

Debra is speaking: I have heard that said before, but I am not sure what that means?

Mr. Pearson is speaking: When most couples say this, what they are saying and what they mean are two different things. To them, they no longer feel the way they used to for one another. What they mean is the chemical reaction in their body has faded, and the adrenalin felt during the time they were together has changed. It doesn't mean the person doesn't care or still love them anymore. It simply means the "way" they once felt is different now between them. I hope I have answered your questions.

Debra is speaking: Yes, you did and then some. You've given me a lot of useful information about love that I hadn't thought about as well as a different perspective.

Mr. Pearson is speaking: To bring my point home, I would like to share a story with you of an experience I went through in high school and college concerning love that many have or will experience. It is a little embarrassing but true. During my teenage years, when I was dating, I learned the hard way that saying "I Love You" could not save a relationship when it was over.

After a breakup, I had a lot of questions but no one to answer them. I did not know the rules, pitfalls, problems and joys that come along with loving someone. I learned through trial and error and the many, many, many mistakes made by assuming I knew a lot when I knew very little. Then, I started to understand that what little information I picked up and learned was not always from the best of sources.

Advice from family and friends only confused me more. For me, I looked elsewhere for inspiration, and I found it in things I liked, such as music, books and movies. Not understanding yet how to express myself in my own words, I often borrowed lines from my favorite songs, television shows and books to pick up and impress those girls I was attracted to in high school. At the time I saw nothing wrong with doing this, I felt until I got it on my own, I would "fake it until I made it." Sometimes it worked, but most times it didn't.

Debra is speaking: Guys still do that today. My husband used to dedicate songs on the radio to me. I knew this was his way of showing me he cared for me. I knew he didn't write or sing the songs he dedicated to me, but I understood what he was trying to say. It made me feel unique and good inside knowing he took the time to do this for me; I enjoyed the attention. Even though we have been together for a while, it is still an effective way for a man to show his woman he cares for her.

Mr. Pearson is speaking: I am glad you said that. You see where I was coming from, right? Let me be clear for those listening. I wasn't using this to run game or trick women into liking me. It was just my way at the time, of showing them I was interested in knowing them. Because I was not seasoned yet, I stumbled through my words. Those I was interested in knowing could see I was not that good at the conversation aspect, and they would laugh. However, those who bought into it thought my not knowing how to talk was cute and gave me a chance. The cuteness wore off quickly though, and I needed to do something else fast if I was going to keep their attention.

By the time I got to college and got involved in my first adult relationship, I was fully aware of the weight "words" carried in a relationship. I got hurt and disappointed a lot because I wore my heart on my sleeve. I made the mistake of telling them exactly all I was feeling for them, but it came off at times as a little too much. It wasn't until later that I realized I felt *eros* and *agape* for them, but I wasn't aware nor did I know the difference between the two.

My mother often told me to slow down. I remember her telling me during that time, "Every week you meet someone and because they show you a little attention, you fall hard for them. Just because you like a lot of women doesn't mean you're in love with them." Once I realized what she was saying was right, I understood, but I never told her. I found it so easy to get into a relationship but extremely difficult to end them.

I remember a girl in high school telling me the reason she wanted to break up was that I was too sweet. I had no idea what that meant because I had treated her right or so she said. I was confused as hell hearing that and wondered, did she want me to be mean to her? I wasn't a bad boy, and I wasn't going to try to be. I just looked for someone who wanted a good guy. I asked my sister, Yolanda, and she told me some girls like "bad boys" because they (the girls) are bad. There is nothing wrong with me being a good guy. Good women are always looking for good men, and one day I would find one.

Debra is speaking: How did you deal with the breakups?

Mr. Pearson is speaking: Over time, I got over it and honestly, despite the possibilities of it happening again I foolishly sought love (eros thinking it was agape) out repeatedly. I hardly ever spent time alone (meaning being single). I would jump out and into another one to avoid being alone. What I thought was love didn't feel that good anymore. I felt there had to be more to love than just being in a relationship with someone, and I wanted to know what "it" was. I learned from my experiences enough to avoid certain behaviors in the next one and hoped not to repeat any past mistakes. To be honest with you, it was years and many relationships later that I truly understood what love was and what it should feel like until I met and fell in love with my wife, Reginae. With my wife (then girlfriend), I felt both eros and agape.

Debra is speaking: How did you know you had found the *one*?

Mr. Pearson is speaking: I knew (or I felt at the time) because I wanted to and made it a point to meet her in the mind before we met in the bedroom. I told her I wanted both love and sex at the same time, not one or the other. It wasn't until I met her that I realized I had been selecting women from an eros perspective and not an agape/eros perspective.

It made sense looking back then, why a few of the relationships ended after a few months. It had been about sex and not love. I didn't realize at that early age that I wanted them both at the same time with someone. I knew when I met Reginae, and I was determined to slow things down and show her I was in this with her for more than just sex. During our dating stage, I understood and educated myself on both the biblical definition and the worldly definition of love to ensure what I was feeling for her was a combination of both agape and eros at the same time. I wanted to grow and build something with her. So far so good. It has been three years going on four and we're still going strong.

Debra is speaking: I am glad I was able to get through today. Your information and stories have been eye-openers, very inspirational and uplifting for me to hear. You got me thinking I am ready to find that "one" person for me. I know most women listening feel the same way.

Mr. Pearson is speaking: I am glad. You see, I took my time with Reginae. We read the Bible together and learned the meanings of the four Greek words as they applied to what I was feeling for her. I made my choice, and I've done my best to show her she is all I need to be happy forever. The funny thing about it is, I felt so comfortable with her on our very first date that I volunteered information I thought she needed to know because I was interested in her that much.

It was a gamble, but I wanted to make it clear to her that I didn't want her just for one night. I wanted her forever. I didn't suggest we live together or play house to *see* what it would be like to be married. I got to know her in her mind, body and soul and then made it official and asked her to marry me. It was clear I wanted to "invest" in her, get to know her and be the man she knows she could depend on and feel protected with. I would commit and be loyal to her, take care of her, love her and honor her for as long as we live. So, before I end this, let me tell you, you need to take your time and try and notice in your dating stage if you two are like-minded. If you believe in God, put Him first when you do make a choice. It will be the right one.

Debra is speaking: I hear you, and I agree with you 100%.

Mr. Pearson is speaking: I thank you, and I appreciate you allowing me the opportunity to answer your questions fully. I hope the information and different perspective helps you in your search for love.

Debra is speaking: Yes, you did and more. I appreciate it a lot.

Mr. Pearson is speaking: Great. Thank you for calling in. We have to take a break now, but when we come back, we will continue with our next caller.

(The lines are lighting up.)

Mr. Pearson is speaking: We're back. Karen, who's on the line?

Karen is speaking: We have David from Alpharetta, Georgia.

Mr. Pearson is talking: How are you doing today? What is your question?

David is speaking: Before I get into my question, I have to ask do you believe in Karma?

Mr. Pearson is speaking: Yes! Why do you ask?

David is speaking: Years ago, I was dating my ex, Essence. She was a good woman, and she was good to me. I will admit that when we got together, which we shouldn't have, I was a womanizer. I know now I wasn't ready to settle down and be faithful and that's why I cheated on her. When I got caught, she forgave me and took me back. I would be constant for a few weeks and then get that itch again and cheat. Now you know for a guy, this is hard to admit, but I lied, cheated and disrespected her on more than one occasion, but I did love her. Eventually, she got tired of it, and she left me.

It took me a while to face up to all I had done, and yes, I tried to get her back, but she wouldn't return. I was single again and able to be with whomever I wanted, but I knew that if I kept up the same behavior, I would probably end up in the same situation with someone else. I needed a change, so I started going back to church to try to change my life.

After going a few months, I met Debra. She was a regular, and we started talking one day at church. Then we'd get together for lunch, dinner, and eventually started dating. We've been together for two years, but lately, things between us have changed. We haven't spent much time together, and she has been going out with her girlfriends more often. The first thing that came to mind was that she could be cheating on me. I thought this way because I remembered when I would cheat on Essence, my behavior was the same way.

So, I am calling in because I am too embarrassed to tell anyone about my situation because those who know me know how I was out there in those streets cheating on my ex. I know if I told them they would say, "It's karma coming back on you." So, I will make this quick and hope my friends aren't listening and tell my girlfriend what I think because I don't know for sure. I know men and women cheat, but I am not sure how to recognize if she is cheating on me. Can you help me with identifying signs so I can figure out IF she is cheating on me?

Mr. Pearson is speaking: When you say, "things have changed between the two of you" what do you mean?

David is speaking: Well, I have noticed sudden changes in her attitude towards me. It's not like her usual manner; this is a more aggressive one without reason. I work and pay all the bills, and she used to show appreciation but lately, she acts as if I am not doing enough and using this to create pointless arguments about nothing.

Just the other day she came in and saw I had made a small mess in the kitchen where I had fixed myself a snack. Usually, she would say, "Hey babe, make sure you clean up your mess." Instead, she blew up and made a big deal out of it. She went from the mess I made into how I wasn't a real man, how I was treating her, being disrespectful, calling me names, questioning and interrogating me like I was a crook or a stranger to her. She started talking about my phone and how I didn't want her to know who was calling or who was calling me. She's telling me that I don't respect her, all from a mess on the counter in the kitchen. She had never done that before, and when she did, I didn't know what to say, I just stood there and listened to her.

Mr. Pearson is speaking: If this were to happen every so often than it could be work-related and she could have just been venting and wasn't really directing her problems at you. But on the other hand, if she has started and continues to do things like this daily, then there is more to it and a reason why she all of a sudden has felt the need to come at you in this manner. If there are issues and concerns, presenting it to you could get the necessary changes needed. So instead she has told her girlfriends or family, and they have gotten her all worked up to a point where she is acting out of character towards you.

In other words, something has started making her feel she has made a bad decision in you two being together and that she possibly could and should trade up. She hung with her friends more often.

David is speaking: Yes, she has gone out with them, and I have met them maybe once or twice during the week, but now they are going out 3 to 4 times a week. They hardly talk on the phone, just a lot of texting and laughing as she reads her texts from someone. It seems strange to me because I have never seen her dress up over the top to hang out with her friends as she has been lately.

Mr. Pearson is speaking: This could be a "tell-tale" sign that she is dressing up to go meet someone else who is giving her "new" attention that she may be feeling she isn't getting enough at home. In situations like this, her girlfriends know she is meeting someone and have agreed to be her alibi. They will cover for her because they want her to leave you.

Now, I'm not saying this is your case, but this change in her attitude and dress, along with hanging out more, could be something you may need to look into. You have to understand that with women, cheating isn't about sleeping with "many." One will do. Now if she were going to leave you, you would have no obvious clue she was going to.

David is speaking: If she is that unhappy, why doesn't she just leave?

Mr. Pearson is speaking: Well, David, I could ask you the same thing. When you were cheating on your ex? If you weren't happy, why did you stay with hurting her daily with your behavior? You stayed because you wanted your cake and eat it too; she is no different. You didn't want to leave your ex. You just wanted the freedom to sleep with other women and still be able to come home to her and "think" foolishly, that she had no clue things had changed between the two of you. Your ex suspected you were cheating because of your behavioral changes in your connection to her, and now you are experiencing what I call "Monkey Arms" of your current girlfriend.

David is speaking: What is "Monkey Arms" and what does it have to do with a woman?

Mr. Pearson is speaking: "Monkey Arms" is a term used to describe when a woman is still holding on to one man until she feels what she has with another is solid enough where she can let go of the first and go be with the second. You know how as a child you would play on the monkey bars? You would swing from one to another but BEFORE you would let go of one bar you would make sure you had a firm grip on the next bar. This is what some women who are cheating on their men do.

The fact is women aren't stupid. They will never let go of one man until they have another to go to. Like I said, women might flirt and hang out with many, but they are looking for the next ONE, not many just one. Foolishly a lot of men help them without knowing it. It is something we all do, and it is human nature. In all relationships, this happens. The more comfortable we are with one another, the more likely we are to take them for granted. I don't feel most do it, but it happens and if you don't catch it, sit and talk to each other and make some much needed changes, more problems will creep into your relationship.

You can see her mysterious behavior such as, always looking at her phone, hiding it from you, turning it face down, keeping it on "silent", taking it with her when she goes into another room. She could be communicating with someone else and setting up times to meet after work, etc., and telling you she has to work late which she has never done before. In reality, only men would use the "work late" excuse. Women would say to you that they are going to stop over one of her girlfriend's house for a moment to pick up something. You know it's a lie when the details are vague, and she gives no time when she would be home. Have you ever said you wanted to send her flowers at her job or drop in for lunch, and she's told you no?

David is speaking: Well, now that you mention it, yes. I sent her some flowers at her job a few weeks ago, and you would have thought I had killed someone. I didn't understand why she reacted the way she did when all I was doing was showing her love. She told me it was "inappropriate" to do so. She didn't want her co-workers to get in her business. I was thinking, what business? I was showing her love. Why do you think she reacted that way?

Mr. Pearson is speaking: Well, women who get upset like that and tell their man, who is trying to show them love at work, could be cheating or lying to their co-workers about their relationship status. Cheating women say it is inappropriate to send them flowers because if they aren't there when the flowers come, someone will sign and pick them up for her. If she has told her co-workers she has a man and the flowers show a different man's name on them, they might question her as to who this guy is who is sending her flowers when she has a man already. They may be nosy co-workers who start telling others that she is cheating on her man, and what she is trying to do is not let anyone know she is doing dirt.

Then she would be explaining and lying not to let her business get out. I say this because what woman would refuse her man sending her flowers and gifts to show how much he cares for her. Only someone who is cheating or thinking about cheating would feel that way. Many women claim to be but are not independent; most of them are co-dependent. They need to be reassured and be receiving constant attention from someone to validate their existence. The behavior she's shown suggests she is seeking "attention" elsewhere. Has your sex life changed or slowed down?

David is speaking: Yes, it has. Before, when I wanted to have sex, she was down but now when I ask, and we do it, it seems more like a task instead of enjoyment between us.

Mr. Pearson is speaking: This could be a sign that she is getting it from someone else. She may still keep having sex with you because she isn't completely ready to leave yet but fewer and fewer times but just enough to make you think she is happy with you. Has she ever talked to you about "What if" situations that include a "nameless" girlfriend whom you've never met or know who is dating someone she believes is cheating on her to get your thoughts on what you would do if you were in her place? Many women who are cheating or thinking about cheating will come up with these multiple scenarios to engage where your mind is if it were to happen to you. She is asking in order to get an idea of what might happen if caught and her next course of action will depend on the answers you give her at that time.

David is speaking: Give me an example of what you're saying.

Mr. Pearson is speaking: Well, the story would be something like, "Babe, I got a girlfriend (she never tells you her name and if she does you've never heard of her or seen her before) and I believe from what she told me the other day that she could be cheating on her boyfriend. If you were in her place and thought cheating was going on, what would you do?

This question is asked to see your reaction to someone cheating. Be aware that a woman doing this will be listening hard; she's trying to understand where leverage can be gained when you catch her. Just so you know, in these scenarios, the friend and the questions are about her. She is not the woman for you, nor is she worth "investing" your time, love or resources.

David is speaking: Hearing you tell it, women can be worse than men.

Mr. Pearson is speaking: Well, I will not say worse. I would say they are much more deviant in their cheating. Most men cheat and get caught because they talk too much. Men get themselves in trouble because there are sloppy. They feel they are getting away with it, and they have to tell someone, and most times, it's the wrong person. Has she nagged you more than usual?

David is speaking: Yes! She has.

Mr. Pearson is speaking: I bet you the difference between her normal nagging and now is that her nagging now is more specific.

David is speaking: Yes, but I am not sure sometimes because she will start complaining about one thing and somehow cover many other things not related to what she began complaining about in the first place.

Mr. Pearson is speaking: Yes, this is a sign she is up to something. She may start out complaining about you not cleaning up after yourself and jump to something like "You don't hold hands anymore," "You don't tell me I am beautiful like you used to," "You haven't told me you loved me in days" or "You don't want the same things I want or want to do the things I want to do anymore." She creates tension and an argument for using as her reasoning for her behavior. When she does this, she will tell you that "you made her do it," it is your fault, etc. all to justify her actions of infidelity in your relationship. She is looking for an out and needs you to give it to her so she can walk away free and clear. Making it seem like you wanted her gone when it is what she wanted in the first place.

Listen, sloppy women doing this and some who don't, think because a new guy gives them a little attention that they feel they aren't getting at home, that they want to date and be with them when all they want is to sleep with them. She is thinking back on the 80/20 rule and going after the 20% she feels she is missing and leaving 80% on the table. Not realizing that it is human nature that once we get with someone in a relationship and are with them for a while, we get comfortable. We begin to take the person we love for granted but not always intentionally. I am not saying you or her for that matter, should stop doing the things that brought you together in the first place, but I do think when one or both are feeling unappreciated that you both should talk things out, not cheat to solve your issues.

Everyone knows that when they first date someone, they are talking and spending time with their "representative" and not the real person yet. They think a few dates in that they know enough about the person to get involved with them and they don't. Instead of her sitting down with you and expressing her concerns of the things she needs that you hadn't been doing, she decided to create a problem and gamble that by leaving you the new guy will give her what she needs. This woman is so smart that she is stupid. Meaning, that she is so greedy (just like most men in the same situation). She is blinded by the "momentary" attention someone else is giving her, so much so that she is willing to mess up her current relationship for it.

David is speaking: Why do you think this is?

Mr. Pearson is speaking: I feel this happens because more often, women in a relationship acting out are focused too much on how "they" are being treated and never think or care how they are "treating" their man. They forget, or should I say, most don't care if men have feelings or not or if they want to be treated certain kind of way in the relationship. These harlots only think about themselves. Many women believe a man is only in their lives to give them sex, take care of them financially, and give them money.

David is speaking: I treat her good and get her whatever she wants when she asks. What's wrong with that? Why would that make her consider cheating on me?

Mr. Pearson is speaking: What's wrong with what you just asked is this: so many men think and believe each time they do something for their woman or give them things, they are building "relationship equity." Something they can pull out and use whenever they are not doing new "things" for their woman. Many men believe the more they spend and give a woman the more she loves them. Often, they think that when she remembers something wrong they've done that she will then remember all they have done that is good to equal

42

everything out when it doesn't. Most women do not, will not nor will not care what you did for them three days ago or three months ago, only what you're doing for them right now.

Men do not get any carryover credit for past things done, remember that. I will also remind you that if your woman is in the relationship for more of what she can get from you then what she can get with you, she will drop you and upgrade the first time you get low on funds, stop doing things you used to or are unable to keep things up. Love has nothing to do with this at all. This is about her surviving you and the relationship. I have told men many times, "A woman may forget what you say to her most times, but she will never forget how you made her feel." I tell men often, never start something with a woman you can't continue because she will expect it to continue if she is going to trust and stay with you.

David is speaking: I don't want to go back to my old ways and cheat on her, but I could.

Mr. Pearson is speaking: Yes, you could but you and I both know, "two wrongs don't make things right"; it could and often does make things worse.

David is speaking: This is true, it may not make things right, but it sure does make things even.

Mr. Pearson is speaking: I hear you but keep in mind, didn't you say that you started going to church to change these old ways? Do you think God would approve of you getting back at her as the solution to your problem?

David is speaking: Yes, I did say that, and no, I don't think God would approve of me doing something like that. So, answer me this, "I am just supposed to let her make a fool out of me? I don't want to get played for a fool.

Mr. Pearson is speaking: I understand, but *IF* you don't know for sure she is cheating, you've got to pray for her, forgive her and ask God to guide your steps. Once you accept God in your life, you don't want to backslide and disappoint Him after all He has done for you. Allow Him the opportunity to work on your behalf. I can tell you from experience. Doing the right thing doesn't always feel good. You stay your own course and do not mistreat her or do her wrong but leave if you must *IF* what you feel she is doing is happening.

David is speaking: That makes sense.

Mr. Pearson is speaking: David, here is something that many men in situations like yours forget. Women will date you for one of two reasons: (1) She will date you *IF* she wants to be in a relationship with you, or the more common reason, (2) she will date you *IF* she wants something from you. How long did you two date before you became a couple?

David is speaking: We dated for one month, why do you ask?

Mr. Pearson is speaking: I ask because many people don't take enough time to check out one another's character. One, two or three dates don't cut it. You need to see if she wants you for you or is it for what she can get out of you? A process like this can and likely will take five to six months for you to know why she is with you. You need (like most women dating men need to know) who she is. During this time, you will no doubt get to see her "default" behavior, meaning what she is like daily and not just when she is with or around you.

You need to look for signs that she is looking to build and own, not rent as it relates to a relationship. If she is into you, she will find (like men should do as well) out what your needs are and give you what makes you happy with her. Women who want you will talk about things that include you, and regardless of her schedule, she will make time for you two to spend a moment to get to know one another. She is willing to invest in you, if you're willing to invest in her.

Listen, whatever a woman is consistent in is who she is. This means that most women know how to flirt with a man and make him feel like a man, and this leads to her getting what she wants from a man. If your woman is consistent in the way she treats you, that is "who" she is and how you will always be (if not better) going forward in your relationship.

A lot of women aren't with the men they are with because they are in love with them. They might care, but many are with their man for financial reasons. Keep in mind no woman is ever going to leave the man she is with to "trade down." She is going to always "trade up."

David is speaking: So, are you saying she is doing all of this because I am not making her happy?

Mr. Pearson is speaking: This is not just about making her happy financially. This is about you taking care of her financially, spiritually and sexually consistently. Women will stay with men mostly but not always who can take care of them in all three areas and will only consider moving on when the man can no longer do it or if there is someone with more to offer them. Men often forget that sex costs money, and if you're going to keep having it with her, you're going to pay a little or a lot for what most other men have gotten for free because she knows you love her not because she loves you.

David is speaking: Are you saying most women want men for financial reasons only?

Mr. Pearson is speaking: Not all but most do. Listen, a woman who loves you will not cheat on you, and the same goes for men. Contrary to what most people think, love is more than just spending money on a person. It is about getting to know one another.

Men need to understand if the woman they have met has her purpose in life, meaning she has goals and ways to achieve them and adding you to her life is a plus, then you might want to see where it goes. But, if the woman you meet has no purpose or is not in her "purpose" when you meet her, it is more likely that she is getting with you, not for love, but financial reasons until someone else better comes along.

Now I can't tell from what you've told me that your girlfriend is cheating on you, but if you want to know for sure, you need to watch her actions and not listen to her words. Women can manipulate you with her words and flirtations toward you. She will also, like most men have mastered, say and do things that lead you to believe she wants you for a relationship when she is trying to fulfill her own needs until someone else better comes along.

David is speaking: I appreciate the insight, and I will have to go back and re-examine what I have seen and be watchful going forward to know for sure. I hope this isn't karma that's happening to me. Do you believe people can be in love and faithful to one another?

Mr. Pearson is speaking: Yes, I do believe we can love one person and not cheat on them, but like anything else, it will take work to resist the numerous temptations and not allow it in your relationship. Listen, I know it sometimes seems that happy endings only happen in the movies, but I know and believe if what you've found with your girlfriend is *love,* it will last longer than two hours and mean so much more. Thank you for calling in David. I hope everything turns out right for you. Pray on it and let God handle it for you.

David is speaking: Thank you, Mr. Pearson. This has helped me a lot.

Mr. Pearson is speaking: Who do we have on the line next?

Karen is speaking: We have Tina from Decatur, Georgia.

Mr. Pearson is talking: Good morning, Tina. What is your question?

Tina is speaking: Hello Mr. Pearson. Well, it is like this. My man and I have been together for seven years, and we have three children together. One day out of the blue, he told me he no longer wanted to be in a relationship with me; it was over, and he left! At first, I thought he was playing, but I realized he was serious when I saw him pack his bags. I was shocked and mystified.

Within two months, I heard from a mutual friend of ours that he had met someone new, and they had gotten married. He had only known her for three months. When I heard this, I could not believe it! I called him to see if this was true, and when I got a hold of him, he confirmed it was true. I wondered when I hung up "why" he didn't marry me. We had a history, memories and children together. I didn't understand. This move of his, it made no sense to me at all.

I started to cry because I remember when we were dating, we talked about having kids, getting married and growing old together but now that dream was just that …a dream. I felt it was just yesterday when I said to him, I wanted to get married. He told me he wasn't ready to get married anytime soon. I took that to mean he'd reconsider marriage down the road for us. I didn't understand. We hit it off so much. I willingly put what I wanted (marriage) off for a while and was willing to wait until he was ready to be with him, and he knew this.

When I would bring up marriage, he would say not yet, maybe in a few months. Now I am mentioning this because he put me off for seven years and then married someone he knew for less than three months. I know you can hear I am still pissed, hurt and mad over this. I can't believe he left me and our family and started another one with her. I felt foolish thinking about the time, love, and money I wasted on him. For a long time, I thought I did something wrong for him to do this to me. I was confused, and I still have no idea why he would do this to me.

So, the question I have for you is, "Why do guys while dating you tell you that they aren't the marrying type? And soon after they break up with you, turn around and marry someone else they've hardly known so quickly?"

Mr. Pearson is speaking: This is a great question and a mystery that has kept many women guessing for years. Although the question is simple, the answer is not. There is no "one answer fits all" in this situation, because we have no idea what factors went into his decision with the history you two had. I have thoughts, and I will share them with you. My opinions may or may not be the answer you want to hear or even consider, but it will be insightful on what factors that could have led to his decision to leave the way he did. If things I say come off offensive, please know it is not my intention to downplay what he did or how you feel at this moment. First of all, what he did was ungodly and not a sign of a real man. Real men don't do silly things like that. Only children pretending to be men act this way.

Tina is speaking: Okay, please tell me something because I am confused.

Mr. Pearson is speaking: Let's take a look at a few reasons why a person would do such a thing. I may ask questions that seem a little too personal, and if you're uncomfortable, please feel free to tell me or not answer. With that said, I may stray during the process of making my point but stay with me. I promise you I will tie it all together.

Tina is speaking: Okay

Mr. Pearson is speaking: Let me begin by saying no one man thinks, acts or reacts the same way in a relationship. I often say to both women and men that when you start dating, you must step back and think about who you're dealing with at the moment. When I spoke at the Women's Seminar a few weeks ago, someone asked similar questions. I shared with them that a lot of our relationship issues come from the fact that many of us are afraid of being alone, to the point where we will jump into a relationship with someone in order to not be alone. Many are so anxious to get one another in bed that we hardly take the time to get to know one another. When you're doing this, you find yourself complaining and arguing a lot because you have no idea of "who" the person is you're dating. You thought things would all fall into place at some point and be alright once you got together.

Listen, a "good" man senses when he has met a "good" woman. Man reactions kick in, and he knows he will need to "invest" in her and that this is not someone to "rent" for the evening. He would take time to show her that she has made the right decision to be with him and that he is worthy of having her love him. He would get to know her likes and dislikes, the things that make her smile, her favorite color, understand what she needs emotionally and spiritually. He would love her and would never be afraid to let her know he "is" fearful of losing her. He would make her feel she can be, as would he, vulnerable with him, trust him, rely on him and that he "got her" through both the ups and downs. All this so she would feel secure and protected in their relationship. Did your man make you feel this way when you were with him?

Tina is speaking: Somewhat.

Mr. Pearson is speaking: If he were a real man in love with you, he would have known or felt if you were willing to trade your youth, be loyal and exclusive to him. He would have broken his back to make you his wife forever. Simply because he would have known he had found a "good" woman in you. A "good" man would never want to lose if he realized what he had, a "good" woman. Many people are together calling what they have a *relationship,* but what they have for most is treated as if they are roommates. It is far short of what couples back in the day that stayed together for over 20 years, had. There is no shame in wanting to know more about someone you're interested in. If you both feel chemistry, it should be no problem to "get to know" one another BEFORE you start sleeping together.

I have told men often that when you meet a woman and you two start to get close, you need to ask them to explain to them their definition of *love*. What is a good man to her? What does "Take care of me" mean to her? You need to find out if for what she wants she is willing to give. We are all wired differently; we must remember we all think differently. We all have a different definition of what *love* is and what we want and need from our mates to *stay* in love with them. Many women I spoke to mentioned that they considered themselves "good" and were seeking "good" men. They said they need to feel financially secure, protected and respected, loved both spiritually and physically to be able to give themselves to their man entirely willingly. I mention this because for some women the amount and level of their love for their man is based on how much money their man spends on them, how many "things" he buys them and how much money he gives to them to freely spend on whatever. Now, this comes as no surprise.

Men have said a lot of women, but not all, do not feel they should show any appreciation or say thank you for anything their man does for them. They see it as if they are "entitled" to all they receive. Many women do not understand that whatever men do for you or give to you is not something he is supposed to. Most do it because they want to please you. Many men believe they give their love unconditionally and that women love them with conditions. This is where the disconnect begins and the problems happen. Thinking that *love* is measured in the amount of money given and spent in the relationship will always badly.

Tina is speaking: I understand what you're saying, but men play so many games when it comes to *love*. All most men want from women is sex, and they will say and do whatever they can to get it.

Mr. Pearson is speaking: Listen, no man is going to sit down with you on your first date and tell you they're a dog. Very few will say to you any part of the truth. Men will never tell you that all they want from you is sex and once done, they're going to move on to another woman. If they did, you wouldn't sleep with them (unless you were horny). I know I have strayed a little, but rest assured, I heard you when you said your man out of the blue up and left your relationship, and soon after, met and married someone he had only known for a while.

You want to know "why" and "what" brought on the sudden change in his behavior. How could he do such a thing? More importantly because it seems you were in love with him, why with your history and two kids together didn't he see you as his wife, right?

Tina is speaking: This is correct.

Mr. Pearson is speaking: Let me state something I heard in the movie, The Brothers, said by Jennifer Lewis (who played Morris Chestnut's mother in the movie) because I agree with what she said. She told the women listening, "A man doesn't even know himself until he knows what kind of woman he wants." It's a powerful statement and 100% true on so many levels. If you break this statement down, it says a lot to answering your question and a lot about men in general. It explains and answers why so many men are single; why so many men are so comfortable with the title boyfriend/girlfriend and not with the title husband/wife. More importantly, it answers the question of why so many men avoid marrying those long-time girlfriends.

Tina is speaking: You're not going to tell me I am not wife material, because I don't believe that. During our time together, I gave and did everything I felt a wife would do for her man. I thought over time he would see how loyal and committed I was to him, and he would make me his wife. I have always felt and shown that I was a good woman. He should have made it official by marrying me. I never put pressure on him, but he knew I wanted to get married. I felt that after we had kids and invested seven years of our time together that marriage only made sense to do, but it didn't happen.

Mr. Pearson is speaking: A lot of what you just said is a big piece of your problem and a factor of "why" he may have left.

Tina is speaking: What do you mean?

Mr. Pearson is speaking: You said you gave him everything you felt a wife should give her man when he was only your boyfriend and NOT your husband. This problem right here is a position that many women find themselves in and yet, have no idea how they got there or how to correct the problem. To understand HIS behavior, I have to examine yours as well. What I am about to say is not to be taken too personally but is meant to be taken seriously. I am going to talk about what I feel is a solution to stop this cycle of women thinking that they will keep a man by sleeping with them, having children with them, continuously allowing the "boyfriend" to receive "husband" benefits before they have earned them. Setting standards will *STOP* this mess from happening. Again, I am not blaming or pointing the finger at women who are in this situation or have been through this situation. I'm merely stating the obvious and suggesting a solution for those dealing with this and who want it to stop.

Tina is speaking: Okay, so tell me what your thoughts are because you've got me curious to know your perspective. I know there is more to it than what I think, feel or understand.

Mr. Pearson is speaking: Let's start with what you told me already. You told me you knew in the beginning from his own words that he wasn't the marrying type. He said he "might" consider marriage one day but no time soon, and with this known, you got involved anyway. You had children with him "thinking" (1) he would see you as a good woman and marry you; (2) he would change his mind sooner than later, and (3) give you the kind of life you dreamed of, right?

Tina is speaking: Yes. What's your point? Because I cannot see how all that you have mentioned would make him want to leave me, get involved with another woman, marry her and start a family with her.

Mr. Pearson is speaking: Yes, it does. Let me explain how. Before I address that, have you heard the phrase, "Some women get married first and have kids, and many have kids and hope to get married one day?" I mention this because so many women today are willing to gamble on what they claim they want (if marriage is what they want at the end of the day) with men. Many buy into the "future promises of marriage for sex today theory" with men thinking kids will make him stay with or marry them when it doesn't. The evidence is out here today. Look around you, and you will find a lot of men with two or more baby mommas and women who have three-plus children still searching for a "good" man. For some women, a "good" man is that fool who they find and tempt with their bodies to step in and give them ALL the things they feel they deserve and didn't receive in their past relationships. It is as if it is THEIR responsibility to make up lost time and things their dead-beat men from before refused to do.

Before I get to the reasons why he may have left, let me first show you some red flags you ignored even though he told you a lot in his actions. The first red flag that should have made you rethink sleeping and having kids with him was when he said to you upfront that he wasn't the marrying type. Now, it doesn't matter that he was or wasn't. If you wanted to get married and he didn't, then he told you he wasn't the man for you. It should have told you that maybe you two should be friends but not sleep together or have children. Your next flag was the time you invested in waiting, and nothing happened; no marriage proposal came from him. Did he ever get you a ring during your seven years and three kids?

Tina is speaking: No!

Mr. Pearson is speaking: Listen, I am not trying to make you feel bad. I am trying to get you to see how serious this man was with you, and how he viewed your relationship. If you had been clear with him, stood your ground and not afraid to walk away if you didn't get what you wanted, this wouldn't have happened. He either would have stepped up and been a real man toward you and courted you the right way or walked away knowing you weren't going to be a thot to or for him. It would have saved you time, love and heartbreak.

What I am trying to tell you is not all love is good love. If this man respected your relationship, you would have seen it. He would have proposed within a year with a wedding date planned. Now, I am not saying everyone must get married before having sex, although if they call themselves Christians, they would know this already.

I know he lied like most men do because he had an agenda which was to sleep with you. Most men will take the information you say you want in a relationship such as marriage and kids and dangle it over your head during romantic moments to get what they want, with no intention of giving you what you want in the order you want it. It is clear from his behavior that he didn't value what you both shared. Honestly, it is good that he is gone because he didn't deserve you. You didn't need him to bring your life down with dreams and lies that he wasn't ever going to follow through on anyway.

Tina is speaking: So, why do you think he did this or felt this way because he never led me to believe he didn't love or care for me?

Mr. Pearson is speaking: I'm not saying he didn't care or love you because he probably did at some point, but you never put your foot down and demanded a wedding date. After you had your first child, he just continued to ride things out. He wasn't going to marry you because he didn't value the relationship that way. It is evident to me that he walked away with no regrets because he did tell you upfront that he wasn't the marrying type. I am not saying this to make you feel lousy, but you must have known that you're not the first and nor will you be the last to buy into men's lies. Many intelligent, smart, and beautiful women fall for the same tricks, lies and games men play even when they know they're playing and lying.

My opinion on why he left is he never saw value in what you two shared. He got before he gave. He continuously got from you "husband" benefits with no intention of marrying you regardless of the fact that he had kids with you. He used your love for him and the fact that you didn't set your expectations for him in the beginning to be involved with you. He took advantage of the situation, as most men do. You were dealing with a weak ass man.

Tina is speaking: I can't help but feel you're blaming me for him leaving because I allowed him to treat our relationship the way he did.

Mr. Pearson is speaking: Well, I am not, and I am sorry if it sounds that way, but this is just my view on this situation, okay? It is a subject I hear about all the time. I have daughters myself and know when I am not around that the men they meet and get involved with could lie and do this same thing to them. So, this is why I am so passionate about getting those in situations like this to understand that this is not something you have to do to be with or have a man. The fact of the matter is men are going to lie. It's what they do and do well, but women can prevent themselves from getting hooked in by having and setting reasonable expectations and sticking by them.

Listen, women, where marriage is concerned, most men see it as merely a "piece of paper," nothing more. They see no reason to rush out and legally commit to you that way when they don't have to. For men in general, marriage isn't something they grow up thinking about, but most do seek the companionship of the opposite sex. I am not saying, married men today do not enjoy being married or value their marriage because most do, but I have heard married men say,

"Women fall in love and get married; men marry and then fall in love." I wouldn't trade it for anything in the world. I enjoy it.

Tina is speaking: So, when you say, he didn't *value* or *respect* what we had, what do you mean?

Mr. Pearson is speaking: Again, in my opinion, you, like most women today, make it too easy for men. You give them what they want before they have earned ANYTHING and then wonder why they, after getting it, act a fool with you. Understand, because it is no secret to other women today, men want sex first and maybe your companionship second. He spent less and got more. He had children with you because "you" said you wanted children (if he wanted them or not) to continue to get from you what he wanted. He probably at some point made you feel you were luckier to be with him then him with you. He saw in you that you wanted a man in your life, and he was happy to fill the spot. That's what appears to have happened from my perspective.

For those women listening, please hear me and pass this on to the younger women. As the Bible said, you should tell the younger women so they can avoid this cycle and not have to figure it out on their own. Teach and show them how to lay down expectations, rules and regulations. Teach them that what they have is worth more than money. In other words, make men work for what they claim they want, which is you. If a man wants to be with you, let him show you by investing in you and not by buying you for the moment. If he does it right, he can have you forever (marriage). There is no amount of money more valuable than the love of a good woman.

And for those women out there playing games with good men, remember when he does "wake up" and see you for who you are, he will take his resources and leave you and give them to someone worth investing in.

Tina is speaking: So, what are you telling me?

Mr. Pearson is speaking: What I am telling you is he needed to leave, and you are better off without him. You may not see this right now because the pain may be still fresh in your mind, but I guarantee you at some point down the road, you are going to look back and ask yourself, "Why did I ignore those red flags or my gut?" You will see that you gave 100% of yourself to him, and he may have given you 20% if that, and that is not being *equally yoked.* You did get three beautiful children out of it, and sooner than later you will find the right guy who is willing to meet you way passed halfway by showing you, investing in you and growing with you in a way you not only need and will accept but the way you deserve.

Tina is speaking: Why do men act this way?

Mr. Pearson is speaking: They act this way with women because they can. The one thing men hate for women to do to them is set or give them "dates and timelines." The reason why is because putting dates and timelines on things moves the relationship forward, but more importantly, it makes men keep their word on things. As we all know, physical attractions are common, mental connections are rare and a verbal commitment is a "commitment" between two people in the relationship. When a man makes that verbal commitment with their woman, they can't come back later and say that "you" misunderstood them or what they meant.

Without commitment, most don't follow through with 95% of what they tell you. Even in some cases, the woman knows their man isn't going to follow through but they sleep with them anyway. Don't get it twisted. I know no matter what I say people are going to do whatever they feel is best for them, but if you're tired of ending up in the same position or you want to avoid it altogether, you might want to listen to what I have said and take it to heart. I took the pressure off my wife by telling her, I wanted "sex and love" at the same time, and I was willing to wait until we married to get it because she was worth it.

Tina is speaking: Looking back, I wish I would have done this.

Mr. Pearson is speaking: Men need to know real men don't act this way. In my book, <u>*Wrong Turn (Diary of a GOOD man)*</u>, I break down a formula/method to help women protect themselves as they search for the right man for them. I said that "the *woman* is the *employer*, and the *man* is the potential *employee*." It's the man who is applying for a "position" in your life. You want to find out if they are looking for "full time, part-time, seasonal or some on-call work" before considering them for a position. Based on their resume and their presence (their conversation) you can determine if they are even qualified. Now be cautious! Don't get too excited because their resume looks good because it is just a bunch of words not proof of actions. Take your time. You're looking for someone who is capable of "leading" and could be a right business partner with you because you want to be able to feel good turning your company over to him and know it is in good hands.

If you hire someone who looks good on paper (meaning they look and sound good) and they get their benefits BEFORE any work has been put in and then quit shortly afterward, don't blame them. Blame yourself. There are men who are only looking for part-time, seasonal or on-call work and will be happy to start and put in very little work or time to get the benefits if you allow them to. However, if you're serious about what you are looking for, you would never hire any of these people because the job has and comes with too many damn good benefits to just give it to a person looking to do a half-ass job.

No job you ever worked gave you a two-week paycheck on the first day you started, so why would you pay them (sleep with them) shortly after you hire them? Most jobs start you out with a probation period. They make you wait for the benefits, make you work for two weeks before receiving a paycheck and if you're not good at what you do, they will let you go. Remember, when you started your job, you didn't get all the benefits that they spoke about right away, did you?

Think about it. A man is looking for a woman like he searches for a job. Do you want someone to come in every so often and do as little as possible and get full benefits? Allowing this to happen wouldn't make good business sense now, would it? Women need to remember you're looking for a *business partner,* a person to come in and grow with the company, someone who understands the job isn't an easy one, but the benefits they receive makes it well worth it. It is a company worth *investing* in, and it gives back high dividends and comes with perks! You are looking for this person to replace you as CEO, to allow you to step down and assume a new but vital role within the organization and run the company (because you'll be married and this responsibility will now belong to him). All women need to know during this process is that just because he applies for the job you have available, looks good on paper (meaning looks and talks well to you) doesn't mean he is the right person for the job. To ensure you get a great candidate with the right skill set for this position, you must ask detailed questions specific to the needs of the job agenda. To start with, just list the job you have available (make yourself seen by dating in person or meeting people online. Show that you are on the market, and you're interviewing), be sure to list the *requirements* for this position (your wants and needs, your desires but be specific), and set up interviews (meaning talk first on the phone; if you're feeling them set up a date, talk and see if the person is worthy of a "callback" or does he need to go directly in the "trash/don't bother" file.) Determine from your interviews if you have the right candidate for the position. Reach out to them for a second interview before you hire them. Are you following what I am saying?

Tina is speaking: Yes. So how do I pick the right person going forward after all I have been through, not to get it wrong again?

Mr. Pearson is speaking: Well, you may need to interview many applicants (go on many dates with potentials) before you find the right person for the position. It doesn't mean you have to pay them for coming to the interview (meaning you don't have to sleep with them). I say this because as we have learned from what you've said, your last employee was the wrong fit for the position. He talked his way into the job (in other ways he lied), thinking once in, he could make a lateral move to get what he wanted (which was to sleep with you).

He sold it well knowing that the job would never get completed (meaning he would never marry), and you told him without checking his references (finding out who you were dealing with, getting to know each other first) he had the job. Based on his actions, he was looking for *seasonal* work not *full-time* and based on his quality of work (not asking you to marry him after seven years and kids together) he was the wrong person for this position. You paid him (slept with him often) for a half-ass job done. Before you could fire him (meaning before you could confront him on the quality of his work) thus far, he quit. He is leaving you with issues and concerns to figure out.

Listen, when selecting the right person for this current position you have open, you need to be clear on the requirements for such a job. You need to listen to see if the potential person is looking for a full-time job. Are they ready to put in overtime and *invest* in the company? Are they prepared to handle the day-to-day responsibilities (meaning be the provider and head of the household) that is needed for you and your current employees (your kids). You must be much more precise, upfront, more transparent and not willing to "pay" them for promises. Read their resume carefully (in other words, "LISTEN" to what they say because in the first 30 minutes of most dates men will tell you the truth and if you are not impressed, then they will go into full lying mode in order to wow! you).

Remember, you have standards and expectations in your head. You know which ones are important and which ones are negotiable. If you do this, when you get up from the table from your first date, you will know who you're dealing with at that moment! Are you a Christian woman?

Tina is speaking: Yes, but I don't go to church as often as I should, but I believe in God. Why do you ask?

Mr. Pearson is speaking: I ask because to do this correctly, you must trust in God to help you find that right person. You cannot "pay" men for part-time work, nor should you look to hire anyone not qualified for such a great opportunity. You and I both know that the person who gets this position will receive great benefits. You make your selection based on his resume, make sure you have checked his background thoroughly to ensure he doesn't bring you or your company down or devalue it. You can do that all by yourself.

Now the tricky part is letting him know he must "show" you that he is the right person before you consider letting him know. Asking God for His help to keep you secure will prevent you from hiring the wrong person and paying someone who isn't worth paying for a job they never knew how to do. Any man who wants the job will put in the effort to get it because they see the potential growth and all the benefits and perks "if" hired. Weak men will fake it and hope you never check their references (to see if they are working for someone else at the same time (dating more than one woman) because they know they don't qualify for such a high position.

Tina is speaking: I see what you mean.

Mr. Pearson is speaking: If you think about it, it all makes sense. No job gives you your full paycheck on the first day, they make you wait. If you want the paycheck, you will accept their terms and conditions, right? And you do.

It is why many women who have been in this situation or are in this situation today feel used or played by men. They have paid these men (giving up their bodies) and then get mad when he quits (leaves you for someone else) for no reason and wonder why they up and went without giving a two-weeks' notice. They did it this way because they didn't respect the job, the employer and felt the "pay" wasn't enough for them to stay. Men who have done this feel no obligation to show up anymore, complete the work or even let you know that they don't want to work for you anymore.

Tina is speaking: I understand what you're saying, but men lie so much, and many of them do it well, so well, it's hard not to believe them. I feel this is why many women pay them BEFORE they have completed the work. Are you saying if we (women) would stop paying men for work they haven't done yet that it would lessen our problems with them?

Mr. Pearson is speaking: That is what I am telling you. I agree men tell more lies than the Bible has scriptures to trick a woman into sleeping with them. All women must understand that they control what work is needed, what the pay is, the rewards and benefits, and the TIMING of when the man gets a check for the work he completes not him. Remember, he applied for a position in YOUR life. YOU decide who "gets" the job and the benefits. You placed an ad (by going out to clubs, getting on a dating site) saying, "Work is available for the right man, not just any man." It doesn't matter what anyone says. Respect yourself. Value and know your worth but more importantly, realize you bring too much to the table to be treated like a *napkin*, then men will not be able to get over on you as much so quickly.

I am not telling you this to gas you up but more to have you be aware of the "games" men (and some women play) to get with you, and how to avoid the problems. It will cut down on you *paying* many different guys for part-time work undone. Who wants to be broke and brokenhearted? Don't blame the guy if you hire him *knowing* he failed the background check, and he lied about what he could and would do if given a chance; that's on you.

If you enjoy being someone else's *thot,* then pay them and be broke. Don't get me wrong. Some women are cool with being a thot, side chick, etc. as long as they get some money and things out of it. If you choose to sleep with men because you have "needs," understand that they don't owe you anything. Don't lie to yourself thinking afterward that you were *in control* because YOU decided when HE got what you gave him. Know that some men are very patient and will wait for what they want and still spend the minimum on you to get it.

Ask yourself this question, "What is the price to be with you?" If you come up with a number, then you've sold yourself cheap. I tell women all the time if you dress like a hooker, you will attract a pimp to rule and run you as long as you both are together. If you dress like success, then you will attract a successful man who sees you got it going on (meaning your life, not your body) and will want to approach you in a manner that is respectful and worthy of your time and effort to get to know them if you find them attractive. Which would you want to be, someone's *thot* or someone's *wife*?

Tina is speaking: I never thought about it that way. I should stop looking and ask God for His help to find me the right man because I do believe in God.

Mr. Pearson is speaking: I agree. Now, this doesn't apply to all women because not all women want to get or be married. There are a lot of women who are okay with casual sex and having kids without being married. Many women in their early 20s and 30s are not thinking about marriage. They're thinking about exploring and living their lives. I understand. I, too, had casual sex and even had two kids with someone to whom I wasn't married but it wasn't because I didn't ask her to marry me. She didn't want to get married.

You must understand something about most men. If the sex was given too easily, it makes us question and say, "If I got it on the first date, how many other men also have?" This train of thought, even though they sleep with you, will not make them see you as a wife but more like a "sex buddy." A sex buddy that is someone they hook up with from time to time but not to seriously commit to them. If you're one of those women who is sleeping with a guy thinking, if the sex is good he will marry me, stay with me and not cheat on me, then you are not very bright. You are using your body much as a prostitute would.

I am not saying good sex will not get you married, but if I were you, I wouldn't want to rely on sex alone to find me a loving and a long-lasting relationship. Just out of curiosity, "What did this man do that was so damn wonderful for you that you lowered your standards and PAID him in full for a part-time gig? You've heard the phrase, "Why buy the cow when you can get the milk for free?" What good man wants to pay a premium price for something other men got for free? Have you ever thought about what that phrase is saying about women who sleep around?

Tina is speaking: I've heard it, and it is saying men want sex, not a committed relationship long term. Women are telling them they can have milk without purchasing anything.

Mr. Pearson is speaking: You are right! Please hear me when I say that I'm not saying in your situation or women in situations like this are wrong for falling in love and having kids but at some point, in this continuous cycle, women must know and realize they are worth so much more to a real man than in-house sex. Investing time in a person and not getting the rewards you deserve from it can be painful. How much pain must a woman experience before she says, "Enough is enough" and move on? His leaving was a blessing for you.

Tina is speaking: How so?

Mr. Pearson is speaking: He wasn't the one you were supposed to be with anyway. God has a better plan for you and your children if you trust and believe in Him. Have you prayed lately for Him to help you get a better understanding of your recent events and to help you through it?

Tina is speaking: No, but now I will.

Mr. Pearson is speaking: Listen, it says in **2 Corinthians 13:5**, (KJV), "Examine yourselves, whether ye be in the faith; prove your own selves. Know ye, not your own selves, how that Jesus Christ is in you, except ye be reprobates?" In other words, you are not alone, and you don't have to do this alone. God has got you and will help you if you ask Him. Whenever you feel what you're going through is too much to handle, you need to call on Him and let Him fight your battle for you.

Tina is speaking: So, what you're saying is I shouldn't focus on why he left or who he is with now because it is not going to change my situation. I should focus on me and my children and how to prevent this from happening again. By asking God to guide me, and with His understanding, He will help me get ready for my future husband. Somewhere out there, someone is ready, willing and able to complete the job they'll apply for with me. Someone is prepared to lead so I can follow but more importantly, someone to love me and my kids full-time not part-time, right?

Mr. Pearson is speaking: Honestly speaking, yes. You know anything in life worth having is worth working for. You will appreciate it more once you get it. We value things a lot more if we've worked hard to obtain them than we do when someone gives it to us. When things are so easily given, we do not appreciate the value or take care of it. In the situation where so many women are looking forward to being wives and being married, they are allowing weak ass men to sleep with them and talk them into having children when they don't know if this man is going to help them take care of a child. It is just sickening. The men doing this to good women are wrong. Many good men are showing or setting good examples of what a man should be in their children's life. Then there are those men, sorry, children, who are showing other growing young boys that it is okay to contribute to creating more broken homes.

Tina is speaking: I agree.

Mr. Pearson is speaking: I know what I am saying for some women listening will go in one ear and out the other. I am glad you understand what I have said enough to think and re-examine yourself and your behavior so that you will do things differently. I am not saying this to offend you or anyone listening. I am merely saying it is time for both men and women to break this cycle of creating broken families where there is very little of a father's positive influence in the home or a child's life.

Tina is speaking: You're right; we must learn from our past mistakes and do better.

Mr. Pearson is speaking: Yes. Don't get me wrong though. As a follower of Christ and a person who believes in the Bible as it relates to marriage, I am not advocating nor am I saying I encourage sex before marriage. I was once young, so I understand. Now why people do what they do will always be a mystery, but one thing is for sure when people play games, someone wins, and someone loses.

Tina is speaking: I understand what you're saying and yes, in a way, looking back, I allowed my feelings for him to dictate my actions. I did believe that one day we would get married.

Mr. Pearson is speaking: I know because when we like someone, it is hard to stick with what we said we were going to do. We want what we want with that person. However, because most men lie, it is damn near impossible and hard for a woman to trust and believe in them or consider marrying them.

Tina is speaking: That makes sense. But there are a lot of women willing to lower their standards in order to not be lonely.

Mr. Pearson is speaking: I agree. Sadly enough things will not get any better. No one wants to be alone and, in some cases, both men and women alike will lower their standards to not be alone. I understand sleeping around seems cool, but for many doing this, they look desperate, thirsty, lonely and easy. While in this state of "I don't want to be alone" is when we make the most mistakes and end up getting and feeling used by the other person "if" they treat us less than how we thought they felt for us.

Let me share this with you. I learned from women at an early age that there are two kinds of women: a *seasoned woman* (and most married women and those in a steady relationship reading this know what I am talking about) and then the *unseasoned woman.* Let's talk about the difference between the two because the differences are as clear as night and day. All women dating today know men prefer to sleep with them and prefer to spend little to no money if possible, to do so.

This is not a secret. Some women use their bodies to attract men thinking that by sleeping with them they will keep them as their man. Men called these women, back in the day, "chicken heads." They give up the sex thinking sex alone is going to make him love them, and they will get whatever they "feel" they deserve. These foolish women often say, "I deserve nice things. Why shouldn't he give them to me if he wants to be with me?" They don't understand that they are *renting* themselves to a man not yet willing or ready to *buy.* Many of them end up getting played and used like this. Let me tell you something my grandmother tells my sister, "A wet vagina and a dry purse don't match."

These women repeat this process over and over expecting different results but never end up with anything more than "things." The men lead with sex, not morals, standards or expectations of what it would take to have a priceless jewel like her in his life. He already got her at sex, why go further?

A *seasoned woman* understands what a man wants and makes it clear what she wants before she considers giving him what he desires. She "needs" to see that he deserves what she has to offer. She will make him *earn* what he claims he wants. If and when he earns "it," meaning she has seen for herself through his actions that he is worthy and knows she has much more to offer than just her body, he has to put a ring on her finger and say, "I do." He then can have what the Bible says is his.... her!

Tina is speaking: Funny but true. It is because men lie so well that many women fall for it. They must take some of the blame. It is not all on the woman.

Mr. Pearson is speaking: I agree. Men should take a lot of the blame, but at the same time, women need to understand and know that they control if and when any sex will be given out, not the man. If you slip once from his lies, okay. Know that if you keep going back knowing and seeing he is lying, that's your fault. In this case, he didn't use you. He may have lied to you, but it was YOU who made a choice to sleep with him repeatedly and gave him what he wanted BEFORE you got what you claimed you wanted.

Now, if you're not one of those women who wants to get married and you prefer yourself a "sex buddy," do your thing because what I am saying does not apply to you or your lifestyle. Be aware that it will wear on your emotional state of mind over time if the person you're sleeping with isn't exclusive to you. Unfortunately, this happens and will continue because many women are willing to gamble with their bodies for momentary happiness and *hope* the guy they are with wants the same thing they want at some point.

Serious men with good intentions will wait and show you mean more to them than just a night in bed. They will get to know you and make you feel and know that you are with someone you can trust and fall in love with, have children with and build a life with.

Tina is speaking: I understand, and I am glad you said that. I know many of my female friends who aren't ready to settle down but want to engage in premarital sex. Then, I have some who are committed to waiting until they get married. I should have been more cautious.

Mr. Pearson is speaking: It is sad because bed-hopping has become the "norm" and is widely accepted as something to be expected in relationships today. I don't want anyone, especially women, to be taken advantage of by a lying man, but it happens; it is part of being in a relationship. I want all women to be more "proactive" and less "reactive."

Tina is speaking: What do you mean when you say, "Women need to be more proactive and less reactive?"

Mr. Pearson is speaking: What I am saying and what I mean is that there are very few, if any, men who will respect a woman who is quick to sleep with them. It says in **Proverbs 31:10**, (KJV), "Who can find a virtuous woman? For her price is far above rubies." In other words, you are worth more than just sex to a man in God's eyes. You have much more to offer than your body in a relationship. Here is what I would like to do if you don't mind. I want to walk you through something I shared with women at the seminar I spoke about earlier in hopes you get a better understanding.

Tina is speaking: Okay, I would love to hear this because as you know, I am single now. I don't want to repeat with my next mate the same approach.

Mr. Pearson is speaking: On your next or first date, a casual conversation needs to include things you feel are important to you and things that your mate should come with or be willing to adjust. You must not feel you cannot ask questions. It is your right. Remember you are trying to get to know this person and the only way this can happen is if you ask questions (gather data to make a sound decision on whether he is a potential mate or just a friend). (1) Ask what you want but make your questions *valued* ones. (2) Don't talk about sex on the first date or allow him to push the conversation in that direction. If he does, it tells you right away that that is all he is looking for from you. Too many women mistake "sex talk" on the first date for interest and lead him to believe you are telling him without saying so that you're an "easy lay," a one-night stand and someone he shouldn't waste time "investing" in for long-term. (3) Get deep on them and ask about things like marriage, kids, sex before marriage, finances, etc.

This is how you will find out his position on the subjects that are important to you. If he has a hard time answering any of these kinds of questions, it means he is not ready for a serious commitment. I don't expect anyone to pour out their hearts on the first date, but both men and women should have an idea of the qualities they want in each other other than a beautiful body. By not asking valued questions, you're hoping they will "be" perfect, and things will fall in place with what you dreamt your next ideal mate would be. Hoping is not the same as knowing.

Tina is speaking: That makes sense, but I am not comfortable asking things like that. What if he doesn't want to answer at all?

Mr. Pearson is speaking: Then you are having dinner or lunch with a new friend and not a potential mate, and that's okay. You need to get comfortable with asking "valued" questions. I can guarantee he is sitting there looking at you and thinking to himself, "I would love to smash her," and at some point if he feels bold enough he may just ask, "Would you like to smash?" just to see what you will say or how you would react to what he asked. Men are not afraid of losing you at this point because you are not theirs to lose yet.

Tina is speaking: I understand what you're saying, but if they are feeling me out, why be so aggressive for sex right away?

Mr. Pearson is speaking: Good question, simple. The answer is that most men are and will always be impatient. Men don't like to wait for what they want from you. Therefore, they will push hard on the first or second date to get you back to their place to "get to know" you better (their definition of getting to know you). Men still think today that if they "spend" on you, you owe them sex. Men pushing that hard are people you should avoid because they have told you without saying, "You're just a thot for the night."

Tina is speaking: With all the lies men tell, how do we know when a man is interested in you for real?

Mr. Pearson is speaking: Another good question with a simple answer. Any man claiming to be interested in knowing you better will show you not just tell you in and through his actions when he is with you. As someone interested, he knows sex is something that "comes with" your relationship, but it is not the only thing. Real men already know getting and keeping a woman happy requires money, patience, and time.

Tina is speaking: Why is acknowledging, respecting and treating us right when we are with them so hard for them to do?

Mr. Pearson is speaking: The answer to this question is at the heart of your original question, but more importantly, it is the reason why so many men hurt so many women so freely. Too many women have convinced themselves that as boyfriend and girlfriend you must have sex while not understanding that as long as you (the woman) keep giving the boyfriend "husband" benefits he will always treat you as such and nothing more. Sure, sex in the relationship is beautiful but, in this situation, and at the end of the connection (if it should happen), the guy comes out the "winner." Why would any man want to renegotiate this agreement when it works so well in their favor, he got sex with no legal commitment, would you if you were them?

Listen, you need to know, and it is a must, so please write this down (4) Men on a first date will tell you the truth in the first 30 minutes, and if you are impressed, they will continue to be truthful. If you're not impressed, they will start lying to you to impress you. (5) There are two types of men you are going to meet in your lifetime. They are the men who will "invest in you" and those who will "spend on you." I touched on it earlier but let me explain a little more what I mean. Men willing to "invest" in you will be those guys who take their time to get to know you for who you are and not for what you have between your legs. The guys who "spend on you" are looking to "rent" you for a period and will, when he grows tired of renting, move on and rent elsewhere. He is willing to spend to get what he wants from you, but at the same time, he will try and spend as little as possible to do so.

Tina is speaking: I agree. But keep in mind that some women are willing to trade sex for things or money.

Mr. Pearson is speaking: Yes, I agree with you, but with that kind of arrangement, there are also consequences.

Tina is speaking: What are the consequences?

Mr. Pearson is speaking: Besides the fact that they could catch something that they can't get rid of, very few men see this kind of woman as a future wife. She is not the woman they feel they can introduce to family and friends. This is why women in this position often ask the guy, "Why haven't I met any of your family or friends or why haven't we hung out at places you frequent?" The reason is that you are his little dirty secret that he doesn't want anyone to know about because of the *type* of relationship you two have. Is this a sign of a man who you want to live long-term with?

Tina is speaking: It is a shame, and you're right, it isn't something a woman considers a "long-term" relationship. I remember you said earlier that those women who believe in the Bible should wait for marriage before having sex, but what if the sex is not as good as I want it to be? Then a woman is stuck in a bad situation if she is sexually active and wants it often.

Mr. Pearson is speaking: Good question. I can see how that would be a problem, but at the same time, what if the woman is bad in bed, isn't he left in the same situation also? Sex alone shouldn't be your reason for getting married. It should be based on the love and respect the two of you have developed between you. Yes, sex in a relationship is important but if your relationship and marriage are based solely on sex, once the sex becomes not so good one of you, if not both, will seek "great sex" with someone else. This would make the time you spent with one another wasted time, a time you will never get back to do over again. I would hope you two had more in common than just wanting to have sex because if you don't, you will divorce or breakup soon afterward.

Tina is speaking: What about marrying someone with kids?

Mr. Pearson is speaking: This is a tricky one, and I will not get too deep into it because there are many ways this could go. I will say this though, some people have a problem with people with kids. I've found that women are more open to accepting a man's kids than men are to accepting a woman's kids from previous relationships."

Tina is speaking: Why do you think that is?

Mr. Pearson is speaking: Unfortunately, in this world we live in, there are *double standards* for both men and women. There are many women with two-plus kids by multiple men, and most men have problems with that on their end. Most men even if they have the same situation, do not want to take on the responsibility of taking care of another man's children. Is it fair? No, but it's the reality we live in that, as far as I know, will never change. I know some women who prefer men without children and will not date them if their kids are younger than 17 years old. We all have our preferences. People who feel this way do not want to deal with baby mama/baby daddy drama.

Women who continuously show a lack of respect for themselves are more likely to end up in this situation more times than they will admit. Women who think sex will keep a man and make him love them the way they want and desire are thinking foolishly. Their thought process is that they're assuming if they "throw it on him," he will stick around and treat them like the queen they feel they are. Little do they know this method hardly ever works for anyone.

These women out here today thinking and doing this need to take down the sale and for sale signs they are currently wearing so that those men who are attracted to them will not think they are someone they can buy. Let me say it this way, "Don't advertise what you don't mean to sell (meaning your body)." It says in **Proverbs 22:1**, (KJV), "A good name is rather to be chosen than great riches, and loving favour rather than silver and gold." In other words, you can ruin your reputation by the way you carry yourself.

You cannot dress and act like a harlot and be seen and treated like a queen. It says in **1Thessalonians 5:22**, (KJV), "Abstain from all appearance of evil." In other words, women inviting men over to their place or you going to his home at 2 am, what do you think you're going over there to do, talk? Do you believe that afterward he will see you as the *one* or just another *thot*?

Women need to stop treating *living together* as if it is the same as being married because it is not even close to being the same. I read an article in a Christian Magazine in 2019. It stated that 69% of Americans felt it was okay to "live together" and not be married, and that is sad.

Tina is speaking: You know how it is when you are young and in love, you do a few stupid things that you later regret.

Mr. Pearson speaking: I understand because I, too, made my share of mistakes in my 20s and 30s. Honestly, there is no excuse when you learn and know the truth. People claiming to believe in God and doing this are telling me that they know but have decided to do things their way and not His. Let me ask you something, do you want to be part of some man's flock of baby mammas? Is this a life you see for yourself? What message do you think is being seen and understood by younger women who are watching older women do this?

Tina is speaking: No, I don't want to be part of some man's flock like R. Kelly. I have more respect for myself than that. The message being sent out to young women growing up is that engaging in sexual activity and having kids before marriage is okay. We shouldn't judge anyone on their choices. We didn't like it when our parents or others judged us.

Mr. Pearson is speaking: I am not asking anyone to judge anyone. I am asking women who know and have gone through this to *teach* the younger ones as the Bible says they should. If they are not taught to respect themselves and their bodies then this process that we see today will continue. The fact is marriage isn't taken as seriously as it should be. Our society sends out messages through television shows, movies and in magazines that sleeping around is acceptable and just a part of life. So, my question to you and those listening is this, am I wrong for wanting better for women? Am I crazy for asking them to ask more questions and make better decisions BEFORE deciding to get involved sexually with a person they hardly know?

Tina is speaking: No, you're not wrong, but like I said earlier, men tell lies so much how can women trust them or what they say?

Mr. Pearson is speaking: Women must ask "valued" questions and understand that sleeping with any man doesn't mean the man loves or cares for you. What most men have told me is that sex is just sex not love with most women.

Tina is speaking: You touched on that earlier. What kind of questions are valued ones?

Mr. Pearson is speaking: Yes I did, and this is number (6) on my dating list. Valued questions are those questions you ask a guy that give you data, the data you need to know to determine if you want to move forward with him or if you two need to be just friends.

Here is a typical question most women ask which is not a question that will get them the answer they are looking for, "Are you single?" This question is asked and is a yes or no answer. It is not a detail question and because the guy wants to sleep with you, what do you think he is going to say? So, your question isn't *specific,* and the answer will always be "Yes, I am single even if he is not." Here is another way to ask the same question to get the response you are looking for: "Are you seeing, dating, sleeping with or involved with anyone else while you're trying to get to know me?" This question is direct and leaves them NO WIGGLE room. It makes them nervous, squirm and struggle to find an answer that they "think" you will accept. If they avoid it altogether, it is your clue and the red flag to walk away. *DON'T IGNORE IT!*

I am not saying he couldn't still lie to you, but this method helps you quickly identify if he is lying or not. Just remember that no guy is going to voluntarily feed you information about himself or what his real motive is because you look good. It doesn't help him achieve his goal that evening, which is to sleep with you. Why would they tell you? Here is a fact few women know if the truth is said, *not all men are "marriage material."* It depends on where they are in their life when you meet them.

Tina is speaking: Can you explain what you mean when you say, "It depends on where they are in their life?"

Mr. Pearson is speaking: This is what I mean when I say that. I am saying when you meet a man, he will be in one of two places, either in the *Search* Mode or *Ready to be Married* Mode. Let me break this down so you can recognize who you are talking to and the difference between the two. What I am about to share with you will save you time and protect your heart from those men who are not ready for a real commitment. It will stop you from giving up the cookie before it's time (if marriage is your goal), keep you from looking thirsty and give you a better insight to know if the man you're speaking to is your potential husband and someone worthy of your love or a guy you need to pass on.

Tina is speaking: Okay!

Mr. Pearson is speaking: Recognizing "who" you're talking to starts with the "language" he is using to speak to you. Many of us are known for having "selective" hearing, right?

Tina is speaking: Right.

Mr. Pearson is speaking: This means we hear what we want to hear and do not hear what we should. It is because many of us cannot handle the "truth or bad news." Some don't like talking or answering questions especially about themselves. So, when a woman asks a man on their first date, "Tell me about yourself?" their answer usually focuses on what they do (their job) because what they do is to them who they are.

Tina is speaking: I am not following you, explain, please.

Mr. Pearson is speaking: Most men identify themselves by their job title and position without realizing that their job is something they do; it is not who they are. In other words, in their head, they will always answer this question this way because they identify themselves by the job and title they hold. This is evident when they lose their job as they get depressed and take it out on their woman. To them, they are nobody without the title and position.

Tina is speaking: Interesting.

Mr. Pearson is speaking: The funny thing is when women ask the question, "Tell me about yourself?" what they are asking about are his inner qualities not about his job. Other areas of their life such as how they grew up, where they are from, their likes and dislikes, if he wants to get married, if so, when, do they have or want kids, his plans with his next mate, etc. As you can see, this is very important to most women because they learn a lot about the man and they're better able to determine if he is a potential mate or if they will just be friends. (FYI: The word "friends" isn't something most men want to hear.)

Tina is speaking: I have noticed that with a lot of men.

Mr. Pearson is speaking: Now men "ready to settle down" will not attempt to approach or get involved with you if they are stable and somewhat financially ready. He'd know if he didn't comment correctly that you would have a lack of respect for him. He'd know that you would take more of a motherly role than one of a companion in the relationship, and that is not what he is seeking in his potential wife. Men like this will take their time and get to know you. They are and will be very patient in their efforts to understand you. In doing so, it gives you time to see if his actions match his words and the promises that he made to you. You can see if he is working on making them come true. He will make it easy for you to fall in, grow in, and stay in love with him. Does this make sense?

Tina is speaking: Yes.

Mr. Pearson is speaking: Remember when you are on a date, you are the *Interviewer,* the man is the *Interviewee.* He is trying to get with you! So, ask all the questions you want. You are trying to find the "right" person for you. Don't rush because they "look good" and talk "sweet." Look for qualities such as compatibility and chemistry. Listen to see if he describes where he sees himself in 5 years, and see if he is going in the same direction you are for starters. Know this. You're not just choosing a mate; you're picking a future business partner.

People who don't want to put in the work to find someone will often revert to an ex. Not because they are so in love with them, but because there is a sense of "familiarity." Returning to and repeating the same process, going through the same issues all the while expecting different results, what's wrong with this picture? They do this because they are afraid of "starting over" and meeting new people. In short, they would be considered lazy. I understand they don't want to put themselves out there and be hurt again, but if you do not get involved or participate in your success, how can you expect to find someone?

Tina is speaking: Why do you think many people do this and do not take more chances if what they had didn't work out the first time?

Mr. Pearson is speaking: I feel the reason most do this is because their ex is someone they already know, and they are already familiar with their faults, moods, etc. They are willing to repeat it and believe that things will be different this time. Is this healthy to do? No! But for many men and women, it is their sad reality. I have said many times that when you feel you cannot do things on your own, you need to pray to God and ask Him to guide you. It may take a while, but when God feels you are ready, He will present someone to you.

Tina is speaking: I have a few girlfriends who have done that, claiming they have found their soulmates. I am not sure I could or would want to.

Mr. Pearson is speaking: Here is a common myth many people believe regarding "soulmates." Many of us believe that when we find our soulmate, they are going to be just like us. They are going to like all the same things, think the same way, be the same in every way and they will have no problems. It is not true. The statement "opposites attract" is really how we all find one another. Accepting the differences and finding ways to deal with one another is what builds a relationship and brings us closer. I have always asked couples, "Why can we not accept the flaws we see in one another?" We already know everything isn't going to always be perfect but if we can be willing to share and be open with one another in our views and opinions, as it pertains to our relationship, our relationship could last and we both may be fulfilled. It is so important to know a lot is riding on your selection of a mate. I advise you to take your time and pick wisely and understand that relationships take work and years together to become what you both expected it would be.

Tina is speaking: I agree.

Mr. Pearson is speaking: I forgot to mention the actions of the guy still *searching* so you can recognize him. It will not take long. This kind of guy is a little harder to identify. His conversation is never about the future and if you were to ask him, "Are you dating someone right now or are you single?" his primary response will be "I do not have anyone special in my life yet, but I am still looking for her." Code for "I'm just having fun with as many women as I can, would you like to be one of them?" Men like this are still trying to find themselves. The women they meet and get involved with are looked at and used as "appetizers" before the "main course."

Tina is speaking: Meaning what?

Mr. Pearson is speaking: This guy treats women like they are an appetizer. He will order and try them all and reorder them over and over again until he is "ready" for the entrée. He wants to try many different "appetizers" (women) to see which one was more enjoyable, and even reorder the some of the same ones repeatedly from time to time. He will put them all in the rotation. I mean he will call or text them before they text him to set up an excuse of why they shouldn't expect a text from him for a period. Each of these women he meets will be distinctively different from the next. You see, in his mind, they all will mean different things to him.

Tina is speaking: Okay.

Mr. Pearson is speaking: With all those he is involved with, he will lie to them. He is good at spotting those women who seem "thirsty" and desperate for companionship. He will take his time to respond to their text or voicemail. He will be the one to set the times and dates the two of you can get together. He will always offer to go back to your place and will never ask you to stay at his home. His position is and will always be off-limits unless he feels by allowing you to come by it will help him sleep with you. He does this, so he can "control" when, where, and how often you two will meet. If you complain about not getting "time" with him or that he has not talked about the two of you getting serious yet, he will deflect and sweet talk you off the subject and will often say, "We will talk about it later. Let's enjoy this moment together now."

He often during this process leaves a few casualties along the way because he only thinks about his wants and needs, not yours. If he has to lie or pretend that he wants what you want in order to sleep with you, he will say anything. Too many women fall for this kind of guy and lower their standards. They find themselves supporting this "kind" of a man financially especially if he tells them he loves them.

Tina is speaking: I believe I have seen this kind of man.

Mr. Pearson is speaking: In my opinion, I feel we, as men, should be honest about the type of men we truly are, know where we are in our development in our lives and be real with ourselves concerning what we can bring to the table. It can only happen if we are honest with ourselves first. We must understand and know the unnecessary foolishness and games we play only makes it harder for a woman to trust and love us the way they can. I know I've said a lot and thank you for allowing me to do so. I hope what we spoke about helped answer your questions and other concerns. Listen, let me say this, "Falling in love is not what we do. We should "grow" in love." I say this because things that fall, break, but things you plant, grow and get stronger. We should care for growing in someone's spirit, heart and character. Please remember because I hear people say this a lot, "I am looking for someone to complete me." Listen, you don't need someone to complete you; you only need someone to accept you completely.

Tina is speaking: It was a pleasure talking with you. *Real Talk* is real talk, and I learned a lot about myself, men's behavior and my next steps in becoming a better me. All that you shared has made me feel better about my situation. Thank you so much.

Mr. Pearson is speaking: We got to take a break right now, and when we come back, we will see who is on the line ... We are back, who do we have on the line?

Karen is speaking: We have Latoya from East Point, Georgia.

Mr. Pearson is speaking: Good morning, Latoya, what is your question?

Latoya is speaking: Good morning, Mr. Pearson. Thank you for taking my call. I am so glad I got through. Before I ask my question, let me give you a little background of my situation so that you can better understand why I am asking my question.

Mr. Pearson is speaking: Okay.

Latoya is speaking: Thank you. Well, I am 37, a beautiful black Christian woman (Queen) married to my very handsome black King. My husband and I have recently come to a point in our marriage where we are not on the same page. I believe we can fix things, but I am not sure how to bring up concerns I have without seeming as if I am ungrateful for all he does for his family. I don't want to appear as if I am complaining or nagging.

Mr. Pearson is speaking: What do you mean?

Latoya is speaking: Well, one of the concerns I have is that he doesn't share with me our finances. Sure, he pays for everything, but as his partner and his wife, I feel I have a right to know what he is spending and brings in. I want us to sit down and have him show me a break down of our finances. I feel I should have access to it at all times. I have asked him to add me to the checking account, but he told me, "At this time, I am comfortable paying bills and taking care of this household the way I am doing it as the provider. You know the bills are getting paid; you shouldn't concern yourself with that. Don't I give you money when you ask for it? Don't you keep all the money you make from your job? Why is what I am doing with the money I make bother you to a point where you feel you should have access to it and be on the account? The way I do things takes the worry off of you, so chill and live life, okay?" I didn't feel what he said was fair or respectful to me.

Mr. Pearson is speaking: Did you two sit down in the beginning and talk about your finances? I ask because if you had, you would have been able to discuss "how" paying the household expenses was going to happen. With that said, let's address your concerns now.

Latoya is speaking: No, we didn't sit down and talk about it, but that shouldn't matter. I am his wife, and I should have access to whatever he has. Another issue I am having is that we are not as intimate as we used to be. It didn't happen overnight, so you know this begins during the time he was out of work. During this time, our intimacy slowed down. It seemed to get worse once he returned to work.

Mr. Pearson is speaking: How so?

Latoya is speaking: Once he returned to work, we spent even less time being intimate. I got less attention. He hardly said any sweet words to me like when we were dating, and love letters stopped. I mention this because I enjoyed reading the love letters that he wrote to me. I am not questioning his love for me. I know what we are going through is temporary. I want to feel loved like I used to feel. We both have had to adjust our mindset from "I" to "we," which is understandable. I don't want to seem like I am begging for attention, affection or him to recognize me. It doesn't feel right.

I have prayed daily to God and asked for His help and guidance through this. I think when I ask him questions just trying to feel included, he sees it as nagging. How do I address my concerns about his behavior towards me lately without coming across like a nagging or an unappreciative wife? How do I get him to see his actions are those of a single man? How do I get him to talk to me about our financials? Just tell me what I can do to get him to act right.

Mr. Pearson is speaking: Well, your concerns and situation are typical ones of married couples and something I hear often. It seems you have a lot of issues to address and we will but first, let me make sure I am clear on what I thought I heard you say were your concerns. Your concerns are:

(1) His behavior toward you – meaning his actions are those of a single man and not a married one.

(2) He doesn't show you attention or affection like he used to.

(3) He doesn't involve you in household affairs.

(4) He hasn't added you to the bank accounts.

(5) You do not feel loved by him.

(6) You want to handle the household bills, and you could do it if you were on the accounts.

(7) You'd like to know what brought on these changes.

(8) You wanted to see if it was something you did.

(9) You'd like to know if whatever it is can be fixed or turn this around, and overall, how do you get him to act right, right?

Latoya is speaking: Yes, that about sums it up.

Mr. Pearson is speaking: Okay then let's begin. Now, as you know the adjustments from going from boyfriend/girlfriend to a married couple and facing real life after the "honeymoon bliss" passes can be a little scary at first and hard to do. The adjustment mentally from not sharing your world to sharing your world and space with someone else takes a moment to sink in. Even though you know it's something you must do, it is still not easy. These adjustments are essential and need to be made as soon as they can to keep you from thinking you've made a mistake. All of this is normal, but to make this transition more accessible, it has to start in your mind first. You both must change your thinking process from a "me" perspective to a "we" perspective. And understand you are now one flesh. Does this make sense?

Latoya is speaking: Yes, it does.

Mr. Pearson is speaking: The issue of becoming and thinking as one can make most people feel they are losing their identity in the relationship. It is hard for a person who is used to "running" and "controlling" their own lives to allow someone else to take the wheel and lead them. When someone feels they have little to no control, they tend to rebel and not accept "their" role in the marriage. Therefore, you see couples like this living the roommate-style life as individuals and not as a married couple. You mentioned "act right" what is your definition of "acting right?"

Latoya is speaking: When I said act right, I am just saying for him to act in a manner that displays our life as "we" and not as if it is still "I." I mean to share with me and stop making me feel like I am a guest in my own home. I am trying to make it feel for him like home is HIS castle and not his prison when he comes home.

Mr. Pearson is speaking: I am asking because I don't want to assume anything. It sounds as if you would feel more a part of the marriage if he would allow you to do these things, right? I would hate to think that all you want is control of him and the money he makes. I am not saying this is your motivation, but many married women say their husband "is" the head of the house, the provider and breadwinner, but she runs the relationship. If you don't mind me asking, has either of you been married before?

Latoya is speaking: Honestly, I don't feel what I am asking is a form of "controlling," but more of me being seen and treated like his partner, not his live-in maid. And yes, I feel it is my job to run the household. I think I can best help him and take the pressure off of him by maintaining order in our house and that includes me keeping a clean home, buying food and paying household bills to keep things running smoothly. Paying bills and buying food requires me having access to money. I am not trying to do his job. I am trying to be more the "helpmeet" of our relationship as the Bible says is my role. As far as being married before, yes, I was married once previously, and this is my second and his first.

Mr. Pearson is speaking: Ok. Let me quickly speak on this paying bills thing first. When you got married did he ask or inform you that he expected you to "handle and pay the household bills" as part of your duties as his wife? Yes, God created you for his "helpmeet," and yes, he should have told you early on what his expectation of you and your role in the marriage was going to be. But if he didn't, then he is saying without saying it that he will pay the bills in the household.

There is nothing wrong with you wanting to expand your role, but that comes through a conversation and if he is willing to do it. Yes, you should at least know what he makes, brings home and the bills he is paying, but your approach to getting this information needs to be in the form of a "workable solution" instead of ordering or demanding that he tell you. It is the same for anyone, always telling someone about problems without following it with possible solutions doesn't make anyone want to consider or make changes to give you what you want. Just saying you deserve to know, and you want to do it isn't going to help you.

To understand him and I am not defending him, you need to break it down to him as to the reason why he should stop doing what he does and allow you to do it. I say this because you're telling a man who pays the bills, gives you money to spend, lets you keep your paycheck, doesn't disrespect you and loves you to STOP and change what he has been doing. That's hard for someone like him to do.

Start small and ask to see the bills. Offer to pay one or two but make a case and don't just try and fix something that is already working.

The man you married may not be "that guy" who wants or accepts help that way. Just maybe if you two were to sit down and talk with a marriage counselor maybe, they could explain how you're feeling by not being involved. They could explain it in a way he can see and understand how important it is to you to "feel" and "get" included in your household life.

Latoya is speaking: Okay, that sounds like a plan.

Mr. Pearson is speaking: In what you're saying to him, it is coming off as if you want access to the money and nothing else. Now whether that is true or not I can't make that call, only you can. Hearing your concerns from an outside source may ease him back of the fact that you're not appreciative of all that he does for you as his wife. Does he know what you make on your job? And would you be upset if he asked?

Latoya is speaking: No, he doesn't know what I make, nor has he ever asked me what I made. I use my money to pay my bills, and occasionally I get groceries, but he does everything else. I feel he should ask me to pay the bills I had before we met such as fill my car up with gas. My uncle told me that is what a man is supposed to do for a woman. He should give me more than $2500 per month to spend on my hair, nails, etc., he should cover that also.

Mr. Pearson is speaking: Do you hear yourself right now? Seems like the man is providing a good life, giving you "additional" money to spend, not to pay "the" bills, allowing you to keep your check for yourself, making sure you're taken care of and all you can do is ask for more. Do you know how rare it is for a woman to find a man to do what your husband is doing for you right now? If you tell any other woman the things this man is doing for you as his wife, and how you feel he isn't doing enough, they would think you were greedy, stupid and ungrateful, and would trade places with you in a heartbeat.

You think a man making six figures, giving you $2500.00 per month to spend as you see fit, allowing you to keep whatever you make on your job to get your nails, hair etc. done, paying the household bills and treating you with respect and loving you would be an ideal situation to be in, right? Keep disrespecting your situation and I promise you some woman will replace you with someone who will appreciate him. You haven't said he was mistreating you in any way, and I haven't heard any real problems he is doing to you other than spoiling you. It is a shame you don't see what you have.

Latoya is speaking: I do know he is a good man but he is capable of doing so much more.

Mr. Pearson is speaking: I hear you, but can you *see* hearing it back how it sounds as if you are not happy with what you have? I'm just saying from a married man's perspective, I don't mean any disrespect, but you sound very unappreciative. Anyway, tell me a little about your first marriage.

Latoya is speaking: I was young when I first got married and was trying to find my way in the church. I had not yet become a quote on quote a Christian woman I am today. At the time we got married neither of us knew our roles in the marriage biblically. We were in love, and we just wanted to get married, so we did. Not knowing what was expected, I did what I thought a wife should do, which was take care of the house as he took care of the bills. We had children early, and for a while, things were okay. I attended several churches before settling on one that I felt fed my faith and beliefs. The more I went, the more I learned and figured out how wrong my husband and I were living our lives as it pertained to the Bible. I shared this information once I found out with my husband. He wasn't trying to hear it. I told him we had to make some changes or we were going to clash and have severe issues in our marriage.

The more I learned, the more we fussed, and the more I knew our marriage needed help or our marriage was doomed. I learned in church about being "equally yoked." It wasn't until I researched this that I realized we were unequally yoked. I didn't want to give up on our marriage, so I suggested to my husband that we go and see a marriage counselor. After a few sessions, it was clear it wasn't helping. He wasn't willing to change his ways to do what the Bible said we should. So, we divorced. We remained friends for our kids' sake.

Mr. Pearson is speaking: I am very sorry to hear that. So fast forward, to your current marriage. With all you've said, did you feel you had a slight advantage over him in this area?

Latoya is speaking: What advantage?

Mr. Pearson is speaking: The advantage I am speaking of is "marriage experience." Because you had been married once before, you had some knowledge of what it felt like to be married and some experience of how to be a wife, but your husband had none. Since it seems you two didn't start out understanding your roles according to the Bible, he didn't seem interested once you got involved in it. I can say it appears once you learned something new and tried to share it with him, he saw it as if you were forcing it on him and not leaving him a choice in the matter. For you, you found out what it was you two were supposed to be doing as a married couple, but for him, he saw the changes in you to be something he wasn't ready or willing to do. You walked into your current marriages, knowing a little more and expecting him to be on the spiritual level you were on. Once you saw that he wasn't as knowledgeable about the Bible as you were, you took his lack of knowledge as him acting out.

It was a little presumptuous on your part to assume without asking him where he was spiritually. Even though he was religious and believed in God, went to church and all that, you seemed to never have asked him how spiritual he was concerning how much he knew on the subject of marriage in the Bible. With him not knowing and not doing what you thought he should be doing, you saw it as a form of him "acting out." All because he wasn't on your spiritual level or didn't know as much about the Bible as you did.

Based on what you said, it sounds as if the first thing he felt he knew was to "provide" for you the way HE knew how, not necessarily in a biblical sense, yet. That included him taking care of you, paying the bills and doing beautiful things for you. He ran with it (without talking to you first to know what your expectations were of him, which was wrong on his part, but I can see why he did things this way) and assumed his role. I can bet when you came to him the first time, he had no idea of what the problem could be when he was doing what he thought were all his husbandly duties. I bet you he looked at you crazy like when you said you wanted to pay the bills as if you wanted to do his role. He probably thought you were losing your mind and were unhappy being taken good care of by a good man.

I don't think he understood your position in this argument. He was providing for his wife the way he knew how, and to him, there was no problem. He was doing what he felt he was supposed to do for you. He needs your help, and you will have to be patient with him on implementing other aspects of his role. Keep in mind when your husband does what he considers to be "good" things you've requested (or not) of him some form of praise and acknowledgment is what he craves from you. In his mind, he believes his good deed done in your eyes has earned him *relationship equity.* He feels that when he isn't at his best in the relationship that he could, and you will allow him to use his past actions to help him out of difficult times. He thinks his good deeds have no "expiration date" on them.

Latoya is speaking: What do you mean?

91

Mr. Pearson is speaking: What I am saying is this is true for most men when they do things for you. They feel they are building *relationship equity* or *credit* which they can use when they mess up with you. Men doing this don't realize that women don't see past actions as built-up *credit* to be used down the road as an excuse or *get out of trouble* equity. Whatever he has done counts only for that moment in the woman's eyes. They will remember it later on, but it is not something that carries over for the man to use to NOT do something new for them. In other words, what a man did three months ago was three months ago and means nothing now. Women will expect them to continue and do more to keep them looking "worthy" to be a part of their lives.

I say all this to say complaining and ordering your husband around in a manner as if he doesn't know how to be a husband will only hinder your process and make him not want to do anything you ask of him. Your goal here is to help him to better understand your wants and needs, not expect him to come and ask you all the time. What you don't want him to do is look and think that you married him for one of two reasons: (1) You wanted and saw a future with him or (2) you got with him for what he could do for you.

Latoya is speaking: How would he know which is which?

Mr. Pearson is speaking: Well, he would have to really think back to when you two were dating and recall what your character was like during that time. As he remembers the conversations you two had and he would recall whether he felt you were interested in him because you saw a future with him or if you got with him because of the things he could give and provide you. This is based on how you two spoke, whether it was in terms of "we" or "I." During your "dating process" of 3 to 5 months maybe he would have had enough time (as would you) to see past your "representative" to better understand your character as well as your true intentions (as should you).

Latoya is speaking: Why do you think this is?

Mr. Pearson is speaking: He was taken by your beauty (like most men with beautiful women) and intrigued with the possibilities of sleeping with you that he (as do most men) failed to get to know the real you and not your representative. Many men like this can't see nor even care if you are in "your" purpose, meaning your career. Many want to smash, meaning sleep with you.

Very few men understand that at some point, a financial and life conversation must take place. It is in this conversation that expectations are brought up concerning who does what in the relationship.

Latoya is speaking: So how should I address this matter with him?

Mr. Pearson is speaking: To start with, every so often you may need to tell him because he may not recognize that you have issues, problems or concerns. He is still learning who you are even after 15 months of marriage, and he is still working on understanding your wants, needs and requirements as your husband. Does that make sense?

Latoya is speaking: So how long should I wait for what I want, need and require from him? It is not my responsibility to teach him how to be a husband.

Mr. Pearson is speaking: You are correct that it is not your job to show him nor can you help him be a husband, but you can help him understand with patience what you, as his wife, require to feel secure and loved as his wife. It will not work if you treat him as if he is stupid for not already knowing this. Remember *love* is why your man is with you. Real men want to do the right thing with and for you. He knew coming in that there were things required of him, but he didn't fully understand them all yet. He was willing to learn if you allowed him to be with you.

With your marital experience, it is your job to reassure him when he does something expected of him. He feels more comfortable and confident and will continue to repeat whatever it was that made you find happiness with him because he is attempting to please his wife. I can tell you that most men don't always open up and share of themselves right away. It takes time. With you guiding him to what is required of him as your husband for you to be happy, it should make him more willing to learn. It is not seen as a form of control but seen as help. Boys are not shown or trained on what is needed to be husbands, but the girls are. Girls are taught and guided on how to be a wife for a man.

Latoya is speaking: How so?

Mr. Pearson is speaking: Young girls grow up playing with dolls. They "practiced" with toy babies on how to feed, change, look after and dress them. As they get older, many of them (and this is true if they have younger siblings) babysit to earn money. With this training, they are somewhat prepared of how to take care of others.

More women think about their wedding day, then men do. I have never heard any man say, "I can't wait to get married." Many men view that day more as their mate's day than theirs. You will hardly see a man concerned about what kind of flowers they should have at their wedding. For boys growing up, they learn how to play games. Every toy they played with centers around "winning or losing." Their games required them to use "strategies" and "manipulation" to achieve their objective, which was to win.

So, it is clear what both the male and female do best. Most men's goal to this day, when trying to get with a woman, hasn't changed. They will do and say ANYTHING to achieve their goal which is to win, and winning, in this case, is sleeping with the woman. Now you can see why so many of them are so comfortable with lying in their relationship, playing head games and manipulating their mates. It is what they were trained as a child to do.

I am telling you this because married men aren't going to "plugin" or "fit" into a predetermined mold you've created in your mind of how they should be and act to suit you. They are not *Ken*, and you are not *Barbie*. Your husband can be "programmed" and "trained" but he is not a robot or someone you can turn on and off or pull out from a drawer when it is convenient for you to use. He is a person who is willing to do and be taught "if" you're ready to help him. I am not saying you have to "hold" his hand, but in your situation, if you continue to push him or make him feel he is no good because he isn't where you want him to be spiritually in your relationship, you can cause more damage and still not get what you want. Is this what you want?

Latoya is speaking: No, it is not what I want. But something must give. It has been 15 months already. I have expectations, and I need them met. If I don't tell him what they are, how can he possibly meet them? Yes, I was married before, and yes, I feel my experience and understanding has served me well thus far. I agree with you. Pushing him too far can backfire and make matters worse, but at this point, what am I supposed to do?

Mr. Pearson is speaking: What you know and how you apply it are two different things. Being married before has helped you understand your role better, but it is reckless of you to think he is going to fall into his role without making mistakes. With you knowing he is "finding his way" to please you, you would think you would be a little more patient with him and encourage him instead of pointing out his faults. Patience and understanding are what is needed here, not discouraging comments or remarks. Are you trying to understand your husband or run over your husband?

Latoya is speaking: I am not trying to run or run over him. I want him to do what I say. It worked for my mother and my dad. My dad listened to my mother and just did as she asked with no questions asked. My experience should count for something, right? Besides, it is his job to meet my needs first.

Mr. Pearson is speaking: First and foremost, your husband is not your dad. It is not his job to emulate his relationship habits. It is his job to understand and run his household his way. Listen to me and be clear on what I am saying. Controlling your spouse in your marriage is not what it is all about. There is so much more to it than that.

Latoya is speaking: This is true.

Mr. Pearson is speaking: From what I am hearing, it reminds me of an article I read that asked the question, "Why are there so many single and unmarried black women." The material posted statistics showing the number for single black women to be 70% and unmarried 42% versus 21% of white women or other races. I know many black women if asked, would probably have a problem with the statistics but would agree there are issues, questions and concerns on how the black man sees black women and why they don't see many of them as someone to marry.

Latoya is speaking: I know what you're saying because I read a few of those articles as well. And although I feel the numbers are off a little, I do believe there is a problem that needs attention and solutions. Yes, I would agree there are slim pickings for good quality men for black women today. That is part of the problem but I also feel and I am saying this with love to my black sister, some of us can and do come off a little crazy to men who we're attracted to. They group many of us as "liars and dogs," and it is not fair to group us all in one category. We don't like it when they do us that way.

I feel although it is challenging for us, the media doesn't help any at all by stereotyping black women as being hard to get along with, bitchy, argumentative, bitter, etc. I think many of us get in our way and can sometimes be our worst enemy. Many of us, from what I have experienced and seen, block the blessings God presented to us in the form of a good man, and we sometimes dismiss them to avoid them hurting us with the lies most men tell. These reality shows depicting us as something many of us aren't don't help men's perception of us or the way many of them see us, come at us and treat us.

Many of these shows portray black women as money-hungry, gold diggers, weak and women who rely on men to give us the life we feel we deserve when we all are capable of getting it for ourselves. A lot of women want a good man for companionship and not for their money. Showing our young women coming up that their life goals are to find a man with money and status, sleep with him, have multiple kids by him and be submissive to him to keep the lifestyle he provides for us (like we're their slaves) is just plain wrong.

Our young women need to see more of the successful black women who run successful businesses and who are doing great things in their community and are great role models, not what the reality shows depict. I know reality television is all for entertainment and staged for the drama effect, but I hate the image it sends out because, for those women who do not see it is for entertainment purpose only, they will go out and try and live that life.

Mr. Pearson is speaking: You are correct. Black men, I talked to while writing this book shared with me, saying black women have too much attitude. They said that it isn't worth dealing with it to be with them. They would rather stay single themselves and have "friends." They say this behavior is evident during the "dating stages" (women use their representative to establish right away that no man is going to run over them and sometimes this is shown) saying this is where some black women display how argumentative they can be and would be in a relationship. For them, it is always about having the last word. They demonstrate how hard they will be to get along with, show you they are still bitter from their previous relationship and then complain that men should accept them for who they are. The men said that that the women were thinking the entire time that we are trying to "get with" them and that "all men are the same." Just like their last man, we will hurt them, so they sometimes come off very defensive toward us before you get to know us.

Having men ask, "How are they going to get the love they desire from a black man when they act like this? Why would any black or any man stick around until she has worked out her issues and sees that he is not the other man?" These are good questions. Now before you think I am picking on black women or that other races don't have their issues, they do, but I am addressing the black women because that's who we are talking about right now. This is not to say black men don't have their issues. Lord only knows I could speak on that and how we make the women who deal with us want to curse us out for the antics we do that drive them crazy, but I will focus on your concerns as it relates to your problems with your husband.

I wanted to know from men what is a solution to this problem, so I asked, "What attracts you to black women?" The majority said, "Their external and internal attributes and how she carries herself." They said the *exterior* attributes that make them stop, look, listen and respond were a woman's smile, her looks, her personality, her confidence, and most of all her non-bitchy attitude, meaning she feels she has to come off that she isn't going to allow a man to control her. As far as their *interior* attributes, many said what attracted them the most would be her spirituality, her loving herself, her closeness to her family, her honesty and respect and how she carries herself, being emotionally stable and being goal-oriented are things men look for but rarely find.

This is not to say black men don't have some work to do for women to be attracted to them because we do, but for now, it would be helpful if we could remove the stigma that "All black women (or women in general) want from and with black men is their money." Some black men say women expect and have high expectations of them and the women don't want them to have any with them. Women call their men leaders, but they want to control and rule them. They viewed their relationship as more of a dictatorship than a partnership. A lot are looking for "yes men" with resources they can use and control. You said he is acting out, he doesn't love you or he needs to change, but you have not expressed the changes you are doing as well to make things better.

We need to get down to the real issues to solve our real problems with our beautiful black women (and other women). I mention this because some women fail to understand this and many end up alone or in a relationship with someone they don't love or respect so as to not be alone. They don't understand that a simple "attitude" adjustment (this is also for all men period.) could make them seem more desirable to the kind of men they want to be in a relationship with.

Latoya is speaking: I understand what you're talking about, but no, it's not like the way it sounds. I am not a gold digger. I want him to allow me a little more responsibility in our household. That's all.

Mr. Pearson is speaking: I hear you, but can you see hearing it back how it sounds as if you are not happy with what you have? I am just saying that from a married man's perspective. I don't mean any disrespect, but you sound very unappreciative. If he is the provider of your household and King of your house, there is a good chance he will respond to his queen with much respect and end up doing much of (if not all) you want him to do to please you if he feels respected by you. You're right. He should get you more involved in household matters but making him think what he is doing as he is learning is not enough is not the best way to get you what you want. Talk to each other to fix your problems.

Latoya is speaking: I agree. I need to do a little more also.

Mr. Pearson is speaking: I remember growing up hearing this from women in my family, "Young boys are raised and told to grow up and "be" somebody and girls are told growing up to go "find" somebody (to be with)." I don't believe all women want men just for their money; some do want to fall in love and grow old together. In an ideal world, men and women would not seek to use one another for money or things. Instead, they would seek out one another for companionship, but we all know this ideal isn't our world's reality.

Women need to understand just because they smile at a man doesn't mean he should hand over to her his hard-earned cash. Telling real men I love you after one date will not do it either. Real men know there is more to you than just your body. If women were to not lead with that to get "trinkets," they would see this and get a quality man they want. It makes you wonder whether those who supposedly are seeking a *relationship*, "Are they looking for a mate? Someone they can "grow" with? Or, are they just looking for someone they can lie, trick and use to get the things they feel they deserve without working for it?"

Listen, I agree with some of what you're saying that your husband needs to open up and share more with you. I understand you both have your way of solving problems, handling bills, etc. but it is never good for either of you to tell one "how" they should act in the marriage. Fussing will not get you what you want. It will get you the opposite. Just because you were married before doesn't mean you "know" everything about being married, nor does it give you the authority to tell your husband how badly he is doing his job. A "good" loving, long-term marriage requires daily work and effort. No one gets it right by saying it should be. You have to put in the work.

Latoya is speaking: I understand.

Mr. Pearson is speaking: Marriage, as you know, is a "partnership," not a dictatorship. Your "conversations" cannot be "interrogations" when you're trying to resolve your problems, issues and concerns. One of the things that upsets people is when they do things out of the goodness of their hearts thinking about you, and you act as if they should have, it was their job or it was only to be expected. It is even worse when you always remind them of all you've done for them as if they are supposed to bow down and kiss your feet for your act of kindness toward them. Just respect them, show them kindness for even thinking about you at all and don't always expect them to do that because they weren't put here to serve you like that. Remember, people do things for one another because they care for them not because you made them do it.

Hearing your mate tell you "I told you so; I told you I was right; I knew my way would work" doesn't say "I want to work with you again; it says they will not do this again." You should *talk* to one another, not *preach* to each other. When your husband comes home, it should feel like his castle, not his prison. He should (as you should also) be able to come home to *be* with your partner and get re-energized by them not to be drained. Not getting or feeling this way is one of the main reasons most men don't come straight home after work. You both should often acknowledge each other's efforts. If either of you boast or brag about all you have done for one another, I can almost guarantee it will not make you closer.

Latoya is speaking: But will this help him act right in a way the Bible says he should towards his wife.

Mr. Pearson is speaking: Yes, but keep in mind that you are talking about two different things, his role and how to act overall. Yes, as a Christian man, he should know from what he has read and learned of what his role as a husband is according to the Bible. As far as *how* to act, you must define what this phrase means to you because the definition is different for everyone.

As far as his behavior toward you, he needs to understand that you react to whatever he gives you. What I am saying is, if he treats you well, you will treat him the same way. What you want from him is not an issue of "right or wrong," it is about how you two understand one another in the marriage.

Remember, you're dealing with a man with pride and he can't be the man you expect him to be if you continuously treat him like he is a child. Neither of you, when you're speaking to one another, can come across as if you know everything, (because you're both growing daily,) and the other person knows nothing. I can guarantee you neither of you will see what you both are doing as helping one another if it is done this way. You will both see it as a form of belittling each other. As a married man, I know how this feels when it is not being done right, but with my wife, she did it right, and it helped us both be better for one another.

Latoya is speaking: Really? How?

Mr. Pearson is speaking: I was in a similar situation when my wife and I got married because she knew a little more about the Bible scriptures and our roles than I did. I shared with her openly when we were dating of where I felt I was and what I needed help on and she helped me in a way where I felt *helped* and not *told*.

Latoya is speaking: So how did she help you?

Mr. Pearson is speaking: She honestly met me where I was biblically and went from there with me. I didn't stop her growth to wait on me. She continues to learn and help me work up to her speed in a way where I was excited and wanted to know more. I never felt she ordered me to do anything or that she was trying to run me. I felt she was sincere, and she wanted to help me get where she was so that we could move forward together. Does that make sense?

Latoya is speaking: Yes, that makes sense.

Mr. Pearson is speaking: A lot of times when people meet other people they expect them to be in the same place in their life as they are and for most, they are not. Not everyone is where they want to be in their life when you meet them. You must step back and allow them to grow from where they are in life. Don't get me wrong. You are not wrong in wanting to help your husband but you need to remember this is a new situation for you both and especially him. Patience is required if you wish to accomplish what you feel you have to work on. As I said and it is a fact of life, "We don't know what we don't know."

Latoya is speaking: I know what you're talking about because recently I suggested something, and he did it. I jokingly said to him, "I was right," and he became upset with me. I wasn't trying to disrespect him in any way nor was I saying he was wrong. I knew I was correct in what I said.

Mr. Pearson is speaking: Stating your fact and saying you were right implied he was wrong. You showed him your so-called help didn't help. It was done for you to be able to say you helped him. Your way made him feel he was stupid for asking you. Now I don't feel you were trying to or meant it that way, but that would be how he would take it. You must be careful. Your efforts, although good, got you the opposite effect. Question: Did you two go through a marriage consultation before getting married?

Latoya is speaking: No. You must understand I was open from the start concerning who I was and all I wanted in a marriage. I let him know that once I became a Seventh-day Adventist, I attended church regularly on Saturdays. The Lord was and still is a big part of my life, and he knew I wanted a Christian man. I had mentioned during our time dating that I had been celibate for seven years since my last divorce, and I didn't plan to engage in sex again until I was married.

I explained how turning my life over to Christ and becoming a Christian helped me through my last marriage and made me a better person. I also told him how I was willing to wait until God presented someone that He thought was right for me. As far as the two of us seeing a marriage counselor before we got married, we did not. We had a good friendship foundation from the start. We felt comfortable enough with each other during our dating process to get married.

Mr. Pearson is speaking: Was he as open with you as well?

Latoya is speaking: Yes! He was. I appreciated it too.

Mr. Pearson is speaking: That's good. I asked about the marriage counselor because engaged couples don't always verbalize their expectations about marriage when they are "boyfriend and girlfriend." Speaking with a marriage counselor helps because they would: (1) ask you questions to see if you two were compatible and had enough things in common to build a strong foundation on. (2) Check and see if you two were mentally ready to share a life merely because marriage is way different from the boyfriend/girlfriend situation. You cannot walk out free and clear when things do not go your way in a marriage.

Some people aren't built for marriage nor do some want to get married, and that's okay. For those who do, they need to understand there are more responsibilities and a lot of work to keeping what brought them together a successful long term marriage.

Latoya is speaking: I learned from my first marriage that I should never see my husband as my retirement plan nor should he be my unlimited ATM. Hearing "no" isn't always a bad thing. Complaining and constantly preaching and showing him no respect doesn't solve issues; it only increases them.

I figured out that respecting and acknowledging his efforts was a good thing. Because of my husband's behavior toward me, it has been hard for me to do what I know is right for him. I want him to be happy with me and see how I need to readjust the way I am doing things to achieve my goals. I will be proactive and help take a little pressure off him so he can be the provider he is trying to be. I feel it is okay for me to help even though he has never asked me to, with every day small things such as food and small bills. He has no problem from time to time coming home and cooking for me, and when he does this, I appreciate it. I do not want to be someone he "pays" for every day. I am not trying to put more pressure on him than need be which could kill him. I would rather have my husband alive than dead. No amount of insurance money is worth more than my husband.

My girlfriends often ask me how we do it. How do we keep our relationship healthy? I tell them, "We work together and balance one another out." It wasn't until my mother told me, "He loves you for you. If all you were to him was his maid, cook and sex partner why would he marry you? He could hire someone to clean his place and find a woman willing to sleep with him and have far less stress without you living in the house. You, as the wife, must do more than *be in* his life. You have to *be* his life. He needs to feel and know you are, so he understands his purpose, which is to please you." Once I was divorced from my ex-husband, I told myself that if I ever remarried, I would remember this information because it was helpful.

I understand that *submitting* to my husband is part of what I am supposed to do because he follows Christ. He acts, does and treats me like his wife and not like his girlfriend. Understanding our roles in a marriage and having a financial conversation upfront, for me, would have helped us cut down on the disagreements and arguments between us.

Mr. Pearson is speaking: You sound like a woman who has learned from her past, and it is now dawning on you how to use it to help your marriage. A lack of communication makes a woman feel her house is not her home, and that is not a good feeling. Feeling secure is a must for women in relationships. I don't feel your husband expects you to BE the provider, but at the same time, he doesn't want to handle all that he does and feel unappreciated. Contrary to what many married women think, there is nothing wrong with a wife contributing or paying for a meal or a movie every once in a while.

Latoya is speaking: I agree with that.

Mr. Pearson is speaking: Patience with your husband is the key to him listening and hearing your concerns and issues of what you need, want and require of him. Remember, it may be easy for you to express yourself to him, but he may find it harder to express himself to you because not all men are good at doing that. It's not that they are not capable of it. Many feel if they did this, you would see their softness/ kindness as a weakness. I find it funny because what a lot of men fail to understand is, "If we hide our true selves from our woman, she will only love what we do and not what and who we are!" because we never showed her our true selves.

Listen, no two relationships are the same. Each is different. Speaking, listening and hearing without judging is fair because we all want to be heard. If the wife's job is to stay home and take care of the household, budget the money to pay bills, take care of the kids, etc., it needs to be defined from the beginning BEFORE (or at some point in the marriage) you get married and redefined if children come later. I know firsthand that stay-at-home moms and taking care of children is just as hard if not harder than a day job. Men, believe it. Not having roles defined causes problems, results in arguing, leads to someone cheating, people lying and families breaking up.

To fix problems in your marriage, you both must first admit there is one. If both of you do not express your concerns/feelings, how can either of you expect them ever to be fixed? People want to believe their marriage will never have problems. These are the people who are fooling themselves. People often forget when there are problems in their life that they are unable to handle, they should turn to God. I know many of us only turn to God when things are bad, but we need to give Him praise regardless. Turn to Him not just when things are bad, but when things are good as well. It is because of Him that we can experience the things we do and can love each other. We cannot do these things on our own all the time. We need His help. You must remember, "What we fix is temporary; what God fixes is eternal."

Latoya is speaking: I have a lot of work to do, but it is doable.

Mr. Pearson is speaking: Okay, I have just one last question for you before I move on, why was it so important for you to get married early on and have kids? Was there pressure to do so?

Latoya is speaking: No, there was no pressure on me, nor did I feel pressured to do so. I just believed I was ready to be a wife and have kids. My boyfriend, at the time, knew before we graduated high school that I wanted to get married afterward.

Mr. Pearson is speaking: I often question and wonder in situations like these what the woman's real reason for getting married is. I wondered if they got married because they were in love or to not be alone? I say this because I often hear when it comes to marriage, "Women fall in love and then get married. Men marry women and then fall in love." I agree with this statement to some degree. I hear how many women get married to complete themselves when it doesn't.

A lot of people feel marriage is a "tool/piece" that completes them, and this isn't true. It is more of a *union* of two people becoming *one*.

Your *union* should be a place, an opportunity to enhance and grow in love with each other over time. Therefore, I suggest to those I counsel to see a marriage counselor before they get married. The counselor can bring out the importance during the dating stage of having a conversation at some point that includes finances, religion, children, careers, the division of labor and where you are going to live. This information will help you both better understand, but more importantly, it will clearly define your roles going into the marriage to see if you both are ready. Communication and not complaining is the key to getting your problems solved. You must be specific, open and honest with each other when you speak.

Latoya is speaking: This is something I am learning.

Mr. Pearson is speaking: Couples must understand that arguing in the relationship isn't always as bad as it seems. Although it is hard not to take some things said personally, it's neither about who is right or wrong nor about winning, but more about understanding and listening. Arguing when done *fairly* tells you how much your mate cares for you. Even though the words don't always sound pleasant, it is how they feel at that moment, so try not to take it too personally. Arguing is never the best time to come up with or solve your current issues. It is best to do that during peacetime because neither of you is thinking straight while arguing.

Your spouse's feelings and you seeing their point of view helps you understand why they are feeling the way they do and makes it a little easier to know what they are trying to say. It enables you to respond and resolve both of your issues (if that is what is required) by understanding them. Arguing to make a pointless point will make you right and alone. As the old saying goes, "You can win the battle but lose the war." It is not always about getting the last word or being right. It's about finding a middle ground to continue to build what you have and share. When it all comes down to it, which would you rather be, right? Or happy in your marriage?

So, as I wrap this up, here are a few pointers to remember because *acting right* and having a successful marriage is much more than just how a person *acts*. It is about the foundation you two have built that determines and provides the direction your relationship will travel.

Remember to apply these things:

1. "Negotiating and Compromising" will always be a part of marriage.

2. Try and communicate calmly to solve your issues and concerns.

3. Your body language and actions are more important than the words you say in determining your resolution.

4. If you argue to win, you will always lose. "If you play this game, just know for there to be a winner someone must lose."

5. "Listening" may not solve all your problems, but by doing so, it can help you learn "how" to better manage and work through them. Just know that sometimes your spouse only needs to vent and not have their problems solved. Venting helps.

6. Being honest about what is not working to resolve your issue is the only way you can find room for what is working to solve your problems.

7. No one can read your mind on how you want to be loved.

8. Working and showing your spouse you are "with them till the wheels fall off" will make loving them more natural to do.

9. Knowing, growing in love and understanding "love" is your full-time career. It will help your intimacy, and should not be treated like any other job you can get fired from.

I know we've covered a lot, but I hope I answered your questions. I hope all we spoke about will help you fix the issues you feel you have in your relationship because loving someone is good and even better when it is reciprocated.

Latoya is speaking: Thank you so much, Mr. Pearson. I have taken a lot of notes, and I will apply what I have learned. You have made a big difference in my life with your suggestions and advice. I appreciate you for doing this.

Mr. Pearson is speaking: Nice talking to you. When we come back, I will read an email I received from a gentleman entitled "Learning to trust again" in our **_Real Talk_** segment. I found this email interesting because these days it has become harder and harder to do, but it is possible. I am talking about trusting someone who hurt you. I will share this with you and give you my responses and get reactions from our listeners.

We are back, and in our **_Real Talk_** segment today, I am reading a letter from a guy in Smyrna, Georgia. It is not that often we receive messages from guys expressing their feelings of hurt, but this is a good one. This letter is expressive, and I had to share it with you. By the way, I appreciate all your emails, tweets and texts. Keep them coming, and we will, each week, try and read them on the air. Anyway, let's begin...

Dear Mr. Pearson,

I recently ended my 8-year relationship with my longtime girlfriend because I found out that not only had she cheated on me, but she was having his child. As you can imagine, hearing this from her, it took me a while to wrap my head around this. I loved her, and I wanted to marry her. Saying I was hurt is an understatement. There I was thinking I had found my soulmate and the woman I was going to spend the rest of my life with, but instead, I felt like someone had just ripped up my heart. Her attitude when she told me wasn't one of regret, but more as if I should be happy that she was honest with me. And if I loved her, I would accept it and move forward. She made it sound as if she had done me a favor for cheating on me.

My anger with her at that moment was beyond words. I felt betrayed. I had done everything I could for her and even asked her to marry me, but she said she wanted to wait, and now I can see why. She seriously thought we should work things out, but I couldn't see any version of where this would happen. Every time I looked at her, thoughts ran through my head in full color of some other guy smashing my woman. I wasn't mad at a guy I had never met. I was angry at her because she knew when she lay down with him, she had a faithful man at home. I mean all I hear most women say is how they want a "good man," someone to be committed to them. She was one of those women who said this same mess to be at the beginning of our relationship. Talking about she didn't want to be hurt. Can you believe this?

It hurt because we had spoken about having children but not this way. She attempted to apologize as if it would help me from feeling like a damn fool for being faithful to this woman all this time we had been together. To think back on how I was working hard so she wouldn't have to is just sickening. Like a fool, I was trying to make sure that she didn't have to worry about being provided for. I had her 1000%. I couldn't at that moment accept her apology. At that moment, I couldn't look at her without wanting to do something which I knew was wrong, so I walked out and went for a long drive with no destination. I told her before I walked out of the house that she needed to inform her "other man" that he was going to be a dad.

Fast forward, it has been 14 months since we broke up. One day out of the blue she called me to see if I had gotten to a point where I could forgive her, and I said to her, "Yes, I have moved on past this, and yes, I forgive you. Once, I loved you, and even though I wasn't pleased with what she had done, I was in an okay place at the moment. I wished her well, and we didn't get much after that.

I took a break from dating to make sure I was over her, and she was out of my system for good. I didn't want to carry any of that baggage into a new relationship. It wouldn't be fair to the woman I was dating. I wanted to give her all of my attention, not some of it. When I started dating again, I was a little out of practice of how to "talk" to women. After a while and a few dates, I started getting my mojo back, but deep down inside, I was finding it hard to trust a woman again the way I had before. I, for sure, didn't want to replay or experience my past any time soon. I knew though, if I was going to meet and fall in love with someone, I had to trust someone for this to happen eventually.

I must admit I felt at times, "love didn't love me anymore." During this point, I prayed what seemed like every night to God asking Him, "Why is it so hard for a good man like myself to meet and fall in love with a good woman? Why is what I want so hard to have?" Just when my faith in the love system was at wit's end, I met someone. Her name was Maya, and she was beautiful, funny, educated, and great to hang out with also. I was scared at first because I didn't want to mess things up. I was feeling her, and I thought she could tell I was a little nervous. I knew it was something special for me because I was finding it hard to speak at first, but over time, hanging and spending time together, things got better for me. I felt I had found someone special, and I was determined not to rush whatever we had or could have. I got excited like a child on Christmas day thinking about the possibilities of being in a relationship again with her. I was "feeling" this woman. I couldn't believe my luck. I felt I had hit the jackpot. I kept thanking God for bringing such a beautiful woman like her into my life from the first day we met.

Everything about her seemed to turn me on. Around her, I felt like a kid. The more time we spent together, the more she restored my faith in love and made me think I was ready and worthy to love someone again. Now before you think I was feeling this way because I had been single for so long, because I was lonely, because I didn't want to be alone or that I was on the rebound, you would be wrong.

Within four months, I had developed strong feelings for this woman, and I felt the need to tell her. Yes, I knew it was a risk because she may not have felt the same or was ready to hear this from me. When I did, she replied, "I can tell you like me a lot, and I like you as well, but I am not quite where you are right yet, but I do see myself getting there. I hope you can be patient with me as I get there. I like you, and I do not want to rush what we have. I did that in my past and got hurt doing so, so I hope you understand. Are you okay for now with where we are in our friendship?" Inside I had mixed emotions, happy she didn't reject me and glad she had felt the same as well. But still I was scared I would mess things up. I let her know that I heard her and understood and that, "I wasn't going anywhere." I told her we would take our time because I want whatever we develop (and she felt for me) between us to be something she wanted with me as well. I felt inside even though she wasn't mine, yet I didn't want to lose her.

Anyway, the more we talked and spent time together the more we got to know about one another and our past relationships. It was six months into us dating when she told me why she needed to wait to start a relationship with me. She told me she had been hurt in her last relationship by rushing and assuming, and with me, she wanted to be a little surer before entering into such a difficult situation with me. Hearing this I could understand where she was coming from and even though I was thinking and wanted to tell her that, "I wasn't her past, but I could be her future if she allowed me to." I didn't because the timing didn't seem right. I knew if I were going to gain her trust, I had to show her and not just tell her. My actions, if done consistently would be proof, and the only way she would see I am not running game on her. I guess you can see she had my nose wide open.

I hoped God would send a message to her heart to let her know, "I want to be her man, and I would do all I can to make and keep her happy if she let me. I needed her to know what she wanted in a relationship I needed ...which was the love of a good person in my life." I know it sounds like I am, but I am not desperate or lonely. I have fallen in love with her. So, my question to you is, "What more can I do that I have not already done without looking desperate or lonely to let her know I understand her pain, her doubts, and that she needs time to trust again?" I told her I would wait, and I will. Any suggestions on how I could help her put her past behind her and let her know she can trust me?

Dave

Mr. Pearson is speaking: David, here are my thoughts.

Let me say because it is essential, congratulations on finding someone. New love is great! When I read your letter, there were a few things that were very clear to me, (1) you both had experienced hurt in past relationships (2) Neither of you wanted to be hurt again. (3) The feelings you both had begun to develop were real, and (4) Patience and time was the key for her to get where you already were.

I do not think desperation or loneliness was the motive for you getting with this woman. You had waited long enough and by what you knew getting your ex out of your system was something that was needed for you to move forward. It is not a coincidence that you two met when you did, it was God telling you both it was time for you both to get up, get out and do something if you wanted love in your lives again. He presented and made it possible for you two to meet and still believe in love.

The evidence of you both learning to trust again is clear. You both are cautiously but willingly allowing yourselves to believe one another.

You both are doing this in the right way, and communicating is a great place to start. Even though at first you felt strange telling her how you felt about her, you did and doing so, you were able to learn that she had begun to develop feelings for you as well, although she wasn't where you were yet, she saw herself getting there with you.

Her wanting to ease into it made sense, and it was wise of you to give her space and time to get herself where she wanted so she could believe in not just your words but your intentions toward her. You seem to realize it is harder for most women than men to get over or past a bad relationship. It appeared you understood her enough and her state of mind to not take her as prejudging you. Knowing most women have been hurt by guys they've liked, it is good you were about to weather the storm for her to see she can trust and believe in you and what you have told her thus far in your friendship as it relates to being in a relationship with her.

The one thing a lot of men don't seem to understand is when a man lies to a woman, he kills the very soul of her and every chance he has of her loving him. Depending on her state of mind and her self-esteem at the time you meet her, it will determine "how" much time is needed for her to trust you. Just keep in mind your efforts aren't going unnoticed, she, like most women, enjoys the fact that you listen, you understand and empathize with what she is saying and have been through and that you seem sincere in all that you're feeling for her. Keep doing what you're doing because you earned your first *brownie point* when you reluctantly accepted your friendship "status" early on. By waiting patiently and still doing what you do with her, she will begin to feel you're sincere in your intentions with her heart and let you in.

So, relax and continue doing what you're doing because it is working. Don't concern yourself too much about trying to fix the past, concentrate more on the future. There is an attraction on both sides. Don't be surprised if in a few weeks or sooner, Maya turns one evening and says, "I think it is time we take our friendship to the next level."

I've got to take a break, but up next is your *Inspirational Vitamin*.

We're back. Before we go today, I would like to thank all our listeners because without you, I wouldn't have a show. I want to thank my staff for all their hard work because without them, I couldn't do this show. I want to thank those who called in, emailed, texted and tweeted, keep them coming. I hope what I shared with you helped you and your relationship.

Up next, I have your *Inspirational Vitamin*.

We're back. Today's message is entitled **"Affair-Proof Your Relationship."** In relationships today, it is hard to get them and harder to maintain them. With so many temptations surrounding us all and the opportunities for us to slip up, it is no wonder why people become weak and give in to their desires and cheat. It can crush your relationship.

Listen, when you find out the person you have given your heart to has cheated on you, you go through many emotions. You want to know most of all, "Why did they do it?" You start to think it may have been something you did or that you could have prevented it. You ask yourself, "What did they see in the other person that they didn't see in me?" Often, you think and ask yourself, "What could I have done to prevent this?" which is nothing because when a person decides to cheat, most times it has nothing to do with you. It's just something they wanted to do. I want to share with you a few ways to help protect your relationship.

Let me repeat a scripture I mentioned earlier from **1 John 4:18**, (KJV), "There is no fear in love; but perfect love casteth out fear: because fear hath torment. He that feareth is not made perfect in love." In other words, human love is flawed. It keeps a checklist of our sins and shortcomings — and consults it often. God maintains no such list. His love casts out our fear because it casts out our guilt. To protect your relationship, you must first understand that there is temptation everywhere and remember the moment you say, "That will never happen to me and my relationship." It is at that moment that Satan enters into that opening you've created.

Here are a few suggestions to help **"Affair-Proof"** your relationship.

1. Communicate regularly with God and your mate and ask Him to protect you against marital mischief. Pray with your spouse because it makes it harder for Satan or anyone to get in between the two of you and Him.

2. Faithfully read His Word. Books about marriage (relationships) can inform you but only the Bible, His marriage manual, has the power to transform your life.

3. Sharing the Bible and reading illuminates your understanding. It exposes, sensitizes and purifies your heart's intentions. It safeguards your relationship.

4. Build "relationship hedges" so that temptation doesn't get a foothold. Establish practical guidelines for interacting with the opposite sex.

5. Be open and honest with each other about your social, workplace and church relationships. Anything that makes your partner uncomfortable should be acknowledged and where possible changed. Although as humans, we cannot prevent everything. What we can do is catch things early and adapt them for the better.

Listen, next to God, you are each other's best protection against failure. So, listen, learn and love! Your faith is in Him, and only He can help you see your errors and provide you with what you need to correct them.

This was your **_Inspirational Vitamin._** I hope you all have a blessed day. We will talk again tomorrow. I will leave you with a song by Pastor Marvin Sapp called "He has His hands on You" ... because I know God has his hands on me. Be blessed.

Session Two

Eyes Wide Shut

Well, the show has ended. I went to the break room for a lunch break before going to meet my client, Ms. Clark, at my office. While eating my lunch, I checked my phone, and I saw I had missed a few phone calls, and that I received a few text messages from my wife, Reginae.

Sexywife69
Great show! Baby, I just wanted to say I love you.
Oh, I forgot if you are free, I would like to treat
you to dinner tonight. Meet me over at the
Cheesecake factory over at the Cumberland
Mall around 6 pm. dinner I am taking "you" to
a movie, it starts at 9:10 p.m. so we will have
enough time to eat and make the movie.

KingDray
Hello sweetheart. I did not think you had
time to listen to my show at your job. Anyway,
thanks and I will be done by 4:30 p.m. and
I will meet you at the restaurant on time.
See you there, I love you!

My office is only a few blocks down from the station. So, as I finished up, I went to my office. When I got to my office, my office manager, Debbie, said Ms. Clark called to confirm her appointment at 1:30 pm. It's 1:00 pm now, so I have time to prepare. I printed her online questionnaire to get familiar with it and her situation.

Note to self: An observation of a situation

As I waited for Ms. Clark, I had a thought concerning people in general. I wondered, "Had the communication between men and women gotten so bad that we're unable to understand each other in our relationship?"

In the book, *Women are from Venus and Men are from Mars*, one thing was clear, women and men think and communicate differently. Women say one thing, and men hear another. It is true that most men have issues communicating. It is not the "words" that most men have problems with. Mostly, it is the number of words used by women to describe and the subjects women want to talk about that bother them the most. When men communicate, we communicate with fewer words than women. We want the "highlights" of the conversation first, and if we're interested in more, we will say, "Tell me more." Women, on the other hand, want the full details from the beginning. They want to hear everything that happened.

Most women, when they are speaking to their man like to share their complete thoughts. Some men listen to the introduction of the conversation, but if the story is long, they will lose interest. Their timeline is somewhere between 15 to 20 minutes, and we all know most women's conversations last much, much longer. As their man waits for the "bottom-line" of their conversation, they begin to hear less and less, and this becomes evident on their faces.

When men do this, it upsets women because it makes them feel they don't care about what they're saying. It isn't that men don't think whatever they are saying is worthy of much more of our time, but it does make women feel we don't want to give them their much needed "attention." Women must understand most men's attention span is short. When this happens, it doesn't always mean they aren't interested. They just feel the "lengthy" stories are too long. They need time to process what they're hearing, and it will take more than a moment to do that. It is in our nature while listening, to "fix" your issue or concern when all you wanted us to do is listen to whatever it is you're saying.

Women can and will hold most men's attention with key words. These are words that men automatically listen for that "benefits" them such as food, sex, money, etc. If what is being said benefits them, then you have their FULL attention. Anything else that is said sounds like a foreign language to them. Most times, men "translate" with their selective hearing the information they hear into something they *want* to hear. I call this *translation* or *selective hearing* as most people say. We all do it from time to time when we're not interested in what the other person is saying to us.

Translation is tricky and can be confusing. It can cause significant problems if you're not familiar with the lingo. Here is a conversation by a couple communicating, trying not to upset one another but wanting to get their point across. In this example, Cedric and Trina have been together for three years, no kids. Cedric works in technology and Trina works in healthcare. Cedric takes care of "everything" financially in the home and allows Trina to keep the money she earns to do whatever she wants with it with no questions asked. We pick up the conversation where Trina has decided she wants to save her money and on top of everything Cedric is providing, she wants him to give her a sizeable weekly budget to spend on herself. Understand that the goal of this conversation for Trina is to get more money.

Trina: Honey, I am getting tired of using my money on my needs. I need you to give me more money. I want to save my money for me.

Translation: I know keeping my money is good, but it would be better if you give me a lot more. How can I save for myself and buy things for myself if I am spending my own money? I already know that I am not contributing absolutely anything to our household, and you will continue to spend on me, but a chick needs more. The more you have, the more I want. You are my financial fool, retirement plan, my 401K and I plan to use you because I know you love me.

Cedric: Sweetheart that makes no sense. I am paying all the bills. You're keeping whatever you earn. I am buying and giving you things all the time, outside of all the things I am doing. Why should I give you more money so that you can "save" money for yourself when we have a savings account together for emergencies, vacation and a rainy day?

Translation: You are a selfish, unappreciative, soulless, heartless fool. It sounds as if you think on top of all I am doing to keep you happy, I am going to give you more. You're sitting here telling me like I can't hear you that you want to save your money for yourself while I cover us both? You want me to believe this is the behavior of a woman trying to "build" with a brother? If what I am not doing is not enough, you need to leave like now.

Trina: It's obvious you don't love or trust me. If you loved me, you wouldn't question "why" I want more money. You would give it to me regardless.

Translation: I am sleeping with you, and that's all you need to know. If you expect me to love and trust you, you need to "show" me I can trust you by putting some more money in my pocket and look the other way. The number of years we've been together means nothing if I am not getting my way. If you don't give me what I feel I require, I will take what you're offering and get the rest elsewhere from someone else. I know you love me more than I love you, so regardless of what you're saying you are going to give me what I want, period.

Cedric: Honey, it's not like that. You know all I do is and has been for us.

Translation: Are you out of your damn mind? Do I look like an ATM? I am giving and doing and you're complaining and asking for more? Don't you think I know you're with me for the money? You don't think I know that if I cut you off you would bounce without looking back? You got me twisted if you think sleeping with me is going to make me "work for you." If you don't want to work with me or I feel you have outlasted your usefulness, I will replace you. I can find another woman who will appreciate being taken care of and not complain.

Trina: I hate you. I wish I would have never gotten with you. You make me sick.

Translation: You are not supposed to recognize that I am using you. You're only supposed to see my body and the bomb sex I am giving you. You're right. My love and trust do hinge on all you do and give me nothing more. The more you give, the more I love and trust you. Sure the sex is good, but I can get sex from any man, so leaving you wouldn't mean a thing. You are lucky and should be grateful I allow you to do whatever you do for me. I deserve to be treated like a queen no matter what it costs you to do it.

Cedric: Really? You hate me, and I make you sick?

Translation: You're deluded. An insecure, bipolar, ungrateful, selfish excuse for a woman complaining about living for free? I am giving 80%, and you're giving 20%, and you got the nerve to think you're doing me a favor for spending my money. You need to stop smoking that crack. I have made it where you don't have to lift a finger for anything, and you think I am not doing enough? I bet you will be lonely if I stopped whatever I am doing and find myself a real woman willing to build with me. You need to get your ungrateful ass up out of here. Go and find yourself another fool to "take care of you" since I am doing such a lousy job.

Trina: So, what are you trying to say? You want to break it off and leave because I am asking for more money to spend freely on me? I am entitled to more! Hell, I am faithful to you. I could cheat on you, and you would never know. I am protecting you. Hell, you got the money. I've heard you brag about it to your friends, so it should be no problem.

Translation: Listen, the more you have to give, and if I can get it from you, I will. You think by telling me "no" that I am going to break things off and give up my golden goose. You're crazy. I will take whatever you give and do for me for as long as I can, believe that! I will be damned if I allow another woman to slide in and mess up my good thing. If I need to, I will get what you're not giving from someone else and still have you. I know I am in a great position, and I am not going to allow a "thot" to take what I have already invested and broken in. You must think I am a fool. I figure I could yell, act out and fuss, and you would give me what I want because I am your woman. I never took into consideration all that I could lose by being greedy. I am good with our current arrangement so let's drop this line of conversation before you expect me, ask or tell me I should pay some bills since I am not comfortable with the way things are.

Cedric: Listen, sweetheart, I hear you, and I will see what I can do but for now let's keep things the way they are.

Translation: You need to shut your ungrateful behind up and stop trying to force my hand or bully me into giving you more money. Keep pushing me, and I will make a decision for you and put you out. I am trying to build wealth for our future, and you're trying to take care of you. You expect me to marry you? If you act like this as the girlfriend, I can imagine how your behavior would be if you were legally entitled to the money I make. You probably would hang out just long enough to get half and then bounce. I need to scale back on you and make you earn what you are getting from me. Sleeping with me isn't going to cut it. The door is open, and you can leave whenever you want. I am too young to be stressing myself out for you. It might be time for you to go.

As you can see, her approach to achieving her goal was a horrible one. Instead of "talking to her man," she "talked at him" and got the wrong response to what she wanted. With her behavior of entitlement when she is just the girlfriend and not the wife was the wrong thing to do when she is trying to get something SHE wanted, which was more money. Even if he wanted to give her what she wanted... the way she came at him made it hard for him to give in without seeming as if he was a weak man.

We all know when we are angry or hurting, we say hurtful things that we may or may not mean, but during the moment, we're upset and want to win the argument. Never thinking of the long term effects and damage we may be causing that will last much longer than the discussion, we just want to win the case. We will say whatever to win and end up losing in the end. You may be thinking, "Why does this happen, right?" The answer is because both men and women have egos that they are trying to protect from being hurt. When you realize you've said some things you didn't mean, it is imperative to "explain" calmly within 20 minutes to one another "why" you're feeling the way you do.

By doing this it does a few things, (1) it stops the arguing, (2) you both can begin to explain "why" or "what's" really going on. Most times when we lash out about one thing, it is the prelude for something else we want to talk about, but because the tension is so high, you are forced to angrily push it into the conversation by default just to get heard. I say this, and if you're honest with yourself, you will agree, arguing "sometimes" is good for the relationship. It lets you know where you both stand... meaning that it brings out issues you may be unable to talk about calmly. It tells you both that you both care for each other. No one purposely argues with someone that they don't have feelings for.

On the other hand, usually but not always, "if" your mate doesn't explain or clarify what was said during this moment of anger promptly, it will lead them to believe you were saying what you meant. Egos or not, this could lead to the death of your relationship. I am not saying people do not have the right to be angry because some people will push you there sometimes, and you naturally react. If you're in a relationship that you feel is worth saving, apologize and mean it.

Don't let your ego or who says it first prevent you from saying, "I am sorry." I know it is hard for either of you to admit when you are wrong, and it is even harder for men because we always think we're right. Guys, I will say this, in your relationship, sometimes, it may not always be your fault, but you may have to carry the load (take one for the relationship) and apologize "first" to save your relationship. Women must understand men aren't sharing because they don't want you to know them, they are not sharing personal information with you because they feel that the moment you get upset with them, you will use what they've told you to hurt them. Honestly, who wants to be destroyed by their own words? No one. Believe me, when a woman does this, it hurts the guy's ego, but he will try hard not to show it.

A rule of thumb to avoid damaging your relationship any further would be to apologize quickly. Talk and not yelling gets you heard. Just continuously yelling and trying to push your point will only make the situation worse. Your goal in an argument is to solve an issue or concern. You have no need to waste more time talking bad and finding faults about one another. Contrary to what most people think and believe "having the last word doesn't mean you are right or that you will get what you were arguing about at all, what it means is if you keep it up you will be right and alone." Is that what you want?

The Bible says in **Ephesians 4:15**, (KJV), "But speaking the truth in love, may grow up into him in all things, which is the head, even Christ." In other words, we need to be kind in what we say and how we say it and speak the truth. We need to give each other the right to talk about our "truth" and at the same time, not make our spouse feel they were wrong for doing so. The reality in all relationships is this, "We are not always going to agree on everything, and it is okay to agree to disagree."

If we were honest with one another and communicated regularly, this would not happen. Although the request is a simple one, it isn't so simple for most men to do. Very few (if any) men understand the problems they cause when they continuously lie to their woman and do not give them the attention they request or desire. Not responding to their spouse's needs makes them feel, think and believe they don't care for them. In situations like this, men say women are complicated, and women say men don't understand. For most women, they feel as if they are wrestling on how to communicate their needs to their spouse.

Quick note, ladies, men's non-response does not always mean they don't care or love their spouse. The reason why men don't respond the way most women want them to is that we are not built that way emotionally. Most men's thinking is "one dimensional." Their thought process is, "Even if I don't say 'I love you,' you should just know how I feel about you" and that should be good enough. It is this way of thinking that drives most women crazy. To keep this matter simple and not work the nerves of the women reading this, I suggest women merely calmly tell their man what they want and need as a reminder every so often. I say this because it's not only accurate, but it is sad to say that most men are not as bright as many women give them credit for when it comes to expressing their feelings.

If you teach him "how," allow him to do it, encourage and acknowledge him when he does it, it will help provide you (his spouse) with the "kind" of communication to put your head, heart, mind and soul at ease. It will also make you feel the work and time you've put in and invested with him was worthwhile. Not to mention, it makes a HUGE impact on him repeating this process. Sounds simple, right?

It's because it is. Now before you say, "I should not have to remind or tell him to tell me how he feels about me, he should already know and just do it."

Let me tell you a secret to keep you from losing your mind as you deal with us (men). Most men aren't that skilled in deciphering, decoding or decrypting your wants and needs. In most cases, you must spell it out for them. They want and need your help. Stop fighting and hoping they will pick it up and tell them. Men who are told hardly forget. How *you* and *your* spouse communicate is really what your relationship should be about, not what the world says it should be. You two need to find the way that works for you both, not go off of how the world thinks you should.

If you, as a woman, find yourself asking these questions and saying these things to your spouse, "Are you listening to me?", "Are you paying attention" or "Do you understand what I've just said?" then you are talking at your spouse, not to them. I know many women feel it should not be so hard or this exhausting to communicate with their spouse, but sometimes it can be. Here are a few suggestions:

Women need to remember:

1. Men do not express their feelings like women do.

2. To tell your man you like it when he compliments you. You would love to hear it more often; he will do it.

3. Men respond better to things when you talk to them and not at them.

4. Expressing your wants and concerns in a calm manner gets him to listen. By doing this, he will not take what you say so personally. You will get what you want because he will not feel you are telling him what to do or ordering him around.

Men need to understand:

1. A woman's desire for closeness and intimacy is not always a sign of clinginess.

2. When your spouse shares her fears and feelings with you, they do not want it to be viewed or taken as they are nagging.

3. If you listen to your spouse for real, ask them how they are feeling, and listen when they speak. Hug them randomly; it shows you love them. This acknowledgment helps her shine and flourish in her femininity in the relationship.

4. Telling her things like "Thank you, I appreciate you, I love you, and you are beautiful..." These are always welcome, and it makes her feel good being with you.

5. Nothing makes a woman feel more inclined to go beyond to satisfy her man than her spouse acknowledging her efforts.

6. Showing her how much you love her outside of the bedroom makes her more willing and freer in the bedroom. When she feels appropriately loved, she is more conscious of her strengths and flaws.

7. Most women want to support you and be that person who when you are sick, she is the one to take care of you; if you start a business, she'll be your secretary, accountant, business partner, and most significant investor. When you're discouraged, she'll do all she can to help you find peace not because it is her job, but more because she believes in you. Your spouse wants to feel and know that if no one else is standing in their corner, their significant other is.

Men need to be very aware of a few things:

1. No woman wants to feel she must endure the hardships of the world with no one to hold her hand.

2. She doesn't want to lie next to you every night and feel alone.

3. A lonely woman can be a dangerous woman.

4. If in the relationship, she is silent and moving in the relationship with little to no noise, she is more than likely at her breaking point.

5. Her silence is her way of communicating that she has just about tapped out of this relationship. Silence to her means loneliness. If you love and want her, her silence is screaming for attention. Give it to her!

What men need to do is:

1. Be more sensitive to their spouse.

2. Be more understanding and not accuse them of being "overly emotional" when she shows a moment of weakness in the relationship.

3. Be a sounding board and be the one to restore and lift her spirits at the end of her hectic day.

4. Realize she is not going to tell you when she is feeling low most times. You must pay attention and be in tune with her energy. And yes, sometimes women are insecure and need you to support them.

5. Understand that nothing drives a woman away faster than feeling dismissed and unappreciated.

It is no secret that how we speak and communicate to each other determines how well we understand each other. Interestingly enough, how we talk to our spouses can be more important than the words we speak. The Bible says in **Proverbs 18:21**, (KJV), "Death and life are in the power of the tongue…" In other words, the words we choose to use when we speak have the power to pick our spouse up or put them down. Knowing "how" your spouse understands things helps make it easier for them to respond correctly to what you are saying or asking of them.

Another critical thing for men to remember is, it doesn't matter how established your spouse is in her career or how well put together she seems. She may occasionally need reassurance from you that she is and always will be unique. If she doesn't hear reassurances from you from time to time, she will question herself. She'll start to wonder if you see her the same way you used to. Has her recent weight gain made her unattractive to you? Do you still desire her like you used to?

It is during these moments of insecurity that validating your woman's position in your relationship (and in your life) is what she needs to hear from you. Let her know that no matter what or how you both may have changed physically, you'll always be attracted to her. She is still the most beautiful woman on the planet, and she is your life. She is…irreplaceable.

Problems are never a welcome occasion in relationships. One thing all couples need to avoid is displaying the feeling of *entitlement* in the relationship. Thinking you are doing them a favor by allowing them to support you when you're not. Taking and giving less is not the best way to make the other person feel valued in the relationship. There are a lot of men who believe when a woman gets married, their new job is to "receive" only, not give. They feel too many women see marriage as their personal "retirement plan," their "401k" plan and their own "ATM." Thinking that all their job consists of is to "be" in their life not *be* their life. Many of them justify their behavior by saying, "I am the wife, I deserve this. You should give me what I ask for and ask no questions." This kind of woman isn't a woman looking to help build something with her man. This is a woman looking to break her man. No man needs a woman to spend their money. They can do it themselves. I am not saying all women are gold diggers, but as the song says, "They ain't lookin for no broke …"

A woman who comes into the relationship looking for a place to unpack her *emotional baggage* isn't someone who is looking to "add" much to the relationship other than additional problems. A good woman in this situation understands that even though the man may make money, part of her job is to help "manage" the money. Meaning, it is her job to make sure they don't lose their wealth but increase it. Any man with a woman with this mindset will never question her. He will never believe that she is in the relationship just for the money. He will always feel they're on the same page, and he knows (as does she) they are in this relationship *together,* till death do us part!

Don't get me wrong some men need help. Many will admit they are bad with finances and prefer that their woman handle the finances. They know if she does, the essentials will get paid. Many prefer that their woman gives them a "me" allowance from their paycheck, so they can have some pocket money and not feel broke. They know, and it's not about their egos, that they can make money but are not good at making sure things get paid on time or at all. For them, it is what works for their household. Doing this doesn't make them feel less than a man because they are the "provider." The scary thing most men think about and do not want to encounter is a woman who is hooking up with them, not for love but financial reasons. Women who want someone to take care of them financially. These are those women who use the Bible's term on men being the providers to take advantage of their man. She is only with him for his resources, not for love.

Being the provider doesn't mean that if your wife was working before you married her that she should stop working. It means that if you follow the Bible, the man's primary job is to provide the finances, meaning make money to run the household. It doesn't say a woman cannot "manage" the money that he brings in, if he feels he cannot or is not good at doing so. It doesn't say she cannot or shouldn't contribute to the household finances. It says it is primarily the man's job to make money, not hers. Unless they have talked about it and the man agrees the woman shouldn't work, she should up and quit her job, once she is married.

In the Bible, the word "helper" or "helpmeet" doesn't mean a wife's job is to create ways to waste the money a man brings in. It means it is part of her "job" to help "manage" all that happens in the house to ensure things run smoothly. It does not mean that she should sit around all day watching the paint dry and waste money on a maid service to do her duties as the manager of the household. If her job is to manage the finances, then do so. A discussion needs to be had to ensure no one feels useless or used in the relationship. Before anyone takes what I am saying out of context, let me say that I believe women who take care of the home and the kids have just as much work if not more than any man working his day job. They are the masters of multi-tasking, often cleaning up trouble before it happens and hardly get any credit for doing so. Even though the Bible assigns both the man and woman their roles respectfully, I just wanted to acknowledge how hard most women in these positions work.

By the way, there is a reason why women outlive most men. "Men who come home to a woman who complains 24/7 about what their man isn't doing, could be doing more of or is no good at doing" isn't the best way to welcome your provider home. I tell people that you have to be aware that there are people in this world whose main job daily is to complain. They will go to bed complaining; wake up complaining, and when you ask, "Why are you always complaining," they will answer, "Because I can." These are those people, and I know you know who I am talking about; people who will find something wrong on a sunny day. Although men complain, women complain the most and half the time it isn't because the man did something. It is because he isn't doing something she wants him to do right then.

Don't get me wrong some men do sometimes give women reasons to complain, but most times they do it on their own to hear themselves talk. Always making pointless points and trying to establish their territory in the relationship. Hardly ever able to tell you "why" or "what" they are upset about or what you did to bring this to this point. Yes, there are men sometimes, who purposely give women reasons to get on them, but 90% of the time the woman complaining about something small is only the prelude to what they really want to talk about. They just are not sure how to express it without seeming or sounding like they are nagging for no reason. All of this takes a toll on men more than it does women. Always complaining will drive him to a quick and early death, make him leave the relationship, have him put his hands on you or have him ending up in jail because he wasn't able to handle the stress. Is it worth all this to be with him or him to stay with you?

As his wife, it is part of your job to share the wisdom God has given and shown you with him. Showing him you have more skills than just the ones in the bedroom is a plus to the relationship. For most men to get it and act right, seeing this is something they need to experience. He needs to see in action all that God has equipped her with to help you. Then he can see the value you bring to the relationship and will respect you more.

A "good" Godly woman would never make her man feel he is worth more to her dead than alive. A "good" Godly man would never die without knowing his wife is fully taken care of for the rest of her life. *Love* should never be measured by the amount of money the two of you have. It should be a tool used to make the good times better for as long as you both shall live.

A "good" woman would never put her husband in a situation that could land him in jail or cause his death. A "good" man would never allow himself to be put in a position where he would jeopardize or hurt his family. A "good" man should always make his woman feel and know he loves her. A "good" woman should never make her man feel he is "useful" as long as he provides for her and "useless" when things are not so good between them.

The one thing that is hurting couples worldwide is when one of the two who took the vows that said, "For better or worse" only stays around for the "better" and creates ways to leave when things are at their "worse." It says in **Ephesians 5:25-29**, (KJV), **25** - "Husbands, love your wives, even as Christ also enjoyed the church, and gave himself for it; **26** - That he might sanctify and cleanse it with the washing of water by the word, **27** - That he might present it to himself a glorious church, not having spot, or wrinkle, or any such thing; but that it should be holy and without blemish. **28** - So ought men love their wives as their own bodies. He that loveth his wife loveth himself. **29** - For no man ever yet hated own flesh; but nourisheth and cherisheth it, even as the Lord the church." In other words, men, love your wife "unconditionally" and provide for them so that they can be a helpmeet to you. Now, although the Bible doesn't say a wife should love her husband, it does say she must respect him. It doesn't mean *if she decides to that it should be with "conditions."*

As a "helpmeet," "communicating" is the key, not telling, instructing, forcing him to or making him feel bad for not doing as you ask. For him to perceive your "suggestions" as something helpful, it cannot come across as a "demand." It is human nature for us all to do the opposite when we feel someone is telling us what to do rather than asking us. It is like the old phrase goes, "You can get more bees with honey than vinegar." I understand that this way, a suggestion, question, comment, want, need, wish, etc. if asked, needs to be in a respectful way for it to be considered and met.

For a *seasoned woman* reading this, you know what I mean. There is a vast difference between a *seasoned* and *unseasoned woman*. Seasoned women get what they want, and they run the relationship to a certain degree all because they know how to talk *to* their man and not *at* him. They understand their role and play it well. Never looking to take because they know all the things they want they can, and most times get, by communicating them to their man. She uses a phrase that begins with "Honey, I like it when you...." to encourage him.

She fills in the gap with the many things he has done for her or that she enjoyed. By doing so, it makes him feel good, valued and important to her and the need to fulfill whatever she "likes" again and again without any arguing, push back or hesitation. Some women would say, "I am not doing anything like this. He should do for me because I asked, period." These would be the kind of women who are soon to be single shortly afterward because they think people react positively to demands barked at them like a dog or demanding them when it doesn't work. If it does, the woman should be concerned because she doesn't have a real man. She has a very foolish man and a weak one at that.

Seasoned women understand that by making their man "feel" appreciated, he is willing to do whatever she wants him to do. She doesn't have to raise her voice, yell or demand. All she would need to do is ask, and he will do. She will make it hard for him to leave the house each morning and more comfortable to come home when he gets off. She will make his home heaven, and he will do anything she asks of him. She doesn't have to be concerned about another woman taking him from her because he will know, feel and understand that his "business partner" is worth her weight in gold and then some.

Her success with him isn't about her sleeping with him to get what she wants. It is not about belittling herself or kissing up to him. It is about how she respects and treats him. It's not a trick or a big secret. It is a skill and an understanding that makes and keeps her marriage running well on all "cylinders." Her man knows her worth and treats her accordingly, as his well-deserved equal, not his employee. She is using the gifts God has equipped her with to get things done without ever raising her voice. This is a skill unseasoned women never seem to grasp or understand. They know being deceitful isn't the best way; straight forward with strength is better.

A *seasoned* woman understands it is hard for a man to share his feelings and dreams and even harder for him to NOT get the support of his woman when he does tell her. When her man shares (which many don't do that often, if at all) his dreams with her, she knows even if she doesn't understand it, agree with it or feel it is something she wants to do, she will encourage him. She will ask him for clarity, to get involved because that's the only way she can stay on top of what is going on. More importantly, it is the only way she can show her skills in enhancing the situation which makes her seem valuable to whatever he is doing. She will stand with him on whatever he is trying to do that will better himself, even if it means suggesting ideas and changes and allowing him to feel that they were his own. In turn, he will look to her for her suggestions, accept them and more importantly, she is and will be thought of because he feels she is "a part" or whatever he is doing. She never has to ask, "Why are you not including me in your project? What are you going to do with the money when you make it? or Why don't you keep me posted on what's happening?" because she will be "involved" every step of the way on whatever it is.

Unseasoned women always fuss and fight for what little they receive from and with their man. They're continuously asking for something because to them, sleeping with their man is considered to be "equal" to all the things they feel they are entitled to from him. I'm not going to call these women prostitutes (but using and trading sex for trinkets or money is the definition of what they do, right?) I will call them the "something for nothing" people. The young, so smart that they are stupid, small-minded thinking and not yet grown using what they have (their body) to get what they want from men and thinking it is the thing to do. Not realizing they are seen and treated as "thots" by the men they are with and nothing more because the men already know they are not around to stay.

These women have not yet acquired these *skills* and often find themselves by themselves. She will be the one who never knows where her man is, what he is doing or what time he will return home. She'll always wonder why he doesn't communicate with her as often as he should. She'll be the one wondering why he doesn't share his dreams or ideas with her, but will with everyone else. She wonders why she isn't asked to get involved in anything he is doing outside the home. She shows no reason why he should keep her around or include her in anything he does because all she is doing at the moment is enjoying what he is giving her, not contributing to all she could have.

Because she has put herself first in their relationship, she is always afraid when he is not smashing her; you're smashing someone else — "always" wondering when her last day will come. She pushes her way into his life and doesn't allow him to see that she could be a significant part of his life. She doesn't understand when her man is sharing his ideas, vision or plans with her. She is concerned as to why she is not part of any of it and why she doesn't seem to be included. The reason for this is because she is continually forcing her way into his life. In doing so, he doesn't see her as an asset, but more of a liability.

He expects her to contribute (and this could be done mainly through encouraging him) and support him not criticize, critique or discourage him because he has a vision and a plan. Instead of recognizing this opportunity to "be" his life, she is more comfortable just being "in" his life. When he talks about doing things to better his life like starting a business, she responds by saying things like, "Who do you think you are starting a business? What do you know about starting a business? What are you going to do? Do you know how to do what you're saying? Isn't something like that already out there? What makes yours different? It won't last long. You will give up if it doesn't pop off right away."

She is so much into herself that she doesn't even see that when he does "get it together" right before, he will trade up for someone who can appreciate his efforts. All she had to do was be supportive. No one wants to be with someone who is a "dream killer." They don't talk to them because they can't keep their mouths shut or their legs closed.

As we know, a man with a woman like this waiting at home is the reason why he will stay out late and spend more time with friends all to avoid dealing with this foolishness after a long day at work. This is why most men will try and stay out until they think their woman is asleep. They don't want to hear negativity, complaining and be questioned for no reason concerning their whereabouts when they told you where they were already. They don't want to be accused of things you made up in your head, explain how they should be living their lives or told who they should and shouldn't be hanging out with. You're the girlfriend not his wife or his mother. Let's be real for a second. Honestly, who wants to be drilled and greeted like that every day? She doesn't work with her man. She spends her time "working" against him on purpose to feel essential and involved. She's always thinking because she is beautiful it's going to last forever. What women like this forget is, "Beauty fades, and love lasts forever!"

Where a *seasoned woman* makes her man's house a home that's worth coming home to, the *unseasoned woman* makes her man's house not feel like his castle but like his prison, a place he would rather not be that often. "Women who meet, fall in love, and marry their husband understand how to keep him, and the man knows how to keep her." Don't get me wrong. I often foolishly fell for an unseasoned woman when I was young. I wasn't at the time, able to recognize which was which. I was 25 years old. She was drop-dead beautiful and based on how we got along, I "thought" I had a good one. I was so caught up with her beauty that I didn't even notice how damaged she was, nor did I see how she was using me. I put this woman through college and took care of her every need. It never dawned on me, nor did I ever think or feel she would use me like that until I fell on hard times.

My friends saw it and told me, but I thought they were jealous. It wasn't until my Aunt Sherry pulled me to the side one day after seeing what kind of fool I was making of myself and said to me, "I see how you are doing everything for her, and she doesn't appreciate it. I know her, and I am telling you this woman is a user. She doesn't care anything about you. She is manipulating and taking advantage of you because she knows you like her. She will be with you for as long as you can do for her but let your money go down or you stop buying her things and I promise you she will drop you like a bad check and quickly replace you with someone else before the sun goes down. Listen, there are some good women out there, but she is not one of them. You need to cut her loose before you end up broke messing with her." It goes to show you everyone plays the fool sometimes.

(Buzz) Yes, Ms. Jackson? Ms. Clark is here.

Mr. Pearson is speaking: Thank you. Show her in. Good afternoon Ms. Clark.

Ms. Clark is speaking: Good afternoon Mr. Pearson.

Mr. Pearson is speaking: From what we said, did you believe her story?

Mr. Pearson is speaking: Come on in and have a seat. Make yourself comfortable. Can I offer you something to drink, water, tea or coffee? Do you prefer Lisa or Ms. Clark?

Ms. Clark is speaking: No, for now, I am okay. Calling me Lisa is okay.

Mr. Pearson is speaking: I have reviewed your questionnaire, and from what I read it seemed your ex had emotionally, verbally and physically abused you. He had control issues. He cheated on you. He was extremely critical toward you, am I right? It seems although this was years ago, it is still affecting your life today, right?

Lisa is speaking: Yes, that's right.

Mr. Pearson is speaking: Why have you decided to talk to someone now?

Lisa is speaking: Well, I recently got married, and I am happy my husband treats me well, but I find myself during simple disagreements with my husband, reacting and saying things to him I wish I could have said to my ex. My ex treated me badly and had me feeling worthless. I would have spoken up at the time, but I didn't know then that the verbal abuse I saw as normal wasn't right. It wasn't until I met and married my husband that I saw what I had gone through wasn't love, nor was it right for me at all.

Now I am not that bad but at times, when my husband says certain things, acts a certain way or grabs me a certain way, I get flashbacks to how my ex handled me and I start screaming and crying. My husband always consoles me and calms me down, but he said to me, "This has gone on for months. You're not sleeping, hardly eating and you're starting to look a little depressed. It is time to talk to a professional in the hope that they can get you through this ordeal. I want you to be happy and if talking to someone can achieve this, I will find someone and stay by your side until you are your old self." He found you and made the appointment for me because I was too embarrassed to do it myself.

Mr. Pearson is speaking: I understand, and I am glad you're here. I know verbal and emotional abuse can be just as, if not more dangerous than physical abuse is in a relationship. For many people when they hear of verbal and emotional abuse, they think of the physical aspect, and because of this, it is hard to recognize, address or acknowledge the long-term damage it causes a person. There are more people than you think out there today going through this. Many are suffering in silence not knowing how it affects them until their next relationship. With that said, rest assured I am going to do my best to get to the root of this and get you peace of mind. Let's start at the beginning. Although it may be upsetting to talk about your ex, I need you to walk me through what you experienced. If I interrupt you, it is because I feel you have said something we should address at that moment.

The goal today is to understand, address and resolve these issues and concerns so you will no longer see yourself as the victim, okay?

Lisa is speaking: Yes, I understand. Well, everything started when I got a new job in Atlanta. I packed up from my hometown in Alabama and moved to Atlanta. I didn't want to leave my hometown, but this opportunity was a good one and would help me provide for my five kids. In between and before I moved all my things from Alabama, I reached out to my sorority sister Valerie. She was able to allow me and my kids to come and stay with her until I could afford a place of my own.

Mr. Pearson is speaking: Did you and your ex live together in Alabama?

Lisa is speaking: Well, in a way. I mean he stayed with a roommate, but from time to time, I allowed him to stay at my place. We were co-parenting the kids and he could watch them while I worked sometimes.

Mr. Pearson is speaking: Was this your first time in Atlanta or had you been here before?

Lisa is speaking: No, it wasn't my first time here. I would come every so often to see my friend Valerie. She was the one to talk me into looking for a job here. She said that with me working in the medical field, I could find a good job with better pay, and I did. It wasn't too bad because during my visits, I made friends and learned my way around a little, so it wasn't too scary. I worked a lot so I had very little time to go out and enjoy the nightlife. So on one of my days off Valerie suggested we get out and have some "me" time. We went to the Greenbrier Mall to shop and hang out. She said, "Who knows, you might meet someone." I told her I wasn't ready to meet other people just yet. I wanted to get myself together first.

While at the mall, I saw this guy. I pointed him out to Valerie and she said, "I know him. That's one of my coworkers. Don't worry, I will introduce him to you." So she called him over. I am not going to lie. He was very good looking, easy on the eyes, toned body, and I was attracted to him. His name was Isaiah. Valerie told me his name was Isaiah as he walked toward us. Then, she conveniently walked away to a nearby store so that we could talk. Feeling a little nervous, I started asking him a lot of questions. He smiled at me, and we spoke for a while.

"Do you have any kids?"

"No. Not yet."

"Why not?

"I haven't met the right woman. Do you have any kids?"

"This isn't about me, but yes, I have kids. How old are you, if you don't mind me asking?"

"I'm 42 years old."

"Ever been married before?"

"No. I am still waiting for the right woman. Do you make a habit of asking so many questions to those you meet?"

"Yes, it is just me getting to know you that's all. Tell me about yourself that you would want a woman to know."

"Well, maybe I can tell you that because it will take some time over dinner?"

"Well, I will think about it and get back to you."

Mr. Pearson is speaking: It sounds as if you were interested in him. You asked a lot of questions because you saw him as a potential mate?

Lisa is speaking: Yes, that's why I asked so many questions. Before we parted, he said he would love to get to know me better. He suggested we get together for lunch or dinner to talk more and asked if it was okay for him to give me his number, and I said sure. Although I wanted to do it sooner, I waited three days before I texted him to see if he was still interested in getting to know me over dinner. He texted back and said, let's talk and discuss where and when.

Eventually, we got together for lunch and hung out more. It wasn't long after, five months, we had become a couple. In the beginning, we were doing well. I thought I had a good man, but I had my guard up because a lot of men "act right" to get you in bed and for now to me, he was no different. During that time, I got my place and moved 3 of my 5 kids in with me, and the other two stayed with their dad in Alabama. I didn't introduce him to my kids for almost eight months. I had to be sure it was okay. I didn't want to bring a man around my kids, have them get attached, and then we break up.

Mr. Pearson is speaking: When the kids met him, did they like him and get along?

Lisa is speaking: Yes, they did. Ten months into our relationship, I asked him to move in with us. For a while, everything was going great, but after a few months of living together, I started noticing changes in him.

Mr. Pearson is speaking: Like how?

Lisa is speaking: Well, first, his behavior changed, and the sweet and affectionate things slowed down as before. He had gotten so comfortable to where he thought it was his place and that he was in charge. He had just left his job right before we moved in together and was in the process of looking for another one, so I thought. I knew something was wrong when he told me one day when I asked for money to pay some bills. He said, "I need for you to hold it down for a while, you make enough money. I am working on my dream of becoming a rapper. It's my dream and something I need to do right now. When I get out there, we are going to be living that life, and we are going to be living large."

Hearing this from a grown man made me hot as hell. He did his best to convince me that he was going to get a record deal soon and soon afterward be making that paper. I asked him, "In the meantime, how are you going to eat, pay bills and take care of my kids and me? What makes you think I want to take care of three kids and a grown-ass man while you pursue a rap career at 42 years old?"

Now to be fair I knew, in the beginning, he liked to rap, and he could rap a little, but I thought it was a hobby of his because he had a day job working with Valerie. If I would have known that he was going to quit his job to try and be a rapper, I would have left his ass where he was. I said, "Listen, I didn't sign up for this kind of relationship. I surely didn't sign up to take care of a grown-ass man chasing a dream." Hearing him tell me this, I couldn't believe he was this irresponsible. I thought as my man he knew coming into a readymade family that "our" responsibilities were to the family, not him alone. I know, the kids weren't his, and legally it wasn't his responsibility, but I was clear that "we" were a total package. Now I see the red flags I missed that may not have been a great idea.

Mr. Pearson is speaking: Had you two sat down before moving in to discuss how it would all work with you having children. Did you talk about bills? I am asking because it seems he wasn't moving in with you to be in a relationship. The relationship was his way in to live off you which many men today seem to be doing and are okay with. He probably thought like many men do these days, that if you're already taking care of everything before he got there, you should keep doing it. Many men feel that if you're handling everything before I moved in, you can keep on doing it. If he helped out a little, you should be grateful. He is your boyfriend and not a family man.

This behavior you're speaking about is the way weak men or controlling men would be because they are trying to train you to believe this way of life is normal. To make matters worse, they will do their best to make you feel they are helping you out by being in your life. They will have the nerve to tell you that you should be happy if they decide to contribute anything. When you bring up bills and tell them they need to help, they will twist the conversation and tell you that they shouldn't have to do much more than "be" your man.

Lisa is speaking: Looking back now, I can see that, but at the time, I was trying not to lose my ever-loving mind. He had me twisted.

Mr. Pearson is speaking: Well, that was a clear indication he wasn't ready to have a family or the responsibilities that come along with it. He seemed like a person who was looking for a place to live and a person to live off of.

Lisa is speaking: I told him that I was not going to take care of a grown-ass man. He wasn't a real man and had no pride if he expected to live off my kids and me. I wasn't going to allow him to live here for free. He was supposed to be my man, not my child. I did not live for free, so neither should he.

Mr. Pearson is speaking: How did he take this new news?

Lisa is speaking: He said he would contribute something if I stopped tripping. He claimed he would straighten up and act like my man if I would chill. I told him if he didn't keep his word, he would have to go.

Mr. Pearson is speaking: A question before you continue, did he explain why he moved in so quickly with you instead of suggesting you both look for a place together? I ask because real men don't

145

move in with women. They suggest that they get a place together. Something new they both can call their own. Now yes, I have known women to move in with men they were dating, but at the same time, the man allowed her to make his house their home.

Lisa is speaking: Well looking back now, it does seem strange that he didn't suggest we find a new place. At that time, I was happy to be with someone and thought we would talk about that down the road, but we never talked about our future, we just lived in our future.

Mr. Pearson is speaking: It's understandable. You were in love and happy to have someone to share your life with at that time. This is the time when we miss most of the red flags flying. In this state of mind, we tend to get deaf, dumb, blind and stupid. This is because even though those we're with are lying a little, seem a little crazy and the situation could be wrong, we want to be with someone so badly that we will give them time to make those lies they told us come true. Okay, let's go deeper. Tell me when did he first put his hands on you?

Lisa is speaking: Well, the first time was one night when he had been drinking. I asked him to not drink so much in front of the children, and I reached out to take the bottle he had in his hand, and he slapped me. As I stood there in shock, he said, "You best leave me alone. You're not my mother, and you're not going to tell me what I can and can't do. Don't you ever talk or touch me like that again."

Mr. Pearson is speaking: Well, that should have been his first and last time. You should never stay with anyone who puts their hands on you. Listen, the first time a man puts their hands on you, you are a victim. The second time they do it, you are a volunteer.

Lisa is speaking: I didn't know at the time what to do. He had never raised his hand to me before, and I just thought it was because he was drunk. However, as time went on, he showed severe signs of jealousy and became very demanding of me.

Mr. Pearson is speaking: Like how?

Lisa is speaking: Whenever I would leave to go to work, he would call or text me. He would ask if I had gotten to work. Then, he would tell me to call him when I got off and was on my way home. He had gotten so possessive that he would question and often accuse me of cheating with my coworker which I wasn't. He used to threaten me, saying, "I better not find out you got a man on the side. If I call you during the time you are supposed to be at work then you better be there if you know what's good for you."

I went from being in love with him to being afraid of him, and I knew that wasn't good. I felt like I was losing it. So I would call my girlfriend because I didn't want my family to understand what I was going through. All they would have done is criticize me for allowing him to move in with me in the first place. That wasn't something I wanted or needed to hear at the moment.

Anyway, I called Valerie to tell her what I was going through. I hoped that she had some excellent advice to help me get out of it. Instead of giving me information on how to get out, she told me, "Girl, you got you a good man, you better hold on to him. He is just stressed trying to get his hustle on that's all. He's just talking girl, don't take what he says personally. Your man loves you, you hear me. He isn't going to do anything to you." I told her I couldn't live like this much longer; I needed to live. After we spoke, I didn't feel any better about my situation, but I didn't know what to do about it, so I avoided him and hoped things would change. I thought I had made a mistake for allowing him to move in.

Mr. Pearson is speaking: At this point, what you had learned, seen and been through should have been enough that if he didn't leave, you should have left. You had kids and you feared that he might do something to all of you and to make matters worse, you walked on eggshells for a while until you could figure out a way to get out. You knew love didn't feel like this. This was a control situation plain and simple.

Lisa is speaking: I know, but I was so afraid at the time of what he would do to my children or me if I asked him to leave or if I left. I just stayed and prayed things would get better and that God would show me a way out of the mess. All of this was affecting my health and my life. I stopped going out with my girlfriends. I felt sad most days, and my friends, when they saw me, said that I looked scared and on edge. I would jump when anyone called my name. I was a wreck, and I knew it, but like I said, I don't rightly know how to change my situation. I couldn't go anywhere without him wanting to know my whereabouts all the time. If I took too long to return from wherever I said I was going, he would fuss at me when I got home telling me I was out with another man, which I wasn't.

Mr. Pearson is speaking: That seems a little too much.

Lisa is speaking: You're right. He would repeatedly tell me, "No one wants you. No man will take you and your five kids. No one is going to treat you as well as I do. I am the best thing you got. I look out for you and your kids. You are not going anywhere. Where will you go? I will hurt you if you try to leave."

Mr. Pearson is speaking: I understand the position you were in and why you didn't leave right away, but it was clear something had to change. Here was the opportunity when you needed to reach out to a professional who handles situations, like yours. Don't misunderstand me. I am not saying you didn't try, but you could see things weren't getting better. They were getting worse.

Lisa is speaking: To make matters worse, he hung out more in the streets and would come home smelling of another woman. When I asked him, "Where have you been?" he would tell me to mind my own business and stay in my lane. Saying I was out of pocket and I didn't know my place. If I weren't careful, he would show me what he meant. He would always tell me I was his girlfriend, not his mother, and he did not have to answer to me for anything. I knew he was cheating on me because we hardly ever had sex anymore. Even if we did, I couldn't enjoy it in the state of mind I was in at that time. This mess was stressing and draining me. I just wanted the nightmare to stop.

Mr. Pearson is speaking: So by this point, if I hear you correctly, you had been abused from all sides physically, emotionally and verbally. With his hanging out and coming in smelling of another woman, you believed he was cheating on you, right?

Lisa is speaking: Yes, you are correct. Did I mention that whenever his so-called rap career wasn't going well or anything for that matter, he would verbally blame me for him not being successful? To hear him tell it, it was always my fault; someone else's but never his. He used to say to me all the time what I was feeling concerning him cheating on me was wrong. It was all in my head and that I had issues. When we would argue, and he always took everything to the extreme, he would make me feel guilty for telling him the problems I had with him. He would come out guns blazing and shoot way below the belt just to hurt me.

Mr. Pearson is speaking: It is unfortunate you couldn't feel safe in your own home. I have known women like you who, under these conditions, would build walls around themselves for protection. However, where there are walls, there are cracks and where there are cracks there are leaks. These leaks, if broken, can cause more problems. So many abusers spend their time fixing and patching cracks to be safe. They want to keep the truth from coming out to others of what you're going through to the point where they feel their situation is never going to get better. I heard you when you told your friend, and she reacted in a way that threw you. I understand how hard it is even when you want to tell others what's going on to get help, but you feel so trapped and you don't know what's right or wrong anymore. It's a fact that abusive behavior robs you of your self-esteem. It doesn't matter if it comes from a man, woman, or a child. I can tell you that it is never acceptable.

Men who act this way, and this behavior they display comes from those who as a child were never corrected. When male children would do something wrong, their parents would quickly defend their actions. Once grown up and involved with a woman in a relationship, in most arguments whether they are right or wrong, they would always feel they were right, and others were wrong. Even if you caught them, they would never admit they were wrong. If you knew then what you know today, you would have known that he was not the one for you. Sadly, we all have to learn these life experiences this way, but we can only hope going forward that we learned something useful to use in our next relationship.

Lisa is speaking: I agree.

Mr. Pearson is speaking: I've learned that when most women think their spouse is cheating they are 99.99%, right. Very rarely are they wrong or far off. I am not saying they are always right because there is a small chance they could be wrong because there are some women who will use this excuse to cheat for themselves. When you are emotionally wrapped up in your relationship, sometimes the decision-making abilities that work so well for you when you are reading others can and will play tricks on you. They will have you thinking and seeing something that isn't there because you need so badly to be right about what you are feeling. Proof always helps, and knowing will also hurt more.

Lisa is speaking: I understand, but I felt I was right because my gut told me so. I got the proof. I needed to be correct. He tried hard to throw me off his trail. He used the fact that I cared for him to act out. He would threaten me and use ultimatums to get his way with me. I stayed as long as I did because he would apologize after the fact and foolishly, I would give him another chance.

Mr. Pearson is speaking: There's no doubt you were in an emotionally abusive relationship.

Lisa is speaking: By now, I felt I would get myself together and leave, but every time I thought about it, I would chicken out and stay.

Mr. Pearson is speaking: You know like I know that insecurities can damage a relationship. Jealousy, although a little can be useful too much is damaging. Being questioned continuously or under suspicion when you've done nothing wrong doesn't help either. Dealing with this kind of behavior as you did, you had to be emotionally drained. He tried to make you feel bad because he was up to no good.

Lisa is speaking: I agree with you. The crazy thing is this man would argue with me all day when we were together, use the silent treatment as a punishment, and pretend he didn't care about me, but the moment I would step out of the house to do whatever or to get away, he would blow up my phone wanting to know where I was, how long I was going to be and when I was coming back. I never thought or looked at what I was going through at that time as emotional abuse, but I did feel and know that loving someone wasn't supposed to feel like it was feeling to me.

Mr. Pearson is speaking: The tactics he was using to control you aren't new, and sadly enough, most men do this to women because it works most of the time. Some would call what they were doing or refer to it as "training" their woman. Listen, he put you through this without you knowing and had you continually thinking about all you had done in order to keep you from seeing and knowing all he was doing wrong. As you can see, this is part of their control package. Men like this use these tactics or methods to punish and manipulate their woman all to get their way.

In your situation, it seems he had your head spinning and kept you always on edge wondering what he was going to do next. He knew you loved him, so he was able to accomplish what he did and take advantage of you. He knew you were emotionally invested more than he was so he knew you would stay and you did. Even though you knew something wasn't right between you two, you stayed anyway to keep the peace.

Here it is years later, and you're still trying to justify why you allowed this man to control you as he did for so long. You've spent years blaming yourself for something that wasn't your fault. It affected your health and is affecting your current relationship, and this must stop.

Lisa is speaking: You're right. I wish I would have realized this sooner than later.

Mr. Pearson is speaking: Trust me when I tell you that you deserve to be loved and to be happy. You did not need to fight for a relationship that tears you down emotionally and psychologically. What you were going through wasn't worth it or healthy. What did your girlfriend say about all this going on with you because she had to have seen something was not right with you?

Lisa is speaking: Although I was embarrassed and not wanting her to see that I saw myself as a victim, I told her pieces of what I was going through. I didn't get the feeling she cared when she told me, "A man is going to be a man." It pissed me off at times because she made my problems seem like they were normal. I couldn't believe my best friend was talking like this to me. She wasn't helping at all. I felt if anyone would be sympathetic and understand my situation, it would be her. When I told her, I cannot do this anymore, her views changed. She then said, "You should leave. I don't know how or why you stayed as long as you did." Hearing this I was confused because the last time we spoke, she was telling me how good a man I had, and now she was telling me to leave, she wasn't helping me. I was confused, listening to her.

Mr. Pearson is speaking: So you left him this time?

Lisa is speaking: Well, in short, I did, but let me tell you what happened. Like I said, I suspected he was cheating, and I was going to get the proof. I followed him one night to the club to see who he was hooking up with.

Mr. Pearson is speaking: Were you emotionally ready to face the truth?

Lisa is speaking: Yes, and no, but either way, I needed to know.

Mr. Pearson is speaking: I understand what you're saying in theory. Most people say that getting to the truth is what they want, but once they found out for sure, they feel worse. Their first thought after hearing the truth is to dismiss it and not believe in your heart that it is the truth. Denying the fact is what we do to lessen the hurt we're going through, but it doesn't help, it just prolongs the inevitable. Knowing this truth turns our world from right side up to upside down. Now is this what you were preparing yourself to go through emotionally? I agree the truth is always best, but in a situation like this, it doesn't make the pain hurt less. I am not saying this because you shouldn't know the truth. I am saying that you should be careful what you ask for as you might just get it.

Lisa is speaking: Anyway, I followed him to the club, **Kapture**. I saw him from my car outside of the club hugging another woman; kissing and patting her on her behind like he used to do to me. I could not see the woman's face, but from what I did notice, she looked familiar to me. I thought about going in and blowing him up, but I knew it would make me look foolish if I did, so I went home and waited for him to come back.

While waiting, I called my girlfriend to tell her I got him, but her phone went to voicemail. She didn't pick up. Thinking something was wrong, I drove over to her place and knocked on her door, and I got no answer. Now I was worried about my friend, pissed about my man, and no one to talk to about it. I went back home and sat and cried. I kept asking myself, how could I be so blind, foolish and stupid to allow this man to disrespect and treat me this way for so long without realizing what was going on?

The more I cried the madder I got. I called. It went straight to voicemail. I texted, and I got no answer. I said enough was enough. I called a locksmith. I had the locks changed, and I put his stuff out on the porch. I was done with him. He did not come home that night, nor did he call or text me to let me know if he was okay. Emotionally I was hurting inside, and at the same time, I worried that something had happened to him. I was over this whole mess.

Two days later, he showed up and tried to get in and found out his keys no longer worked. He beat on the door and called out my name. He wanted me to tell him what was up with all his stuff outside. I didn't let him in because I was afraid of him. I asked him to leave or I would call the police on him. Hearing this, he started apologizing, asking what he did wrong and saying, "You know I love you." I told him he needed to return to where you were last night, tell her your lies because we were through. It was over.

I tracked down my girlfriend finally, and when I asked her where she had been because I had come by her house and called her half the night, she told me she was at home. She had taken some sleeping pills and didn't hear the phone or me knocking on the door. She said she had just gotten up and gotten home from somewhere. I got a weird vibe from her, but I couldn't put my finger on what was bothering me.

Mr. Pearson is speaking: What do you mean?

Lisa is speaking: She seemed a little jumpy. I told her that I had followed him to the club last night, and I saw him with another woman. She asked, "Did you get a good look at her?" I told her, not really, but something about her was familiar to me. I said he didn't come home last night, didn't call or text to check on me at all. I told her that when she didn't return my calls or answer her door when I came over, I started worrying about her, and I wondered if she was okay.

Lisa is speaking: Sure, why wouldn't I?

Mr. Pearson is speaking: Well I find it strange that when she woke up and saw you had called so many times that she did not call you back right away to see what was going on with you that you had called her so many times. You got her when you called her yet again the next day that sounds a little weird to me. She is your best friend?

Lisa is speaking: You know now that you mention it, it does sound strange now. I never looked at "why" she didn't call me back when she saw I had called so many times.

Mr. Pearson is speaking: So, you put him out, and he was now out of your life?

Lisa is speaking: Yes! It was not soon after that that I met my Aaron. He owned his own magazine company, TCM Magazine Company, based in downtown Atlanta. I would see him on Fridays at my job when he would come by to see my manager. I had noticed him many times, but I wasn't sure if he saw me. One day when he was on his way out, he struck up a conversation with me and formally introduced himself. We talked for a while. He was sexy, very polite and straightforward. He didn't waste any time asking me if I was single. He told me he would like to get to know me better and if I was free, he wanted to take me out to dinner. At first, I looked at him sideways because I had heard that before and look where it got me.

I told him to slow his roll. "We hardly know one another. Don't you think asking me out is moving kind of fast?" I said to him that we should talk a little more first. He apologized and asked me if it was okay if he gave me his number and when I was comfortable enough with him, we could talk. I told him it was a little too soon. He said, "No rush. Take your time" because he wasn't going anywhere. I thought that was sweet of him to say that. A week later, we exchanged numbers. When we did speak, we got along like old friends. Although we only talked for a little while, it seemed like hours when it was about 45 minutes. He told me so many interesting things about himself. He said he felt comfortable talking to me, and I told him I felt the same. He was different, and I mean in a bad boy way.

Mr. Pearson is speaking: How so?

Lisa is speaking: First of all, he asked me about me, and for the first time, a man listened as I told him about myself. I couldn't believe it. After a few days of talking over the phone, I decided to take him up on his dinner invitation. I told him that when I saw him again, I would give him my answer. He said he would be back in the following week. A few days later, he returned, and this time he was there to see me. He asked me out for lunch, and I went. We had lunch and talked more, and it was beautiful. When I got back to work, I found myself smiling for no reason for the rest of the day. It was a Tuesday.

With all I had been through the last few months, I was relieved to meet someone like him. He was moving slowly, and I appreciated it. I didn't want to rush and jump into something because I didn't feel I was ready. I did my best though, not to show how much I was interested in him when we were together. I don't think I did a great job. I felt so blessed, and I thanked God for bringing him into my life when He did. Don't laugh when I say this, but I suddenly felt the need to go to church to thank Him in His house. I knew the LORD knew me but had not seen my face in a while. It was time I visited His place. My life had become better. I was in a better place, and I thanked God for this. I made sure I showed up in church on Saturday because it was long overdue.

Friday morning came, and sure enough, Aaron was back to see me and pick up payment for our advertisement. With a big smile on his face, he asked, "Have you decided on my offer to take you to dinner?" I said that after giving it some thought, I decided if we could do it early, I would go. I needed to be home before sunset. He asked "by chance, are you a Seventh-day Adventist?" I said, "Yes, I am. Why do you ask?" He laughed, and for a moment I thought he was making fun of me being an Adventist but it turned out that he was a Seventh-day Adventist also.

He said he attended church over on Beverly Road NE in Atlanta. I told him I worshiped over at Hamilton E. Holmes drive in northwest Atlanta. He said he knew where that was. He said he would have never guessed I was a Seventh-day Adventist. He was glad we finally talked. We had dinner around 5 pm (sunset was at 7:20 pm), talked and had a good time. I knew it might have been too soon to be feeling comfortable with him like I did, but I just did. Over dinner, I asked him if he would like to attend church with me Saturday and he said, "Sure".

Mr. Pearson is speaking: It seemed your life was looking good, and you were feeling better.

Lisa is speaking: Yes, I was feeling better, and my life had turned around. I had met a wonderful God-fearing man. He was interested in me, he listened to me, he had a good job and I felt so blessed to be me. I couldn't believe after everything that I had been through that I felt wanted and desired by someone.

Mr. Pearson is speaking: Well, you may have felt it was luck, but I believe what happened to you was by design. You see, God has a way of "presenting" when He feels you're ready to receive the right person in your life. So how was your date?

Lisa is speaking: Our date was terrific. He was more than I could have asked for in a man. I called Valerie because I had been MIA for a while, spending time with my new man. Things between us were going well. I was feeling good, and I felt the need to share it with my girl. I told her to come to church so she could meet my new man on Saturday. She agreed to come. She said she had a surprise for me as well. When I tried to get a hint to what it was, she told me I had to wait.

Mr. Pearson speaking: So what was Valerie's surprise?

Lisa is speaking: Well, when we got to the church, and I saw her, I went over to say hello and to introduce her to Aaron. The closer I got to her, I saw that she was pregnant. I said, "OMG girl! You are pregnant! When did this happen and why didn't you tell me?" She said she had been busy. She said this must be the guy who has got you glowing. I said, let's all sit down because I want to hear all about this baby coming. She got quiet and said she was here with the father of her child. I said, "Where is he?" No sooner than she could say anything, over walked my ex. I stood up and asked him, "What are you doing here?" He said, "I am here with my lady, is this your new man?"

Mr. Pearson is speaking: I take it you never imagined the two of them had hooked up?

Lisa is speaking: You're right. I never thought my best friend would be with my ex and pregnant on top of it. I was at a loss for words. I didn't know if I should be mad or hurt. Either way, I felt sick through my whole body. I told Aaron I wanted to sit somewhere else. Aaron could see I was a little bothered and that something was wrong. He asked if I was okay and if there was anything he could do to help me. I told him I would be fine, to give me a second to catch my breath.

Mr. Pearson is speaking: It seems to me you were putting the pieces together in your head and you were in disbelief.

Lisa is speaking: You're right. I was doing just that. I started thinking back, and I realized I was right when I thought that Isaiah had been cheating on me, and I had no clue. The two of them had been lying to my face and laughing at me behind my back. Cheating on me was one thing, but sleeping with someone I considered to be my best friend just wasn't right. It hurt me in my heart to find this out this way. I couldn't believe someone I called my sister and family would do me like this. Thinking back, the reason why the woman looked so familiar to me was that it was her.

I felt like a fool thinking about it. This woman sat there with me many nights as I cried over this fool, knowing she was the reason I was crying over him. She saw me doubt myself, live in fear, and hurt while caring for someone who she knew was cheating on me with her. Now, she is pregnant. I guess it was a good thing we didn't have children together. I don't know if I could have dealt with the two of us being pregnant around the same time by the same guy.

Mr. Pearson is speaking: I know it hurts to find out even though you were with someone and learning this secret the way you did. It is obvious you had mixed emotions because you cared for them both.

Lisa is speaking: Honestly, I didn't feel all that good knowing the truth. I felt depressed and numb inside. I could not get over or past the fact that my best friend and my ex had deceived me for so long. I felt as if the whole time they were cheating, they were laughing behind my back at how big of a fool I was that I didn't know what was going on between them. I loved him, and I thought we were working on a future together. As I sat in church looking and feeling like a fool, I was so hurt and shaking. I wondered why they would do me this way. Aaron asked me if I wanted to leave, but I said no.

Mr. Pearson is speaking: I take it, Aaron understood because you two ended up getting married. Believe me when I tell you this, there aren't many men who would want to deal with that kind of drama to be with someone. Aaron loves you. His willingness to help you work through your issues only shows you how much he is invested in you and your marriage.

Lisa is speaking: I agree. It's why I am here. I want to turn my attention and love to the man who treats me like the queen I am. When things went down at the church that morning, I wasn't going to allow my past to stop me from spending time with the Lord. Now the rest, you know. Now you are caught up, what's next?

Mr. Pearson is speaking: Well, being here, admitting and talking openly about your issues makes you ready to make a change. I know you probably would feel better if they hurt like you did, right?

Lisa is speaking: Yes, I do feel that way. Why shouldn't they hurt? I hurt.

Mr. Pearson is speaking: This may be easier said than done, but you must take the high road and forgive yourself first and then forgive them. You need to allow God the opportunity to heal you and deal with them. Let Him fight for you on this matter. He knows how you feel and all that you've been through in your life. Believe it or not, He started healing you when He presented Aaron into your life. Think about it. You met, fell in love and married. Let me ask you. Are you not glad you two met? Are you not happy with him? Does he not make you feel good? Isn't that what you said you wanted? To be loved by a good man?

Lisa is speaking: You are right. I did say that, and yes, I am happy with my husband, but this forgiving those who hurt me is hard for me to do. I am not sure I can do it.

Mr. Pearson is speaking: I am sure you can. You see, forgiveness starts the healing process. If you believe in God, continue to ask Him for His help. Let him know you are asking for His help because you are unable to do it alone, and He will help you. I understand what you mean and how you feel. The hardest offenses to forgive are those committed by the people who are closest to us. I know it is not easy, but you must do it even if they don't.

When you began sharing your story with me, I felt your past issues had consumed you, and you were carrying resentment and anger toward someone no longer in your life. You thought about it so much, to the point where you unintentionally lashed out at those you loved and needed most in your life. Listen, I know it is hard, but you must forgive them. By doing so, you take away their right to hurt you. By forgiving them for the wrongs they have caused you, you are healing your wounds.

As we know, God's willingness to forgive us depends on our willingness to forgive others. I know you are probably thinking, "If I forgive them, I'm letting them off the hook." This isn't true. The fact of the matter is that by doing this, you are letting yourself off the hook. You are setting yourself free from the pain and resentment you feel. You are allowing yourself the opportunity to love and receive love. I want you, right now, to stop concerning yourself with getting back at them. It's wasted energy and time for you to do so. He will handle them on your behalf. Remember, He understands what has happened, and how you're feeling. He knows all you have gone through. God knows the role you played in it, and He is the only person who can fight for you. So, let him.

Lisa is speaking: I hear you, and I agree with you. I need to pray more and allow Him to guide me. I know.

Mr. Pearson is speaking: I know my words cannot take away the pain you've felt or may be feeling, but what I feel I can do is pray with you if you don't mind. I need you to ask God to give you the strength to deal with this. Turning to Him and not from Him will allow you to turn to your husband and not from him. You will have the kind of loving relationship you've wanted and the kind you both deserve. You can turn to Him for any situation and only He can and will heal your brokenness.

Lisa is speaking: I thank you so much for listening to me, and for the advice you have given me. I am glad we had a chance to talk. I feel so rejuvenated. Our talk today has helped me see the light at the end of the tunnel and is helping me to get past this. My husband will be glad. He will benefit from my progress and see a difference in my demeanor. If you don't mind, I would like to continue with our conversation next week if you have some time available. I feel I my purpose and direction have changed for the better. I've enjoyed our time together.

Mr. Pearson is speaking: Thank you. We've made some good progress. We have taken our first step in the right direction. I am here whenever you need me. Have a blessed day!

Session Three

Two wrongs don't make it right!

It has been a long day, and I am looking forward to my "date night" with my wife. As I was packing up my things to leave, I received a text from a college friend who I had asked to appear on my show next week as my co-host.

Smart woman
Hello Ondray, I got your text about coming
on your show on Friday. I wanted to say I
would be honored to hang out with you.
Email me the details, address and I will be there.
Can't wait to see you and catch up. Tell Reginae I said hello,
and she needs to call me sometime because it's been a while.

KingDray
Cool! I am looking forward to catching up also. We all
should get together for dinner soon. You know, I haven't
seen Reggie since we all, Erik, Cedric, Rodney, Z, Humberto
and I hung out at Friday's for the NBA Finals. Before I forget,
let me invite you both to our anniversary party in a few
weeks. Nothing big just a few close friends and family.

Smart woman
That sounds like a plan. We will talk
more after your show. Ttyl

(As I was walking to the elevator, I got another text from my wife.)

Sexy wife 69
Are you about done? I am hungry.

Ondray Pearson

I will be leaving shortly. See you soon
for dinner.

KingDray

Hello beautiful it's 4:50 p.m. and
I am finishing up. If I get there before
you I will get us a table because you
know how packed the Cheesecake
Factory gets on a Monday. Text me

when you are in the parking lot. I will meet you upfront. Love you!

Sexy wife 69
I have finished, and I will be leaving shortly.
That's cool to see you soon, baby.
Love you too!

With some time to spare I drove to Hallmark to get her a card, some roses and our movie tickets for our movie. It started at 7:00 p.m. or we may end up doing a movie night at home. I got to the restaurant around 5:20 p.m. I went in and got a table within ten minutes. I asked our waitress if she could put my flowers in a cool spot until we ordered dessert. I wanted the roses to be a surprise. So, as I waited, I played a game on my phone. I already knew what I was going to order. We often ate here. It was not too long before I got a text from Reginae.

Sexy wife 69
I have pulled in and parked, be in shortly.

Kingdray
Cool. Meet you upfront.

I met her upfront, and we walked to our table. She sat down.

Reginae: Baby, it's crowded tonight. It's not usually this many people on a Monday.

Ondray: I know. How was your day, beautiful?

Reginae: My day was good, and yours?

Ondray: It was interesting as always. Do you remember Reggie and Patricia Jones? Remember I told you Patricia and I went to Georgia Tech University together. She's a Psychology Professor at the college, and her husband Reggie owns their private practice over in Buckhead. We went to their home for their office parties last year, remember?

Reginae: Oh, yeah, I remember them. How are they doing?

Ondray: Well, they are both good. The reason I mentioned them is that I reached out to Patricia and invited her to be a guest speaker on my show next week.

Reginae: That should be fun. I don't mean to cut you off, but let me ask you something. Do you remember my friend Nina, who used to work at Bank of America?

Ondray: That's Joel's girlfriend, right? We used to meet up at the gym on Thursday after work, but we haven't seen him lately. Why do you ask?

Reginae: Well, Nina says she thinks he has been cheating on her.

Ondray: Cheating on her, really? I know they have only been together for a few months. What makes her think that he is cheating on her already?

Reginae: She says when they go out, she sees him checking out other women. He flirts like he wants to get with them or something. She says when they're not together, she wonders if he goes back to wherever they were to see if he could see them again.

Ondray: I am confused.

Reginae: She says when they go out, she sees other women looking at him, and he looks back while he is holding her hand. She says even though they have been together for a short period, his behavior makes her feel as though he doesn't love her like he says he does. This behavior is leaving her feeling very insecure. She says she has no proof he is cheating on her, but his behavior makes her believe he is. What do you think?

Ondray: Babe, you know I do not like getting into our friends' business and even less, giving "one-sided" advice.

Reginae: Come on, Dray. I know you, and I know you have an opinion. Besides, you "getting into" people's business is your job, remember? You do it every day on your show.

Ondray: That's different. It's my job, and you know it. Now, this is a different situation. I know these two people personally. For you, I will share with you what I am thinking from what you've told me. Please don't go running back to her and say that Ondray said this or that because it could cause problems that are not there.

I don't want to get a phone call from Joel asking me why I'm coaching his girl against him. I don't want him to feel we can't talk or that he can't tell me things anymore. This kind of thing can go south quickly if you are not careful. Saying or implying something that isn't true can make them both distrust one another. That would not be good. Neither of us needs to be in the "center" of their mess or the cause of them breaking up, all because we had opinions about their business.

Reginae: I will not run and say you said anything, but I will share any helpful advice you give me with her as if it is coming from me.

Ondray: Now depending on how you relay it, she takes it and believes what is said, she could think because we are friends that I am protecting or covering for him. You know how women think in situations like this, they say, "all men stick together."

You must be very careful when you are relaying and giving this advice. We are all close. We know Joel and Nina both would want each of us to take their side on all issues, right or wrong if we are their friend and this a real issue. By sharing my thoughts with you, by no means am I saying or admitting he is doing anything because I honestly don't know. So, sweetheart, my thoughts and opinions are for your ears only until either of them asks me directly for advice.

Reginae: Okay, stop stalling and spill it.

Ondray: Both men and women glance at people they feel are attractive, but very few will disrespect their mates by staring or trying to get a phone number from them. This kind of action happens by a man (or woman) who is not committed to their relationship.

As you know, people select their mates based on their attraction to the other person. Hardly anyone seeks beyond that fact to determine if they are the right one for them or not. I'm saying this because if she picked him based on his looks alone, this could be the reason why early on she feels a little unsure when she is with him around other women. I mean she could be thinking he wants someone else because she doesn't feel she has what it takes besides her beauty to keep him.

You know how much time she puts into her looks, which is cool. Who doesn't want to look suitable for their mate? But a person's appearance or looks don't determine if they are going to treat you well. It doesn't mean that they will love you the way you want to be loved nor does it prevent them from cheating on you. It just means you are attracted to them. I am not saying men should be out with their woman looking at other women, but sometimes a look is just that, a look.

An excellent example of this is the actress Thandie Newton. You know I am a big fan of hers, and I think she is beautiful, right? I know we don't travel in the same circles but even if we did, you and I both know that I would never leave you to be with her even if she wasn't already married. I chose and love who I selected and married.

Remember how you talk about how fine an actor Idris Elba is, but I don't feel threatened that you would leave me for him. Well, I'm not sure. I am just joking, but you get my point.

Reginae: True, but this is different. We're married, and they're not. Also, maybe it could be possible he is not ready to commit to her as he should yet. Perhaps he wants to play still. You know have a thot on the side from time to time.

Ondray: I agree, but the question I would ask is, "what brought this 'feeling' of cheating or non-trust up, and what made it go straight to 'he is cheating' without proof?" I don't believe what they have is superficial. I think they are in the early stage, that's all, and they just need some time to grow into whatever they're going to be. I do agree though that it is very disrespectful to be checking out women, period, but even more so to do it when he's with her knowing she can see it.

That is not the best way to make her feel at ease and secure with him, nor will it give her the message that he wants her and no one else. Before we jump the gun and accuse someone of something they may or may not have done, does she have any proof or evidence other than her assumption or gut feeling to back this claim up?

I think before she accuses him, she needs to sit down and express what she sees him doing and tell him how much it bothers her. Next, she needs to tell him she would like him to stop it because it's making her feel insecure. She'll see if he does it for her so she feels more secure with him and their relationship. Accusing him without proof says to him she doesn't trust him. If he feels she doesn't trust him, how can he possibly think she loves him and that what they have is worth pursuing further?

People in the street can do it (meaning accuse you of anything) and because you have no real connection or a relationship with them, most times you dismiss it. When you do this to the person you are in a relationship with and claim to love, and you are wrong, you're telling them, "I don't trust or like you." I am not sure the trust and love you once shared can be repaired. It's possible, and anything is possible with God as they say.

Reginae: So how would she know if he has crossed that line?

Ondray: Well, if Joel is really into her, he will not get upset with her for bringing her concerns to his attention because he would want her to be happy and feel secure with him in their relationship. He may be a little defensive at first because he didn't think she noticed, but if Joel loves Nina, he will listen to her and stop doing what bothers her.

If he is not into her, he will defend his action and say something stupid like, "I am a man. I am just looking and looking is not the same as touching. If I wanted someone else, I would go be with someone else." I can't say this means he is cheating, but I do believe this behavior confirms he is up to something.

Innocent people do not defend the truth. Guilty men, when caught will turn EVERYTHING around and make the woman feel she has done something wrong in order to deflect the real issue which is his behavior. "Caught" men will also try and switch subjects. They will bring up past issues that have not one thing to do with the current conversation to confuse the discussion.

Their goal is to get her in a state where she doubts herself, what she has seen, and what she feels she knows. He knows by her arguing with him about NOTHING that she loves him, and push comes to shove, she isn't going anywhere. Meaning he knows and sees she is emotionally caught up and fully committed to their relationship even if she feels he is wrong in what he is telling her. He knows she isn't going anywhere.

Reginae: Explain what you are saying.

Ondray: As you know, men take advantage of most women because they know women are emotional. When a woman loves a man, they love him for real. Their heart is all in, and even when the man is wrong in many situations, they will stay with him and give him one more chance, saying, "Things will get better..." Women in cases like this fool themselves into believing this man will change his ways and realize he has a good woman and act right. To be honest with you, very few do. Men who do this are users and don't deserve the good woman they have.

I know I am going more in-depth than the situation is, and it is because I see and hear this it seems almost daily for so many women with no end in sight. Women do know the extreme lengths that men will go to protect themselves. If this situation continues and his behavior stays the same, I would suggest she start planning her exit strategy because at some point, he will find a reason to cheat or do wrong, and he will blame it all on her.

Reginae: You think so for real? Do you think from what I have told you he is cheating on her? Do you?

Ondray: I cannot say yes or no because I only hear one side of the story. I am just laying out a few scenarios that could or could not be true. Remember and understand, without the whole story, I can only give advice based on what you are telling me.

Reginae: What else are you thinking?

Ondray: Well, if people in the world only picked one person and stayed faithful, there would be no need for marriage. However, we know this is not how the world works. One of the many reasons people get married is because they feel they have found that particular person to share their life with forever.

Keep in mind there are many reasons why a person would cheat. They have their own, and I doubt they would tell their mate BEFORE they do it, but I will say this, infidelity is not new. People have always struggled with this in their relationship when things aren't going well. People can recover from, change and get past their spouse cheating, but for this to happen, forgiveness must be the focus because it is hard but not impossible, to restore trust and love.

Like I said, before she does something she might regret, she needs to sit down with him and talk things out – express her concerns and feelings. I would hate for her to allow her fears and insecurities to cause her to sabotage her relationship subconsciously. When someone feels suffocated, they often will search for an outlet or a way to be free.

Reginae: Well, I am just trying to help my friend because I don't want to see her hurt. Do you think it could be that serious though?

Ondray: Yes, it can. I really can't believe we are talking about these two. When he is around us all he does is talk about how fine she is, how good she is to him, how special she is and how good the sex is. He sounds like he's in a monogamous relationship and speaks as if being with her is where he wants to be, but I could be wrong.

Reginae: Knowing her as long as I have, I know she has had some trust issues in her past relationships because men have cheated on her. It makes sense. This is why she is cautious about trusting him. His behavior around other women has gotten her thinking she has made another mistake again.

Remember her ex, Aaron, the one who runs TCM Magazine in downtown Atlanta? Nina said it wasn't long after she introduced her co-worker and friend Lisa Clark to her ex that she felt Aaron was interested in her. Come to find out he was. Now she said he didn't cheat on her by having sex or anything, but he did start flirting and talking more to Lisa and a few months later said he had found someone he felt was a better match for him and broke off the relationship. Within a few months, she heard they had gotten married, and she thought it should have been her.

Ondray: Listen, I would feel a whole lot better if Nina just called my office and made an appointment so I could hear all this from her, do you think she would do that?

Reginae: I will ask her but don't tell her that we've talked if she asks, okay?

Ondray: Okay, enough about them. I'm finished eating. Would you like to share a dessert?

Reginae: Sure!

I ordered and gave the waitress the cue to bring the flowers back also. When the waitress brought out the flowers, Reginae was surprised. She had no clue, and she appreciated them.

Reginae: Honey, these are great! Thank you so much!

Ondray: We'd better get going ....

Our date night was a success. We decided to watch the movie, _War Room_, On Demand. There was a part in the film that caught my attention and made me ask myself, and it was when the lead character mentioned about "fighting fair" in your relationship. I wondered how it would be if we (those in relationships) knew when we argued with what was considered "below the belt" tactics and what was our "safe zone" would it be easier to resolve our issues? I, during a disagreement with my wife, never wanted to say or do anything hurtful. I just wanted to be heard. I wondered if apologizing helped or hurt as it relates to the amount of trust and love we shared going forward after this incident. I made a note to put the question to my listeners on the show.

It's Friday morning, July 19, 2019, and I am on my way to the radio station to do my show. It's just a few days before our anniversary. Patricia had texted me to let me know she was on her way to the station. I had some time, so I stopped at McDonald's for breakfast. I got to work, and I prepped like I always do, and shortly afterward Patricia arrived.

Mr. Pearson is speaking: Hello Patricia, how are you doing? I'm glad you made it. It has been a while.

Patricia is speaking: How is King Dray doing, as I remember from college?

Mr. Pearson is speaking: I have been great! How is teaching these days?

Patricia is speaking: Good, but between it and running my business, you know, it keeps me busy.

Mr. Pearson is speaking: I am glad you got here a little early. So today, I will introduce you to the callers, and when the calls come in, we can take turns responding. I'll go first and bring you in to give your take on it also.

Patricia is speaking: Okay.

Mr. Pearson is speaking: We go on in 20 minutes. Let's go to the booth. You can meet the producer, Karen. Patricia, this is my producer Karen. She is going to get us ready. Let's go have a good show.

Patricia is speaking: Let's do this then, afterward, we will catch up.

Mr. Pearson is speaking: Good morning, ATL. Once again, I am Ondray Pearson, here on K103 and I want to welcome you all to *Why does love hurt so good?* We have an exciting show lined up today, and a personal guest is joining me. For the next two hours, I will take your calls and answer your questions on relationship issues, the good, the bad and the not so good. My guest today is a Professor at Georgia Tech University, a trained psychologist. She is a college mate and a good friend of mine. Please welcome to the show, Professor/Dr. Patricia Jones.

Patricia is speaking: Thank you for the gracious introduction. I am so happy to be here.

Mr. Pearson is speaking: Dr. Jones and I will both be responding to the calls today, giving perspectives from both the male and female perspective. We are going to take a quick break, but when we return we will go to the phones and take the first caller.

We are back! Before we take our first caller, I have a few book signing dates to share with you. I will be at **Brookstone** in the Lenox Mall on August 9th between 1 pm and 2 pm, Barnes & Noble, over at The Peach Shopping Center on Peachtree Street, August 14th from noon until 1 pm, the Cumberland Mall located off Cobb Parkway on August 16th from 3:00 pm to 5:00 pm and Town Center located off Barrett Parkway, August 21st from 3:00 to 5:00 pm.

Also, I will be speaking at the Men's Ministry held on Sunday, October 13th, 2019. Doors open at 6:00 pm at the Georgia World Congress Center. My friend Greg Hogan is the organizer and host of the event. I was hoping to get him on air with me to tell you more about it. I will keep you posted on this as information is available.

At the conference, I will be talking to our men on the subject of "Manhood: As it relates to Love, Life and Relationships." I am one of many speakers that evening. I go on at 6:30 pm. I want to make sure the men are there because you don't want to miss it. I will be speaking at **For Sisters Only** in November right before Thanksgiving. When I get the date and speaking time, I will let you all know. For the latest details, log in to our website ***www.whydoeslovehurtsogood.com*** and check it for more information.

Anyway, let's take our first caller. Karen who do we have on the line?

Karen is speaking: We have Robin from College Park, Georgia.

Mr. Pearson is speaking: Good morning, Robin. What is your question?

Robin is speaking: Good morning, Mr. Pearson and hello! Dr. Jones. My question is concerning me getting back with my ex, Marcus. Let me explain. My ex and I have been friends since high school. We dated off and on during that time but didn't get serious until around our third year in college. After we graduated, we broke up, but stayed in touch. He hit me up a few years later to see if I was interested in trying it again. I am not going to lie. I thought about it hard because I still had feelings for him, but I wasn't sure if I should give him another chance.

Mr. Pearson is speaking: I do not mean to interrupt, but I have a question. During this off and on situation, were you two sexually active?

Robin is speaking: No, we weren't. I told Marcus when we first started dating. I was not having sex until I get married.

Mr. Pearson is speaking: Was he cool with a non-sexual relationship?

Robin is speaking: He said he was, but I felt he wasn't. I feel that's what and why we broke up. When we did, I heard from my girlfriends that he had told a mutual friend of ours that it was because of me not sleeping with him. Marcus said, "I don't want to have sex, nor am I ready to get married anytime soon." I heard around campus that the girl he got with was more or less a "friends with benefits" type of thing if you know what I mean.

Mrs. Jones is speaking: After hearing this, how did it make you feel?

Robin is speaking: I was hurt and a little surprised because I thought what we had was more than just sex. I guess I was wrong.

Mrs. Jones is speaking: Did he ever apologize for his actions toward you?

Robin is speaking: Well, yes, he apologized and said it was nothing personal. He didn't mean to hurt me, but he wasn't looking for a sexless relationship.

Mrs. Jones is speaking: I guess if you want to see a positive side of this, he may have lied in the beginning saying he was cool with it but he broke up with you so as to not cheat on you. He was not ready for the kind of commitment you were, that's all.

Robin is speaking: I thought the same thing but not right away. I thought it was kind of him to breakup instead of cheating on me. I was a little disappointed because we didn't give our relationship a real chance.

Mrs. Jones is speaking: So why are you considering now getting back with him?

Robin is speaking: Well, like I said, we had stayed in touch after college, and sometimes we talked about possibly trying it again. Marcus told me he wasn't as mature as he should have been our first go around, and he can admit now. Marcus also felt we never did give it a real shot, and we should try it again. He said he still has feelings for me, and I believed him. I tried to find a reason not to try it yet again, but I couldn't.

Mrs. Jones is speaking: It is obvious you still have feelings for him, and it seems you've already made up your mind. Why are you asking this question if you already have?

Robin is speaking: Well, I just wanted to get a second opinion if you all thought I was making a mistake. Now don't get me wrong I know there are pros and cons to letting him back into my life.

Mrs. Jones is speaking: I understand the mixed emotions you're having, but I have to ask why is it so vital for you to be with him and not someone else?

Robin is speaking: I am not sure why, other than the fact that I still have feelings for him. I am single, and we already know one another somewhat well, although, it has been a few years since we were close. I dated others after him, and like I said, I'm single with no real prospects, and he's single, so I felt, why not give it a try?

Mrs. Jones is speaking: I can hear in the way you're talking you want this to work out. He seemed to be sincere based on what you are saying. I wonder if you are seeing this reunion being successful after so many years. Do you feel you two can pick up from where you left off or start anew and be happy together?

Robin is speaking: Honestly, I am not sure, but I am willing to try if he's willing. I cannot say if we will reconnect the same way as before, but so far it looks promising.

Mrs. Jones is speaking: That's good. Just take your time and don't rush things. You want the relationship to develop on its own.

Robin is speaking: I know it sounds like I have already made up my mind, but I haven't yet. Talking with you has helped. It's made me think a little more and see things differently. I know there are pros and cons to my decision. I was hoping you both could help walk me through what they are.

Mr. Pearson is speaking: That sounds like a plan. Okay, Robin, when we come back from a commercial break, we will break it down. So get a pen and pad ready to take some notes. Here is how we are going to do this. I will give you the pros, and Mrs. Jones will provide you with the cons.

Before we begin let me say this, because I have been listening, and I agree with all the information Dr. Jones has said thus far. To add to what she has already said, I can tell it's hard to know if it's best to take someone back or let them go for good. Your decision depends on why the person you're considering allowing back into your life again, left in the first place. Now, based on what you've said, it seemed to me that the break up was bittersweet. You felt hurt, but it passed. Now the time has passed, and you're feeling pretty good about round two with him.

I cannot recall a good experience of taking someone back. When I did, the "newness" and excitement were never the same the second time around. I am not saying that there wasn't room for us to reconnect and form a new romantic connection, but it was different. You both have remained friends and kept in touch however, so who knows, something could be there. Anyway, let's begin. If you give him a second chance, let it be because:

1. He Deserves a Second Chance

You need to realize and understand something I have told many people in your position. Human love is flawed. It keeps a checklist of our sins and shortcomings and consults it often. Understand that by doing this, you are saying you have forgiven or moved passed what happened before. It helps when you know there's power in forgiveness. By doing this, it is a great place to start. If you have any doubts about his intentions or question his sincerity, no pill, pep talk, psychiatrist or earthly possessions can put your mind at ease. It all comes down to your gut feeling as to whether he is worthy of a second chance.

2. If losing you, helped get himself together

As the old saying goes, "You never know what you had until it is gone." Many times, when people lose someone, they tend to rethink after the fact, of what went wrong. Many of us try hard to understand why the person left them. At first, we'll fault the other person, but over time, once we have time to take a hard look at what happened, we'll see and admit to ourselves that we may have had something to do with the breakup. This realization comes after we've gone through some deep soul-searching. We realize we may have been wrong, and we could have done better. We believe if we had another opportunity, we would change and treat them differently for sure.

3. You're having second thoughts (regrets) of what could have been

As we all know, this is something that we all go through if we are genuinely in a meaningful relationship with someone. It happens because we are human. We would hate to think we missed out on the person we were meant to be with. It is this fear we have that makes us feel it is worth taking the risk of allowing them back. We still may have regrets later if things don't turn out right, but for now, it beats wondering *what if* you didn't try.

4. It's harder to say goodbye, then hello

When we have feelings for someone our heart wants what it wants even though sometimes, we know it may not be the best for us. We still seek and want it anyway. Love makes it hard if not downright impossible to say "no" in situations like this, but that's okay. Just remember and understand, if you say "yes," what the risks involved with your decision are. Do not be surprised if you get what your heart wants, and it doesn't work out the way you hoped.

5. Who knows it could be better than before

It's real and rare but not impossible. Most cases, a break in a relationship sometimes helps you take a good look at yourself. It enables you to sit back and take stock of your life. It is during this period, we "assume" we've learned something, grown-up and we're ready to be the person we should have been the first time around. If this is the case, then we might be successful this time.

But we must ask ourselves, are we mentally and emotionally prepared if things don't work out? If we choose to allow our ex back in our lives, we need to put our relationship on a "90-day trial period" until we feel they have earned and deserve our love yet again. I broke down how to do this in my last book, *Wrong Turn (Diary of a Good Man)*. I called it the "90-day Interviewing Process".

It is during the first 90 days of dating that you are interviewing the potential person for a position in your life. During this time, with your questions, interactions, etc., you will learn who you're dealing with and if they are sincerely looking for a full time, part-time or seasonal relationship. Based on their (attitude, goals and actions) answers, you're able to determine if they will receive a second interview (your phone number and a second date).

It is up to you not them whether they get a second chance to impress and show you, they are the right person for this critical position in your life. You must be clear on whether this person has what you're looking for in a mate. If this person chooses to resign on good terms, rehiring them may not be that difficult to do, if you felt they had a good reason for leaving in the first place. When you allow someone back on a job they quit, it puts your trust in a weird position because you're gambling that they will do better the second time around. The rehired "employee" can redeem themselves and be better than the first time around or fizz out and get fired once again, leaving matters worse off than before.

I lean toward moving on with your life. It's essential to move on and meet new people and gain experience. However, I find it incredibly romantic when two people are separated by circumstance and time and overcome the odds to end up together. That's just me though. I have been known to be a foolish romantic, because I believe in love. Are you still with us, Robin? Well, when we come back from break, Mrs. Jones will give you her take on the cons. Stick around. We'll be right back.

Mrs. Jones is speaking (during the break): Good advice, Ondray. I got my list ready, and I will try and tag along with what you said.

Mr. Pearson is speaking: Ok, cool. Okay, we are back. Mrs. Jones, are you ready to give Robin your views?

Mrs. Jones is speaking: Yes, I am ready.

Mr. Pearson is speaking: Okay, Robin, are you ready?

Robin is speaking: Yes, I am.

Mr. Pearson is talking: Okay, Mrs. Jones….?

Mrs. Jones is speaking: Here are my views on this situation as I see it. I would not take him back because:

1. You can never make it like it used to be

It is very rare but not impossible that relationships can recapture the magic they once had. Nothing would make you feel worse than not being able to regain that kind of heat that made it so special the first time. If it doesn't happen for you as you want, you could feel you're trying to revive the dead.

2. Lust is not real love!

When you have familiarity with one another, it's easy to believe that it is possible to rekindle what you once had. You start to think to yourself, "We are comfortable with one another. Marcus knows me, and I know him." That's good, but generally, people like this often get back together because of mutual loneliness. They are just tired of being alone, and because you both are available, and you had something once before, you think, why not give it a shot? Believe me when I tell you this, it is not a good idea. Lying, thinking and saying we don't have to be a couple, we can just be sex buddies is just another way we set ourselves up for heartaches.

This kind of arrangement is nothing more than a temporary *Band-Aid* and leads to a false and loveless relationship. Here is the myth many of us focus ourselves on believing that few understand. "Good sex will keep you in a 'situation' that you shouldn't be in. *Sex with benefits* doesn't grow into a loving *relationship*. It is just what it is, a temporary pleasure. In this situation, I tell people to do what you do but do it for the right reasons.

3. It is possible you could be hurt yet again

Apparently, and it is no surprise if someone hurt you before, they could do it again. So, when this happens on top of the pain of being hurt again, you feel like a fool for the second time for allowing it to happen again. You then sit around and try to understand "after the fact" how you didn't see it coming. You wonder how you could have been so blind as to allow it to happen once again. Therefore, your choice has to be thought out with your head and not your heart. I have heard said and I agree, "Loving someone is not supposed to hurt, but sometimes it does."

4. Fool me once shame on you, fool me twice shame on me!

Many of those who get a second chance with you, walk in knowing and often think they can treat you any old kind of way again. If they come in with bad intentions, they can also already know how to push your buttons and break your heart with a blink of an eye, if they choose to. They know the right buttons to push on you emotionally to pick you up or hurt you. Why would you want to give them back this power over you? Not being mentally and emotionally prepared, all you can do is keep your eyes open until you're sure they're not repeating your past together in your present. You don't want to be or feel like a fool a second time, so think hard before you take that risk.

5. If you're not growing, you are dying

If your past relationship didn't allow you to grow, moving on was the best thing you could have done for yourself. I'm not saying people cannot and will not change, but how much time, effort and love do you want to waste to find out if the person you've allowed back in your life is going to lift you up or pull you down? Meeting new people helps you grow. You learn from each new relationship. Going back to the old relationship might stunt your growth as a person and prevent you from meeting the "one." Are you willing to risk your heart like that?

Mr. Pearson is speaking: Robin, I hope the advice we've provided helps you with your decision.

Robin is speaking: It has made me want to do some soul searching before making this decision. I agree with you both. I don't want to do something foolish and mess up the blessing God has for me. I will think about it, pray on it and wait for God to tell me what I should do.

Mr. Pearson is speaking: Well, that would be a good thing to do. We thank you for your call. Let's take our next call. Karen, who's on the line?

Karen is speaking: We have Aniya from Kennesaw, Georgia.

Mr. Pearson is speaking: Hello Aniya, what is your question, and how can we help you?

Aniya is speaking: Good day, Mr. Pearson. My situation may not seem like a big problem to most, but it has become a concern of mine. I am referring to "sexting." My problem with my boyfriend is this. He spends a lot of time on his cell phone and laptop on Facebook talking to lots of people. He's having conversations and exchanging messages as though he knows them when he doesn't. When I asked him, "Why are you spending so much time talking to people when you can talk to me? I am not getting "my attention time." He says, "It's just entertainment. I like commenting on topics people are talking about." For a while, I accepted that as the reason, but lately, he spends more time talking to strangers than he does talking to me.

I am thinking he is meeting people that he has met online in town or nearby and hooking up with them when I see him on his cell phone so much. I feel this current technology is causing problems between us in our communication. So, I guess what I am asking is, is sexting the new way men and women cheat on one another?

Mr. Pearson is speaking: That is an excellent question, Aniya. It's a tricky situation because with social media these days, it has made it easy to connect with new acquaintances and reconnect with old flames.

I feel the answer to your question is, YES!, but this is not to say that everyone on social media websites is cheating. I am just saying technology has made it easier to cheat if a person wants to. It seems as if you're feeling your man has crossed over from just chatting with people he is meeting to trying to hook up or has already started hooking up with someone, right?

Aniya is speaking: Yes! I don't know for sure, but I have a strong feeling that something is going on. He spends way too much time online. Don't get me wrong I trust my man, but I don't trust other people he is connecting with online, especially women. They are always looking for a fool to give a sad story to in order to try to get some money.

He could meet some woman and befriend her, and she ends up using him. I know firsthand, how women meet men online and talk to them for a few weeks. Then, they ease in stories about how they have hard times. They will come up with stories claiming they have no money to eat, need their cell phone paid or they need money to go to the hospital, etc. and all the while it is a scam to sucker some man out of cash.

You know it is a scam when they have no problem asking someone they have never met for money and expect them to send it to them. It's like women search for those men who are lonely to prey on, hoping and thinking because they are so desperate to be with someone, they will be more willing to send them money to keep talking with them. Who knows? It may not even be a woman who is talking to them. It could be a man for all they know. The pictures they post and send to these men may or may not be real.

Mr. Pearson is speaking: I know of this scam done by both men and women to people seeking attention from someone outside of their homes. It's common practice for most women and men to try and trick you into sending them money, buying them gifts and paying their bills. I can see you're thinking your boyfriend can be fooled into doing something like this.

Aniya is speaking: Yes, definitely.

Mr. Pearson is speaking: Why do you think he could be a victim of something he feels and says is just entertainment for him?

Aniya is speaking: Because, a few years ago he did get taken by some woman online. He told me shortly after we started dating. He met a woman online that was into music, (Oh, if I didn't say, my boyfriend's a musician, and he played in a band), anyway, online he befriended her. He said things at first were cool, just two musicians talking shop and exchanging music skills and notes. They eventually exchanged phone numbers and spoke offline. According to him, he was transferring videos of their band's performances. He told me things got weird because out of the blue one day, she told him she might not be able to talk to him anymore because her phone was going to be cut off that Friday.

He said it's too dangerous and then asked her, "Well, how much are you short from paying the bill?" He said she told him $121.00 dollars because she only paid a little on it a few weeks ago. He told me he offered to pay it for her if she would pay him back. I asked, "Why would you offer to pay someone's bill that you've never met or know that well?

Mr. Pearson is speaking: I can tell you why, he felt he had bonded with a friend. He felt they were and had bonded because they played music. He had no clue that she was sizing him up for the kill. You see those women who have been doing this for a while and have been

186

successful at it, they know they are more successful if they "set the scene up."

The goal is to suggest what she wants or needs and let him *offer* his help. This way, once he caught on to what she was doing to him, (which is using him), he couldn't say she asked him for it or used him because he offered. In her case, sadly enough, she is right. He couldn't say that she used him because he volunteered. Now you're right. It wasn't the best thing he could have done, but like I said, he thought he was helping out a *friend*.

Aniya is speaking: Yes, yes, but you get what I am saying. Now you see why I asked him questions, and why I think he is about to make a not so right decision? I said to him, "What are you doing? Where are you going?" When he is not with me, I am hoping that he doesn't try to make a large purchase without me.

It's not that I am trying to keep tabs on him or that I don't trust him, but sometimes he will make a decision that affects us both or what and where we are trying to go in our relationship. I feel he needs to run things by me to get feedback before doing them. That's all.

Mr. Pearson is speaking: I understand what you're saying, and you're right to some degree. Sometimes, "the way" it comes across can make a grown man feel you're trying to keep tabs on him, but more importantly he feels and hears you don't trust him as a whole.

This can be more damaging than whatever he could have bought or money spent because if you don't have in your relationship, some form of trust, what do you have? I am not saying you should know. What I am saying is that sometimes explaining "why" you want to know helps make him hear you better before he decides to do something big or small. I say this because "when and how" we ask for things in our relationship from our mates determines if we're going to get what we want or what they want us to have and know.

Aniya is speaking: I understand what you're saying, and I can see from a male's perspective, how what is being said or asked can be taken out of context.

Mr. Pearson is speaking: Anyway, finish your story.

Aniya is speaking: Okay, as I was telling you. She propositions him, saying or making him feel if he enjoys their conversations, he can help her by sending her the money to pay the phone bill that this would be the best way they could continue their friendship, and he did. She instructed him to go to Western Union and send it to her that way. She said not to pay the bill himself and foolishly, he did it the way she asked him to do. A few weeks later, he told me she sent him a picture of some boots priced at $900.00 that she liked. She asked him what he thought of them and did he think they would look good on her. He said he told her, "They look nice, but he wouldn't spend that much money on no boots."

He said she then asked him, "You wouldn't buy those boots for me, baby?" He told me that he told her, "Nah, I wouldn't. We're not in any kind of relationship. We're friends. Helping you out of a jam is one thing but buying you high priced items because you like them is another." She was upset, according to him. She thought she had a real sucker and that he was going to send her that much money. He said she told him, "Well, I can't be dealing with you anymore because I need a real man who can spoil me with gifts, and who can spend money on me when I want him to." He said he told her, "Okay, then we can no longer be friends anymore. Lose my number."

The funny thing is, he said, within 40 minutes, she sent him two nude shots of her by text saying, "I was going to give all of me to you, look what you missed out on." He said he texted her back and said, "I have seen a nude women in pictures before. Pictures of someone I am not involved with don't move me." He said she never called him again. That was the first time this had happened. He told me about another woman he met online who did the same thing. This one threw into their conversation, after about two months of knowing and never meeting him, that she "loved him." He said when she told him this, he started laughing. He told her, "Seriously, you love me, and you have never met me?" He said their friendship, if you want to call it that, didn't last long. He told her she should stop texting or calling for about two weeks. He thought to himself that this was just another scammer and that he was through with her, but she texted one evening he said, and apologized for not communicating for so long.

He said that when he asked her where she had been doing since communication had been cut off, she told him she had been in the hospital and was getting out. Now that she was home, she was worried. Of course, he asked her why, and she told him that she called because she had no one else to call. She borrowed the money needed to be released that evening, saying she would ask her friend for it and she would return it to her.

Now understand she had yet to say what she had gone to the hospital for in the first place. Tyrone told her that if she is your friend, she would understand and give you time to get back on your feet and pay her back. He said after hearing that she told him that he didn't recognize what her friend had loaned her, her bill money, and her friend needed it back right now. So he asked her this time, "What does that have to do with me?" She replied, "I was hoping you could pay my friend back for me, and I will pay you back later." He said point-blank, "I don't have it to give. How much are you asking for?" She told him, "$350.00." She said that's how much the bill was.

I said, "She said the bill was $350.00, no more, no less?" He said he thought then that she was lying and told her he didn't have it. He said that she then said, "I have no money to pay my friend back, no money for food. I am starving. Are you telling me you're not going to help me?" He said he told her, "Before you heard from me, how were you feeding yourself? Aren't you working? How are you now starving?

What and how did you eat the two weeks you didn't talk to me?" He said that when he started talking to her like that, she said okay and hung up. They didn't speak any more after that, and he didn't send her any money, he said.

Mr. Pearson is speaking: Well, hearing this information, and how he was taken in and gave a woman money that he was propositioned for sex to send money, I understand how you could be worried. If he continues "befriending" people, especially women, it would be a concern that he could fall for this scam again and possibly cheat on you and ruin your relationship. You're right. He should spend more time with you than the people on Facebook.

The scams you touched on are just a few that men and women both use to sucker someone into sending them money. Promising them sex if they send them money and sexting are valid problems. They can do more damage than good in relationships these days. So, I, and you are right. This is something you may need to keep your eyes on. At the same time, you shouldn't have to be the responsible one in the relationship nor the only one to see the "value" of what you two have together. He should be just as aware, if he genuinely loves you, to listen to you a little bit because what you're telling him makes sense. It happens to more than a few people now. With that said, let us also not jump to conclusions without knowing how deep this rabbit hole goes.

Let's examine both sides to see where you feel he is. Is it more "entertainment" or something else? Is it a repeat of what he has already openly told you, happening again? It's funny because depending on whom you ask, some would say to you that sexting is the same as physically cheating, while others would say it is not as bad. To determine how much harm it is or could cause in your relationship, it depends on the individual and their habits and intentions while surfing the web and connecting with other people. Not every person on the internet is up to no good.

Aniya is speaking: Okay, then let's look at it from both sides and see if I am overreacting. Maybe, I need to trust that he knows and has learned from his past mistakes. If not, do I need to step in and prevent something from happening before it does?

Mr. Pearson is speaking: Have you talked to him about your concerns and the lack of attention you're receiving from him? Have you talked about how you feel it affects you which could also affect your relationship?

Aniya is speaking: No, I haven't. I wouldn't know where to begin without him taking what I am saying as nagging him or begging him. I don't want to seem needy to him. He spends at least 3 to 4 hours surfing the internet, and I know that not all of it is job-related.

Mrs. Jones is speaking: Aniya, there are ways to get the answers to your concerns without him feeling you don't trust him and in a non-confrontational way. As a trained psychologist, it is part of what I do with my patients and that is to *listen* to what my clients are saying. I speak to many people with a variety of issues, concerns and problems. In order for me to provide the best advice for them, I must use specific skills or methods I have learned over the years to determine the truth to better help them. I say this because at first, many people, when talking provide information that may be surface information and often sound one-sided. After a few hard words during our conversations, they begin to tell me the whole story because as you know, there are three sides to every story, yours, theirs and the truth. Now I don't question my clients as if I was an FBI agent, as if they are not telling me the truth, but I do use similar methods to get to the bottom of a situation which is the real reason they are there, and all that happened.

The responses I get from the questions I ask do not make them feel uncomfortable or make them think they cannot talk to me. The methods I use don't accuse or make them seem like liars, but it does reveal to me if they are telling me the truth or not. Most times, people who lie will show you they are lying without knowing it. Now I am not saying my method is fool-proof, but it is beneficial. Some people find it nearly impossible to tell the truth about anything big or small. What I am about to share with you includes a list of cues and clues that will help you get to the bottom of your concerns with your boyfriend right after Mr. Pearson concludes his advice.

Aniya is speaking: Okay.

Mr. Pearson is talking: For some men, browsing the internet gives or makes them feel empowered because on the web they can be whoever they want to be with minimal backlash. I will not go into why men use it to hook up or cheat on their mates, but I will say this, most people, both men and women, cheat because the other party is willing and because they want to, period. Sometimes, the other person involved may or may not know they are part of this person's foolishness. Some know and don't care as long as they get what they want out of it. Some have no clue that they are a part of a huge mess this person has put them in the middle of until they're caught. It is then, that a person learns how they have been played and put in the middle of a mess, but that's another show for another day.

Very rarely do men (or women) follow through with extra-marital affairs from sexting. I'm not saying a person wouldn't follow through, but rarely do they from the studies I have read on this subject. I do believe it is inappropriate for any man (or woman) in a relationship to be sending nude pictures of themselves to someone with whom they are not involved sexually. Let me say this regarding these so called new friends. Sure, we all have friendships we form when we hook up with someone, but at the same time, once you do hookup, you both should "introduce" everyone to everyone else at some point in your relationship to keep them from thinking you're trying to hide something from them.

I can tell you from experience my wife accused me of doing something with a female co-worker because she had never met her. She had only heard me talk to her over the phone. Now, I wasn't trying to hide or do anything with this friend, but we didn't hang out outside the job like that. She would call me to get my advice on her relationship and didn't want anyone to know. To my wife, however, she thought when I was on the phone talking to her and advising her that I was speaking in code and making plans to hook up. It took me purposely setting up a meeting between the two with other friends for her to see and meet the woman and her husband to finally set her mind at ease.

Aniya is speaking: Well, at least you recognized whatever she thought was bothering her and attempted to correct it to put her mind at ease. He hasn't done anything to set my concerns at ease.

Mr. Pearson is speaking: I understand, totally, and I agree he should have recognized there was a concern and chilled a little on the time he spent on the internet and spent more time with you. Now, for him to even consider what you're feeling, he has to know you're feeling something because most men are not that bright. Let me show you what I am saying and how we, as men misunderstand what you're saying from what you mean.

Here's a typical conversation when your man comes home.

"Hey, honey, how was your day?"

"It was fine."

"Anything exciting happen today?"

"No."

"Are you okay?"

"Yes, I'm okay."

Okay, I am going to take a shower, get dressed and catch the game, alright?"

"Okay, I will fix you dinner."

Now, here is what I have learned, and I try and pass it on to most men. When you answer your man when he asks you "How are you feeling?" and you say "I am fine," what you are looking for him to do is understand that the word "fine" really means not everything is fine and you want to talk. You want him to dig deep and ask you questions so you can give him details on any issues, problems or concerns you have on your mind, but he doesn't do it. Now you're thinking he doesn't want to know. You're thinking, "How could he not pay you attention?" He doesn't know you want it at that moment because you told him you were okay.

Now, without making excuses for men, I have told them many times that whether they want to or not, that they ask you, their woman, about their day, and take the time to listen without trying to solve anything unless they are asked or told their help is needed. Most women want to talk and be heard by their man. However, women must understand that what she's thinking is never what she says. Men need to know what you want and mean, *precisely*, to give you what you ask. When you say you're okay, we understand that everything is fine and that you two are fine. There are no issues, problems or concerns for him to address or answer today nor did he do something stupid he shouldn't have — for him, it's a good day!

Aniya is speaking: I know most men don't pick up on signals as much as we hope they would, but he doesn't even seem as if he is interested in my day. If he was and allowed me the time to talk, I would get some of the attention I crave.

Mr. Pearson is speaking: That is understandable, and I get it, I do. Here is another example. When he asks you, "How was your day?"

and you tell him, "It was okay," you're telling him there is nothing more he should ask or know. What you wanted was for him to ask more questions. You wanted him to beg you to tell him about your day because you want to talk right now and him to listen to whatever it is you did, saw or heard, but he doesn't because you didn't tell him to. Again, men should pick up on when their woman wants to talk, but many don't. I am not saying this is every woman. I am just sharing what men hear from the words you say to us.

Aniya is speaking: … and his friends, why is it so hard to think I should know them?

Mr. Pearson is speaking: Well, this part can be a little tricky and if mishandled, damaging. You see men with friends don't like sharing. They like to think "their friends are their friends," and you have your selective friends they know of but hardly ever meet. Listen, most women believe once a man is in a relationship, he shouldn't have a female friend, period, or single male friends at all. Many feel the female friends are out to manipulate you, and the male friends would influence you into doing something foolish that you shouldn't be doing, which could mess up your relationship. I understand the thought process, and some of what they feel and think is right. Some female friends who may be single may not want them to be in a relationship because they're not in one.

Some single men can get you thinking and doing something a boyfriend or married man shouldn't be doing that could break up your relationship, such as hang out longer than you should or talk to other women when you shouldn't, just to name a couple. They don't have to deal with you once they get you in trouble. It is all on him for allowing himself to be tricked into a situation he should not have gotten involved in in the first place. All I know is a real friend would respect you without ridicule for not wanting to put your relationship at risk over some mess.

At the same time, I don't feel all (both men and women) are out to sabotage your relationship. Married men must understand their foolishness could put their marriage in jeopardy and possibly break up their marriage. Married men and those men in a relationship must know how to control and react to anything harmful to their relationship. The wife/girlfriend must have trust in him, making the right decisions even when she isn't with him.

Aniya is speaking: I can agree with you.

Mr. Pearson speaking: If there is something that bothers you, you need to tactfully address it however you see fit to prevent things from getting out of hand. The Bible may call you the weaker vessel, but you are very wise and have gifts most men don't understand. We sometimes feel that being sneaky and snooping is our right to do. Women do it more than men. Most women have said they don't care if their man gets mad or upset because it wouldn't matter if they didn't have anything to hide. However, this behavior, if you're caught, can damage your relationship. It sends the message to your mate that you don't trust them. Remember to *think* before you *do* and ask yourself, "Is that the message I am trying to relay to my mate because if it is, did he hear it loud and clear?

With that said, let's not get twisted thinking that "sexting" is the reason why a person cheats or will cheat. It is more complicated than that. People who plan to cheat will find a way to cheat with or without technology. So, don't blame it on technology. Pay attention and know your relationship so you can see or prevent problems before they happen (if you can).

The internet allows people who may "cheated" 20 years ago in a conventional way, (meaning sneaking around behind their mates back) the opportunity to talk and/or text before even deciding to meet the person and/or do anything together. I am not condoning sexting by any means because it can affect a relationship and possibly, end it. The reality is this. Technology is another of many tools for people to use who are looking to cheat on their mate. I know what I said doesn't seem encouraging, but I don't want to lie or mislead you into thinking that there isn't an issue when there maybe is one. I get the sense there is more you are concerned about than your man sexting.

When we come back from a short break, Mrs. Jones will return with her tips for you to know if you should be concerned about his sexting.

We are back. Dr. Jones, break this thing down so women listening will understand how to know if their man is lying and cheating.

Dr. Jones is speaking: Aniya, let me begin by saying that I agree with Mr. Pearson. I also feel there is more to your story, but I will address your question and if you choose to share more then, you can afterward. You do not have to have psychic powers to know if your man is cheating on you. Trust your gut. However, be careful because sometimes, when you are in love with them or have strong feelings, that same passion can and will cloud your judgment and confuse your stomach. I say this because most women will ignore obvious red flags. They want the lies told to be true *IF* it is something they want that he is talking about. So, for that reason, here are a few signs you can observe to confirm your intuition.

If a man tells you he is not looking for a relationship, believe him. Don't try and force something that is not there. Be friends if you must and move on. Don't get involved and expect or think he will change his mind. If you do not listen to him, he may end up hurting you. Don't think you are going to "change" him and mold him into what *YOU* want him to be because you will be sadly disappointed. If he says you are the *one,* let him show you. Actions speak louder than words.

I know every woman likes compliments, but real men, who see a real future with you, will describe and act on it. They will show you, (as you walk with them), how the future looks because they are taking you to it sooner not later. When talk turns into reality, and a ring is on your finger because *YOU* also feel it is a good situation for you, then and only then, does he show he sees you as marriage material for him.

1. If your man volunteers a lie randomly about anything you *never asked about*, he is setting up a future alibi. Ironically, this is so when he does something stupid you didn't know about. He will say, "Remember, I told you a few months ago about..." This is just another way to cover up his foolishness.

2. If your man takes his phone (in your situation, his tablet) with him every time he goes anywhere, (meaning he never leaves it in your presence) this is a sign he doesn't want you to see or snoop around in his phone or tablet. He doesn't want you to search or come across any evidence of any possible wrongdoing he may be up to. His action, when done like this, leads you to believe he is seeing other women, and he doesn't want you to find out. Another thing, if you see his phone in the airplane mode, it's another way for him to see incoming messages without giving you a clue anything has come in at all.

3. If your man has more girlfriends than you do, he isn't serious about you. You're just one of many.

4. If your man has more excuses than the Bible has scriptures on why YOU can't reach him, there is a good chance he doesn't want you to contact him because ... he may be busy *<smile>*. You see, he's the kind of guy that will have lots of reasons why he is unable to meet up with you when you want to be with him.

5. If your man calls you at the last minute to go somewhere or he tells you to meet him somewhere, it means his first choice canceled on him, and you are his back up. He knows you will drop whatever you're doing to be with him. These kinds of guys will give you just enough attention to keep you around but never push for a real commitment.

6. If, when you catch your man in a lie, he turns it around on you by saying you are too clingy, this is a sign he is up to something. He will stop initiating sexy one-on-one time because he has someone else. If he is serious about you and your relationship, he would tell the world and have no problem posting it on his social media page. Committed men have pictures of their woman on their social media page, at work on their desk and in their phone. They will show anyone who will look because they are proud and happy to be with you.

7. If your man takes forever (more than 15 minutes) to text or call you back when you reach out to him, you're not that important to him. Now, there is a leeway here. If he is working and unable to hit you back right away, keep that in mind BEFORE you get lit with him. Most men, if they are serious about you, will take a second to tell you when they will be free to talk and call you when they are free and not just text. Even if he is busy, he can text and tell you that. He will let you know when he will touch base with you shortly and do it *IF* he seriously cannot speak now.

8. If your man makes plans to have sex with you like a job, then sex is all you are to him. If he is MIA for a while, he is spending time with someone else.

9. If he has his text message rerouted to his iPad and he listed them as "Business notes" (something like that), he is hiding the text messages from you.

10. If your man has a lot of numbers without a name attached to them, those are the other women. If you've never met his family or friends, you are the "side chick." If he gets weird text messages asking random things such as "Did you see my keys?" As you can see, this could be a code from one of his female friends to see if he is free to come over or talk.

11. If your man is uncomfortable and lashes out at you when you try and talk to him about your concerns or issues you're having, this is his way of deflecting his problems. He has an inability to communicate and resolve problems and concerns constructively and in a healthy manner. In short, your relationship is not that important to fix.

I know you only asked about "sexting" and the effects, and I shared a lot with you. I did this because I want you to have a full picture and range of behaviors men have and display in their relationship. This is good even if you have been in your relationship a short or a long time. This information can help clear your view on the kind of man you're dealing with at the moment.

12. If you ignore the signs, it's on you. Don't get caught up on what a man says, see what he does. Being on the internet for 3 or 4 hours, and it is not job-related, can be a sign of problems beyond the internet. I can't tell you how many times I've said this to women and how many didn't listen and ended up getting hurt yet again by the same guy. Just because he is useful to you, doesn't mean he is right for you.

Mr. Pearson is speaking: Great advice. I couldn't have said it any better myself. Aniya did you get all of that?

Aniya is speaking: Yes, you both had different but similar points of view, and it has made me rethink a few things. Thank you both so much for the advice, you've given me some homework to do and things to go back and reevaluate.

Mr. Pearson is speaking: Thank you for calling in. I am glad we could be of assistance. Have a great rest of your day. Who do we have on the line next, Karen?

Karen is speaking: We have Sheila from Marietta, Georgia.

Mr. Pearson is talking: Hello Sheila, what is your question or concern today?

Sheila is speaking: Good afternoon, Mr. Pearson and Dr. Jones. My story goes like this. I broke up with my boyfriend a few months ago because I caught him cheating. We broke up. I still think about him, and during those moments, I cry, wondering how he could have cheated on me when I was kind to him. So, my question is, "How do I or what can I do to get past this pain?

Mr. Pearson is speaking: Well, first, good afternoon to you. Your problem is a common one that happens and that should not happen "if" your mate loved and wanted to be with you. I'm not saying he doesn't like you. It means his love for you wasn't enough to prevent him from sleeping with someone else. Anyway, it has happened and here is how I suggest you move past this affair.

Dealing with the emotional aftermath of an affair is not easy. Feeling guilty and being afraid to let it pass can keep you from actively participating in your life when the other person has moved on with theirs. There is no need to punish yourself. There is no need to feel as if you have done something wrong. There is no need to hang on to the pain because all it will do is make you feel down. Why would you want to do this to yourself? Now, I am not trying to be intrusive, but did you catch him cheating or did someone tell you he was cheating on you?

Sheila is speaking: I found out firsthand. He had told me he was working late, but when I called his job, they said he was off that day. Hearing this, I asked my sister to go with me over to his house to see what was going on and to find out why he would lie to me like that. When we got there and knocked on his door, he yelled out, "Who is it?" I could tell he wasn't expecting me, of all people, to show up.

When he came to the door, he cracked it a little, and once Michael saw it was me, he would not let me in. He hardly had any clothes on, and I asked him, "Why are you half-dressed?" He replied that he had just gotten out of the shower. I knew I was lying because his head wasn't even wet. I heard another woman's voice in the background asking him, "Who is that at the door?" He turned and told her, "It's my crazy ex."

When she asked, "Why is she here if she is your ex?" He told her that I was stalking him, which was a lie. The more I pushed on the door and tried to get in to see who the other woman was, the harder he struggled with the door trying to close it on me. By now I am pissed because just the other night he was lying in bed with me talking about our future, and now he is with this woman claiming I'm stalking him. How crazy is that? Now there I was standing at his door looking and sounding like a hurt fool because of him, and he didn't care or give a damn what he had done to me.

Mr. Pearson is speaking: Okay. Once reality set in that whatever you had was gone, you should have left because there was nothing more you could do. You now know he lied, and he was cheating. I know what I am saying sounds harsh but be honest with yourself. What more could you have done to make things better for you? The damage was done. If I had spoken to you before you went over there, I would have told you it wasn't going to end well for you if what you suspected was true.

I mean you must have had some clues that he was lying to you, and you overlooked them. Very few men are smart enough to not leave evidence when they are up to no good.

Sheila is speaking: I just wanted to know. He didn't have to hurt me like that. He could have come to me like a man and told me the truth, that he wasn't happy anymore with me.

Mr. Pearson is speaking: Do you really believe that if he did that, you would have taken it better and been okay with it? Listen, one thing women ask for and say is, "Why don't men tell me the truth. I'd rather hear the truth than a lie. If he tells me the truth, we can work it out." When women say this, it sounds good to say, but I know many of them are saying this without understanding the pain involved in knowing the truth. They think that asking for it and receiving it will make things better. I do not know many men if any who would willingly admit they are cheating on you as they are doing it and expect to have a smooth relationship at home. Sure, they will tell you afterwards, when they have moved on with another woman. Telling you at that time, and not having another woman to go to, doesn't benefit them, so they will not share that information beforehand with you.

Listen, no one wants to be alone. Men are no different. They will not admit they have cheated even if you catch them red-handed. They will buy time, and during this time, they are seeking and setting up their next mate. Someone they can move over to once you two have called it quits. Keep in mind the other woman he is cheating with most times, doesn't know that he is cheating on you or that you even exist. Getting mad at her for not knowing is angrily directed in the wrong place. Whatever you're feeling should be directed toward him for disrespecting your trust. It's not like the guy will broadcast to her, "Hey, I am a dog. I am cheating on my ex and using you to do it." You and I both know, not too many women with this information would appreciate being the "other woman" and party to this kind of drama. To help you get past this kind of pain,

Here is what you *shouldn't* do during this process:

1. Do *not* carry this pain forward. Go ahead and cry, get mad, shout, do whatever you need to do when you are alone, but get it out of your system.

2. Do *not* sit back and dwell on what could have been. The fact of the matter is he chose to cheat. You didn't make or ask him to do so. There is nothing you can say to someone who has made up their mind to cheat. People often sit around and blame themselves and say, "I did something to lead them to cheat." It may or may not be correct, but worrying about it now will not help you move forward with your life.

3. Do *not* start a new relationship with anyone until you feel you have gotten past the old one first. If you do, you will carry this baggage over to the new relationship and set yourself up to fail before you begin.

4. Get back in the game! Hiding and withholding who you are is not going to help you get over him or make you feel better. If you do this, you are cheating yourself from the happiness you deserve. Understand that when something like this happens, it is not a reflection of what you have done poorly but more of God's way of telling you that person you were with is not the one for you.

5. More importantly, forgive yourself and pray for him also. Learn from the experience because this is something you cannot do alone, and it is always a good thing to ask God for His help. Pray and ask God to help you get past this ordeal so you can move on with your life.

Is there anything you would like to add Dr. Jones?

Dr. Jones is speaking: Yes, thank you. Sheila, I agree with all that Mr. Pearson has said. I want to add though, that it seems you're *not* ready to move on. It also sounds as if you are holding onto a grudge. It seems to me like you want him to explain himself. Hurting as you are right now, I can understand, but you must let this go to move on peacefully with your life.

Sheila is speaking: Yes, I will admit I do wish he could feel the kind of pain he has put me through because it isn't fair.

Dr. Jones is speaking: Listen, holding a grudge can be costly and you and the people in your life will be the ones footing the bill for this mess. Realize that this guy has moved on, forgotten about what he has done and could care less if you are carrying around the pain he caused. In reality, the grudge you're holding will be more of a problem for you, then it will ever be for him despite the fact that he is the one who cheated. Until you can understand and accept it, you will continue to be upset at the world and most men who approach you during this time.

Sheila is speaking: Yes, I am still a little angry. I am trying to move past this, but it hurts.

Dr. Jones is speaking: I understand the hurt and pain you're feeling. Being hurt by someone you care about is never a good or easy thing. I don't want you to allow what you're feeling to fester into:

1. Self-victimization. Meaning, you are allowing your feelings to drain your energy. When you do, it will rob you of your chance to be happy the way God intended you to be.

2. Bitterness. Meaning you, right now, have "minimal" trust in people to the point that you are unable to allow new relationships to develop in your life.

3. Isolation. Saying you are so angry and defensive that no one wants to be around you. You feel this way and blame any and every one for your life choices.

4. Being Negative. Meaning you have very little to say that is positive. You're not happy, and you find it hard to be happy for others in their relationship because you aren't happy or in a relationship. You have a hard time realizing it wasn't your fault he cheated, and it is not other people's fault that you feel the way you do. It is okay to allow others to help you and those closest to you will, if you allow them to.

Now, I know all that was said may not have seemed or sounded as if we are on your side but in this case, "tough love" advice helps more than it hurts.

Mr. Pearson is speaking: Thank you, doctor. Sheila, I hope you know we understand. Most people in a relationship have either been where you are, are going through it right now or hope it never happens to them. Unfortunately, the song by the R&B group, **The Main Ingredient,** said it best. "Everyone plays the fool sometimes. There's no exception to the rule. It may be factual, may be cruel ...." We all hope and try to learn from our experiences to avoid repeating them. So, again, I will suggest to anyone going through something they are finding hard to handle on their own to pray on it. God will hear you and help you through it. Thank you for your call.

Next up, we are going to read our email in our **Real Talk** segment. I have an email from a listener entitled, "Soul in Love," and he writes:

Dear Mr. Pearson,

I have recently met a beautiful woman through an online dating service. We have been talking for a while, and so far, we have gotten along great. In the beginning, I was a little skeptical. I wasn't sure how seriously she would take me being we both met online. We live in different states, and I knew if I pursued her, there were a lot of things that could go wrong. (1) She could just lead me on because we didn't live in the same state, (2) She could end up only wanting just to be friends, (3) She may not be looking for anything serious and (4) She could pretend to care for me and try and get money out of me just to mention a few.

I know it seems I have put a lot of thought into this when we are just friends who haven't met yet. I want her to see if she likes me. I am all in. I knew meeting someone online was a gamble and being careful is an understatement, but I was willing to see where it went. Anyway, we exchanged emails for a while and soon after, we exchanged phone numbers and started talking over the phone. Strangely enough, we would talk for hours about whatever. I couldn't help but hope our conversation would transpire into much more. During our talks, she never asked me for money or even hinted she needed me to give her anything, and that was refreshing. Instead, she was straightforward and very open with me about many things such as what she liked and didn't like and what she was looking for in her next man.

We hit it off, and things progressed wonderfully, to the point where we talked about me making a trip to see her. Yes, the move was a risky one because she could have been crazy, and it could be a set up to hurt me once I got there. Knowing this was possible, I didn't feel it would be, but I would take precautions anyway. I knew there were no guarantees that when we did meet our phone chemistry would transfer over, nor could I predict if we would be compatible, but I was hopeful.

After a few weeks, I took a couple of days off and flew out from Atlanta to Chicago to see her. I got my hotel room and rental car because I didn't want her to think I expected to stay with her. I know it is crazy to fly to meet a stranger when there are so many women in my state, but I was curious. In my mind, if we didn't click or have any chemistry, it would just be a weekend getaway for me, and I had never been to Chicago. I texted her from the plane to let her know I would arrive by 5 pm. I asked in my text if she wanted to meet me for dinner at The Capitol Grille at 6:30pm. She texted back, saying she knew the restaurant. She would meet me there.

Now, we met for dinner, and when she walked in, I recognized her right off from her picture. I've got to tell you she looked good in her photos but better in person. We sat and talked and like on the phone, we got along great. It was a warm night, so we went to the park after dinner to spend more time together. I've got to tell you she was amazing. She told me she thought I was handsome, I sounded like I did over the phone and she was happy that I flew out to see her. She asked a lot of questions which I knew she would. The one I was waiting for her to ask was, "Why did I decide to fly all this way to meet her? Why was she so special? How and why did I pick her out of all the women on the website? Why not someone locally? Why not settle down with someone in my area?" and she did.

I said to her, "Why not you? You caught my eye, and after talking to you over the phone, I decided I wanted to come and see if there was anything there." I told her I was glad I did and that I felt I made the right choice. We had a good time. I can tell you this, after that weekend, I returned home feeling lovely about "the two of us." I was so wide open for this woman that I seriously felt she could be my girlfriend and future wife. So, for myself, I was okay with putting myself out there and trying to get with this woman for real. I wanted her to relocate and come to

Atlanta, Georgia to be with me. I knew I had to convince her and show her why she should. From our short time of knowing each other, I was ready to settle down with her yesterday, you feel me? I knew I might have been moving a little too fast, and I needed to think it all through because I was asking her to relocate to a new state and share a life with me. That was a lot to ask someone you hardly knew.

I did not want to scare her away, but I wanted to know if she was feeling me. I hoped we could take what we had to the next level. I knew my task was a huge one to make happen, but I was willing to try. I knew she had heard lies from men professing their love. I did not want her to see me as just another guy trying to get her in bed. I wanted to invest in this woman if she would let me. So, with all that said, any advice on what I should do to get her to see, feel, and know I am serious about her without sounding like a desperate man?

- Uncertain

Dear Uncertain,

As you know, there are lots of pros and cons with online dating, some good and some not so good. With all the games played today, it is hard to know who is serious and who is not. Consequently, caution is something I tell everyone to follow when meeting people online. If you decide to meet up with them, always make it a place where there are lots of people like a restaurant, mall, etc. Now for you, in your situation, it is a little different and tricky because you both live in a different state. It is good you two have talked, met and spent some time together to get to know one another. With the time you have had together, you said you both have started to develop feelings for one another, and you are at the point where you want to take it to the next level. You want to ask her to move in with you and be your girlfriend. You see and feel she could be your future wife.

The question is, does she see, know and feel she sees you as her future husband? It is clear, if nothing else, this woman has gotten your nose wide open. I am not making fun of you, just saying I am happy for you. Let me break my advice down because it has two sides that I need you to see and understand if this new friendship/

relationship is going to work. First, let me talk about what you are feeling right now. Many people talk about and very few believe in love at first sight, and I understand, but it is real and possible. You have found this yourself, and suddenly, you find yourself thinking about her a lot and the possibilities with her. Relax and do not panic or worry because these kinds of feelings are typical.

Let me tell you something, new love is good, and being in love is even better. At times, love gives us the kick we need to get over obstacles we may have as we try to develop a friendship/relationship. Yes, you can make bad decisions during this process because of love's blindness, but you can also make good ones. We all need an extra jolt of passion from time to time to get over our inhibitions and move further into what life has to offer. Taking your time and being patient enough to allow her the opportunity to feel comfortable with your idea of relocating because it is a big step is a good thing to do. You are asking and giving her a lot to think about so soon.

Before making such a big decision, I need for you to ask yourself some key questions to ensure you understand what this means for the both of you, if she decides to relocate to be with you. Can you imagine sharing her life with you and raising children together? And, can you appreciate your differences? You two have emailed each other, talked on the phone, met in person, spent some time together, talked seriously about "a life" together, and taking the right steps to make it happen. Slow down. This is a good sign that she is considering the opportunity with you.

I would say, before making a final decision on the move, invite her to Atlanta for a weekend or two to spend time with you where you live. Allow her to see if it is a place she can call home. It will take more than just your words for her to relocate. She needs to trust you and believe this is a good move for her as well. When you two speak, you must talk about and consider her job. Find out if she can transfer and if not, make sure you can support her until she finds a new job. I will not get too deep into the particulars, but this move, if she decides to do it, needs to be well thought out.

Secondly, as it relates to the new-found feelings you two share, you two have been dating for a while, and I know it can be hard at times to make good decisions. You often need to step away for a moment to get clarity on the situation. In this case, it makes sense to do so because you're asking her to relocate and leave a place she knows well to come to a town she has never been in or lived. That can be scary if you're not sure if the person you're moving in with is going to be good for you.

Now usually the blindness of what you're feeling lasts only for a certain period. Then it is gradually replaced by the realities of making life decisions and getting along with the person on an everyday basis. Think about it. This is important to you because both of your lives would change drastically. Your situation is a little different because it started online, but it's possible to nurture what you are feeling to build a future with her. Many couples who are in an online situation such as this will think once they get together, they may lose the feeling that brought them together. This can be true because contrary to what people think, love changes tone and color all the time. Love is also a constant. Any romance can transform into a more profound, steadier desire if worked on together. The pleasant potion on cupid's arrow works instantly, but the working out of a relationship could take years. So, you both must be ready to put in work for the long haul because loving someone is not a sprint. It is a marathon.

So, with that said, let me conclude by saying if she is on board with relocating, show her your full support. Help her by not only telling her but showing her, you are worthy of her trust and love. Remember your house cannot be a home until you two make it one. So, keep talking the same language and communicating the same way. I believe what you both see for your new friendship will be. Don't allow those who have had a not so good experience bother what you two have. I believe you two and the direction you are going in is the right one. Be safe and in love.

Next up is your **Inspirational Vitamin** for the day. Today's **Inspirational Vitamin** message is entitled **"Ask God for a Mountain."**

In our lives, we face challenges every day. Some problems are more stringent than others. These obstacles in our lives are here it seems to distract, confuse and deter us from getting what we want and feel we deserve in life. Many of us are afraid to face or take on new challenges simply because we don't know the outcome. It is this "unknown or not knowing" that sometimes keeps us from having what we want and desire for ourselves. When you think about it, anyone can occupy the *flat ground*, but it takes faith in God to tackle a *mountain*. This is the main reason we need to ask Him for a mountain. He knows once we stand up and defeat our fears we will grow and be better.

The mountains in our lives could be many different things and will not look exactly like anyone else's. You will recognize it however, because it lies at the intersection of your greatest strength and your greatest passion. How do you know when you have found your mountain? It is when you are afraid to do whatever is needed to get what you are seeking. This kind of fear comes on in you when you are thinking about applying for a better job, asking for a raise at work or asking someone out on a date. It is that fear that tells you, "You cannot do it," or makes you wonder, "What if it doesn't work out?" Or have you asking yourself, "What's the point?" In cases like these is when you must stand up and take on the challenge, start making plans and dare to dream. Stop saying "No, I cannot" and start saying "Yes, I can!" Listen, life isn't about comfort. It's about saying, "Lord, give me another mountain."

Not trying simply means, you don't believe in yourself or the fact that you deserve whatever it is you claimed you wanted in the first place. Someone once told me that if everything is coming your way – you are on the wrong side of the road. Facing challenges in life is normal. There is no reason why you cannot live the adventurous life He has planned for you. It's the reason you were born. What we all need to do is stop asking Him for a problem-free experience. We need to understand it is in working to solve our problems and overcoming the challenges that help shape us into who we are and will become. So, ask Him for your mountain and be who he intended you to be.

That is your **Inspirational Vitamin** for today. Before I sign off, let me thank Dr. Patricia Jones for sitting in with me today, my staff because without them I could not have such a great show and my listeners because honestly without you, there would be no show. To close the show today, I will leave you with a favorite song of mine by Bishop Paul Morton called *Your Best Days Yet*. I am Ondray Pearson and from all of us here at K103 F.M., thank you for listening. Join me tomorrow, here, on ***Why does love hurt so good?*** You have a safe drive home. Enjoy.

As the show closed, I texted my wife. I was on my way to meet her for our date tonight.

King Dray
Hello sweetheart I was checking to see if we're
still on for dinner out or would you prefer to stay in?
Hit me back shortly. I will be heading out in about 30 minutes.

Sexy wife 69
Hey babe I am leaving work now. I would love to go
out to dinner. What are you in the mood to eat?

King Dray
I thought we could go to **Carrabba's Italian Grill**
over by Cumberland Mall, what do you think?

Sexy Wife 69
That sounds good! I will be there in about thirty minutes.

King Dray
Ok see you there in 30. Love you!

On my way to the restaurant, I thought about the weekend I had put together for us. I couldn't wait to tell her over dinner and get her thoughts. As I sat and waited, the waitress came over and asked if she could get me anything while I waited. I said, not at the moment. I was waiting for my wife. I got a text from her saying she was parking and would be in shortly. I asked the waitress if she could come back in ten minutes for our drink order.

Reginae: Hey love

Ondray: Hey, love. How was your day?

Reginae: It was good, and yours?

Ondray: It was good. Listen, our anniversary is coming up on Friday. Since we already invited our friends and family over for our get together to celebrate with us on Thursday, how about we celebrate it the whole weekend at the Bed and Breakfast over on Piedmont Ave NE called **Stonehurst Place**? We can celebrate our special day over dinner and a movie there, just the two of us. What do you think?

Reginae: I like that idea. Look at my baby, you got our whole weekend planned out.

Ondray: After work on Friday, we can meet at home, pick up something to eat once we are there (or order in) and be in our room before the Sabbath begins. We can wake up and go to church on Saturday and come back. Later, we can either order in or go out. Are you ready to go home? If you want, we can watch a movie.

Reginae: So, wait. You are not going to give me a hint about what you got me for our anniversary?

Ondray: Nope, it's a surprise. I will give it to you after the party.

It is Saturday, 4:30 p.m., the day before our anniversary. I will be getting off soon and going over to meet my wife for dinner at one of her favorite restaurants, **Maggiano's Little Italy** over at the Cumberland Mall. I'd already called ahead early in the day and reserved a table. I had a dozen beautiful red roses dropped off, spoke with the manager, chef and waiter who will be working with me to make this night special and run smoothly. I requested a few non-menu items and a few of her favorites as our meal. I told the manager to say the meal was on the house knowing I had already paid it to look good in front of her, and he did. I know I overpaid, but she is worth every penny! I texted her to tell her right before I left that we should go out to dinner.

King Dray
I am on my way home see you there!

Sexy wife 69
See you soon love. I can hardly wait!

After we got home and changed, we headed out to dinner. Once there, we sat and talked a little. Shortly before we ordered our drinks, the manager came over to our table, welcomed us and said, "Happy Anniversary!" to us. He shared with Reginae that I had pre-ordered our meal, including the appetizers, for the night, and that our waiter will bring over our drinks while the chef prepares our anniversary meal. When he walked away, Reginae asked me, "When did you have time to plan this for today?" I told her, "I made time. I wanted to make sure I showed you how special you are to me, and how much I love you. I wanted you to know how much I love and appreciate you, and I thank you for loving me yet another year."

By this time, the waiter had brought our drinks. When the first course arrived, she was surprised. She said, "This isn't on the menu. I didn't know they served this. You put some thought into this. Did you ask them to prepare this just for me?" I replied, "Of course, I told you I would move mountains for you." "Ondray, you keep spoiling me like this I am not going to know how to act." After dinner, Reginae reached over and kissed me, and I could see she was happy, and that was the goal.

Like most times when we go out, she had food leftovers to take home. I looked at her and started smiling and laughing. She asked me,

Reginae: What are you smiling and laughing about?

Ondray: I was just thinking about our first dinner date back in June, 2015, and how nervous I was to meet you for the first time.

Reginae: You remember the month and date of our first dinner date?

Ondray: Yes!

Reginae: You did not seem nervous to me. I do remember though, when I walked into **Bonefish**, how you looked sitting in the booth. You looked like a little kid.

Ondray: Well, I was sitting, thinking and hoping you liked what you saw. Hoping we clicked because to me you were beautiful.

Reginae: I remember I ordered a tuna plate, and you didn't order anything. I wondered why you didn't order. I thought you had already eaten, which was crazy since you asked me out to dinner and didn't eat with me.

Ondray: Well, the truth be told, I did not order anything because I didn't have enough money to order a meal for the both of us. I didn't want to take a chance to order me something and then be embarrassed when the bill came, and my credit card ends up getting declined so that is why I told you I had already eaten. I had used my last dime for gas to get to the date. The truth is I was starving.

Reginae: I never knew that. That was so sweet of you. You should have said something we could at least have gotten something that we both could have shared.

Ondray: I know, and I thought about that, but I was trying to impress you. I would have looked very foolish if I had told you the truth. I would rather not have eaten and left you with a good impression of me then look foolish in front of someone I found so damn attractive. I knew I had enough money to cover your meal.

Reginae: I still wish you would have told me.

Ondray: I don't, but I was cool with the situation. So, are you ready for your gifts?

Reginae: Yes, I will take my gifts a day early, please.

After dinner, the manager brought over the flowers and gave them to Reginae. She looked surprised and happy. He then told us the meal was on the house. I said to her that wasn't all. I have more to present to you. I took the old ring off and placed on her finger her new Leo Diamond Ring Setting 1 CT. TW Round-Cut 14K White Gold. She couldn't believe her eyes.

Reginae: I don't know what to say.

Ondray: You don't say a word. I wanted to give you something that expressed how much I am still in love with you. I know I haven't been the best husband I could be, but I am working on it. With your patience and help, I will get there. You have brought me happiness these past four years; you have brought me nothing but happiness. You loved me sometimes when I probably didn't deserve it. I still feel now as I did the day you said "I do," that you are and always will be the most beautiful woman in the world. Please know I will do anything I can to keep you happy with me. So, continue to love me, be patient with me as I do my best to continue to show you the love you deserve as my wife. Can you do this?

Reginae: Every time I think I know you, you surprise yet again. I have always known from the first time we kissed, you were the man for me. I fell in love with you shortly after our first date and have been ever since. Yes, there are some days when I want to shake you <*smile*>, but overall, I would not trade you for the world. I love you Ondray, and I am proud to be your wife and have you as my husband.

Ondray: I am glad to hear that. The gift giving isn't over yet. Open the box. Now I know you did not ask for it, but when I saw it, I thought of you, and that it would look good on you and like you, I had to have it.

When she opened the box, there was an open heart one ¾ CT TW diamond platinum necklace.

Reginae: Ondray, I do not know what to say. You caught me off guard with this, and again it is beautiful. Thank you, thank you, baby.

Ondray: There's more...

Reginae: You are kidding! You went all out, didn't you?

Ondray: You know how I do. I have bought us tickets to Hawaii next month for two weeks. Don't worry, I have not only booked the trip, but I told your boss and asked if you could get the time off. We never got to take a real honeymoon because we didn't have the money. That bothered me, so I made a point this year to try and make up for the missed time.

Reginae: Honey.

Ondray: I know you didn't complain or even bother me about not being able to, you just loved me, but you deserve this and then some. I hope you are okay with this since I did not ask you about it. I hope you are not upset. I spoke to your manager about our trip. Like I said honey, I love you, and I will always do all I can to show you.

Reginae: No, honey, I am not upset. I am surprised you had time and took the time to do all of this for me.

Session Four

When a Man lies!

Note to self: An observation of a situation

As I waited in my office for Ms. Bridgeway, I wrote down a few notes. I wondered if the *white lies* or *harmless half-truths* we tell are as harmless as we think they are. We all know people lie for many reasons, but it is unclear why we tell a lie in the first place. The consensus says we lie to avoid trouble, to keep from hurting those we care for, to save face but mostly, we lie to protect ourselves. Lying for most of us is our way of manipulating the way we want people to see us. The question over who *lies* the most, men or women is still being debated, but studies have shown that both men and women lie, but women are much better at it.

It is no surprise that women are better at keeping secrets than men are. It is also no surprise that most men will lie before telling the truth. This drives women crazy simply because they do not understand why men would do this. As to the *why* of why they would do this is simple, "When most men tell the truth, most women, based on that man's track record of lying to her, see it as an excuse and hardly ever believe them. If men give a "believable" lie that seems plausible, women will accept it much more comfortably.

Here is an example of what I mean:

Carlos found out that his longtime girlfriend of 5 years had cheated on him. He broke up with her and moved on with his life. He met Tiffany. They dated and soon became a couple and moved in together. Three months into their relationship, Carlos got a call from Blanca, his ex. She said she needed to see him. He talked with Tiffany to get her feedback. Carlos told her he was thinking about going, but before he did, he wanted her to be okay with it. In typical situations, when an ex calls, everyone knows if they don't have children together, the ex is up to something, and it usually is not good. It makes sense that your current girlfriend would want to go with him, not because she doesn't trust her man but more because she doesn't trust his ex. In this case, and even though she was suspicious of the ex's reasons for wanting to meet and the fact that Carlos had not given her any indication in the past 3 months not to trust him, she reluctantly told him it was okay to go and see what she wanted but she wanted to know what was said when he got home.

Carlos and Blanca met at a nearby restaurant. Carlos was nervous because he didn't know what to expect. He hoped nothing was seriously wrong. When she sat down, they talked. Blanca told him he looked good and everything seemed to be going well with him. She asked him about Tiffany, and how she was doing. He asked her, "Why did you call me after doing me the way you did me? What do you want?" She said first, let me apologize for the pain I caused you. It wasn't right because you were good to me. With that said I got to tell you something and I am not sure how you're going to take it. I know you're in a new relationship, but I am pregnant with your child.

The worst news Carlos could have imagined hearing at this moment was this. Sitting there with doubts because she had cheated on him (and it could have been the others guys) he asked her, "How do you know it's mine? It could be that other guy?" She said, "That's true, but I feel it is yours." "You don't know for sure," he replied. "I will, when he is born. Are you going to tell your girlfriend you might be a father? How do you think she would feel knowing if the child is yours, I will be in your life forever? You think your relationship is strong enough right now to handle this drama or do you think she will leave you to avoid this mess altogether? I heard you two were trying to have children. How would she feel knowing she isn't the only one having your child?"

Sitting there listening, Carlos tried to comprehend what she had just told him. Many of the questions she asked made sense. He wasn't sure how Tiffany was going to react if he had a child with his ex. He wasn't sure if she would want to have children or stay for that matter after hearing this mess. Carlos wasn't sure how she would handle this news or if she would stay with him, but losing her over this wasn't something Carlos wanted to happen, especially based on a presumption. He played it cool, but he was worried and concerned whether he should or should not tell Tiffany about this conversation. Blanca told him, "Go home and tell your little girlfriend what we talked about and see what will happen. When she dumps you, don't worry. I'll take you back. We're going to be a family soon."

Now, I know what you're thinking. He should have gone home and told Tiffany the truth and allowed her to make up her own mind whether she wanted to stay and be a part of this drama, right? To be honest with you, if he did tell the truth to Tiffany the situation could have gone a few ways: (1) He could have told her the truth and asked her to stay with him to see if the child is his. If the child turns out to be his, he could have asked her to stay with him anyway. He could have still asked her to have children with him and hoped she would be okay with him having children with both of them. They could have dealt with Blanca being a part of their life and moved forward. (2) If he told her the truth and she decided this wasn't for her and broke it off with him, and the child ended up not being his, he would have felt foolish for telling her when he wasn't sure. If the child were his, he would be alone and a father, but without the woman he loved because a vindictive woman wanted to get back at him. (3) He could have told a partial truth and omitted things when she asked him what they discussed. He could just tell her she wanted to apologize for everything and hoped they could still be friends and nothing else because he wasn't sure about anything else. Why create problems based on an unsubstantiated doubt in her head when he didn't know for sure? This is how Carlos thought, so number 3 is what he said he did.

Now, I know you're thinking that by him omitting key facts, he lied to her. He should have told her everything. If he trusted her, she would have understood. Who believes if he would have said, "Honey, my ex told me she is pregnant, and I could be the father. She doesn't know for sure but is thinking of waiting until she has it to know for sure. If the child is mine, I need you to do a few things for me. I know we've only been a couple for three months, but I need you to stand by my side through this, and if the child is mine stay with me afterward. I know Blanca will be a part of our lives, and I would have to pay child support, but between the two of us, we would be okay financially. We can still have children together like we planned. I know you're thinking, how far along is she? When did she get pregnant? You're thinking there is a chance I could have been seeing her while I was dating you, but you would be wrong. I know everything I am asking is a lot, but I love you and need you to stand by me through this, can you do it?"

Now seriously, after hearing all of this from the man you are dating, would you stay and wait for the outcome? Would you knowingly stay if you knew he had a child with another woman? Would you seriously have a concern about having children with him knowing what you know? I doubt it, but maybe you would have, I will never know. Now here is where he messed up and things got worse. Blanca thought about it and knew the other guy whose child it could be was married so he would never claim the child, and Carlos didn't want to have a child with her, so she decided to abort the child without either of them knowing. Afterward, she called Carlos, and he went, but this time he didn't tell Tiffany about his visit. He figured the baby scare was over and sitting with her, helping her get through this ordeal was a small price to pay to make sure Tiffany never heard about this. He was wrong. Like a fool, he told Blanca that he didn't tell Tiffany they were meeting again because she would misunderstand why he was helping her. Blanca asked him, "Why did you help me when I put you in a bad situation with Tiffany?" Carlos told her, "I decided to help because I may not be with you, and even though you hurt me, you are my friend, and you needed my help." This was the truth, but it backfired on him.

Weeks had passed, and things seemed okay for everyone. Blanca hadn't called, and Carlos and Tiffany were doing great until the two of them went to visit Carlos' mother, and Blanca was there. Blanca was feeling some "type of way" about Carlos and Tiffany's relationship. Tiffany was pregnant now, and they were having a child together. Upset, Blanca soon regretted aborting her child and hated the fact that he was having a child with Tiffany and not her. Blanca decided when she saw them that she was going to bring Tiffany up on what "her man" had been doing for her without her knowledge to make trouble for Carlos. Tiffany, hearing this, asked Carlos if this was true. Even though some of this was a lie, it didn't matter when she felt foolish not knowing. Carlos had hidden this from her. He told the truth, and yes, Blanca did abort a child a few weeks ago. Once he said "yes," though, Tiffany didn't hear anything else, and she wanted to go home. She started crying and saying to Carlos, "You've been lying to me! What else have you lied to me about?" In this case, with him omitting certain details and not telling her the whole truth at that time, she now feels he lied to her about everything going on between him and his ex. Now she knows why they really met and what they talked about, and she feels like a fool for not knowing then.

When they got home, Tiffany told Carlos how foolish she felt hearing information from his ex that he should have told her himself. Carlos tried to explain that he didn't lie. He just didn't go into the details of the conversation, and he now knew that this was wrong of him. Carlos told her, "Telling you this would have made it look as if I was trying to get back with her when I wasn't. You would have jumped to that conclusion when I didn't even know if what she said was accurate. I didn't want to put you through that." Tiffany responded by saying, "You should have told me everything and allowed me to make up my mind on how to handle it. You took away my decision and made it for me, and that was wrong. You didn't trust that I loved you enough and would stand by your side. You decided for me what you thought was best for us without consulting me in that way, and I am hurt. I don't think you did it on purpose to hurt me really, but you did, and I need some time to get over it. Don't worry, I am not leaving you, but I will need time to feel I can trust you again. We're having a child and going forward, you better not lie to me anymore or I will leave you and take our child with me, you hear me?" Yes, Carlos replied. They did stay together, and Carlos going forward told her the truth in a way to not hurt her feelings.

We have learned that telling the truth is the best policy, and that lies are lies regardless. Even though Carlos's intention was like most of us, which was not to hurt her, it seems to protect her that he may need to not say much at all. Our cultural stereotypes tell us, "If a person will lie, they will steal, if a person will steal, they will cheat." With this said, I wondered, "Is lying worth it if it is to protect someone?" If your mate was to find out and most times they do, is it worth risking your relationship, friendship and hurting them more to avoid telling the truth? The reality is we all are going to lie about something to someone at some point. We take the chance and gamble that the person we're lying to will never find out. No matter how we flip it, the pain we cause is hurtful, selfish and intentional when it is done deliberately. It makes things worse when the person telling the lies, keeps lying thinking that by omitting details their partner has a right to know, it isn't lying if you don't tell them.

Most people are merely covering up the fact that they are unable and afraid to communicate their true feelings to their partner because they fear being honest with them leaves them vulnerable and open to being hurt by them. I don't believe that who lies the most between men and women is the point. I think the point is or should be that if you're in a relationship, how much lying can one person take before they have had enough and end the relationship? Remember a relationship that lasts and uses trust as its foundation and not lies makes sense.

When women lie in their relationship most times, they have a viable reason to do so. Women in new relationships are learning to trust and communicate with their partner, and are very wary and guarded when it comes to sharing personal information about themselves of their past early on, which is understandable. No one wants to have what they've shared become ammunition to hurt them during an argument. Both men and women when they first meet or start dating, exaggerate their achievements and their success to protect their self-esteem and the image the potential mate has of them, but men do it much more. It is no secret that both parties will lie from time to time to protect their partner's feelings and will sometimes flat out lie to make their man feel like a man. If they are in a loving relationship, rather than her telling him what she is feeling, true or not, many women will flat out lie and say, yes, to make him feel good. It is common for those in relationships to protect their partners from engaging in situations that will not end well.

Let me explain what I mean from the wife's perspective. If her co-worker flirted with her on the job, and she is a little uncomfortable with her male co-worker doing this, (this part depends on how bad it is), to not make matters worse because she knows if she tells her man he will come up to her job and make a scene, she attempts to handle things through the right channel. If she has to have her man intervene, then he will do whatever is needed because he will ensure she feels safe at her place of business. How harmless are half-truths? "Harmless half-truths" are the same as lying but we do it anyway to again protect our mate's feelings, like when your mate asks you, "Does this dress make me look fat?" or "Do you like my cooking?" or "Do I look like I am getting older?" Some lies told, in hindsight, could be viewed as a "good lie" if it is used to protect your mate's feelings. I remember when my ex once asked me, "Does this dress make me look fat?" I remember replying saying, "I love the blue dress on you. It makes you look young." So yes, it works and keeps the peace, and most women know this.

Overall men, when a man lies to their woman on purpose, it never ends well. When I think back, this reminds me of a conversation the fellas and I had one evening. My friend, Eddie, said, "I feel most men tell lies to sound interesting, to get their woman's attention and to keep from looking and being boring. The problem is once the lies work, and if they work well, they figure why tell the truth when the lies are working so well. So at some point, they might mix a half-lie with a half-truth to see how she reacts. If she believes it, then he will continue doing it, hoping that when she finds out the full truth, she might overlook the lies told early on. I feel women want and expect men to lie to them. The man who tells the best lie wins them over. Now they will never admit it because they often have said, "I want a man to tell me the truth" when really what they are saying is "Tell me a believable lie." Listen, they know good and well if men told them the truth, they would never get what they want, so that's why men lie. They see no benefits in telling the truth until after they get what they are after. Grown women know what men want from them. They want him to work and sell the idea to them and convince them to be with them.

James jumped in saying, "There is not a grown woman who doesn't know men lie for two main reasons, "sex and convenience." A man will say whatever and do whatever to smash a woman, and most women with a brain know this. These men are out there, thinking they aren't paying for "sex." "I'll never pay for sex" is what they say, not understanding that when they are spending to impress them, feeding them or buying them trinkets, they are *renting* not *purchasing outright.* They're just putting down a required down payment that ensures they can walk away with something if the woman is okay with the terms of their arrangement. Convincing men will spin a lie faster than you can blink your eyes to get themselves out of trouble. You all remember the mess Jerome got himself into sleeping with two women at the same time. One pulled a gun on him. He had to beg and sell the lie to save his life. You all remember how we told Jerome God *saved* you, not you, and we laughed at him. Listen, women are not stupid that a man can trick them into doing anything. If they sleep with a man, it is because they choose to. Now, I am not talking about rape cases. You all know what I am saying.

Listening to them talk and their views on the subject, I can agree to a degree. I have said that some men are very persuasive and convincing in their lying abilities to get what they want, but not all women fall for it.

Why men lie is the million-dollar question and has yet to be answered truthfully by any man. One thing is clear however, most men will volunteer lies for no reason when it is not always necessary. Telling lies for most men is nothing but a "temporary" solution to a temporary problem that they will worry about later. Those who are doing this have no regard for the woman's feelings, the pain they could cause or the friendship they could lose. They only care about getting what they are after. Yes! Telling the truth is the right thing to do but not always practical or should I say, beneficial, to the person lying. It is hard to find someone to love and love you and even harder when they introduce lies into the friendship/relationship. It is hard to be 100% truthful all the time because (1) No one wants to put themselves out there like that nor be hurt or rejected by the person they are interested in (2) no one wants their own words used against them to destroy them.

My mother once told me, growing up, "When you find a woman you're interested in, you need to tell them the truth. Tell her the truth about yourself, what you can and cannot do, and what you're willing and not willing to do. Be honest about what you feel you currently have to offer, and what your intentions are with her." At the time, I got it, but at the time, it wasn't practical. When you think about it, people, in general, will lie to be accepted. If the person we like doesn't reciprocate the sentiment, we're feeling for them. Some feel as if they have committed love suicide. No man wants to finish last, to be that "good guy," who told the truth and is missing out on being accepted by someone.

Good guys are the ones who meet those women, who have been lied to, cheated on, mentally wore down and verbally abused. And to have a relationship with them, they have to pay for the past men's mistakes continually. They don't want to spend a lifetime fixing, repairing and unpacking that woman's emotional baggage just to be loved by them. To get an idea of how hard it is to love a broken woman (or a broken man), a black man has a better chance of joining the KKK then fixing a damaged person. I am not saying it is impossible. I am saying it's hard. The sad part of "good men" vs "bad boys" is that good men (those who consider themselves good) have to PROVE themselves a hell of a lot more to get the opportunity to help heal that person.

My mother would often ask me, when I told her of someone I was interested in, "Do you think lying to her will make her love you? Are you willing to lose the very thing you claimed you wanted with her by lying? Are you telling me you would be happier living a lie with her, and she not know who you are?" Understand your words can pick her up and provide you with the kind of love you never knew existed or bring her down and make her cheat on you and lie to your face. Decide what kind of relationship you want to have.

Listen, no woman wants to question her man's love. It is a fact. If you love her the right way, she will love you more, but if you mistreat her, she will hurt you back … more. Be respectful to her because, "a woman can and will forget what you say to her, but she will never forget how what you said made her feel." A man's lies hurt more profoundly than a woman's. Women are emotional, and when they give their heart to their man, they do it 100%. They hope their man will do the same with them. There are no real justifiable reasons why anyone should lie to another, but we do. The question I would ask men who always lie for the hell of it is, "Would you date yourself, knowing how much you lie?"

(Buzz)

Yes, Ms. Jackson? Mr. Pearson, Ms. Bridgeway is here.

Mr. Pearson is speaking: Show her in. Good afternoon Ms. Bridgeway, how are you doing?

Ms. Bridgeway is speaking: Good afternoon, Mr. Pearson. I am doing well.

Mr. Pearson is speaking: Have a seat and make yourself comfortable. Can I offer you something to drink, water, tea or coffee?

Ms. Bridgeway is speaking: Water would be good.

Mr. Pearson is speaking: Would you prefer I call you Ms. Bridgeway or Pamela?

Ms. Bridgeway is speaking: Pamela is okay.

Mr. Pearson is speaking: You seem a little nervous. Is this the first time?

Pamela is speaking: Yes, I am a little bit, and yes, it is my first time.

Mr. Pearson is speaking: Well, don't be nervous. We are just going to talk. Before you arrived, I took a moment to go over the questionnaire you filled out. I understand you have been divorced for a few years from your ex-husband, but still, you are having problems getting him out of your system, right?

Pamela is speaking: Yes, that is correct.

Mr. Pearson is speaking: It seems to be more to your story than just your concerns about your ex-husband from the way you filled out your questionnaire. The goal today is for me to listen and understand your concerns. We're in no rush. You can take your time. Together, we will take the steps best needed to resolve your problem and put what you are feeling in perspective.

Pamela is speaking: Well, it was Tuesday, April 6, 1999. I was out with my girlfriends celebrating my birthday at the nightclub, **The Loft**, in Atlanta when I first met Keith. He walked in on us all and introduced himself to us. He asked, "Whose birthday is it?" I told him it was mine, and he asked if he could buy me a drink as his gift to me. I told him sure. He asked my name, and I told him my name was Yvette. He asked, "Would it be too forward if I asked you to dance before you leave this evening?" I told him to let me think about it. He smiled, and then went back over to the boys with whom he was drinking at the bar. Then, he looked back over at me and smiled. I would say about an hour later he returned and asked for that dance. I took him up on it. We slow danced. Afterward, I asked him, "Are you a sports player, you look familiar?" He smiled and said, yes. He had just recently signed to the Atlanta Hawks.

I asked, "Do these women here know who you are? If I didn't take you up on this dance, would you have picked up another woman?" He laughed and said, maybe, if we're honest about it. So, I asked him, "Why did you set your sights on me? Did you think if you brought me a drink, I would go home with you?" Well, to keep 100% honest with you, it was because when I spoke to you, you didn't seem to know who I was or what I did when I introduced myself. Believe it or not, I was very impressed with you. I meet so many women since I signed, who know how much I make before they know my name."

Mr. Pearson is speaking: I take it you two exchanged numbers?

Ms. Bridgeway is speaking: Yes, I gave him *a* number.

Mr. Pearson is speaking: What do you mean you gave him *a* number? Was Yvette your real name or your club name?

Pamela is speaking: Well, I gave him my middle name, Yvette, but not my first name, and yes, the number I provided him was my Google number, not my actual cell number. I didn't want to give out my real name or number just in case I wasn't feeling them so they wouldn't be able to call me once I blocked them.

Mr. Pearson is speaking: I understand.

Pamela is speaking: Anyway, he called, and we talked. Soon, we decided to meet up for lunch. We had a good time, and I was feeling him. When we spoke and shared things, and during our conversation, I learned he was born in Seattle, Washington but grew up in Atlanta. He was three years old when his family moved here. Although he was born in Seattle, he said Keith called East Point, where he grew up and went to school, his home.

Our time together, dating, was like a fairytale romance. He brought me flowers, gifts, showed me attention and took me out to dinner when he was off and in town. I saw him as someone I could be with long term. I told him upfront that I was saving myself for marriage, and if this was a problem, we could be friends. He said he was cool with it, so we became a couple officially on October 30, 1999. I felt I had found my prince. He said to me, as his wife, he would continue to take care of me, buy me things and show me the world. Everything was wonderful.

We didn't get to spend as much time together during the basketball season, but we did talk, and we texted daily. I often wondered though while Keith was traveling to these different cities, whether those "thirsty" women, who knew who he was, would throw themselves at him. Not too many men can or will turn down free sex. I wasn't sure as a man he could resist. I could only hope he would stay faithful to me. I had to trust he would do the right thing. Despite my concerns, when we were together, everything was great. I found out our birthdays were in the same month. We are Aries. His birthday is

April 11th, and mine is April 6th. I knew there was a reason why we both got along so well.

Mr. Pearson is speaking: Were you into Zodiac signs like that?

Pamela is speaking: Yes, to a degree. I believed more in the traits than anything else because people do share characteristics. We had a lot in common, and we shared similar views on many things. We were so compatible and likeminded. You see, Aries people are very courageous, determined, confident, enthusiastic, optimistic, honest and passionate.

Mr. Pearson is speaking: You are smiling.

Pamela is speaking: I am smiling because I remember it like it was yesterday. We were like teenagers when we first got together. He showed me so much attention and passion, and I loved every bit of it. He would write me such beautiful love letters. I brought one of them with me to show you why I fell in love with him.

A letter to My Girlfriend,

I heard it said there is a "right and wrong way" to love a woman. I hope you can teach me the right way to love you so that we can make what we have last forever. I believe if we feed one another's souls with true love, thank God for helping us find each other, communicate daily and be honest about what we are feeling for each other, then our relationship will develop into what we desire it to be. You see, my Angel, until you say "I Do" you're my girlfriend, but in my mind, you're already my wife, believe that. I don't want you to just be in my life, I want you to be my life. You're the reason I do the things I do, for you and with you. You're the reason I feel every day so damn glad we met and fell in love. More importantly, you're the reason I yearn for the day you become my wife. I hope you tell me "yes" when I ask you to be my wife, when I ask you not because I expect you to but because you want to.

I know it's hard for you to know and understand how much I love you, how important you are to me or how much you mean to me. So, until it sinks in, just me knowing you feel the same way is more than just my mission, it is my eternal goal! I know my future sounds like a line a guy would say to sleep with you, but I want much more with you than that because I know you have more to offer than just your body. I know you feel in your heart what I am saying is true. It's not just your beauty I love; I love everything about you! Tell me when and where, and I will marry you today! If it sounds as if I am begging for your affections, I don't mind, but I am not. I am just telling you how to love me. I just wanted to express to you one of the many ways of how I feel about you. I don't care who knows I love you! I am willing and ready to be loved by you for the rest of my life.

This letter doesn't replace what I need and will show you to prove forever how much I love you. It is just a written reminder which you can repeatedly read when I am not at my best. Understand something. No matter what, through our ups and downs, I am not going anywhere. Just know this, like the pastor knows his words, I plan to get to know you and the things I need to do to make and keep you happy with me for the rest of our lives. If I have anything to do with it you will be the last love of my life, you heard?

Mr. Pearson is speaking: Interesting. It seems he was feeling you badly.

Pamela is speaking: Now you can see why I fell so hard for him early on. He was everything I could have wanted in a guy. We met each other's parents and talked about when we were going to get married. Life was good. He proposed to me on Valentine's Day 2001. He did it so smoothly that it caught me off guard. A few weeks earlier, he took me to Jared and had me pick out what would be my wedding ring, and he got it sized. He told me we were going to put it on layaway and get it out months from now. Then on February 14th, we returned to the store supposedly to make a payment on the ring, but when the salesperson brought it out for me to see it again, he took it and put it on my finger and asked me to marry him right there in the store. I was surprised. He said to me, "Pamela Reese, will you marry me and be my wife?" I looked at him, smiled and started crying for many good reasons and said, "Yes, I'll marry you."

I was on cloud nine and so happy. We got married on my birthday on April 6, 2001. I was 22 years old, and he was 24 years old. I was looking forward to being a wife. We moved into a beautiful home over in Buckhead. For a few days, we stayed in doing what we had been waiting to do for over a year <*smile*>. A few months later, I found out I was pregnant with our first child. Our son was born on December 28, 2001. Less than three months, right around March, 2002, I found out I was pregnant again, with our second child who was due December 14, 2002.

For the next four years, I was a stay-at-home mother while he traveled with the team. I took care of the kids and our home. We talked on the phone and *Facechatted* seemingly every night when he was on the road. For a while, we were your typical family enjoying life. He took care of us, and we had no conflicts at all for a long while. I never questioned, nor felt he would be unfaithful as most of those basketball wives said he would be. But, in the fall of 2006, he seemed a little more stressed and preoccupied than usual because the team had lost 9 out of 12 games. I wanted to help him, but I didn't know how. Things between us were strange, and I felt different, as if something had changed, but I couldn't put my finger on what it was.

Mr. Pearson is speaking: Explain what you mean?

Pamela is speaking: By now, he had been in the league going on six years, and we had no problems or drama in our life, but something had changed. When he was home, he wasn't spending as much time with the children like he had before or with me. I noticed our bank account balance had gotten a little lower than it had ever been, so I asked Keith, "Do you know why our balance has gone down?" He said, "Yeah, I have been helping out family members. I didn't want to tell you because I was trying to avoid an argument." I trusted in my man and didn't question the situation because regardless, he was still taking care of our household. I was concerned with him taking out vast sums of money every few weeks in cash. So, for a few months, I just let it go, but money kept going out each month.

His behavior changed, and he seemed upset about something when he was home with us. I was worried, so I reached out to his mother to see if she had any idea of what was going on with him. I knew he was close to his family. They said they had noticed him looking a little more stressed, and it didn't look like it was pressure from playing ball.

Mr. Pearson is speaking: Did you have any idea what was going on with him?

Pamela is speaking: Not really, but when he was home, he got a lot of phone calls, and he often took them outside, away from me. After he would get off the phone, he seemed distracted and a little concerned about something. Our sex life and intimacy between us had just stopped. I worried that he was cheating with some other woman. I called and asked his sister if she had heard any sports news about him that I could help him with. She told me she hadn't heard anything, but she wouldn't be surprised if something was going on because he was, and always had been secretive.

Mr. Pearson is speaking: Did she tell you something helpful?

Pamela is speaking: Not really. She did, however, tell me that she wasn't going to talk about him until she spoke to him face-to-face. She wanted to get to the bottom of this and wanted to know why he was acting so strangely. She said Sherlock Holmes had nothing on her skills in finding out the truth.

Mr. Pearson is speaking: When you checked back in with her, had she heard anything useful?

Pamela is speaking: Yes, she said there was some news about him seeing another woman, but it looked like fake news to her. I needed to talk to him face-to-face and get to the bottom of this.

Mr. Pearson is speaking: Did you?

Pamela is speaking: Yes, I did. He was my husband, and I trusted him. However, there was just too much news all over to ignore what they were all saying on all the sports channels. I knew they would not report it, if they couldn't prove it. Another rumor, I caught on TMZ was that he had another woman on the side, and she had kids by him. I was dumbfounded to hear this, and I had to find out because now we're talking about other children. The reports showed she lived somewhere in Florida and that he had been taking care of her for two years.

I started putting the pieces together and asking myself, "Could this be where all the missing money has gone to help out some other woman?" It only made sense because it was about that time our bank account started going down in the balance. I didn't want to believe everything I had heard, before I heard it from my husband first. The facts were adding up, but I still needed to confirm this mess with my husband first before I believed it.

Mr. Pearson is speaking: Before you accepted all you had heard and seen on television, did you speak to him about it? And if so, what did he have to say about it?

Pamela is speaking: He denied it at first, but the more we fussed about it, he eventually broke down and admitted the rumors were true. He said he did have another woman living in Miami, Florida. They had a two-year-old girl named Bella. Her mother, Brenda, he met during a trip there for a game during the slump. He said she saw him, struck up a conversation and stayed in touch for a few months. I knew then, that must have been her calling when he would take the calls outside where I couldn't hear. I told him, so you needed to talk but you didn't think to call your wife? You considered telling a stranger woman your business, and sleeping with her was the best thing to do since you were feeling bad. I said to him, "This isn't right."

Mr. Pearson is speaking: So what happened next?

Pamela is speaking: I put him out, and we separated for six months while I decided what I was going to do next. I was hurt. I hated him and wanted a divorce, but when I calmed down and thought about it, I concluded, because he begged me during that time, I foolishly decided we should seek help and work things out. I gave our marriage another chance. For the next year, we saw a marriage counselor. I hated what he had done, but I still loved him. I wasn't ready to give up on my marriage yet. I felt we could fix it. Now I had to deal with the fact that he had another child with another woman. At times that was hard to deal with, but I prayed on it for God to give me the strength to do what was right.

Mr. Pearson is speaking: So did the marriage counselor help your marriage?

Pamela is speaking: Yes, for a while, everything seemed to be getting back on track. His marketing team turned his image around and acquired companies to endorse him again. The team started winning again, and they were in the playoffs. Although things were going good at home, we still had our issues, and I had my trust concerns of him going out on the road again. For a whole year, things looked okay. Going into 2008, and after I accepted his other child as part of his family, I felt he had learned his lesson, but I was wrong.

Mr. Pearson is speaking: What happened? Did you find out he had yet another child?

Pamela is speaking: No, but he started acting out again. I worried he was back with another woman. I told him, "If I catch you with another woman or hear you have another child out there somewhere, I will leave you for good. I will take our children and leave you. I can't look like the foolish wife again for you." He swore he was not messing around with another woman nor did he have any other children anyway. For a while, during the year he got back to his routine and started calling and texting me like before.

In March of 2009, I heard rumors of him cheating yet again. This time I did not allow it to get out before I found out what was going on. So, I took a flight to Cleveland, Ohio, to confront him face-to-face. I had the hotel person let me into his room saying I wanted to surprise him, but when I got in, I heard voices. When I stepped around the corner to see who the voices belonged to, I couldn't believe what I saw. I couldn't believe my eyes, and what I was seeing. Here I am thinking he was cheating on me with another woman when he was cheating and apparently in a relationship with a man.

I didn't know what to do other than run out of there. Keith put on some clothes and chased after me trying to tell me what I just witnessed wasn't what I saw. With all the noise we were making other people came out to see what was going on. Camera operators were taking pictures, and others were trying to stop him.

Mr. Pearson is speaking: What happened next?

Pamela is speaking: I got in a cab and went straight to the airport and flew home. I didn't tell anyone, nor did I want to. I knew once the press got wind of this, they were going to make us all look bad. I would look like a complete fool for not seeing this. After allowing him to return in the first place, after allowing the affair to be okay, I knew I was going to look worse from this mess. I was so hurt, and now, confused. My husband was a freak, and I didn't even know it. He had cheated on me with both a woman and a man. What was next? I wondered. I didn't know what was worse, that he had cheated again or that he had cheated with a man. My man was bisexual, and I never knew. I had so many questions, but I didn't want to talk to Keith right at that moment.

Mr. Pearson is speaking: Did you two sit down and talk about what had happened?

Pamela is speaking: We did. I was still mad. I had questions. I asked him, "Why did you do this to me?" I told him that my family thinks I am a fool for allowing you to bring shame to our family like this. Do you know how much I am hurting right now over this mess? First, you cheated on me with another woman and have a child, then when I think everything has calmed down, you cheat again but this time with a man. I asked him could he tell me why both a man and a woman? And why stay married if what he wanted to do was cheat? He tried to explain why he did this, but nothing he said made any sense at all. I just told him, for now, he needed to move out until I could think about what I wanted to do, and he did.

Mr. Pearson is speaking: Even with everything that went on, did you consider leaving the marriage?

Pamela is speaking: No. I know it sounds stupid, but I still loved him. We had been married for ten years at this point, and I just wasn't ready to walk away even after everything that had happened. Does this make me a fool for doing what I did knowing all I knew?

Mr. Pearson is speaking: No, you're not a fool. You're just a good woman who loves her man despite the situation he has put you in since you've been together. I can only imagine your emotional state at that moment. Your husband of ten years cheated on you with both a man and a woman and fathered a child. It was a lot for one person to take.

Now I don't want to sound insensitive but was your decision to stay based on your current lifestyle or love for him and your family? Both you and I know that under the circumstances no judge would have refused you both spousal and child support.

Pamela is speaking: I hear you, and no, my decision I was thinking about had nothing to do with my lifestyle but more about my family. I didn't want to rip my family apart and have it be another fatherless home. I know I deserve better, and you best believe I was confused about what to do. Our sex life by this point was nonexistent. I felt undesirable and unattractive. We were hardly speaking, and when we did, all we did was argue. I didn't know how much longer I could go on living like that.

Mr. Pearson is speaking: Did you speak to his parents about your situation?

Pamela is speaking: Yes. I spoke with his mother, Lula. I told her everything, and she didn't look surprised at all, which made me look at her sideways. I asked her to tell me what I should do, because I loved her son, but he had embarrassed me, broken my heart, fathered another child, and slept with a man. I didn't even know how to deal with that. She said, "Babe, come on by, and we will talk." So I drove over to their house.

Mr. Pearson is speaking: In your conversation with her, did she say anything comforting?

Pamela is speaking: Here's the thing she said to me, "Baby, let me tell you a story. I believe once you hear what I am about to tell you, it will shed some light on your situation. I am not defending him by any means. He was wrong in what he did. Let me explain. Years ago, when his dad and I got married, we were young and in love. He had just become the head coach of the Atlanta Hawks. Times were going well for us. I was pregnant with our first child, and we had just got this house. I was an NBA wife, and meeting those other wives of the players was a new experience for me. These women were all into the lifestyle, spending and enjoying the perks of being the wife of a player."

Now, as she was talking, I am thinking to myself, what does this have to do with my situation? She went on to say, "The ladies showed me the rules and regulations, I guess you could say. They all seemed comfortable talking about their men's infidelity as if it was normal and acceptable. While they are telling me all the *on the road* stories they have heard and seen on television about their man, and how, once they caught them cheating all their man did to keep them, I was thrown back a little. They looked at me and told me, you'll get used to how this all works. I wasn't a little concerned because my husband called me every night, and we video chatted when we could."

She then said that after the child was born, things changed. He hardly communicated at all, and she said something was wrong. She said no one changes like that overnight, but she was going to get to the bottom of it. She said, he told her that there were times when he was home, but he wasn't, and I understood that. He seemed, she said, as if he was ready to go as soon as he got back. She said she sensed something was going on, but she didn't want to believe it was another woman. One night while he was asleep, she went through his briefcase to see if she could find evidence of him cheating. She came across a letter from the IRS addressed to him only. She said she opened and read it and found out her husband had purchased a townhome and a new car 15 months ago. The address of the townhome was just a few blocks from their home in Buckhead.

When she found out, she said she was pissed and said, "I know this fool didn't buy another woman a house and car and put her ass close to me and think I wouldn't find out." She said she got in her car with her child, and drove over to her sister's house. She dropped her child off, because there was business she needed to handle. She said she went over to the house and knocked on her door. When the woman opened the door, she told the woman, "You don't know me, but you know my husband. Can I come in, I think we need to talk?" The woman looked surprised and said, sure come in. She told her that her name was Linda, and she thought it could have been some mistake.

241

Listen, let me get to the point. I think my husband is cheating on me with you.

She said Linda asked, "Who is your husband?" She told her Keith Bridgeway, Sr. Linda looked surprised to how this could have happened since she wasn't even from Atlanta. Lula said she asked her, "Where are you from, and how did you get in this house?" She said, Linda told her she was from Austin, Texas, and she had just relocated six months ago. Keith had asked her to come, and he took care of all the arrangements. Linda said Keith told her she was his girlfriend. Linda said they met a year ago, became friends and stayed in touch during the season. They hung out, and Keith would often fly her to where the team was playing when she was free to go, and she did.

Lula said she asked Linda, "What kind of job did you do to make you want to up and move here?" Linda said she was a Marketing Representative for the San Antonio Spurs at the time. When she and Keith started to get serious, he asked if she could relocate and work for the Hawks. He would talk to the front office for her and get her in. Lula said she asked her, did he tell you he was married? Lula said Linda said, no. He said he was divorced and had been quite a while, over a year. Lula said she couldn't believe what she was hearing, but it sounded like some mess Keith would tell her to get her. Buying her a house, car and flying her and her stuff here seemed like something he would have done to impress her.

She said she told Linda that Keith was her husband, and they were still married. Whatever they had is over, and she would see to it. She said she apologized for coming off the way she did because it was clear Keith had lied to her and moved her nearby based on a lie. She told her since you didn't know, I'll let you handle how to process this but understand, if Keith sees you again, I will divorce him and take this home and the car in the settlement because no judge would side with a cheating ass husband after hearing this story. Lula got outside in her car and cried. She couldn't believe this woman lived about

30 minutes from where she lived. Keith had been cheating with her, given this woman a car and bought her a house, and no doubt had been giving her money. She was hurt, pissed, and mad. He had broken her trust yet again. She didn't believe the rumors or those women telling her that her man would eventually cheat on her. She trusted her husband to make the right decisions knowing she was pregnant and having his child.

She said she called his voicemail, and left a voicemail telling him she knew all about his other woman. If he knew what was best, he better call her back a.s.a.p. When he got her message, she said he called her, and said they could talk about it when he got home. She said he didn't even try to deny any of it. She said she cried and threatened to leave him. He begged her to stay and give him one more chance. He told her they could fix it. He was sorry for hurting her and suggested they go for marriage counseling. He said he didn't mean it and didn't want to divorce. He still loved her, and she stayed. She said it took them over a year to work things out. The trust, Lula noted, was a little hard to rebuild, but for the sake of her marriage, Lula was willing to try. She stated that Linda moved back to Austin, and they broke things off. Around the time she had Keith, Jr., she said she sensed he was back at it again.

Mr. Pearson is speaking: Hearing her tell this story did you get a sense this was something the men in her family did to those they dated? She was telling you that since she accepted it and stayed, you should do the same?

Pamela is speaking: Yes, I was thinking just that, but at the moment I wasn't concerned. I didn't care why she stayed. I was concerned about me and what I was going to do because this situation didn't seem right. I told her I wasn't sure if I could stay if Keith cheated on me like that. She said, "When you love someone deeply, you will convince yourself that it is worth saving. You become tolerant of things you would otherwise not tolerate for your family."

Mr. Pearson is speaking: You know she is right about love. When you genuinely love someone, you will tolerate a lot of mess. Though you feel foolish for doing it, you do it because you love them, until you've had enough. It is when they push you to a breaking point that you will start to see how loving this person is unhealthy. She wanted her marriage to work so badly that even with him cheating, it was not enough to make her leave him. She accepted it as if it was HER new norm. Some here would call her a fool for allowing this to happen. They would never let their man mistreat or disrespect them like that.

Believe me. If I got a $1.00 every time I have heard that statement and seen how many women have stayed and worked things out, I would never ever have to work again. I'm not saying that because she's content with her situation you should be in yours. After hearing her tell you in a nutshell, "like father, like son", what I'm saying is IF you felt this was too much were you, "were you mentally prepared for this if he was cheating on you yet again? I'm only saying this because some men will get to the point of you leaving them and change their ways and be better, but many will see it as if they can do anything. They know you aren't going anywhere."

Pamela is speaking: I picked up on that. It caught me off guard, the fact that she made it sound as if it was okay to be disrespected by a man. I know she didn't mean it like that, but that's how I took it. Hearing her story, I felt nervous and scared there. I was having child number two with a man, and I wasn't sure if this would make him stop and act right. Hearing her talk about his father's ways, I wasn't sure if having another child was the right thing to do.

Mr. Pearson is speaking: Fast forward, his mother's advice and the story only made you more confused as to what to do. Next, you were having your second child. Did Keith Jr. pull it together and step up to comfort you in any way?

Pamela is speaking: Well, he seemed excited, and he was there when the child was born, but he had to go back on the road soon. I was nervous as to what he was going to do with everything we had just gone through. Was he going to do right or act out again? Time would tell.

Mr. Pearson is speaking: Would you like to take a moment. I see this is upsetting to you.

Pamela is speaking: No, I am okay. Can I get a tissue? As I was saying, the season had a few more months to go and for the moment, I had to trust him. I had to concentrate on my kids and me at the moment. I called my mother and had her come by and spend time with me to help me get myself together. It was good having her with me. She didn't judge me. She just listened and talked to me. It was hard raising my child alone, but I had to because he was on the road a lot. I pulled myself together for my boys, got them straight and in daycare, and I started volunteering at my church. During this time, Keith and I didn't talk as much as we used to. I still loved him, and I wanted what we had to work out, but we were in a strange place now.

Mr. Pearson is speaking: Strange like how?

Pamela is speaking: Well, I wasn't feeling the family vibe anymore that I thought would come back after the second child, but we were okay. I could wait until the end of the season. The team got knocked out of the playoffs in the second round. He got so depressed that he started drinking heavily. We found ourselves fussing more and more about nothing. He started hanging out all night and sleeping during the day. Financially we were okay, mind you, but it could be that handling two homes, three kids and a side chick, but he said "I" was stressing him out. I tried to encourage him and be supportive, but nothing was working. I wasn't sure what I could do, and I wasn't sure if in this state of mind, he would use it as a reason to cheat again.

Mr. Pearson is speaking: I can understand that based on his past history. With all of this going on, did you figure out if he was cheating on you yet again?

Pamela is speaking: Yes, I found out most inexplicably.

Mr. Pearson is speaking: How?

Pamela is speaking: Well, one night, he came in hung-over from drinking with the guys, and he took a shower. I decided that it was time to snoop. As I was going through his phone, a text came in from some woman named Kenisha. The message asked when he was going to come by because she needed some money for diapers. When I saw the text messages, I wanted to go in the bathroom and beat the living mess out of him, but I didn't. I couldn't believe he was cheating on me yet again.

Mr. Pearson is speaking: So what did you do?

Pamela is speaking: Well, I went through the text messages to see how long they had been communicating. They had been talking for a few months. I said to myself, "Not again, another woman and another child." I texted back as if it was him and said, "I don't have any money right now" to see if she would text back. Sure enough, she responded, saying, "Well, you need to find some because your son needs milk and diapers." As I read the message about his son needing milk and diapers, my heart started beating faster. I wanted to confront him then, but I waited to see if I could get an address on the other woman without him knowing. I couldn't believe he had a son with her. If this was true, enough is enough. I texted her back again and asked, "What size do I need to get him? I'll call you tomorrow." She texted back, "Newborn size, it doesn't matter the brand. What time can I expect you to come by tomorrow? Don't forget you have to pick up Chris from daycare because I don't get off until 5:00 pm."

Mr. Pearson is speaking: So now you're hearing he has yet another child with another woman who lives somewhere near you? What were you going to do now?

Pamela is speaking: Well, first, I copied the messages and sent them to my phone and the girl's name, number and address. I then deleted the text messages I had done and hers that came in so he would not figure out that she and I had texted each other. I went into another room and sat there hurt, mad and shaking. I was trying to figure out how could Keith have cheated on me for the third time? I couldn't believe there was a newborn child. This meant he was cheating still during the time we supposedly were working on our relationship. She just had this child recently if it is a newborn. I needed to talk to someone, so I called my Pastor, Pastor Tucker.

I told him what was going on, and he said to me that before I get myself all worked up, I needed to calm down and breathe. He said the both of you should sit down and talk, see if you can get him to come with you this Saturday for church and afterward, we can sit down together and talk about what you two are doing in your marriage. After talking to him, I read my Bible, put my boys to bed, and went to bed. He got in the bed and went right to sleep without saying a word to me. As I lay there, I was hot. I couldn't wait to get to the bottom of this, and I knew if I asked him directly, he would probably lie to me as he has been doing in situations like this.

So, the next morning I got up, and he was gone out of the house. I called his sister and told her what I believed was going on. She didn't seem surprised at all which again seemed strange. It was as if she expected her brother to do these things. I called Kenisha and lied and said I was a friend of Keith's and that he gave me this number to reach him. She said okay and told me he was coming by. She said that if I don't get him beforehand, around 5 pm, if I wanted to, I could come by then to talk to him. I told her sure, text me the address, and she did. You're not going to believe this. The woman lived just

30 minutes away from me. When I got to her house, she invited me in, and we talked for a while. I couldn't wait for him to show up so I could catch his ass red-handed. I sat there mad, hurt, and scared, hoping this wasn't true. She excused herself and went and got her baby and brought him into the room to feed him. I tell you when I saw the child, I knew it was his without a doubt.

I was so upset that I quickly made up an excuse and got the hell out of there. I felt I was going to be sick. I told her to tell Keith his sister would call him later. When I got in the car, I broke down and cried. I couldn't believe I was in this mess with him yet again. I went back home and waited for him to show up. All those nights he told me he was hanging out with the guys, which was bad enough, he was spending time with her and his child. When he did get in, I didn't waste any time. I asked him where he had been, Keith said he was with the guys. I said, oh. I asked him was one of those guys, Kenisha? He asked me, "Who is Kenisha?" Yes, I said. Oh you don't know a Kenisha? He said, nah. I said well she knows you and when I was over there today, I talked to her, and I met your son, your son, Keith. He then said, "Let me explain. I do know her and yes, the child is mine, but it was a mistake."

I said to him, a mistake? You happen to have sex and father yet another child with yet another woman, and you're saying THIS was a mistake? So, what was the other I caught you with? Errors also? Was the woman in Miami a mistake? Was the guy I found you with a mistake? Oh, what's wrong? Cat got your tongue? Can you believe this man TRIED to get an attitude and defensive with me about his cheating ways?

Mr. Pearson is speaking: So, what happened next?

Pamela is speaking: Well, he stood there, trying to explain his cheating. He apologized, had the nerve to say, "We can work through this, trust me, babe." I looked at him and told him, "Trust?" "Work things out?" "We are way passed working anything out. It's time for you to leave. Pack your things and go tonight. I will be filing for divorce tomorrow morning." I told him to leave before I call the police. When he left, I got my kids together and went to my parent's house to spend the night, because I didn't even want to be there anymore.

Mr. Pearson is speaking: I can understand you were hurting inside at that time. It was a lot to take in. Now, once you cleared your mind about everything, there was no real reason to continue this marriage, but I can tell from the way you are holding your head down you didn't want to nor did you let him go. You forgave him, didn't you?

Pamela is speaking: Yes, I did, and I don't even know why. After a few weeks of thinking about the situations he'd put me in, I met with him and sat and talked yet again. When we sat down, and he tried to speak, I told him, "STOP and listen. You've done enough talking, lying cheating and making mistakes as you call them. I am going to talk calmly and leave here at peace. I told him, "We can't stay married." You have hurt me and worn me down so that I can't do this with you anymore. I thought long and hard the past few weeks, and I realized you are not healthy for me, and we are not healthy together.

I am so hurt and mad at you right now that I don't know what to do. It will take me a long time to get over this. I am doing my best not to cry while sitting here talking to you. I have given you ten plus years of my time, love and loyalty, and how did you return the favor? You lied, cheated and fathered two children all while we were still together. You told Pastor Tucker and me that you wanted to work things out because you loved me and wanted your family to be back the way it was, but you lied. You lied to me, to our Pastor, and most importantly, you lied to God. I can't look at you right now without crying. I feel sorry for you because you've got a problem and YOU and God will have to deal with it, because I can't anymore. I have no more love to give to you right now.

When you cheated on me the first time, and I went to your mother to talk, to get some comfort, she told me then, and I wasn't listening. She said in so many words but I didn't hear her, that you were a dog, and you didn't want to change even if you could. You would have thought after you cheating on me and fathering a child and getting caught sleeping with a man that you would have learned your lesson, but you somehow did not, at all. Let me ask you something, "Did you ever love me at all?" Because I am not seeing how with all that you have done to embarrass me, hurt me and make me feel like a pure fool for giving you all those chances to hurt me again just because I loved you. You're selfish, Keith, and I don't feel you have the ability to love anyone. Listen, I've got to go, but I will pray for you and hope one day we can be friends again.

Mr. Pearson is speaking: Yes, you did the right thing by getting a divorce. It seemed to be long overdue. You did a great job by forgiving him. You see when we forgive those who have wronged us, it acts like medicine, the kind of medicine that heals our deepest wounds. It allows us to close the door on the past and gives us grace and motivation to move forward to live and enjoy our lives again. The Bible says in **1 Peter 5:7**, (KJV), "Casting all your care upon him; for he careth for you." Meaning you need to pray and ask Him for his help because if you keep trying to control your anger on your own, your stress levels will keep mounting. When you turn to Him for His help, you will see and be able to let go of all your anxieties, all your worries, all your concerns, once and for all.

Understand something. Anger is Satan's way of telling you that you are beyond the reach of God's grace, when you're not. Growing up, my mother always told us when we got in a situation we felt we couldn't handle, "When you are going through things that you feel are too much to handle, turn to Him. Ask him to help you. Once you do, you will see things start to get better and you'll wonder why you spent even a single day worrying." I didn't understand at the time when she said it. Like you, I tried to handle problems myself, and I failed because I was afraid to ask for help when I shouldn't have been. We must all deal with the consequences of our actions, and your ex-husband is no exception. He will, at some point, have to answer to God for what he did to you. He knows you didn't deserve it. Do you think you can pray and ask Him for help? Better yet, do you think you can really allow Him to help you?

Pamela is speaking: Yes, I believe I can do that.

Mr. Pearson is speaking: He helped me, and I know He will help you if you ask. Listen, it says in **1 Peter 3:10**, (KJV), it says, "For he that will love life, and see good days, let him refrain his tongue from evil, and refrain his lips that they speak no guile." Meaning you cannot think or say negative things about him around your children because you are angry and upset with him. God pays attention to the way we treat one another. Be a role model to your children by showing them how to handle difficult situations and not be a victim of your circumstances. Let your example teach and show them that asking Him for His help in tough times is an option of their situation, not a sign of weakness.

Understand something, because I know, anger encourages exaggeration and makes us say things we can't retract. Long after we have moved on, our harsh words maintain their power to wound and divide. When I said, you must control your anger, I say this because it doesn't just affect you but those around you. In this case, it changed your kids and the way they thought about their dad. I don't feel that you are the kind of person that wants her kids to take sides of whose love means the most, daddy's or mommy's.

Regardless of how your relationship ended with your husband, the kids are not the problem or the issue of your anger. You seem to me to be a brilliant woman from what I have been able to gather. I feel it's time for you to start taking care of yourself before you burn out. Failing (talking about your marriage) doesn't make you a failure.

It's just part of learning and maturing as we all go through in life. Mistakes are nothing but opportunities for us to learn from. If we repeat our mistakes, if we do not let go of the hurt and pain others have caused us, we will forever live and wonder why we can't see or live in the future. *It is our job to take power away from those who hurt us and for us to become personally empowered.* You must regain control of your life. Don't allow anyone to drain, disrespect or divert you from the experience God has for you.

Pamela is speaking: As much as I hate to admit it, what you've said makes sense and is correct. I can see now how the anger I have carried around for this person, who is no longer a part of my life, has severely affected me. I can now admit it has been hard for me to realize this was my problem. I can see telling others didn't help me get past it, but more importantly, I can see how I seemed to bring in others to be victims.

This talk has given me a different outlook and take on my actions concerning how to deal with my ex and our co-parenting. Going forward, I will not say anything terrible around them about their dad. I will pray to God for His guidance because I genuinely want to change my ways and be all He intended for me to be in my life. Mr. Pearson, I do appreciate you listening to me, your advice is invaluable. It was the kind of kick I needed to get myself back on track. Anyway, I will not take any more of your time. I will make plans with your office manager to schedule another session within a week.

Mr. Pearson is speaking: Well, I am glad we were able to get to the root of your issues. I look forward to speaking with you soon. Have a great rest of your day!

Session Five

Love will make you do wrong!

It is Friday morning, September 13, 2019, my day off. Reginae is at work, and I am hanging around the house working on my message for the upcoming **Men's Ministry**, Sunday, October 13, 2019. I put my television on the music channel, **Music Choice**, as I often do when I am working on projects when my phone buzzes with a text message. It's my friend, Rodney. His text message reads:

Silky smooth
Are you busy?

KingDray
I am at home writing, what's up?

Silky smooth
If you got a minute, you feel like lunch?
I want to speak to you about something.

KingDray
Cool where do you want to meet?

Silky smooth
let's meet over at High Note Rooftop Bar
over on 53 14th Street NW, Midtown.
You remember we watched the
Super Bowl there.

KingDray
I remember the place. I can
meet you there in 40 minutes.

Silky smooth
Lunch is on me! Thanks
see you there.

We haven't hung out for about two months. I figured it was severe because Rodney offered free lunch. Anyway, I stopped my writing and took a break to go and see what was going on with my friend. We got there around the same time and went inside and sat in the bar area.

Ondray: What's going on, man. I haven't seen you in a while. You have been MIA for about three months.

Rodney: Funny. I am good. Yeah, I have been chilling for a while.

Ondray: What's going on? You made it sound like the FBI were after you, and you needed to get out of the country or something.

Rodney: Nah man, it's nothing like that. I wanted to talk to you because I have a relationship situation that requires your expertise. As you know, I have been MIA, and the reason for this is because I met someone. We have been spending time together for a while. Her name is Michele. We've been kicking it for a minute, and so far, things are looking good. I'm feeling her, and I think she feels the same.

Ondray: Oh, okay, cool.

Rodney: Get this. She listens to your show. She heard you give out some advice to someone, and it seems as if she's trying to use it on me. Now, of course, I missed the show she got this information from and needed to know what you said that day to your listeners, so I can pick up where she is going with this. Michele's trying your advice on me.

Ondray: Is it not working?

Rodney: It is working, a little too well. She was telling me about a response you gave to a guy's letter on "Learning to Trust Again" and talked to a woman about "Why men don't act right." Michele spoke about the advice you gave as if you were talking to her directly and afterward asked me what I thought about what you said to them. Do you remember the show? Do you remember the points you made?

Ondray: Sure, I remember it, and what advice I gave out. What's the problem?

Rodney: Now you know I didn't tell her I knew you because she would have wanted to meet you and talk about my faults to get you to tell me how to act. So, my situation is this. We have only been dating for about three months now. We met at **Seasons 52** one evening. A few coworkers and I got together after work for a few drinks. I spotted her at the bar with what looked like two of her girlfriends. I walked over and introduced myself, you know how I do, and offered to buy her and her friends a drink. She said her name was Michele and she was out with her girls. I asked her if I could speak to her for a second alone. She said sure, and we moved down the bar to talk.

Now I knew we were not going to hold a long conversation, so I got right to the point and told her I found her very attractive and I would like to talk more and get to know her outside of the bar. I gave her my business card and asked if we could talk later, maybe tomorrow, and she said sure. I said okay, and walked her back over to her friends and went back to my friends. I didn't want to seem too eager, just interested.

Ondray: Okay.

Rodney: So, we did speak over the phone the next day and made plans to meet for dinner. At dinner, we shared information and talked about what we both were looking for in a relationship. Over the next few weeks of talking and going out to eat, movies, etc., we started talking about possibly being exclusive.

Ondray: Well, everything seemed like it was going well. What's the issue or problem? The things she asked are normal because most women want to know if you want the same things in the relationship. So, her questions and concerns at this point in your friendship are valid. So, again, what are your issues?

Rodney: You're right, get to it. Although she seems as if she's got it all going on, I sense she has trust issues.

Ondray: How did you come to this conclusion?

Rodney: Michele told me in the last relationship she trusted her boyfriend, and she would often catch him in lies over silly things, and this made it hard for her to believe his so-called plans for them.

Ondray: Okay, well, this sounds again, normal because you two have only dated a little while. She seems as if she is trying to trust you. She needs you to show her, while she is deciding that you are trustworthy and you're not looking to hurt her in any way. I have said this often to many people, a little jealousy in your relationship is a good thing. It is a nice feeling to know the person you are with is willing to stand up for you/protect you to a degree to avoid losing you.

However, though, it gets old after a while. If you don't address it, it can and will emotionally drain your relationship fast. Now, based on what you have said so far, it sounds as if Michele has been lied to and cheated on by her last boyfriend. In this case and a situation like this most guys come in or meet these kinds of women in this stage of their life, you're fighting the battles of past men's issues and all that they may have done to her. I know it's unfair to have to do it but if she is interested in getting to know you and you, her, you are going to have to repair her trust in loving someone first, then help and hope she sees you can be trusted. It may seem hard but it's not impossible.

Rodney: Man, don't you think I know this. She is always, when we talk, questioning me about "what if" scenarios and what I would do and how I would react to things that haven't happened yet. It's like she wants me to predict and guarantee something that hasn't happened, so she can "know" what's going to happen next. Now, I am not trying to lie to her, but I don't have the answers to future events yet.

Ondray: What kind of scenarios?

Rodney: We'll be looking at a movie and talking about the film itself and out of nowhere she would ask me, "Would you cheat on me? Do you plan to hurt me? Sometimes when we're out on a date, she'll see a beautiful woman and assume I saw her too and then she'll ask me, "Do you think I look better than she does?" She is always comparing herself to others, thinking I'm trying to replace or leave her for someone else.

Ondray: What do YOU think when she breaks out of nowhere and asks you these kinds of questions?

Rodney: At first, I was surprised and shocked that a grown woman would blurt out something like this when we have been dating for over three months. It is evident to me that I want her because I am with her, but she doesn't see it that way. I am not shocked or anything by her asking, but it has gotten old. Let me tell you what happened last week when we went out to dinner. I mean listen to this. Our waitress came over to take our order and the moment she walked away she asked me, "Why did you smile at her so much? How can you flirt right in front of me as if I didn't see you checking her out? You think she is better looking than me?" In the beginning, it was cute, but now it has become a severe problem. She will ask me a question, and before I could or try to answer her, she replies for me based on what she thought I was going to say and runs with the answer she comes up with as though it were the truth of the situation.

Ondray: You got you a crazy, insecure, low self-esteem woman with jealousy issues rooted from way back, so don't think this is just you that this happened to. I bet you this is way before she met you. She wasn't in a serious relationship simply because most men would have smashed and moved on and not settled down with her. To answer this question, "Is she worth all the baggage she comes with to be with her in a long-term relationship?" Are you prepared and willing to put up with this behavior?

Rodney: Honestly, man, I like her enough to try. I wanted to share this information with you. I hoped to get your feedback on what I should do because she is following and trying out the advice you share on your show on me. I need to know how I should handle this behavior with her as we try and build a relationship.

Ondray: When you first noticed this behavior, did you sit her down and talk to her about what you see happening, and let her know you're a little concerned? Because she might have deeper issues and other things going on within her, but for you to help work through them, she must first admit she has issues. Michele must tell you she wants your help to fix them for her to accept whatever you're trying to do in the betterment of the relationship. If not, your mountain to climb will get higher and higher going forward.

Rodney: I can see this. What can you suggest because if she doesn't admit or feel she has a problem, then what? We have been together for a reasonable length of time, and I know she knows I am feeling her. Why would she keep asking me these kinds of questions day in and day out?

Ondray: Okay, let's break this down: (1) I will share with you "signs" of a jealous woman. I'll share with you how to understand her to know why she feels the way she does. We'll go over what I think would help you in turning her behavior around so you can help show her you are not her past but would like to be her future, if she allows you. (2) I will suggest a few things that could help you help her see you for who you are because she needs to feel and know you are different from what she believes "guys" are.

Rodney: Okay, Dr. Dray, talk to me.

Ondray: A jealous woman, even with you as her man, will constantly think, feel and fear you will leave her for someone else. She will see those people, especially other women you've known before her, as a danger to the relationship. In some situations, she can view the closeness you may have with family members as a threat. A good example – do you remember Trina from college?

Rodney: Yeah, I remember her. She was crazy about you. I thought you two would get married one day.

Ondray: I thought that also. The thing that no one saw or knew because you didn't live with her was that she had trust and insecurities in our relationship, and I got this kind of treatment for the five years we were together.

Rodney: Man, what are you saying?

Ondray: Remember a few years ago when we were dating during college, Thanksgiving, I believe it was, when we invited everyone over to our place, and she invited her friend, Jennifer.

Rodney: Yeah, Yeah, I remember her, she was beautiful.

Ondray: Well, you know we all talked and had a good time, right?

Rodney: Right.

Ondray: Well when everyone left, and we were cleaning up, Trina had an attitude with me for the rest of the evening, and I didn't know why.

Rodney: Why?

Ondray: Well, when I questioned her, she told me that I was flirting with her friend and everyone could see it. I embarrassed her in front of her friend because I paid too much attention to her and didn't give her time to spend with her friend.

Rodney: What? Man, that's crazy. I wish you would have said something. I would have defended you.

Ondray: Well, at the time, I thought she was playing. I thought she was telling me I talked too much. In reality, she was mad as hell because she thought for a good while that I was trying to get with her friend right there in front of her.

Rodney: Man, come on. It was her friend, and we all talked to her and other people that evening, just being friendly. Please tell me she didn't think you were trying to get with this girl for real. How stupid would that be, at that moment, in your house with your girlfriend standing right near you?

Ondray: Yes, she did think just that. Now at the time, I didn't know what to say to get her to realize I wasn't trying to get with her friend. I wanted her and was with her, and she was all I wanted, not her friend. She let it go, or so I thought after a few weeks, but one thing was for sure, she didn't bring her friend around me again.

Rodney: Man, that's crazy. It's funny you mention that because my lady questions everything I tell her. She asks me often, if I've thought about cheating on her. She thinks when I am out with the guys, I am trying to pick up women, and to make matters even worse she is really defensive when I talk to any other woman, period. When

I speak to her or share things happening at my job that involves a woman, she looks at me sideways as if I am trying to hook up with them, not paying any attention to the story because all she heard was there was a girl involved.

Ondray: Well, that's common of a jealous woman. She is always thinking and is fearful that you are going to drop her and get with some other woman at any time, no matter how often you tell her she is the one you want and are with.

Rodney: Normal for whom? I am not used to being questioned about my whereabouts, checked on like a child, having someone doubt me as if I am up to something when I tell her the truth to keep her informed.

Ondray: Well, you have a jealous woman with a very suspicious nature, and it will take a long time for her to trust your words. Based on what she knows from her past relationships, your actions are the only thing she believes. Even then, she may ask a lot of questions at times. She is just trying to trust what you're saying to her. To understand how she thinks and reacts to what you two are doing as you grow a little more, let me give you an example. This will let you "see" what she thinks when what you say doesn't go according to what you told her. Do you remember Jacqueline, she worked with us over at AT&T, her nickname was Jolly?

Rodney: Yeah, I remember her.

Ondray: Well, you remember when we were watching the football game a while back?

Rodney: Yeah, what of it?

Ondray: Hold up, and I will tell you. That night, I told my wife we were getting together to watch the football game at **Buffalo Wild Wings**.

Rodney: I remember. You said Reginae was upset with you because you came home later than you told her. We were sitting in the parking lot of your building just talking, but she didn't know that.

Ondray: Right. Okay, we were outside just talking. Remember I texted her and told her we were outside and that I would be in shortly.

Rodney: Yeah.

Ondray: When I walked in, she was still upset.

Rodney: Why?

Ondray: She was upset because when the game ended, I didn't go straight home. She said the game was 3 hours, and I should have been home in 3 hours. I was 40 minutes later than I said I would be even though I texted her and told her that I was sitting right outside in the parking lot, talking to you.

Rodney: Why was she upset? I don't understand.

Ondray: It had nothing to do with the time but more to do with what she thought and felt. She concluded I was late because I was talking not to you, but Jolly. She thought I was spending time with Jolly instead of her.

Rodney: What? Are you serious right now?

Ondray: Yes! She thought because I didn't come home by the time I said I would that I was with Jolly. She assumed that I would jump up and run away shortly after it ended, so the 40 minutes I was late from outside talking to you she assumed I was with Jolly.

Rodney: Man, that's crazy.

Ondray: Listen, I am not saying your lady is that way, but if you plan to be with her until she "gets there" with you, you may have to walk on a few eggshells to keep the peace. She is not going to change, relax or trust you overnight. She sounds like Reginae from a few years ago, with me. If so, I can tell you she will get angry if you can't give her an exact record of your whereabouts. If you listen to me and heed what I am saying to you, you will be able to manage and deal with her until she trusts you.

Rodney: Okay man, what should I do and look out for until she calms down and trusts me?

Ondray: Watch for signs and defuse them quickly. Okay, listen, some women suffer from irrational fears not just over what YOU may do but more about what the other woman may do to get you to go home with her. She doesn't trust any other woman around you, and she feels if they "put it on" you hard enough you will give in, drop her and get with the other woman and in the process, hurt her.

She may come across as being very suspicious of who you're talking to, even if it is innocent. A jealous person could do more damage than good if they were to violate your privacy. Petty suspicions can kill trust in a relationship. Because she is insecure and has yet to deal with it, you'll find that she will go through your things, your mail and even your phone looking to see who you are talking to and what you've said in your text messages to others as if she's getting paid to do it.

Every time your phone rings or a text message comes in, and it doesn't show who it is coming from, she will fear it is someone reaching out to you for a hookup or that they are up to no good. She may even, if you don't answer right away, believe YOU'RE up to no good.

Rodney: Damn, Dray. You've got me afraid to do anything around her if she isn't involved.

Ondray: Remember, you are dealing with a woman who has trust issues, and telling her straight out can and will seem to her as if you're trying to hurt her. Her behavior may seem intense, and even the smallest things such as having a conversation will seem forced at times.

Rodney: What do you mean?

Ondray: When I called you a few weeks ago about getting together to watch the football game, I heard her in the background asking you who you were talking to. After you hung up, did she act a little strange even after you told her it was me on the phone?

Rodney: Now that I think about it, she did. I couldn't put my finger on it at first, and I soon after ignored it. She did seem for that evening, as if she had something on her mind. We still went out and had a good time. I remember asking her what was bothering her, and I remember her answering me and saying "nothing." A few minutes later, I asked again, and it led to us arguing about something unrelated. Until you brought it up, I had forgotten about it and thought no more of it.

Ondray: See what you learn when you think about it and see the signs? Women like this wonder why a guy pulls away. When he does, she blames him for not being able to deal with or handle a real woman like her instead of thinking she may have been the reason for him backing off. Here is what I suggest you do when you have some time IF you decide to stay with, invest in her and build a future with her.

Rodney: What would that be? Dray, let me get some paper. I didn't expect to be writing down a list of things. I just hoped you had a quick fix to my issues with her.

Ondray: Well, you know you are my boy, and I'm going to keep it 100 with you, if you feel she is worth it. You ready?

Rodney: Yeah, I'm ready.

Ondray: Listen, you cannot lie to yourself.

If you feel like when you two are together that her jealousy or her behavior makes you feel on edge instead of happy, you might want to rethink your decision. Remember this:

1. If you feel emotionally drained just thinking about having another pointless argument over something that is yet to happen, she may not be the one for you.

2. If you are planning to stay and work through Michele's jealousy, you need to acknowledge and be direct with her on what you're feeling. When she responds, listen carefully and be courteous to what she says and respond to what she said before continuing with any other concerns.

Your goal is not to talk or respond as if you are accusing her of anything. You're trying to take the pressure off her of what she may be feeling concerning the direction of your relationship. By doing this, it doesn't make her think you are directing anything towards her, and you are saying without saying, that you're not blaming her for anything. Ask questions, but allow her to bring up her faults.

Rodney: What if she doesn't?

Ondray: Then shift the focus off of "her" and make it about how you feel about her. Tell her she is who you want, and how happy she's made you. Reassure her that you want the relationship to work. By doing this, it will allow her the opportunity to see, hear and feel you are with her in this no matter what. You are making it easier for her to open up and share more with you. Ask her if she feels the same about you. Tell her you are in a "good place" with her, and you want to have a real chance for the relationship to grow.

Rodney: Man, it sounds like I have the problem and not her. How do I get her to understand that "she" has an issue with her jealousy and that IT alone right now, is what is keeping us from knowing if we are meant to be together?

Ondray: I know it sounds like it's all your fault and that you are putting out a lot to get her to see her faults, but think of it this way. By being open about your fears and concerns, it encourages her to do the same. By her understanding the things that bother you, it makes it harder for her, if she is truly into you, to keep hiding from you.

Rodney: So, I hear the do's and I know you have a few don'ts, tell me what you think.

Ondray: Okay, first, in trying to minimize her behavior. And understand, I am not saying you have done anything to make her feel she should be suspicious of things you do when you are with her but this is to cut down on the confusion in how she interprets your actions.

Do not:

1. Compare her to any other woman you know, have seen or feel is attractive, this includes actresses from television/movies. The reason why is because you don't want her to feel she is competing with any other woman for YOUR attention. It puts a lot of pressure on her to live up to an image she's created in her head. It will keep her on edge in the relationship and feeling unwanted or desired by you.

2. When dealing with other women in her presence, limit your conversation with them. Be careful not to seem as if you are paying more attention to them then her. A move like this isn't right, and it will make her feel as if she is just in your life and not your life.

3. Although we all would like to see a few new looks or changes in our mates, how we ask them or tell them about what we love is a primary key in getting it done. What you don't want to do is make her feel you don't accept her, flaws and all. Remember, we all have our

tendencies, weaknesses and fears. For the most part, being accepted with all our faults is what we want. Simple things like changing our look, our style of clothes, losing weight, etc. can be done if we don't make our mates feel that when we ask, we are secretly wishing that they were someone else. Be careful. Trying to change your woman into your fantasy can hurt her feelings because she will think you don't like her the way she is.

4. Knowing how jealous Michele she is, she will purposely look at another woman when she is with you. She may have a jealous streak but she is not stupid. She will see through your game. It would make her feel more on edge with you if you did this because all she sees is that you are looking at other women. Information such as this could push her down the road of cheating with someone who makes her feel "wanted" and "desired" if you keep that mess up.

Remember, we all get a little jealous sometimes about many things. The key is that during this process, do not focus on or make our flaws the end-all to our happiness in our relationship. It is the flaws that make us who we are and learning to deal with them and exploring them helps bring couples together to form a solid foundation of what they have and will have more of down the road.

Rodney: Man, every time I ask you something like this, you give me homework to do, but I've got to say, your advice is always on point. I appreciate the free consultation. It was worth the cost of the meal. What are you going to do for the rest of the day when you leave here?

Ondray: Well, I am going home to continue to work on the message I will be giving at the **Men's Ministry Conference** coming up in October, you should come and check it out.

Rodney: That would be cool. Hit me up with the information, date and time, and I will be there. Alright, again thanks for coming out.

Ondray: No problem. Remember to take things slow and not judge her. Talk to her.

It is Sunday, October 13, 2019, the day of the conference. I go on in just a few minutes after the other speaker. I am glad Greg called me. I reworked my message. Now I had enough time to get into it.

Greg is speaking: Good evening. I hope everyone has enjoyed themselves so far today. Our next and last speaker of the evening is a personal friend of mine. He has his radio show on K103 here in Atlanta. He is a published author with a new book out entitled ***Why Does Love Hurt So Good?*** It is my pleasure to introduce to you, Mr. Ondray Pearson. Let's show him some love.

Ondray is speaking: Let me first thank Greg Hogan for inviting me this evening. As a Follower of Christ, I am honored to be here. The message I will be sharing with you this evening is entitled *Manhood: As it applies to Love, Life and Relationships*. Before I begin, let us pray:

Dear Lord, I ask that you guide me as I deliver this message this evening. I pray the message fills those listening with the understanding of your Word, for we all need to know your glory and how without you, there is no us. In your Son's name, we pray, amen!

I feel my message is important to share because there are men in relationships that still aren't sure "what their role is in their relationship." What I am sharing I am not implying I have all the answers or that I am perfect. I do believe though that you will find my perspective and views on everyday situations in relationships most interesting. I plan to define, explain and answer questions through both scriptures and my opinions to ensure you get a clear understanding of:

(1) What a man's role is in the relationship, (2) What his duties are according to scripture, (3) The reason why God created man first, (4) What a man's *purpose* is, (5) Why sometimes you encounter detours in your life on your way to your *destiny* and what they mean, (6) Why having a *plan and vision* in your relationship is so important, (7) Why the greatest gift God has given you isn't your *sight* but your *vision*, (8) Why so-called *good guys* finish last, (9) The difference between your *work* and your *job*, (10) What is a virtuous woman? What is her role and why it is vital and much needed for success in your relationship? (11) The choices men and women have to choose from and why it's hard for them to find that *good* man, and lastly, (12) Why reading the Bible and having a relationship with God first is the only way to get and keep your marriage in alignment.

My message aims to begin the process of undoing or reversing ideas and concepts that have been programmed in your mind concerning marriage by our society. Between religious statements and church doctrines, many of you have been conditioned to believe things about marriage that aren't true. You have been programmed to reject things you don't already know. Many of our men today are so confused that many are not sure what is real, factual, spiritual or historically correct as it relates to scriptures on marriage. I am hoping that after tonight when you leave here you will have a better understanding of what the Bible says about marriage vs what you've learned concerning "your role" in your relationship.

As you can see, we have a lot to talk about this evening, so let's get to it. Let me ask those men who are married and those looking to get married a few questions. When you hear the words *Provider, Head of Household,* and *Kingdom Man,* what do these words mean to you? When you decided to get married and said, "I do," were you aware of the duties and requirements of a husband? Were you aware that having a successful marriage started with you?

I don't expect any of you to answer these questions right now, but for those who are unable to answer them, it is okay, I will answer tonight. I feel many of you are scratching your head, wondering why I ask these questions. Listen, *we don't know what we don't know*, meaning, no one knows everything, but we all know a little bit about something. It's no secret, having *a plan and a vision* and sharing it with your mate makes your relationship congruent. George Washington Carver once said, "Where there is no *vision*, there is no hope." In other words, if you have no idea what or where you want to go or know how you're going to get there, why do anything at all? Listen, for those who don't know, start where you are and with what you have (meaning an idea) and make something of it. Your plan, in other words, is the *direction* you are leading your family.

Now write this down, for a woman to follow you willingly, and understand, many women have no problem following a righteous man in Christ, but to do so, they must feel secure and confident that you can lead. Unfortunately, this is an area most men struggle with at times, not knowing it is essential to the growth of your relationship. I know it's hard, but men need to understand good women will endure with you, if you have a plan and they see where you're going. They know and understand the difference between *endurance* and *ignorance*, so don't play them short. Write this down. *Endurance* for her means that she recognizes that as a couple you may hit a few bumps in the road and even may have to alter your route taken, and it is okay, if you continue to the destination. *Ignorance*, on the other hand, as she sees it, is you telling her you are unable to "Practice what you've preached" or follow through with what you told her, making following you pointless. If she doesn't know where you are going, why would she follow you?

Now your *vision* you see from your lips to her ears is your *purpose with pictures,* your *road map* of your *finished* future. Your *vision* helps ensure you stay on point to get where you're going. From her view, she has a "destination," and even if there are variations, she has a clue of what you're trying to achieve for your family. You can see this in **Joel 2:28-29**, (KJV), where it says **28** - "And it shall come to pass afterward, that I will pour out my spirit upon all flesh; and your sons and your daughters shall prophesy, your old men shall dream dreams, your young men shall see visions." and, **29** - "And also upon the servants and upon the handmaids in those days will pour out of my spirit."

Here where it says, "old men shall dream dreams; your young men shall see visions," it is telling the difference between the two people. In this passage, when it says old men dream "dreams," it is telling you they've seen their past. They know what has already happened or something they wish they could relive. When it says "a young man shall see visions," it is saying the younger men see themselves, where they are going, in other words, their future. To put it another way, they are chasing their dreams to make them a reality. Don't get it twisted. Your vision doesn't become real to you until it is written down and spoken into existence by you. You see when you talk it into "existence," it means you believe in what you are saying. Saying it out loud gives you the confidence and self-discipline you need to achieve it, and writing it down confirms what you see for your life.

When you have a vision for your life, you must be careful who you tell it to because not everyone sees or cares about what you're doing. There is no need to get upset if who you shared your vision with doesn't understand. You need to realize it is not anyone else's job to get excited about your dreams. The only way you would get upset is if you are telling your vision to gain acceptance of others and not because you believe in what you're saying. If you don't believe in yourself, you will allow those you are telling and hanging with to influence the direction you take in your life without even knowing it.

Listen, we all know if you hang around positive people, positive things will follow you, and if you hang around negative people who are doing harmful things, there is a good chance you will emulate that behavior and view it as normal and okay to do. When you hang around men who aren't driven as you are, who don't support your vision, they can and will slow down your momentum; even stop you from completing what you see as your future. Not everyone is strong enough or convicted of their vision, and for those who accept their present as the future, they can be swayed very quickly and not even know it. If this continues to happen over time, your actions of "not completing" things becomes normal and acceptable to you as though it is the way things are supposed to be.

Listen and write this down. You block your momentum and your ability to move forward with every incomplete promise, commitment or agreement you fail to keep. The worst thing you can do is not complete a task you start. When you don't finish what you start, you make it return to you for you to do over again. This keeps you from moving forward. When you do this, it makes you question what you saw for yourself and if it was really for you. Don't fault your friends or family for not seeing what you see for yourself, it's not their fault. They, with their eyes, are looking through their current sight, not their future vision.

It says in **Habakkuk 2:2-3**, (KJV), **2** - "And the Lord answered me, and said, Write the vision, and make it plain upon tables, that he may run that readeth it. **3** - "For the vision is yet for an appointed time, but at the end, it shall speak, and not lie: though it tarry, wait for it; because it will surely come, it will not tarry." In other words, for anyone to understand what you're saying or doing that involves them, you must be clear. The point I am making is this: If you are in a relationship with someone and have no idea of where you're going, you don't have to worry. They will gladly take you everywhere "they" want you to go. As the man, you should be the one driving the car not riding in the passenger seat. As the man, if you're a passenger in your relationship right now, you cannot complain if your mate takes you somewhere you don't want to go. By not leading, you've told them it is okay.

It says in **2 Corinthians 5:7**, (KJV), "(For we walk by faith, not by sight :). In other words, "we need to believe before we see, not see first to believe." If we believe in God and feel that He will bless us, then we should do as the scripture says and not question Him. Listen and understand. I believe God has a plan for your life, a destiny for your life, a place He wants you to be, a purpose for your existence and a purpose He wants you to fulfill. You being here right now is necessary because He has something He wants you to do. His *purpose* for you is the source of your *vision*. Your *vision* is your reason and *purpose* that helps drive you to where He saw you when he first created you. In short, your *vision* shows you what could be (meaning your future), and your *sight* shows you what is (meaning your present). Does this make sense?

The problem why so many so-called Christians struggle with God's instructions is because they view them as mere suggestions, something they can or cannot follow. God wrote his instructions of what He wanted us to do and how we were to act in our lives. Many of us however, want to have one foot in the world and one foot in heaven. It makes it hard for us to stay disciplined to Him. When those who want to "do their own thing" and call it biblical not scriptural, they will say the reasons why they are doing things their way is because we all interpret the Word differently. These are no more than willing excuses to remain in the "world" and stay lost and misinformed. Being unwilling to accept God's Word as it is written and reluctant to make any changes because they desire to be in the world, this is not God's Word.

Another way to look at it would be many people do not want to know God's Truth because by not knowing, it continues to give them free will to do wrong and claim they didn't know. It is sad because many who do this are telling and showing God that they are not as dedicated to Him as He would like them to be. It says that they are okay with it. It gives them more of an excuse not to do right. Many know once they are exposed to the Truth, doing wrong is no longer acceptable to God. If, following the Word conflicts with their current lifestyle, they will give as their reason to not do right, "God knows my heart," as if that is a perfect excuse to use for their foolishness.

It's not a onetime deal. It happens all the time. People do this to avoid "knowing" the truth. Telling God, "Bless me and excuse all the wrong things I know I am doing because I am a good person at heart" is not going to be acceptable to Him. These actions and behaviors say you want God to adjust to you, not you adjust to Him. Do you believe God would write a Bible for you to follow and then say, "Don't worry about what I wrote. You do what you want and I will follow along?" No, I don't think so.

This incorrect interpretation continues to be perpetuated today by many of our Pastors saying, "The Bible was written for those in their times. We're in different times and must adapt the Bible to our times." These would be men who *work* for companies telling them point-blank to misdirect people so that they will accept and believe what their being told is God's Truth when it's not. Pastors doing this are willingly leading them to hell on the A-train. They know it is not God's way to mislead or direct them from His Word, the Word of the Bible. God doesn't expect us to take His words literally because something doesn't apply or may be harder to do, but He isn't, on the other hand, going to allow you to do whatever you want and still cover you. He will forgive us if we make mistakes because He is a forgiving God, but He is not a fool. People who are living their life their way are under the impression that "the word repent means to repeat" and it doesn't. Are you telling me that you cannot show up or call on your job (and not give a real reason why you didn't show up) and still expect to have a job?

Yes, we all have read that God is a merciful person. You think we can keep playing with Him, and He will continuously allow us to do this without any consequences to our actions? I don't think so. We cannot consistently do the opposite of what He asks of us, by having one foot in the world and the other toward heaven and assume even though we know it's not right, He will always forgive us. Scripture says if this is so, He will allow us to go on our own and "do us," but He will also make way for us to return to Him to receive His blessings but a change in us is required. Do we think He is unaware of what we are doing? Do you consider adjusting His words is following in the footsteps of our Lord in Christ? Changing and following the "worldly ways" is not the same as following in the footsteps of our Lord in Christ. Either you are trying to live your life politically correct or you're living biblically correct, you can't do both. As men, changing how we think and being open to advice is a good thing. As men and leaders following the word of God, we must "believe before seeing" not see before we believe.

If you can only do for God after He shows and does for you, then you do not believe in Him. You just want Him to give you something or help you out of a tough time. Belief such as this is not "faith," it's foolishness. If this is your train of thought, keep thinking this way and you will be waiting for a long time for help that may never come. Listen and write this down. It is when God knows we believe in Him that He shows us our purpose and guides us to and through it. When we do the opposite, the devil can enter in and mess with us by filling our head with doubts. The reason he would mess with you like this is that he has taken a look into your future and has seen how God has ordered your steps and all the things He is about to bring us into and bless us. He is doing his best to prevent this from happening. We have to show patience and wisdom to prevent Satan from messing up our blessings.

It says in **Proverbs 17:24**, (KJV), "Wisdom is before him that hath understanding, but the eyes of a fool are in the ends of the earth." **Proverbs 12:15**, (KJV), "The way of a fool is right in his own eyes: but he that hearkeneth unto counsel is wise." In other words, "listening" can benefit you. Listening and taking advice can be wise of you sometimes. Understand something. You do not waste your time correcting a fool because they will hate you. If you correct a wise person, they will appreciate you. Write this down. Constructive criticism is made to improve. You should always welcome it. The reason most men don't listen is that they view advice or criticism of any kind as you're telling them they don't know or understand a situation. They have yet to understand the difference between helping and hurting. Listen, because this is true. You will never be criticized by someone who is doing more than you. Only those who are doing less than you, will criticize you.

All men need to understand this fact, "A man's greatest strength in his development in his relationship is the encouragement of his woman." The woman God put in your life is put there to be to you a "helpmeet." He put her in your life at that moment because He knew she had something that you needed to be successful in the relationship, but most men never see her in their life this way. Listen, because this is important. God "equipped" her with gifts, and it is these "gifts" that will help us, not hurt us, if they are used correctly, but only if we recognize them. A long-lasting relationship consists of compromising, negotiating, adapting and making changes "if" we want it to grow.

Does anybody remember the movie *Why did I get Married?* Do you remember the scene where the guys were talking about the "80/20" rule in a relationship? It was Gavin (played by Malik Yoba) who mentioned, "We're only going to get 80% of what we need in our relationship. It is when we start to think we're missing something that we want that other 20%. Not knowing that when we make that choice to try and get that 20%, we end up losing the 80% we had that we needed in the first place. You will not realize your mistake until after the fact."

I took this to mean, and this applies to both men and women, many of those who engage in this type of behavior are those who are willing to gamble their whole relationship for a moment of pleasure. Creating a situation or excuse if you will, to cheat instead of working out the issues to save the "relationship," this is a selfish person making decisions without any consideration or thought to the consequences of "how" much they will hurt their mate. For the moment in their mind, it's all about their pleasures and not their relationship. It's sad but real, and it happens a lot. Don't get me wrong. Many of us have done things we regret, but willingly and often hurting those we say we love isn't a mistake. It is intentional.

Listen and write this down. All successful relationships need "good soil" to grow spiritually. In **Luke 8:4-16**, (KJV), Our Lord in Christ tells a parable of the farmer scattering seed, and how God's Word can sprout even in rocky or thorny soil. This parable can also apply to our relationships. In **Luke 8:15**, (KJV), it says, "But that on the good ground are they, which in an honest and good heart, having heard the word, keep it, and bring forth fruit with patience." You see, whenever the soil is right, meaning the foundation you start with, a good friendship, honesty, open communication, your relationship will flourish both physically, emotionally and spiritually. Whenever your soil is bad, meaning you start out planting lies, deceit and distrust, your relationship will fail and produce bad fruit. In other words, if we feed our relationship with positive things, build on a good foundation from the start, it will grow and be what you hope it would be.

To do this, we must, while building this foundation, make better choices and consequences. We must, mostly men, must think through the results before making the decision we make. Most men will go through with their choice without considering the consequences of their actions. They end up gambling their relationship that took a while to establish for a momentary pleasure. This indicates they do not value what they have with their mate or their mate enough to avoid the temptation. This is because at that moment they don't appreciate what they have or care if they lose it. When we no longer see what we have is not worth losing, then it is not worth saving.

Believe me when I say, "The grass is *not* always greener on the other side."

Strangely enough this behavior helps explain why some women are attracted to "bad boys," why so-called *good* men finish last, why men and women cheat on one another so freely and often think nothing of the hurt they've caused each other and why so many women with kids aren't married.

Many women have said they are attracted to "bad boys" because they bring a little much needed edge to the relationship. They believe that some bad boys make them feel a bit more protected, in some cases. Some said they are better sex partners because they are more sexually aggressive in the bedroom, and some women say they like it when a man takes charge in the bedroom. Many have said, "They want a little thug in their life. They want their man to be a little rough with them at times." This is understandable because we want what we want.

So-called *good* men, on the other hand, many women say are often boring. Many women have said *good guys* finish last, and some aren't even considered to be in the race because they have been labelled *simps.* These friendly guys are seen to be weak and dull in many women's eyes because they place or treat the woman they want to be with respectfully. Other men look at these men catering to these women, telling them they're beautiful, liking their photos on Facebook, Instagram, etc., giving them compliments as *simps,* weak ass men. These men make our job (those who are disrespecting them) easy to attract and sleep with a woman because they know "these kinds of women" aren't attracted to them. In a way, they are correct. Women like this will waste their entire youth chasing a man who doesn't want them, doesn't want to be with them, who treats them like crap, seek that validation of acceptance from them and this is crazy. "Seeking men who don't want them, instead of seeking men who will adore and love them."

It's not because they are not attracted to them, it's more because they're being given what they want and expect and it is not challenging to them. Many like the challenge of trying to get the guy to provide them with respect and validation. I know those women reading this can't believe a woman would sink so low as to chase a man who doesn't want them, but many have and still do.

Don't get confused. There is a difference between the *good guy* and the *simp*. The good guy pursues the woman for a purpose which most of the time is for sex. The *simp* wants a relationship with them. Many want it so much that they will sit back, wait and watch the woman they want go through countless encounters with other men as they run through her like the Harlem tunnel, treat her like crap and disrespect her. They will be there when she needs a shoulder to cry on, all hoping that she sees them as the person she should get with in a long-term relationship.

She, however, has labeled him her "Use in case of an emergency," man. She will only use him that way when the other men show they don't want her. When she does "get with" him and sleep with him, she sees the whole encounter as mercy sex, not love. Afterward, she will ask herself, "Why did I do this?" Most times, the reasons why she would do it and get involved with him is for financial and security purposes because many see them as being more stable, dependable, and reliable. Most said they would still cheat on this guy, even though they have provided them with all they requested just because they can. These are the same women who would say if he did it to her that he was wrong or a dog.

Don't get it twisted. Many of the men who called this kind of man *simp* are jealous. Jealous because many of them who are considered simps can afford it, and don't mind it. Men who aren't able to financially do what the simps can, point them out, make fun of them but deep down, for the most part, they wish they could afford to be one. Successful people with a lot of money can attract the most attractive women in the world. Those with a little money or who make good money can attract beautiful women but those with "short" money can only attract women who the other men don't want. So, if you are paying more attention to those men who you refer to as simps, then even though you may get the girl over them, you are concerned enough about them to talk about them and make them relevant to some women.

Studies show women in their 20s and 30s have a different definition of a *good* man, but it changes as they get older (around their 40s). Good guys are respectful. They treat women right, give them attention, compliment them often and bend over backwards to please them. They give and ask no questions, all to show her she is valued and loved by him. They are not known to dominate their relationship, but they are not a pushover either. They see and treat the woman as an equal. Sad to say though, these same guys are the first ones to be used, taken advantage of, disrespected, talked loudly to in front of others, run over and controlled in the relationship. They never get the last word in an argument and get cheated on. The mess-up part of this is that even if the woman doesn't love him, she will stay because he has resources she wants and needs.

Good guys lose out to bad boys because they give the woman what she asks for without a fight, and many women don't find that attractive. A good guy gets ignored when they compliment a woman. You see most good guys who approach the relationship drama have not figured out that most women need "drama" daily like a crackhead needs a hit. Many will fight for "drama" (after they claim that they don't want it) as if they are getting paid to do so. In most cases, good guys are not prepared for this and end up losing the woman.

Many see this behavior as "normal." Chasing men to get them to validate them and to get their acceptance is challenging to them and worth wasting their youth. For some, this disrespect is exciting and something they need as much as the air they breathe to function daily. They will create it if it doesn't naturally happen. They end up getting with a guy who puts up with it for a while and getting used like a two-dollar whore and calling it love. I am amazed at how many women are willing to endure being disrespected and treated like crap. They're loyal to someone who shows them hardly any attention. They think their mission is to get him to compliment and validate them and will put up with this kind of treatment for years even if it kills them, which is just stupid.

For whatever reasons the attracted good guy who compliments them, gets rejected. These same women's attitudes and needs change as they get older. Looking for men who are stable, reliable, and somewhat predictable is the new goal. Even if the sex isn't mind-blowing, it is more important to be in a financially secure relationship. Being with someone who loves you is better than being alone and unhappy worrying about how they are going to take care of themselves. A lot of men who are with these women refuse to compliment their woman or give them the attention they crave. They use the "compliments" every so often like they are distributing a drug to them, when they want something from them and to keep them in line and around. By not giving her this simple compliment, she will continue to stay and fight to get it.

She needs him to validate her existence in their relationship. Now, some would say these kinds of women have low self-esteem, and this may be true, but, sadly, a person who would subject themselves to this kind of treatment to be with someone when some men who they are attracted to are seeking them is hard to understand. Even if he cheats on her, she will find or create a reason to stay and will forgive the guy as long as he says something sweet to them. I am not saying all women allow this, but there are enough who do it for me to be able to talk about it. Their view drastically changes once they reach their late 30s and early 40s after being mistreated by those so-called bad boys. Many start to question their choice. They wonder "what if" they would have taken the good guy? What would their life have been like? To many women, the "bad boy" is a "good guy" to them.

They've stated that there are benefits to dating the "bad boy" but feel "good guys" come with more unlimited resources that long term, they want and need to survive. Many times, and in some situations, once the thrill of being with a bad boy wears off, these women realize they have two or more kids (by 2 or 3 men,) and their beauty has faded. They now need this bad boy to be more responsible but very few are.

Women I have spoken to have told me that many of them are with good men they don't love or much like, but because they have the financial resources to take care of them, they can tolerate them. The sad part about it is that many of these "good men" they are with have no idea (some do and don't care) the woman with them is only with them to fulfill their wants and needs, not his. They have no idea that as long as she has a "need" for him, not love for him, she will keep him around. In other words, as long as she sees him as "useful," she will stay with him, but the moment he becomes "useless," she is gone without even saying goodbye. Men like this, to some women are no more than vehicles that carry them to their desired destination. If he fails in getting her where she wants to go, she will find another who will.

The reason for this is that today's modern woman has been seriously misguided and allowed her fear to guide her. Social media and television with shows like **Love and Hip Hop and Basketball Wives** have contaminated and brainwashed women into believing life is about getting "trinkets." Love has nothing to do with the interaction or relationship as they call it at all. Men who are looking for a woman to build with find it harder and harder because so many women today will bounce and or run from this guy, when they aren't ready or willing to "build with" (more like "take what they can get" from) the guy and then move on to the next man. It's the guy's fault in this situation because many know when they talk to these kinds of women what they want and are about but mess with them anyway. Many willing to play this game will *spend* on them, sleep with them and move on to the next one. The few good men seeking a good woman will look for her to build a life with her.

A lot of women have been made to believe all they have to bring to the table in a relationship is sex. Many will say, "They are looking for and want 'perfection' in their man when they aren't themselves." All they want is a man with status and resources, and if you noticed, I didn't say they want to be loved because again, love has nothing to do with this. Foolishly enough, some men are willing to take on these kinds of women (and some will marry them) hoping they have found love and thinking they have a "virtuous woman" the Bible speaks of which most don't. I will talk about what a "virtuous woman" is according to scripture a little later because you need to know what the characteristics of this woman look like to know you have a good woman.

As I was saying, these women who got with the bad boy and were played by him like a new deck of cards now want and seek out the good guys (simps) to fix their brokenness, provide them with their resources to raise someone else's children, and take on the responsibilities the other men wouldn't give her while she likes and disrespects him in more ways than he can count. He still isn't who she wants to be with. She still wants the other guy. She expects him to pay for things (sex) when she has spent years giving them away for free. She expects him to take care of her and the children, feed them, cloth them, cover them medically, etc. but the moment he tries to discipline the children he is taking care of, she will quickly remind him, "These aren't your children, and you can't discipline them. Only I and their father can."

At the same time, this good fool who is "the one" providing a roof over them all, feeding them, covering them all medically, going to all the children's school events, helping them with their homework, doing the family thing cannot discipline because they aren't his children. Listen, any man can be a father, but it takes a real man to be a dad. Men have told good guys to be careful and not to be a simp for these women. They've been told not to marry these women with kids unless they are prepared to use ALL their resources to raise someone else's children with no benefits. They say this because in the event the woman ends up leaving the relationship after so many years, it will hurt. He has built a bond with the children and loves them and yet, he has NO legal rights to stay in contact with them if she decides he can't.

Some women will stay with the guy and cheat on him with the kids' father or someone else because she doesn't want to be in the relationship, but it has financial benefits. The sad part of this situation is that many of these men, who find themselves in this trap, care for her, but she doesn't care for him. Even if he spoils her, treats her right, she will always see him as being weak, dull and easy to use. Women like these can't be trusted. Listen, you've heard women say they measure a man's character and believe more in his actions than his words. That's fair but at the same time, when he shows her all she claimed she needed to see, she needs to do him right, but many don't. To make it fair across the board, men should treat women in the same sense. Trust their actions, not their words because women can spin a good lie also.

Some women feel and believe that good guys are stupid, desperate and lonely enough to take on extra baggage, both emotional and low self-esteem issues, financial issues and colossal debt that she accumulated with other men to have love in her life — thinking that she is doing them a favor by allowing him the opportunity to fix her problems. These women know the beauty they have relied on for so long has faded and their opportunities to attract that bad boy to take care of them has disappeared. So, they look for that simp or good fool, sorry I meant to say good man, as their means of still having that good life.

You know you have met one when you've heard one say, "Where have all the good men gone?" Assuming there aren't any left or they are married. By this time, they are probably right. Most of them have found other good women who saw the potential in them and married them. The question is why are they now looking for this good guy? Now that they are worn out, used up, and run through by Tyrone, Chad and John when they overlooked them years before? What makes them think they deserve a "good guy" like that now later in life? I'll tell you. They need someone to take care of them financially.

Now don't get me wrong I am talking to you mainly about your character. I am not talking about a "right or wrong" situation. I'm talking about "choices and consequences." Men can no longer make choices and be careless about the consequences afterwards. They need to "think" before they act on something they are considering doing, and contemplate for a moment, the consequences of their actions. Many of the choices we make in our lives, including those we choose to be in a relationship with, often determine our path in life.

Some of the options are good, and some are not, hence the phrase, "live and learn." The sad truth about this phrase is as it applies to relationships, most times more women end up with the short end of the stick than do men. Write this down. It's essential. Fact: Women today are tired of meeting and getting with broken, lying and lazy men who continuously make promises they know when said, they are not going to keep. Women in this age range can no longer afford to rescue men. Women cannot continually be unexplainably loyal to them, to the point it causes their downfall, to show them that they have value in society. A lot of times, these women with so-called bad boys get involved and waste a lot of their time and loyalty to men who will drop them for a younger woman in a heartbeat for no reason other than it's just what they want to do.

Men today put women in compromising positions in their lives at times, positions they really can't afford to be in and the men don't care. Men promising to show them a good time but who are using them financially. Many don't realize it at the time because everything seems so exciting, but as time goes on, they realize it is no fun being that woman he calls when he needs a place to crash or needs to borrow money. He makes her feel like it's her job to save him.

Now, for those who follow the Bible, they know it says a man is supposed to take care of the woman, not the other way around. Listen, good women seeking good men know they are worth protecting, worthy of being treated like the queen they are but more importantly, (but only a few learn this early on), they deserve to be loved not used. Some women get this early on, but for many, it takes years and much heartache before they realize this. I am not saying if you date a bad boy, you're doomed. I am saying studies have shown that many women waste their youth with these guys and then seek so-called good guys. They are not realizing it until later that they often have allowed their 20-year-old self mess up their 40-year-old self by their choices and consequences made during that time.

The fact is, boys who grow up with their father as their role model see firsthand "how" they treat their mother and tend to model their behavior and treat the woman they get with the same way both good and bad. They learn how to respect, hold doors open for women, provide for them, protect, love them, mistreat them, hurt them, etc. Boys who grow up in a broken home don't have that person to "show" or "teach" them what it means to be a man or how to treat a woman in a relationship, so, they end up teaching themselves and learning from friends, television or music on how they should treat women and most times, it never shows the woman's worth or value.

Women growing up with no father figure in the home watch their dad (or men in their lives) mistreating their mother and so she tends to believe it is normal. Not having that fatherly love, they search for it in the world and most times they seek it in the "bad boy" first before the so-called "good man" because they represent the closest image to what they grew up seeing. For many, the good guy doesn't get noticed right away because they have never seen them before. Now with all this said, this doesn't let guys doing this off the hook. Men can't continue to blame and use the way their woman is acting out as their excuse not to provide. Many of you need to understand that a woman's greatest fear is getting played by the very person she is loyal to.

Listen, this is important. A person doesn't abandon someone they love. They abandon those they are using. Men cannot feel like real men who women should respect if they are acting like they are the woman in the relationship. Let me be clear, "No man in a relationship should ever feel comfortable 'living off' a woman and allowing her to take care of him when he can work." Many women have thought about it and felt there was a reason why so many men aren't behaving as real Christian men should, why men treat women the way they do and blame them for their shortcomings. There is a reason why "men" are unable to be the kind of men God intended them to be in their relationship. There is a reason why there are so many men still angry, upset, confused, lost and struggling to regain their identity, their purpose, their direction and getting respect from their woman and being acknowledged. The answers for these actions aren't things that happen by accident or by chance. It is done by design.

It says in **Proverbs 16:27**, (KJV), "An ungodly man diggeth up evil: and in his lips, there is a burning fire." Meaning they always use the past to explain the moment. **Proverbs 27:5-6**, (KJV), 5- "Open rebuke is better than secret love." 6- "Faithful are the wounds of a friend; but the kisses of an enemy are deceitful." Meaning you need to take accountability for the things you say and do. Apologize for your actions and make the correction, don't blame your mate for your inabilities when you're wrong. **Proverbs 19:11** (KJV), "The discretion of a man deferreth his anger; and it is his glory to pass over a transgression." Meaning as the man, you need to know how to put your anger aside and be the leader. **Colossians 2:8** (KJV), "Beware lest any man spoil you through philosophy and vain deceit, after the tradition of men, after the rudiments of the world, and not after Christ." Meaning you should not allow this world's behavior dictate the way you handle your relationships. God said men need to be men and provide for their family and not force the woman to do it.

Here is why I say this. The world we live in has changed, and women's views on what a real man should look like have changed also. Many women no longer believe they must depend on a man to be successful or to have the things they want or feel they require anymore. It's hard for some women to believe in men when they can see so many men don't believe in themselves. As long as there are still a few women who will give lying, no good, child acting, no plan having, visionless, game playing, non-bill paying, momma's boys, money begging, no job having men a second chance and the benefit of the doubt, they will never change their ways. It is crazy to think or wonder after the fact, how did they get stuck with such a person.

Listen to me. This system in America has glorified the woman and devalued the man. In giving women Food Stamps and Section 8 housing, it has devalued the man's role in the relationship down to a point where the woman doesn't need them for anything — taking away the man's purpose as the provider. Women in this position don't respect their man, and see him as a child they are taking care of, if he is living with her and bringing nothing to the table.

It says in **Jeremiah 31:22**, (KJV), "How long wilt thou go about, O thou backsliding daughter? for the Lord hath created a new thing in the earth, A woman shall compass a man." In other words, God is asking men and women, how much longer will you repeat the same process in your life and continue to go nowhere before you will do right? It is talking about the men messing up the natural order of relationships by allowing the woman to lead. It's the man's fault that this is happening. It tells you this in **Proverbs 8:4,** (KJV), "Unto you, O men, I call; my voice is to the sons of men." that God is talking to the men and not the women.

Let's look at **Revelation 14:4,** (KJV), where it says, "These are they which were not defiled with women; for they are virgins. These are they which follow the Lamb whithersoever he goeth. These were redeemed from among men, being the firstfruits unto God and to the Lamb." God doesn't want you to trade places or roles in the relationship. He wants you, the man, to be the provider and run your household. You may think this is by accident, but it's not, it is by design. You are contributing and buying into the "worldly" ways and putting your relationship out of alignment.

These low-down men doing this seek weak-minded or inferior self-esteemed women who they feel they can control. These are the women who allow men to lie, trick and use them and once caught, they make excuses, claim they love them and the woman believes him, and lets him stay to continue to mess with her and break her spirit. These kinds of people I am talking about doing this are not men. They are boys pretending to be men. Real Christian men wouldn't rely on using a woman to be with them. Real men know the goal in their relationship as a couple is not to *think* alike but more about the two of you *thinking* together.

Think about that, a moment, and you will get it. Thinking alike doesn't mean you are thinking together. This is expressed in **Philippians 2:2,3,** (KJV), **2-** "Fulfil ye my joy, that ye be likeminded, having the same love, being of one accord, of one mind." **3-** "Let nothing be done through strife or vain glory; but in lowliness of mind let each esteem the other better than themselves." Meaning this "couple" growing in love must work as one. They must accept the roles God has assigned to them and not allow the "world's" perception of families to reverse them. It is the man's fault for this current "role reversal" and broken families. Although the woman is to blame some, mainly it's all on the men. We are the ones God chose to lead in our relationship, not follow.

If they knew Him and their role according to the Bible, they would not act this foolishly with their woman, nor would they want their woman to observe or experience this in the relationship. The scripture doesn't say anything "financially" about your woman splitting the bills "50/50." God assigned you the job of providing. It doesn't matter how much she earns, nor should you be concerned about what she does with it. You are the provider, not her. That's not her role according to the Bible. These men who are comfortable with allowing the woman to take care of them are not real men in any religion. Women call men like this "low down" and "no good," and I agree with them. I am not saying women who want to contribute shouldn't because real women would regardless, but it is their choice to do so, not a commandment of God.

It is sad when the woman is tricked by the man into thinking she should pay and do his job. I know some of you think I am a little hard on all men when it is just a few men doing this, but I disagree. God tells you it is your job to act right, treat your woman right and provide for your household. You read this in **1Timothy 5:8**, (KJV), where it says, "But if any provide not for his own, and especially for those of his own house, he hath denied the faith, and is worse than an infidel." in **2 Thessalonians 3:10**, (KJV), where it reads "For even when we were with you, this we commanded you, that if any would not work, neither should he eat." And in **1 Timothy 3:4,5** (KJV), **4** - "One that ruleth well his own house, having his children in subjection with all gravity;" **5** - "(For if a man know not how to rule his own house, how shall he take care of the church of God?)" In other words, men need to work and be the providers God intended them to be and not assume or rely on their woman to "take care of" them.

Christian men, don't get it twisted. Real Christian women read the Bible, and they have read for themselves what your role is. They are watching you closely to see if you are allowing Christ to rule you so that they can submit to you. It is hard for them to give you what you want of them when you're trying to switch roles with them. These kinds of men doing this don't understand that a woman cannot respect their man when they have to step up and do their part. They see you as useless. If you are one of those kinds of men doing this, how can you get mad at them when you don't want the responsibilities?

There are those men who get mad, and you hear say their woman is crazy, bossy and angry all because they failed to be the man in their relationship. This kind of thing is happening across the globe, and it is causing conflict in the home. Most men don't want the responsibilities of being a provider but can lay down with a woman and help create a child. "Weak men will say and use as an excuse saying, "Women want to be equal to a man and get paid like one, and so they should expect to be treated like one. The Bible says we're equal doesn't it?" Sure, in God's eyes, both men and women are equal, but in the marriage, you each have different functions and roles to perform.

Because the roles have been reversed, you hear the woman say to you when you ask her to do things your way, "My mother taught me this way" or "My dad told me I should do it this way." If men fulfilled their role in the marriage, this would not happen. Sure, everyone has opinions, but no one wants to argue daily on who is going to be the provider or head of the household and which one is to follow and who is the leader. Creating confusion in your house, the so-called leader (you) has been fired and replaced (by her), and you don't know how to get your job back. If God wanted the woman to be in charge over the household, He would have created her first and not you. She is supposed to "help" you, not do it for you. A home running this way makes you ask, "Who is the man in the family?"

It is no secret a woman's "position" in the home today has changed from what women were doing years ago. There are still homemakers, but now there are also more women doing duel duties than ever before, working and taking care of the home. The title, "Head of Household" has become just a title that no longer applies to the man only. Many women have been "forced" to assume the responsibilities of "Head of Household and the role of "breadwinner" not because they want to but because so many men have left them no choice. *A man without a plan, a vision or a purpose is useless to any woman.* I wouldn't blame any woman who looked at a man like this sideways calling himself a man when he isn't ready to take on the responsibilities of one. If this is happening in your home, it is a clear sign of the relationship being out of alignment of what God intended it to be. I will talk about *being out of alignment* a little later.

Men out here today who are having multiple children with multiple women and handing the woman a few dollars every so often thinking they are men and that they are "taking care of their responsibilities" are dead wrong. It makes them a deadbeat dad and a no-good man, undeserving of their kids calling him, daddy. Listen to what it says in **James 4:8**, (KJV), "Draw nigh to God, and he will draw nigh to you. Cleanse your hands, ye sinners; and purify your hearts, ye double minded." Let me explain it this way; this kind of action is seen by God as sin. It is this kind of "sin" that changes the course of the thing and the ideal intentions He has meant for your life. God wanted us to be married and to have children, not have children and hope one day to marry. Our goal, even if we sometimes fall short, is to be like God like it says in **Matthew 5:48**, (KJV), "Be ye therefore perfect, even as your Father which is in heaven is perfect."

Listen, being a father is not just about giving your kids money and presents. It is about being there, present, in the child's life. Being a part of and taking part in their lives as they're growing up makes a huge difference in the direction they take in their lives. You're supposed to be there to guide and keep them on "their" path to greatness. Stop being that man who lies to women, has children with them, never marries them, leaves them and your children and then gets mad at her when she "gets with" or finds a new man who ends up raising and supporting "your" children. They end up calling him daddy because he is the person they see every night before they go to bed, the person who attends their school events, and the person who takes them to the doctor when they need it. He's there when they need help with their homework and so much more that you miss out on because you have "other" children to pretend to take care of with other women.

It doesn't matter if you are her boyfriend or husband, if you are in a relationship with her, be the man and do what a man is supposed to do for his woman and family. Don't be the dad the child grows up searching for to find out why you were never around. If another man is fulfilling your role, step off and allow him to do it until you're able to become and play an active role in the child's life. Don't confuse them or make them choose between the biological dad and the person who is taking care of them. It is this kind of foolishness of men that have made the term "baby mamas and baby daddies" the norm among many people today. Now it is not all the man's fault. The woman plays a role in this also. The woman knows when she sleeps with a man if she should use protection to keep from having an unwanted child. They know they can prevent it from happening just like a man can. She allows it to happen "thinking" by having his child it will make him stay with her not knowing that 99.99% of the time it doesn't.

Women need to stop asking the question, "Why aren't men looking to marry them instead of just dating them?" The reason why this is, is simple. According to a recent study, it showed that 21% of white women get married as early as 22 years and start a family as opposed to 70% of black women who have children who are not married. In my opinion, women in general, who want to get married aren't because many of them are giving these so-called "boyfriends" "husband" benefits. In most men's eyes, this makes marrying you seem pointless to do because they are already getting what they wanted, which is sex without a "legal" commitment. They tell the woman who said she wanted to get married to "wait" and promise them that somewhere "down the road," they will get married. Sadly, most women believe this lie. Many women are looking to get married but have not found that "right one." They say they can't find any "good men," but this is not true because they are being found somewhere by someone and are marrying quickly.

Many women feel by giving them what they want makes them see them as "marriage material." Their thinking is that they will marry them soon after, but very rarely does this happen. A lot of women allowing this, seem or act confused and surprised, why, after sleeping with them, they are not rushing to marry them and take them off the market. Why would they? The women are confused and the men doing this to them are saying (without saying it) that they don't respect them because they don't respect themselves. Too many women think and believe if they have a child (or children) with the guy they're sleeping with, that it will settle him down, and he will eventually marry them.

These are the same unmarried women with kids by different men, thinking it is cute to be degraded by men. To make themselves feel less of a fool, they will say, "I didn't expect to marry him." These are the same ones up in church talking about and asking God to bring them a good man. It makes you wonder, "Why didn't they start and wait on God to present to them that man BEFORE they slept and had children with someone?"

They can't see how they are contributing to the vast abundance of young mothers having children out of wedlock. By not teaching them to wait for the right man, they continue to send the message through their actions that it is okay to sleep around and to have many babies by different men when it is not. They don't understand that their children emulate what they see in their household, and this goes for both men and women. If growing up, their dad loved and respected their mother. This is what they will try and "emulate" in their relationship. Seeing their married parents stay together and in love with one another gives them something to strive for in their relationship. However, growing up *not* seeing this, changes their views and understanding of how they should treat someone and how others should treat them. The young woman growing up without her father in the home lacks the love most fathers give their children. Fathers are many things to young women growing up. They are their dad, the first "man" she loves in her life; he is her first real male friend and a person she looks up to for protection. Her dad shows how others, especially young boys and years later grown men, should treat them.

For young men, their dads must be in their lives growing up. You see, although men who aren't around may leave their son for their ex's to raise, (and many do a damn good job), they cannot teach them how to be men. They can tell them all day long, but for many, they need to "see" or "hear" it from their fathers for it to resonate and stick. Some women recognize this and do their best to get the fathers to spend time with their son/s. They need their dads to show them how to respect and treat women. They need to explain to them "why" they should, and what their role is once they're in a relationship with a woman because they need to know how to relate to the opposite sex respectfully. Without the father in their lives to provide them with this practical information, they grow up taking what society, friends, the media and their surroundings say is "okay" in how they should treat a woman. Because they have never experienced love growing up, from their father, most are unable to express it to their mate, not because they don't want to but more because they aren't sure what it is, what it looks like or how to.

Now, this is important as the leader and provider of a family, if they have never "seen" what leadership looks like, how can they emulate it in their relationship? It is already hard to "be" a man in this America but even harder when you are playing a game and don't know the rules to survive, compete or win. Men need to know the basics of communicating with women to be able to relate in some way and not feel they don't belong. Too many men today are playing "tough," talking slick and "faking it until you make it" will limit what you make of your relationship because you do not "know" enough about what you are trying to accomplish.

They say "opposites attract" and I agree to a certain degree, but I also agree that if you get together with a person who has trouble relating or communicating in a relationship, you will not have one for long. The young man growing up seeing this image will think and believe that this is the kind of behavior HE should display. For those women in a "fatherless" situation, it is best if the women found their son a mentor, someone he can talk to and feel comfortable asking questions; someone he can respect and listen to the things that will help him. If not, they will grow up thinking disrespecting a woman is the norm.

Overall, it is the man's fault that this is happening because no doubt, in the beginning, he is filling her head with future promises for sex today, and she bought it (believed in what he told her). Why would I say this, you ask? I say this because God created you first, and as so-called Christian men, you have to be the one to break this unhealthy cycle. Listen, this generation has not been shown or taught because if they had been, it would seem not normal to "shack up" and create more broken families. However, this is not the case today. Over 69% of people today see no problem having a child with multiple men, shacking up and pretending to "be" married while waiting to get married. Too many women are sitting around waiting and believing AFTER getting what they want regularly, that this will be the one to "change" their situation, meaning, marry her. Why would they? They are getting the benefits of marriage without getting married, and since you (the woman) have no problem with it? Why would they? Men doing this are sending the message to young boys that, "It's okay to sleep around, have kids with many different women, leave them alone to raise your children on their own as you move to another woman and repeat the process."

Many men who are doing this, know if they can skate by and convince that woman not to file court papers for child support and wait it out long enough, some simp will show up and take care of HIS kids for him. He will be the guy who genuinely falls for this woman, accepts her problems, situations and issues and she, not being used to a guy like this, will mess it up with him by creating drama to make him leave AFTER he has used ALL his resources to support them all. Even though the ex is not the man she needs him to be, he is the one she wants. It doesn't matter how much the good guy does right. She doesn't feel he is right for her.

Listen to me. Men without fathers in their lives don't always make the best choices. Since they don't have that fatherly direction, some often choose other means to find what they feel they are missing, which is love and a sense of belonging somewhere. Many, depending on where they live, join gangs. Here's a fact though, there would be no gangs today if the fathers of the children in these gangs were to go out and get their child and bring them home. Show them how to respect and love themselves. Teach them how to be a responsible man. Help them develop the habits they need to be a man, and show them how to treat their woman. It's essential because our influences affect our choices, which in turn control our behavior which directs and guides us to the kinds of habits we learn and do throughout our lives.

In today's world, it is clear on so many levels, the "role" of our men and the men themselves have changed so much that real Christian women seeking real Christian men cannot find them. They do not recognize many of us anymore. They want, more or less, to submit to us as stated in **Ephesians 5:22**, (KJV). I said earlier that this is the man's fault. We (men) are the hunters! We chase the woman, very few chase men. We pick them, they don't choose us. It is men's behavior and actions that give them away, and lying is one of these bad traits that doesn't help get and keep a good woman in our lives. It says in **1 Corinthians 15:33**, (KJV), "Be not deceived: evil communications corrupt good manners." Men and women meeting today lie to each other so much about everything. They hardly follow through with anything but expect everything to be handed to them. They expect their woman to submit and follow them as the Bible says they should.

The funny thing is, and hardly any men know or understand this, many Christian women are willing, readily waiting and wanting to follow and "submit to their husbands" not to their "boyfriends," but they cannot seem to find too many Christian men who follow Christ. I've heard many men say, "In the Old Testament, men had more than one wife, why can't we?" They're comparing their cheating to **Solomon** in the Bible as found in **1 Kings 11:1-6** (KJV), where it says he had over seven hundred wives as their leader. They are trying to use this as their excuse to cheat and have children with many women. What they fail to read is where it says, "These wives turned him from God...his heart was not perfect with God...he did evil in the sight of God." In other words, this was not what God wanted for him. It was what he wanted for himself.

Have you heard a typical conversation of men and women trying to get to know one another and possibly be a couple these days? It is crazy. Men are trying to buy and treat women like slaves (meaning control them), and women are trying to find and work her man until they die. (Meaning have them get two or more jobs to keep up with their growing wants and needs in the relationship). The unsaid word of a man in this transaction is "How much will it take to buy you?" (meaning, what all do I need to spend to sleep with you?) The woman's unsaid words are "How can I get what I want to be guaranteed without giving up anything?" (Meaning, if she can get out of you all she needs without sleeping with you she will.) In this situation, scriptures have very little to do with either of their transactions, but this will not stop either of them using scripture to get the other to do as they want them to.

Many men looking to "control" and get their way with their woman will often "pick and choose" from scriptures the ones that best support their agenda. Trying to "sound" as if they know what they are talking about — using and misinterpreting scriptures to sell their pointless points to a Christian woman to get with them and trick them.

It says in **Titus 1:10-11** (KJV), **-10** "For there are many unruly and vain talkers and deceivers, especially they of the circumcision:" **11-** "Whose mouths must be stopped, who subvert whole houses, teaching things which they ought not, for filthy lucre's sake." In other words, men need to stop using the Bible in the wrong way when explaining their anger to their mate. They reinterpret their understanding of scriptures based on their "worldly" needs. A woman's role is to assist, not lead, according to the scriptures.

Those doing this believe they are walking in a Christ-like manner. Men, let me hip you on to something. Christian women are not stupid. They can see if you are following Christ or not. When they see you aren't living Godly, you will get push back. So, stop trying to play them like they are dumb because they are not. God gave them a specific skill set, and one of those skills is to know when you are lying to them. It is because of this foolishness that women have so few choices today when looking for a husband.

Listen, if you are unfamiliar with women's choices these days, let's review what they have to choose from for potential husbands.

There is the true **Christian Man**. This is the guy who knows that in order for him to know his wife's needs, he must spend quality time with her. By doing this, it helps him to improve and understand her self-worth and her confidence in their relationship. He knows by him doing this regularly, he will get his wife's full attention and cooperation. Thus, the phrase, "a happy wife, a happy life" is a true statement.

There is the **Pretender.** This is the man who THINKS he knows everything when he doesn't know much of anything but refuses to admit it. He is too proud to ask for help. He is the one you'll find creating problems in his relationship by lying to his woman, trying to control her and blaming her for his lack of knowledge of his role in their relationship. He is the one who, during an argument, will say hurtful things and take it too far. He says to his spouse, "If it wasn't for you, I could have done better." Men like this are trying to say, "I am not going to be responsible for my duties or choices in this relationship." He chases money, thinking it will get him more women. They have no idea that "A man will never lose a woman chasing money, but he can and often will lose his money chasing a woman." Here is where having a mentor or someone in his life to teach him "how" to treat and deal with a woman in his life is an important advantage. Without that mentoring, it is evident that he doesn't know how to deal with his role's duties.

Next, we have the **Angry Man**. He is the one who has been so broken by society and women for so long that he feels lost and without an identity. He is the weak man who seeks out low self-esteem women because he feels he can easily manipulate and control them. He continually lies and plays mind games with them. He does all he can to bring their self-esteem back up just to a point where they feel good about themselves, and then tears them back down again. He is the one you will find continually abusing his woman because he thinks it makes him a man in her eyes. He is the sad soul who is so wrapped up in his value that he cannot see all that she brings to the relationship. For him, it is about fear. He'd rather be feared by her than loved because strangely enough, some men believe fear is a sign of love.

Lastly, we have the **Confused Man.** He is the one who has given up on trying to "be" a man. He has taken up a gay lifestyle and claims the reason he does this is that "society made him do it" or that "he was born this way." This same person who claims to love God foolishly believes God is cool with this behavior when He is not. This is shown and confirmed in **Leviticus 18:22**, (KJV), as it reads, "Thou shalt not lie with mankind, as with womankind: it is abomination." In other words, God didn't design nor intend for men to sleep with men or women to sleep with women. Society, however, is doing their best to push this kind of behavior on us as if it is *normal* or biblical by approving same-sex marriages, movies and televisions shows. Instead of our pastors today standing up against this behavior, they have overlooked it and accepted those doing this in the church, claiming "God loves and accepts everybody as they are," when nowhere in the Bible does it say He said this.

Let me sidestep for a moment because many of these false doctrine so-called Christian men quotes come from *bad* principles they learned in their church. Write this down. It is essential to know that God gave us commandments, statutes and laws, not a religion. Man gave us "religion." Understand this, "religion is based on Christian standards, not biblical scriptures." Many of the "churches" today are more concerned about money and being accepted, then they are about knowing God's Truth. If the "Truth" gets in the way of the church making money and the people's acceptance, the Truth will be rejected quickly and dismissed.

Today's Pastor's job is to build up their congregation and get the money by using God's words as the "product" to entice them to keep coming. They tell the "congregation" only feel-good stories, get their money and send them on their way knowing hardly anything about God and His Word. Have you ever noticed when the Pastor wants a new plane or car, he asks YOU for the money? The moment you ask for help or need help many of them tell YOU to pray to God and ask for His help? I am telling you all this because if you "read" for yourself, you will know and see God has given all of us instructions. He wants us to follow His directions as it concerns a relationship and our duties. If you read for yourself for your own understanding, you cannot be tricked or lied to by false prophets claiming they are doing God's work.

I tell you this because for most of us our understanding comes from our Pastor, very few read for themselves. If he misled you, then you will mislead the woman following you. Don't be fooled, "The traditions of man are not biblical." You can't "lead" effectively or expect a woman to go with you when you don't know where you're going. "One of life's greatest mistakes is to embark on a life journey with someone who is not going anywhere in life."

The reason so many relationships are having issues is that they do not know the Word of God. Let's not be mistaken, splitting hairs and thinking that being bisexual or on the down-low does not make a difference to Him is ridiculous. Gay is gay, and it doesn't matter what title you give it. If this is who you are going to be, know that God doesn't support your decision, nor will He allow this behavior in heaven. You keep forgetting that the government doesn't run heaven, God does. If those living this lifestyle want to get to heaven, they must repent and not repeat.

Anyway, this is why so many women are wary of men. This is why they have trust issues with men, feel they can do bad by themselves and be afraid to "submit" because they do not know who we (men) are these days. This predicament is all on the man. If there are men here tonight looking to get it right before they get a woman, please read all of **Chapter 5 in Ephesians**, (KJV), to know what both of your roles are according to the scriptures. If you are one of those men who is not ready for marriage, that is okay, but I need for you to stop lying to women and using the lie, "I want to get married someday" as a means to sleep with them. It is not fair for you to waste a Christian woman's life who is tied to you through loyalty to a promise you made when you aren't ready to "be" married. Now she is stuck with you, trying to do right while you're continuously doing wrong. How is this fair to her?

Turn in your Bibles to **Genesis**. I want to reexamine and walk you through a story you already know, to bring home the point of why God created you first. This shows you your purpose, why He put you in charge, what your duties are and explains to you why everything starts with you. It will help you understand that even if in your relationship, it is not your fault. It is your *responsibility* to get back in alignment with what He designed it to be, and more importantly, the consequences if you don't do these things.

Let's start in **Genesis 2:7**, (KJV), where it says, "And the Lord God formed man of the dust of the ground and breathed into his nostrils the breath of life; and man became a living soul." Here, it shows you God's foundation, which is you. In **Genesis 2:15**, (KJV), it says, "And the Lord God took the man, and put him into the Garden of Eden to dress it and keep it." Notice here how He "put" man in the garden. He didn't have him search for it. God gave him a job which was to dress it and keep it up, in other words, He assigned Adam "work" to do. Because He walked with Adam daily, Adam wasn't told to worship or told to pray to Him.

As we continue to read in **Genesis 1:28**, (KJV), it says, "And God blessed them, and He said unto them, Be fruitful, and multiply, and replenish the earth, and subdue it, and have dominion over the fish of the sea, and over the fowl of the air, and over every living thing that moveth upon the earth." Here we see God has given Adam "dominion" over everything but not "ownership." His dominion, as you read, was over everything but not people. Dominion meant Adam's job was to "manage" God's property, protect it, work and cultivate it. In my opinion, I feel He did not give Adam ownership of these things. If Adam had "ownership" of all things, there would be no need for Adam to report to Him for anything.

We read in **Genesis 2:16, 17**, (KJV), that Adam's job came with rules and regulations, restrictions and consequences. **16** - "And the Lord commanded the man, saying, Of every tree of the garden thou mayest freely eat:" He is warned here in **Genesis 2:17**, (KJV), of what not to do when he says, "But of the tree of knowledge of good and evil, thou shalt not eat of it: for in the day that thou eatest thereof thou shalt surely die."

Let me make a quick point because it is crucial to know. BEFORE God introduced the woman to Adam, He knew he had equipped Adam with all he needed to take care of someone else. Are many of you, before you approach a woman, equipped with what you NEED to be the man of the house and the relationship? Financially, are you ready to support her or provide a place for her to call home IF you plan to "get with" her? I believe God did this because He wanted to ensure "first" that Adam understood "his" role clearly before being presented a helper (woman) into the equation.

With these instructions, provisions and consequences (that included death) given to Adam from God, it was clear what he could and could not do in his job. As you read on, you see it wasn't until He felt Adam was able to handle his new position, that He created and presented the woman to the man. You read in **Genesis "2:18**, (KJV), why God created a woman for the man, "And the Lord God said, it is not good that the man should be alone; I will make a helpmeet for him."

He did so, and we see this in **Genesis 2:21-22**, (KJV). He created man a helper, **21**- "And the Lord God caused a deep sleep to fall upon Adam, and he slept: and he took one of his ribs, and closed the flesh instead thereof;" **22**- "And the rib, which the Lord God had taken from man, made He a woman, and brought her unto the man." Once done, God brought her to Adam to classify what he would call her. You can read in **Genesis 2:23**, (KJV), "And Adam said, this is now bone of my bones, and flesh of my flesh: she shall be called Woman because she was taken out of Man."

Now, let's recap for a second to ensure we are all on the same page. God created man. "Put" him in the garden, did not let him find it on his own, assigned him "work" (gave him a job) all before bringing in Eve. God gave Adam the rules, regulations and guidelines of this position and the consequences, if he didn't do his job. I said this to point out and show that Adam had a job and was doing work BEFORE Eve came into the picture. It was his responsibility to teach Eve, go over the rules and regulations and consequences given to him by God as it pertained to them living in the Garden of Eden. It was his job to make sure none of God's instructions were misunderstood, but as we know, he failed.

As we continue to read in **Genesis 3:1-24**, (KJV), we observe how the devil, who was looking to disrupt God's plan of family and marriage, approached Eve and not Adam, convinced her to eat from the forbidden tree, telling her if she did, she would know all that God knew. She believed this as we know because she proceeded to eat of the forbidden fruit. She then shared it with Adam only to find out after the fact, that she had been lied to and tricked. Satan's mission was then complete. I am telling you this because I want you to understand that even though Eve was the person tricked into eating the forbidden fruit first, the fault of this happening was still Adam's. He was supposed to watch over her (protect her) to prevent this from happening.

It is evident when we read how when God comes into the garden, He knows something is wrong. He called out to Adam, not Eve. Remember and understand, God had put Adam in charge of everything, including Eve's protection, and he failed. God wanted an explanation of how this could have happened to him knowing what he knew. It reads that God reiterated the consequences to Adam of breaking His laws. Adam even tries to save himself by blaming Eve. Even with Eve's mistake, they both would suffer because it happened as you know. He did not say, "I was playing, you too can have a "do-over" for breaking my rules" or "Don't worry about it. Pray on it, and things will be okay." No, He cursed them both, and they had to leave the garden and never return.

Many of us today get tricked and break God's laws as if it means nothing." Many of us feel because "God knows our hearts, and He is a forgiving God" that we can break His laws set out for us and nothing will happen. Many think His love and protection comes without consequences. If this was true, why even read the Bible when you treat it like you would any other book? Just as Adam and Eve were told right from wrong, so were we. We don't concern ourselves because God's consequences aren't right away. We feel we've gotten away with whatever it is we've done. We don't think that God knows and remembers because the world we're in right now doesn't seem to care what we've done. However, God does.

Sure, God's given us the ability to make our own decisions, but He also expects us to respect Him. Marriage, as we see today, has been and continues to be disrespected. Christians or real men, period, in a relationship with a woman should know that women and marriage need to be treated with the utmost respect as it is explained in **Ephesians 5:28,29**. (KJV), 28 - "So ought men to love their wives as their own bodies. He that loveth his wife loveth himself." **29** - "For no man ever yet hated his own flesh; but nourisheth and cherisheth it, even as the Lord the church:" He is telling you it is not okay for you to mistreat your woman. Those men who may have heard this without reading it for themselves may not have gotten the full understanding of how real this is according to God's Word. I suggest, if you haven't read this, take a moment and start at verse **20** and read to **32** for more understanding, but right now, let's deal with these two scriptures. In verse **28**, when it says men should love their own wives as they love their own bodies, it is telling you "how" to love your wife. You would never mistreat yourself, so why would you harm her? **29**, says if you hate your own flesh. Do any of you hate your flesh? Do you abuse yourself? Then, why do you feel the need to mistreat your wife?

I know there are men out here today who do not understand how to accept love from others. Since it was hardly if ever shown toward them, it is hard for them to believe someone could and does love them for real. I understand, and it makes sense why they would hold back or reject what they are not used to having from their woman. Not knowing is not an excuse for not trying, and in this world we live in, it is damn near impossible to do what is right when so much around us rewards us for doing badly.

Men who say they are *trying* to do anything are saying, "I don't want it for real." *Trying*, as I see it, is an excuse, and when a woman says this to the man who says he is *trying*, she is accurate. I will suggest this for those who are *trying*, and give you the benefit of the doubt that you want to do right. Instead of saying you're *trying*, tell her and yourself, "I am in *training*." I am *training* myself to do the right thing. I guarantee this small adjustment and change will make a difference in how you see and view your actions in your relationships.

If you read in **Ephesians 5:20-33**, (KJV), you will understand that your wife's behavior mirrors your own. You give to her what you give to yourself, and she will treat you the way you treat her, if she is a Christian woman. If you show her love, she will give it back in return ten times over, more than you could have imagined. Keep this in mind the next time your wife has issues with you. Listen and write this down. When you ignore your woman, you're not just hurting her. You're teaching and helping her to adjust to living without YOU! Ask yourself, am I treating her the way I would like her to treat me? Treating women the way most men do, there is no way a woman will submit to them, follow, love or reverence them acting the way they do. How can you be her savior? How can you sanctify and cleanse it with the washing of water by the Word if you are treating her as if she's the enemy?

For you married men and those seeking to get married, understand something. God gave us our wives so we wouldn't make fools of ourselves. He tells you to love your wife, but there are no scriptures where God tells her to love you. He does tell her she, as the wife, is to reverence you, in other words, respect you.

I am amazed how many of us don't want to accept the Word of God. We reject or dismiss it by saying, "We all interpret scriptures differently." I agree. We do *understand* things differently. However, the only time this is brought up is when someone doesn't want to accept or make any changes in their lifestyle to coincide with the Word of God. People think that the Bible should adjust to "today's times." This is reckless and very foolish thinking because it doesn't matter what "time" we are in, biblical days or today's, God's word will never change. It was then as it is now *the* guide we either follow or not. God is no fool, and He knows when you are using this excuse as your reason for not making any changes in your life.

It is sad that even if we see His words written in the Bible, we will still fight what we read to avoid doing right, all because it doesn't line up with what we are already doing. If you find yourself in a position where you are not sure what you've read, ask Him to guide you. Ask Him to show you or bring someone into your life to help you get a better understanding of what He is saying to you. Don't reject it because everyone else is. You're not everyone else. Your salvation isn't determined by what they do, it is based on what you're doing. Never go by what anyone tells you as fact. Read it for yourself.

Now, before I continue, let me say, men, I understand sometimes your woman can and will get on your last nerve. They know what buttons to push (as do we of them) to get us to act out of character and do wicked things when we shouldn't. Regardless of the situation, it is evident in the Bible. It is our job to turn whatever is wrong into right in our relationships. Turn to **Ecclesiastes 9:9,** (KJV), where it says, "Live joyfully with the wife whom thou lovest all the days of the life of thy vanity, which he hath given thee under the sun, all the days of thy vanity: for that is thy portion in this life, and in thy labour which thou takest under the sun." Also, turn to **Ecclesiasticus 30:24**, (The Apocrypha), "Envy and wrath shorten the life, and carefulness bringeth age before the time." In other words, it makes no sense to hold onto anger because it is going to shorten your life. It is our job as men to put our house back in order as God intended it to be. Anyway, let's continue.

As I was saying, God wanted Adam then as He does for men today to become what you were created to be through self-manifestation. If men were to follow this example, of working first (meaning have a job) before they look for a woman, they would be more prepared to support and provide for their woman and family (if it leads to marriage). Many, surprisingly, would lie less (because they would be able to "walk the walk" and follow through with all they promised their future wife). They would have a real plan and direction in place on how to get there. They would be able to accept help from their woman in areas they "know" they are lacking without feeling less manly when they do. What I am telling you is this. You shouldn't be looking for your woman or relying on her money to have a life with her. It is (in marriage) your job to provide not hers.

When I say prepared, I mean you need to be financially able to handle and provide for your woman regardless whether she can help economically or not. It is your job to show her you can and will do what IS expected of you according to God's Word, not the "world's" way of marriage where she kicks in "half" of her earnings to satisfy YOUR ego. This is important, so write this down. When she meets you, you should be able to show her you are financially independent and do not NEED her money to support her. If you are unable to provide for the both of you, don't take her from her parent's house. Don't move her into a place you could lose because you cannot afford the rent or mortgage, hoping she will stay by your side until you get it going on. That's just stupid.

Remember this, when you met her either she was comfortable in her parent's house or her own. She was doing well without you. Why would she want to give up being well-taken care of in order to come to a place she isn't sure you can afford? Listen and understand something *Hope* is not a strategy. You get her to come with you based on a lie and promise her the world you know you can't afford all to be able to "keep her" and sleep with her? If men are going by what the Bible says *provider* means, you are not getting with her for her to help you pay bills. You're getting with her because you're able to provide for her. You're telling her by handling things on your own that she will be well taken care of. If she works and wants to put in something to feel she is contributing to her household, let her pick something.

If you get sick or lose your job, your wife should be able to "maintain" things for a short period while you rebound. She shouldn't put additional stress on you. She should be able to step up for a little while (until you get yourself back on your feet) and help out as best she can and not complain about it or tell you she is doing you a favor.

An example of this can be seen in **Tobit 2:10-14**, (The Apocrypha), "**10** - And I knew not that there were sparrows in the wall, and mine eyes being open, the sparrows muted warm dung into mine eyes, and a whiteness came in mine eyes:, and I went to the physicians, but they helped me not: moreover Achiacharus did nourish me, until I went into Elymais." **11**- "And my wife Anna did take women's work to do." **12** –"And when she had sent them home to the owners, they paid her wages, and gave her also besides a kid." **13** – "And when it was in my house, and began to cry, I said unto her, From whence is this kid? Is it not stolen? Render it to the owners, for it is not lawful to eat anything that is stolen." **14** –"But she replied upon me, It was given for a gift more than the wages. Howbeit I did not believe her, but bade her render it to the owners: and I was abashed at her. But she replied upon me, Where are thine alms and thy righteous deeds? behold, thou and all thy works are known."

You're both in this for better or worse, not just for better. A real wife knows her man and her family. She will do her best to encourage you along the way, to find something else or possibly something better. She will help you emotionally even if you are unaware of it because it helps balance out her family — a sign the man has a good woman. You see this in **Ecclesiasticus 26:26**, (The Apocrypha), "A woman that honoureth her husband shall be judged wise of all; but she that dishonoureth him in her pride shall be counted ungodly of all." Meaning this, if her man is unable for whatever reason to fulfill his duties for a short while, she should still honor him and support him not abandon him in his hour of need like many women do when their help is needed. It has been shown and proven, "A man will save (care) of a woman, but a woman will not save a man" in the situation.

History has shown one of the things men aren't good at doing is handling themselves when they lose their job. To most men, their role is more important, if not more than, them having a woman because the position is their identity. It doesn't matter what kind of job it is. The point is it makes them feel "valued" as a man. A man's self-esteem is high when he has a good-paying job with a suitable title. It is because they believe in that moment and time, they have found their purpose, and with this, they don't need any outside approval from anyone. The opposite effect happens when they lose their jobs. Some get depressed and feel worthless and less of themselves.

In most cases, their woman is the one who suffers because of it. A significant problem and the reason they go through these changes is their lack of understanding of the definition of their "Job versus Work." Many men fail to understand or even notice the difference between the two because when things are going great, it doesn't matter. If you know the difference between your *job* and your *work,* you wouldn't get depressed when you lose a job. Let me explain, because it is very important that you understand this. Your *work* is "your gift" from God, which you never can lose, nor can you be fired from it. It is what you were born to do. It is within you! Your *job* is a "skill" you've learned that you use to get paid.

Let me give you an example of what I mean. If you have a job and you don't perform well, you can probably get fired. The reason why is because your pay is based on your performance. Based on the skills they taught you, you can, and most do, get another similar job again and again. Your *job* besides helping you to pay your bills is just preparing you for your *work*. In other words, your gift is your ability to work, and your *work* is in your skills. Many men lack the understanding between the two. They have no idea which is more valuable to them, the "gift" or their "skills." It makes it hard for them to understand and know what their woman's position is, and how she is to be a "helper" to them if there is no work for them to do.

Even when you (the man) get back on your feet (and also while you were out), you should never wonder or ask your wife what she makes or what she is doing with her money. If she believes in you and the marriage, she will tell you on her own and even try to help when she can to take the pressure off of you. That's not something you should be focusing on at all. If she is your wife and someone who respects and loves you, she will tell you and share it with you but not because you asked her to, but because she feels you are her man and it is the least that she could do to show you she appreciates all you do for her. To this day, I don't know what my wife earns, nor have I asked her. I say this because it doesn't matter. It is my job to provide for my family's needs, not hers, but if I "need" her help, I know she will step up with no problem, no questions asked.

Let's talk about what a *virtuous woman* is and why her role is essential. Turn to, if you have it, **Ecclesiasticus 26:1**, (The Apocrypha) where it says, "Blessed is the man that hath a virtuous wife, for the number of his days shall be double." I mentioned earlier that I would share with you the characteristics of *virtuous women* and why God finds favor when you have one. Here are a few scriptures that demonstrate this:

Proverbs 31:10, (KJV), **10** – "Who can find a virtuous woman? For her price is far above rubies." **Proverbs 12:4** (KJV), "A virtuous woman is a crown to her husband: but she that maketh ashamed is as rottenness in his bones." In other words, she is more valuable than money or anything you hold dear. She will always make her husband look good. **Proverbs 31:26-28** (KJV), **26** -"She openeth her mouth with wisdom; and in her tongue is the law of kindness." **27** – "She looketh well to the ways of her household, and eateth not the bread of idleness." **28** - "Her children arise up, and call her blessed; her husband also, and he praiseth her." Meaning when your mate speaks, she speaks with wisdom or kind, respectable words. She appreciates what she has, a husband, children and her home.

Proverbs 12:14 (KJV), **14**-"A man shall be satisfied with good by the fruit of his mouth: and the recompense of a man's hands shall be rendered unto him." **Ecclesiasticus 26:6**, (The Apocrypha), 6 "He that hateth to be reproved is in the way of sinners: but he that feareth the Lord will repent from his heart." **Ecclesiasticus 26:13-15**, (The Apocrypha), **13** "The grace of a wife delighteth her husband, and her discretion will fatten his bones." **14** "A silent and loving woman is a gift of the Lord, and there is nothing so much worth as a mind well instructed." **15** "A shamefaced and faithful woman is a double grace, and her continent mind cannot be valued."

Leviticus 19:18, (KJV), **18** "Thou shalt not avenge, nor bear any grudge against the children of thy people, but thou shalt love thy neighbour as thyself: I am the LORD." **James 5:16** (KJV), "Confess your faults one to another, and pray one for another, that ye may be healed. The effectual fervent prayer of a righteous man availeth much." **Ephesians 4:31** (KJV), "Let all bitterness, and wrath, and anger, and clamour, and evil speaking, be put away from you, with all malice:" **1 Timothy 6:6** (KJV), "But godliness with contentment is great gain."

In other words, a *virtuous woman* understands her role as the wife as directed by God. He has made it clear if you have a *virtuous woman*, He says she is in His eyes, worth more than money or anything you hold dear. A *virtuous woman* is worthy of the title she has been given, meaning her husband would never have to worry that she would cheat on him. She will take care of her husband's health. She doesn't complain of their current lifestyle (a man must put her in a beautiful place and not a hell hole to call home). She will be comfortable with what they have as her husband seeks more and improvement (better lifestyle). She will always keep family business in-house and not tell others. She will do her part if he is doing his role. He will not need to worry or concern himself of what she is doing with her own money.

Although she may disagree with her husband on some matters, she will not hold grudges or be bitter towards her husband. She can admit her faults (as the man should do as well when they're wrong). I say this because when couples argue, they both feel they are right, and the other person is wrong. This makes it harder to repair or fix the problem. Couples must be able to be real, and keep it real with one another. It's not about who is right or wrong. It is more about the two of you at the end of the day agreeing with "how" the relationship is and can be better. Couples who understand this will realize, "A good and growing relationship requires both of you, and as long as you both understand that you win and lose together and not apart, you will always win."

As I was saying, yes, God created man a "helper," and yes, there are some women, both married and single, who will take advantage of this situation when things are good but run when things aren't. In short, women should stay and not run when a situation like this in the relationship comes up. Many of you know the Bible refers to the woman as the "weaker" vessel. "Weaker" in this understanding is not referring to her strength. It is saying that she is "delicate."

In some situations, her "strength" for you can be as strong if not stronger than your own. Not understanding this is where many men fail to see in their woman the "gifts" God has equipped her with for him. These attributes that He has provided her with such are Intelligence, Intuition, Plans, Wisdom, Ideas and Suggestions that benefit YOU in your work. We see this accentuated in **Ecclesiasticus 26:16**, (The Apocrypha), "As the sun when it ariseth in the high heaven; so is the beauty of a good wife in the ordering of her house."

God knew if and when you were ready and once accepted her skills, you would be a better you for her. She would no longer be viewed as your "competition," but more as your "companion." Weak men who are not ready or mature enough for this kind of woman will observe and see her skills as aggressive and hard to work with, all because they aren't worthy to receive help yet. This kind of reaction exists because many men are intimidated by strong women. You would think that a strong man would want a strong woman, right?

Let me back up a second because I am assuming when I made this statement that I was talking to strong men when many of you may not be yet. You see, strong men understand that good women are attracted to strong men. Let me break this down for those who aren't sure if you are or are not a strong man who is well suited for a strong woman. If you think you're ready for a strong woman and you're not, this could be YOUR issue, not hers.

Let's examine a few facts. A strong and smart man - (1) Will deal with a woman on a first date asking what seems like millions of questions because he understands she is trying to get to know him not just get into his business. (I am not saying you must answer EVERYTHING she asks because some questions asked can and will be pointless. You must use your best judgment to determine which is which.) (2) Realizes (if he is feeling her also) his responses will be the determining factor on whether she sees him as a "potential mate" or a "waste of her time." (3) Will know, understand, welcome and value the fact his woman has her views on things in the world. He is not looking for a "yes" woman. He is looking for a woman to challenge him. (4) Loves a woman he doesn't have to control, smother or supervise when he is not around. Her independent spirit is something he wants to help her with because it builds her up and does not bring her down. He sees her as his equal, not his child. (5) Includes his woman in situations that affect them both. He trusts all decisions made by her because he knows she has their family's best interests in mind at all times, not just her own. You read this in **Proverbs 5:13** (KJV) where it says, "Happy is the man that findeth wisdom, and the man that getteth understanding."

This man understands that in a marriage, "It is not smart or healthy (as does the wife) to make decisions in their household without the support of his wife." No marriage is perfect, but we all aim to be the best for our mates, the best we can be. We know victory in marriage is longevity, the length of time we're together living and working together to be on the same page at the end of the day. The goal is to "be" one flesh in the sense that you both understand one another and love each other. Based on what I've said, who thinks they are a good strong man?

As I said earlier, the men many women have to choose from are slim pickings. Now saying all this, you can see where the strong, smart man is far different from those men. I said earlier that women do not see many strong good men from which to select a potential mate, and that's sad. Active, smart men seek strong, intelligent women, plain and simple. He sees her value and worth, and she sees in him his plan and vision to love and be loved as they grow their relationship. If you are intimidated by a strong woman, it means you are not on her level, and she need not waste her time on you, no matter how fine you may look or how nice you may be.

Honestly, I don't feel a woman should be forced to lower her standards to be with a man unequally yoked with her. She should never have to settle for less when she is worth so much more. Is that not what the Bible tells you about the women we marry? Don't get me wrong. There are a lot of strong men who deserve strong women, but they must "act" right and know what their role is with their spouse. Sure, like most women, men also can meet and get involved with a woman whose intentions are to use him. She can take advantage of his kindness as his weakness and play him like a violin out of tune.

It is a fact many women but not all see marriage as their personal "retirement" plan, meaning they no longer have to work or worry about bills or take care of themselves. They use the "provider" and "head of household" as their means to just "be" in the relationship and hardly do anything. Their husband is their "personal" ATM, meaning their unlimited source of income to buy and obtain all that they feel they deserve or did not receive in their last relationship. They will say, "I deserve nice things..." I can agree with many of them, but I never understood why men should be the ones to provide them with these things they said "they" needed. These money-hungry women will insist, before or shortly after they are married, that their man quickly put their name on everything, including life insurance. They then put as much additional pressure on him as she can to get themselves more and more things knowing they cannot afford it, hoping he stresses out and dies trying to keep up. All this because they know that once you're dead, they are set for life and well-taken care of from the insurance. Finally, they don't have to deal with you. It's a fact, if women can have a man's money and not have to live or deal with them until they wanted sex from them, they would.

Many of these foolish men will go into debt and stress themselves, thinking the more they get their woman, the more they will love them. They don't understand that the more they get, the more they will want. Many women like this will expect you, once you start spoiling her, to continue it because YOU (the man) have made her feel you could keep it up when most men can't. As you can see this is the main reason, and why many women outlive their husbands.

Men have added additional stress because of the lies he has told, and women stress them even more, forcing and enforcing them to do what they say.

The Bible talks about this in **Proverbs 31:11**, (KJV), "The heart of her doth safely trust in her so that he shall have no need of spoil." In other words, men need not lie about what they can't do, and women should show some appreciation for all her man does for her. At the same time, she should encourage her man (as he should do her as well) to reach for bigger and better things. For this to work, they both must be humble and appreciative of what God has provided for them thus far as they strive to obtain more. My understanding of the biblical definition is that a man as a "provider" needs to provide a home for a family, food for them and clothes and the necessities to live comfortably as a family.

Now, if he can go above and beyond, meaning taking the family on expensive trips, buy them expensive gifts, etc. then he can do so, but that is considered "extra," not a requirement. A woman who pushes her man to work two and three jobs only because she wants expensive things isn't a good wife. She is a user and no good to him. We see this in **Ecclesiasticus 26:22**, (The Apocrypha), "An harlot shall be accounted spittle; but a married woman is a tower against death to her husband."

In other words, a woman who is unappreciative of what her husband is doing is ungrateful. Women who disrespect their husbands by talking loudly to them as if he is their child, act out by clapping her hands to express she is not one to be messed with in front of others, all to get attention, is a self-centered person. Thinking she is setting him straight saying, "He is not going to rule or run her!" is nowhere near or close to being a Christian woman. No doubt this will be the same woman that will wonder AFTER she has embarrassed him, why he beat her ass for doing so.

Some women just don't get it. Even though no man should put his hands on a woman, at the same time, no woman should put her hands on him either. I feel if you are that upset with him for whatever, for your safety, you should walk away, as does the man. It is sad to say this because it is wrong for men to do this, but some women talk themselves into an abuse by the way they act. By running their mouth, acting out and being disrespectful instead of discussing the problems at home, they can often walk themselves into a backhand slap or worse. I am not saying it is right, but some women push men to react this way because it is what they want them to do. It's their way of getting attention from them, but the unwanted way, I think.

Now at the same time, no man should be shouting and belittling their women in public. Disrespecting her in any way to show they are the man and in control of her and the relationship to those who are looking on is wrong. Neither of them is a Christian, according to the Bible. People doing this haven't read in **1 Thessalonians 5:11**, (KJV), where it says, "Wherefore comfort yourselves together, and edify one another, even as also ye do." In other words, disrespecting one another in public or private to gain control of each other isn't what He wants us to do. He expects us to love each other and grow together. We can't do that if we're always fighting and jockeying for position in the relationship.

Let me share this with you because in the world we live in, these are the facts. Unlike most races, (1) Black men are the most underrated, respected, appreciated, undervalued people. (2) Black women are the most disrespected, unprotected and neglected people in America. Just being black in America is hard enough. We don't need to make it even harder by disrespecting one another in a relationship. Men, I need you to learn how to touch your woman in ways that have nothing to do with sex, but rather everything to do with comfort, understanding and protection. It is our job in our households to be the Provider, Protector and Priest. We must understand that the best "gift" we can give to our wives is our time, attention and love.

Understand that to ALL WOMEN in relationships, "attention" for them is critical, and something that is a must have. Just because she has and displays confidence doesn't mean she is your competition. A woman needs to bring a sense of calm to her relationship because she is his sense of escape from the world. A man who is providing for his family shouldn't have to fight the world and come home and fight with his wife.

All men must know this, we all make mistakes and if they were real "mistakes" and not our new "behavior habits," God says we need to repent, and He will forgive us. We see this in **Acts 17:30**, (KJV), "And the times of this ignorance God winked at; but now commandeth all men everywhere to repent;" In other words, He is telling you, the person He put in charge to be the man and repent your wrongs and make things right. I am sorry to say to you there will be times in your relationship where you will have to fall on the sword, take the blame even if you didn't do it, for the sake of your relationship.

I understand how it feels to "provide" and not be appreciated by your woman for you doing the right things. Listen, my ex and I were in the mall one day, and she saw a dress in the window she said she liked. When she saw the price of it, she put it back. At that moment, I felt kind of bad because even though it wasn't in our budget, I wanted to get it for her if it was something she wanted. Understand she never told me to get it for her, just that she liked it. So, me thinking about "her" happiness, I went out and bought the dress and surprised her with it. Maybe I should have asked her "IF" she wanted me to get it for her, but I thought it was a good thing to show her I loved her. I took it home excited about what I had done, thinking she would appreciate the fact I heard her, and I acted on it, but I was utterly wrong. When I took it home and gave it to her, this is what she said to me concerning my efforts, "I said I liked it. I never said I wanted it."

Now, as you can imagine, I went from being excited at doing something for my woman to being pissed and feeling like a pure fool for trying to make her happy. I say this to say, I know it is hard for men to be men these days and the pressures we are all under trying to "be" that guy for our women. We have to remember having a successful relationship requires hard work and very long hours but the rewards if successful are worth it. Terms such as "give and take" are words we all must get used to hearing and doing to make it work. If only one is giving and the other is taking, the one receiving will be happy while the one giving will feel used. That is not a good recipe for a good relationship. The sad thing is many of the women today have no clue what we go through being us, but they need to find out. If you are like me, you want to hear every so often, "Thank you!" or "I appreciate all you do for your family and me..."

It is no secret. Men and women speak and understand things differently. It has often been said, "Men say one thing, and women hear another." It's not uncommon or hard to fix *IF* we understand how we think, react and comprehend what is being said to us by our mates. Let me explain. Women, when things are bothering them or they have something on their minds, will often speak it out loud because they are "external" people. This is how they communicate and prefer to express their thoughts and feelings to their mates. When she shares her thoughts with her man, it isn't for him to solve her issues or concerns but more for him to listen and acknowledge what she is saying. For most men, when a man says, "No, I don't need any help," he means it but when a woman says "no" she is asking you to dig deeper to get to the root of what is bothering her, and most men don't do it.

For men, this process is much different; men are not built to talk of their problems out loud BEFORE they fully understand and have solutions for them. They handle their questions, issues, and concerns "internally." We know this to be because it is evident when things are on a man's mind or something is bothering him, he will get quiet, get real closed-mouthed and won't talk that much at all. We want to fix it *internally* first, then share it with her. Men do this for the most

321

part because they feel if they were to say something that is bothering (a thought) them before having a solution to their issue, she will do as they tried to do, fix it or suggest ways to fix it. Their woman starts asking unwanted questions for details on something a man is not ready to share. Since he doesn't provide her with the details and information she requests, she feels he doesn't care for her enough to share what he feels when that is not the case. I know this may be a little confusing to most men because, by nature, we are "problem solvers." Most men hear and try and solve their woman's problems. The way we see it, it is what "we" are supposed to do.

As men, we're thinking we are helping, but in reality, we are hurting by not just listening to her. I believe most men will try and make their woman happy if they can. Making her "happy" makes most men feel like men. Failing to do so makes some feel worthless. For some, making her happy sometimes is for him to understand, appreciate and feel her pain. Many of us feel this way about our woman, but few will admit it. Our woman's smile is the sexiest thing about her. It's no secret. All men need to feel needed and desired by their woman. In short, many women think because we love differently, we don't love equally, and this is not true.

Another area many women forget or omit is the fact that part of their many jobs (their role) is to "encourage" not "discourage" their man. Many successful men will tell you, "It was my wife who encouraged me to push beyond what I thought I could do to get where I am." It's why you hear football players, when they win the Super Bowl say, "People see me and think I did this alone, but I got help from family and friends. They also made a lot of sacrifices for me to have this opportunity to be here today." They are telling you someone encouraged them not discouraged them from their destiny, and it helped them get there.

Many men who have huge egos will never see their woman's importance and all they bring to the relationship as essential pieces that complete them until it is too late. Others will never see it, and that is sad. I make this statement because I am not sure many men understand what the scripture in **Ephesians 5:23**, (KJV) is saying, "For the husband is the head of the wife, even as Christ is the head of the church: and he is the savior of the body." Remember the word "savior" because I will show you the importance of it later.

Understand something about being the Head of Household, it doesn't mean the husband has the right to treat his wife any old kind of way, put her down or disrespect her. There is much more to it. The Bible explains the "head of the household" by saying the man has the authority, and he is responsible over which he oversees in his home, and this means everything. Even if he is not directly accountable when things go wrong (as in the case of Adam and Eve), it is still his responsibility. It is the man's job to get his household back in "alignment" with what God says is the "order" of marriage for him to advance His purpose of marriage. Did you know when she rebels and acts out, it is the result of what you have shown her in your behavior? She gives you back what you give her. So if you are respectful toward her and treat her lovingly, she will respond in a loving way toward you. If you mistreat her or do something to her that is not Christian-like, she will react with the behavior you have shown to her. In other words, she copies and responds to you the way you did to her.

These kinds of actions mean your relationship is out of "alignment." When your woman is out of alignment, it is your responsibility to find out why and fix it to get her back in alignment. I know what you are thinking, "She is a grown woman, she should fix herself, right?" Men talking like this are speaking from a "worldly" perspective and not a "Biblical" perspective. It is this kind of thinking and the reason why so many married men are out here today acting single. They are thinking and operating within the marriage as if they are only responsible for themselves. This is a clear sign of men who do not understand their role and responsibilities that they agreed to when they said, "I do."

Men, let me ask you something, "Have you ever thought about what it would be like to date and be with yourself? Would you date yourself knowing all the hurt you've caused, the lies you've told and the broken promises you have made?" I don't think so. I know for a fact, many of you, if the woman you were dating lied to you, you would do your best to hurt her heart and make her feel sorry for doing so. You would not care how it made her think either. It happens because many of you, you start day one when you first meet them by gambling, lying, setting up a false expectation, not knowing you're setting the friendship/relationship up to fail. Do you remember all the things you promised her and said you would do and give her if she were your woman? Do you remember how much "game" you kicked at her (aka lies) as you were trying to impress her, for her to see how worthy you were of her love?

I know someone here tonight knows they can relate to what I am saying. You know when you first met you introduced your "representative" to her and he was willing to do and say whatever was needed to get with her. Tell a lie and make it sound like the truth. The woman listening to you wants to believe you mean all that you said. After you get together, you fired your representative, and did it on your own. Therein lies the problem, now you must prove and do what you said.

You were hoping that AFTER she learned and saw who she was dealing with that, she would be so in love with you, that she would accept you as you are. You hoped she would forget all the promises made and things you said you would give her, but she isn't going to ignore them. You don't know that though, yet. The moment she brings up all you said and the promises you made, you have the nerve to get mad at her. Let me ask you something, have you ever asked yourself, how would you feel if she lied to you? Made promises and never kept them? Said hurtful things and never apologized for them? Would you still believe and have faith in her that she will turn it around and do right by you? The answer is no, and you wouldn't stay around or give her a second chance. So, my question to you is simple; why do men continually do this to their woman and expect different results?

The sad part about this is when you hurt her, you think it's the right thing to do. You feel as if you've shown her and that she isn't going to get the best of you. You feel good, like you won something for hurting her. Even while she is sitting there crying, in pain and hoping you'll fix this because you didn't mean it, you don't care. It doesn't bother you at all, and you could even go to sleep, and while you're sleeping, you're thinking to yourself, "She doesn't know who I am or who she is messing with." Here we are in a relationship with this woman, and we are finding ourselves spending time trying to make the lies right. Arguing is good sometimes because it lets you both know where you stand with one another. However, arguing too much can make you both not only fall out of "love" but out of "like" as well. We know this happens because "we" as people are controlled by our "emotions" and not our "will." Listen, it has been said, "People who allow their emotions to rule over their will, are weak-willed people."

Let me give you an example of it this way, there are times in your life where you "feel" like doing something you know isn't right, but you do it anyway. You do it because it makes you "feel" good not because it's right. We are human, and I understand. Depending on the person, they might feel badly about it afterward, but at that time it's too late, it's over. You know as men we will tell whatever lie we think is needed to get us what we want, and if it works, it does. The woman you're telling this lie to knows you are stretching the truth but because she is at a time in her life where she wants or needs what you are saying to be accurate, she gives you the benefit of the doubt and gives you a chance. Your "will" in the situation told you to tell her the truth, but your "emotions" and the fact that you didn't want to lose her told you to lie to get her.

The thing most men don't understand, care or think about are the aftereffects of her learning the truth about who you are and believe me, she is going to find out. You will lose everything because of it. You're not thinking about what will happen if you get caught as you need her to buy what you're selling at the moment. Why is this, you ask? It is hard for most men starting out in a friendship/relationship to be "responsible" in the things before and after they are in a relationship. A lot of times their emotions will be so keen on that person they want that their "will" to do right is not a factor at THAT moment, only what they want and feel they need is.

We all at some point have done it, lied, tricked or deceived someone to get what we want. We've all played someone for a fool, taken advantage of someone to get what we want and been played ourselves, and it is very irresponsible of all of us. Here is the deal and a little-known fact. It is because of our persistence that many women give us a second look, to begin with, most times. Many of them, if you were to ask, would tell you they didn't like us that much when they first met us, but we grew on them the more we pursued them.

Some men are so arrogant. They think women aren't listening and watching their every move when they are. Understand something. It is during this time, she starts to question her choice, our leadership and friendship for being her future husband. If she stays after knowing the truth, she will always wonder if you are lying to keep her from being with someone else or if you love her and want a real future with her. In this situation, most men will take her willingness to stay, knowing you lied, as a weakness and an open door to mess up again and again. If you're doing this now, you are a "trifling" man and do not deserve her. It will be your foolishness, when you two do break up, that makes her bitter towards other men. Here's a newsflash. Real men don't act this way.

To avoid all this drama, tell the woman the truth. If you are not ready to settle down, tell her. If you don't want to get married, tell her. If you see no future with her, tell her. Figure out what you two have and are doing "IF" you decide to get together. No woman wants to believe she has found her Prince when you are a wolf in sheep's clothing. There is a good chance if you're honest, that she will wait with you as you both continue to get to know each other. She may see you as someone she could love and be with because you were honest upfront. Men write this down. A woman wants a man who is willing to "invest" in her. If he did, he would learn the wisdom, abilities, attributes and skills that she brings, and he would understand she is capable not only to enhance his life but both their lives. The fact of the matter is if men took the time to observe and learn their woman, they would know she has much more to offer and something much more significant than her body to bring to the relationship.

Too many men think their woman is in their life to be their maid, slave, lover and fool. They think she is someone who allows them to do whatever they want to do, and she is not to question them. If you're single, thinking this way, you can see now why you are still single and will probably stay single, thinking like that. It's you're way of thinking and how you perceive the women's role in a relationship that determines the success of it.

You might want to write this down because you must understand this. I said this earlier. If you've read the Bible and come across this part in it where it says the woman is a "helper" then you should have figured out the word helper means "to help." You do not have her do it for you. If you have no work for her to help you with when she meets and gets with you, how can she fulfill her role according to the Bible in your relationship?

How can she "help" you or be a "helper" to you if you don't have yourself and your life together? When you had her, you were too blind to see or recognize that as your woman, she was willing to "help" you achieve YOUR goals because those goals included her. The reason she is willing to do this for you is that she is your equal partner, not your employee according to the Bible. If you treat her efforts in the relationship as if it is her JOB, she will eventually quit and seek better employment elsewhere with better benefits. Women often tell me, "They want men to grow up."

My grandmother had a phrase she used to say that went like this, "You don't have a pot to piss in or a window to throw it out of." She went on to ask me a simple question that made me think hard about it, she asked, "Why would a woman leave her parent's house to end up without a place to stay?" She is your wife, and she needs to know or at least want to know where you plan on taking her. By telling her, it makes her feel she is in good hands. It is the same question many successful women who are seeking men today are asking, but they aren't getting any answers other than, "Trust me, I got you." Men don't seem to get it. Love is good to have, but love doesn't pay the bills or make a woman feel secure or safe in the relationship. A man with a plan, vision and actions does. Try paying your rent by telling the landlord your wife loves you and see how long you will stay there. My question to men here tonight is this, "Why would you intentionally waste a woman's time knowing you are not going to do anything you promised for her?"

You have heard the saying, "Behind every good man, there is a good woman." I have changed the phrase a little by saying, "Beside every good man is a good woman." I need my woman beside me not behind me, and here is why. Beside me, she can relay to me what's on her side, and I can communicate what's on my side. I am her "ride or die" dude, and she's my "ride or die chick." Your thought process should be this, "She is my equal (and she needs to know you see her this way). Her job with me is for life in a growing organization bound to prosper. She will never feel (and nor should you) that she could be fired from her position."

Something most men still to this day aren't good at is realizing that if they were to listen to their woman, they would understand their wants and needs. Three of their needs, in particular, are explained in the Bible, and they are:

1. In **Ephesians 5:25**, (KJV), it says, "Husbands, love your wives, even as Christ also loved the church, and give himself for it." Meaning this, as her husband if anything is wrong with her, it is your job to be her savior and fix it.

2. In **Ephesians 5:26**, (KJV), it says, "That he might sanctify and cleanse it with the washing of the word." In other words, you need to sanctify her. Set her aside and show her she is essential in your life. She is to be treated and know that she comes first, and friends and family are second. She needs to know and feel you understand this.

I am not saying neither of you can have friends as a married couple, but your wife must know her position in your relationship is "first." Be careful, because some women knowing this will take advantage of you and misuse the fact that she is number one to mess up your relationships with your friends and family out of spite. Whenever you want to spend time with them, she will remind you that she is first. She will use this power of being "first" to shut you off from them, not because she loves you that much but more because she wants to take ALL of your time, and that is not right. Yes, men, your time is the most valuable thing you can give to her. Giving her attention is well and good but not to the point where you are under one another 24/7, that's not healthy. You both should create boundaries, days and times you can see and spend time with your friends and family. Create a "date night," a time dedicated to your love.

Anyway, remember in **Ephesians 5:31**, (KJV), where it says, "For this cause shall a man leave his father and mother and shall be joined unto his wife, and they two shall be one flesh." This is where men get things twisted. What I mean is those men moving in with the woman and allowing them to take care of them is not the way God intended it to go. It doesn't say anywhere in the Bible that the woman should leave her father and mother. It says the man should do this. The reason why is because God wanted you to create a place for her to come and make her home BEFORE she left home. Asking her to go from a place that is already giving her a roof over her head, clothes on her back and food for her to eat, you best be able to provide the same things because if not, why should she leave to come live with you for less than what she had?

You can't expect her to have faith in your leadership when she doesn't know or have proof you are capable of leading her or a family. You must earn it through your actions. She must see it for herself and not take your word on it. She shouldn't feel her leaving to be with you is a gamble but a sure thing. What you need to do first and foremost is take a moment to clear any doubts in her head of your intentions and ability to lead, if you plan to keep promises previously made.

3. In **Ephesians 5:28**, (KJV), it says, "So ought men to love their wives as their own bodies. He that loveth his wife loveth himself." Meaning if your wife has legitimate needs and you can meet them, you need to satisfy your wife and fulfill her needs. It should be clear by now that it is the man who is the "initiator." Another example of this can be found in 1 **Peter 3:7**, (KJV), where it says, "Likewise, ye husbands, dwell with them according to knowledge, giving honor unto the wife, as unto the weaker vessel, and as being heirs together of grace of life; that your prayer be not hindered." In other words, this is saying as the man, he is in charge and responsible. It is your job, according to what God has instructed, to love your wife and treat her right.

I mentioned earlier that I would explain the behavior some men have concerning the actions on subjects of:

(1) Why many of them treat women the way they do,

(2) Why many feel this is something they most do.

(3) Why many believe both women and society have contributed to the changes in themselves, and

(4) What they feel they need to do as men to correct it going forward.

First off men, in your relationship, you must be "productive" and not just there. From the day you are born until the day you die. You need to leave a legacy for your family and not only bills when you pass. You see there is more to "providing" than just paying some bills. As part of the "Protection" you provide your family, it must include what will happen after you're gone as well. Who here has heard the Temptations song, *Papa was a rolling stone*? The lyrics for the chorus read, "Papa was a rolling stone... wherever he laid his head was his home, and when he died, all he left them was alone..." Is leaving your family with bills your idea of "protecting" or "providing" for them? Is this all you want to leave your family with a lot of bills?

I started by asking a panel of men a simple question to get them to "see" the attitude of men years ago, as it pertained to marriage. I asked, "Did you feel men back in the day took their marriage vows more seriously than men today?" Most of them said, yes. Those who said yes, said they felt that back in the day, there was no question about their role was. They felt men took their position more seriously. Their role was being the breadwinner, paying the bills, bringing home the food, protecting the family, taking care of the things needing to be fixed around the house and taking care of his wife's needs as well. The wife took care of the home, cooked his food, cleaned the house and managed the kids and her husband's needs.

At that time, it was clear there was a level of respect on both sides as it related to the everyday duties and their "position" in the relationship. The wife had no problem with her role, and occasionally would say to her husband, "Thank you for providing for your family, paying the bills, bringing home the food and taking care of all of us." That simple acknowledgment gave him a sense of purpose as to why he did what he did daily for his family. It made him feel valued by his wife and kids, and he felt that he was needed in the home.

These kinds of actions are the reason many of the marriages during that time lasted so long for so many years. How much "influence" the Bible contributed to this, I do not know. However, this I do know, men took pride in their role as a father and head of the household for their family. There are very few men today who think like this. They have gone from leading by example to handing over their responsibilities to anyone who wants it in order to avoid being held responsible for anything. With these changes in men and their views, women have changed also. With their empowerment, many see things a lot differently than their parents did years ago, and herein lies the problem. Many of the women in these relationships are wearing the pants, and these weak men are allowing it to happen as if it is normal.

It is clear that men are feeling the changes in the dynamics in a relationship with their woman. It is because of this "change" that many men don't feel like men anymore. Many of them have lost their self-confidence, few feel wanted by their woman, and most know now the title of "provider" can apply to either of them. Do you see how what was once known as the man's role and the woman now having assumed it, are not prepared to give it up for the man to be, unless he can prove he is capable of doing it? Now I am not blaming women for their progress. As I said earlier, I blame men for not stepping up and being who God created them to be…leaders of their family.

Instead of men being honest with themselves, which by the way is all women ask of us, they come at women sideways and catch an attitude when they don't accept their tired, outdated non-believable game to get with them. Men tell more "lies" than the Bible has scriptures. They misrepresent themselves, make more false promises, lie about where they are in life and what they really have, hurt their mate's heart, waste their time, criticize them for educating themselves and then feel useless when the woman uses her education to elevate herself somewhere they were unwilling to take her.

All the while not understanding that it is your foolishness that makes it harder and damn near impossible for real Christian women seeking real Christian men to meet, date, fall in love and marry because you have created the impression in their minds that all men can't be trusted. Many of us are our own worst enemy. We point the finger first, at them without understanding that in most situations, we created this lack of trust in her toward men. It is why a lot of women say, "All men are the same." Until they see evidence that suggests otherwise, I don't blame them for acting in some of the ways they do toward foolish men who act like children. These men out here with kids, who are not paying child support, are lucky and should count their blessings. I said they're fortunate because they have brainwashed and convinced their women not to take them to court to get support for their child/ren. Many believe, and I agree, most women use the money that they do receive from the man not as "child support," but more like "child/adult support." They misuse the money to try and cover all their monthly bills and to avoid having to make up their income if they work.

These are those women who see their child as a paycheck and not just as their child. This crafty lying man convinces them that if they took him to court and he can't pay, he would go to jail. That's not good for the child. The woman, feeling emotional, gets sucked into this mess and allows him to stay free, if he promises he will give them whatever he can afford to support his children, which is yet another lie. Listen, it is a fact. Jail is the one place many men don't want to go, (but it is where you can find most of them). You need to remember, "The woman you are "courting" today (trying to get with), could one day be the same one, if you don't act right, who ends up taking you to "court" to help you (if you will) fulfill those many lies you told her about your finances."

Listen, I say this out of love for you. As a man, in this situation, you must take your responsibilities seriously. Let me ask you this. How do you think you would feel standing in front of a judge, hearing him state in front of other people how much of a deadbeat dad you are, have him tell you how much of a low life you are for not willingly taking care of your child (or children)? It is because of your arrogance that you are here, in court, and he will give you ONLY two options to fix your situation, and they are (1) pay the money or (2) go to jail. Should a judge be the one to inform you that you need to provide support for your children? No, he shouldn't. You should just do it.

Let me give you a tip for when you meet a woman with kids. (FYI: There are very few women these days, over the age of 25, who don't have kids from a previous relationship.) You need to understand a few things starting with (1) What the position you are applying for in her life entails, (2) Asking yourself, are you prepared to step into the role of the "Provider and Head of Household?" (3) You understand that she and the children are a total package. (4) You must accept and be prepared to enhance her life and not drag her down, and (5) more importantly, you need to be prepared, able and willing to love her and not hurt her. Remember, when she allows you into her life and heart, what she is doing is handing you the keys to her kingdom. She is saying she is willing to let you run it, if you can do it the right way. She believes in you, and if you handle your business correctly, her kids will listen and see you as someone of authority to whom they should show respect. You will have respect for your new "position" as the man of the home, and they should obey you. Don't allow a bad moment, an argument, outside friends or anything keep you from doing her right as God intended. We will never agree on everything, but we can agree to disagree.

Let me say it another way. When you allow one bad season into your life, it consumes your thoughts. Eventually, it will overpower the good ones. During this time, you will wonder to yourself, "When will it end and when will I win?" not knowing there is a process you must go through to get to where you need to be. Believe me cause I know, this is a complicated process to understand. Many of us do not realize, "If all we see is what we see, then we do not see all there is to be seen." In other words, for you to see differently, there has to be a shift in our perspective of how we see things in order for us to see what the *cause* of the problem is instead of *what* the problem is.

Listen to me because this is important. Even in our bad season, some things can never be understood. However, we must remember, believe, understand and know our situation may seem hopeless and gloomy, but it is not. With God, we know our present "situation" is not our future. It's all a test by God for the measure of our character. What we must understand as men is that we cannot allow our "character" to destroy our purpose. Yes, when this happens, we will feel pressure. We react to that pressure by changing our methods to match our situation. It will come to a point where you, like the Israelites, will question why God is doing this and why He would allow you to go through this and make you wait.

What you must understand is God doesn't make you wait for the sake of waiting. He is simply during this time, shaping your character. I know many of you right now are looking good on the outside and wrestling with things on the inside. Not understanding what it says in **Matthew 23:28**, regardless of your issues, concerns and/or problems we're going through, God can and will guide us through it, if we allow Him to. We must stop fighting Him, repent and genuinely regret the choices we've made that got us in the situation in the first place so He can step in and help us.

Let me say this because I had a gentleman tell me something I found disturbing. He told me that when he met this woman, he moved in with her and saw nothing wrong with it. I had to sit him down and tell him that men who are doing this are making the biggest mistake of their lives. Listen, I know it seems like a good idea at first because you're walking into a readymade life, but when you do this, your life will be a mess. Do you think she will never bring up the fact that you didn't have enough money to find the two of you a place? You, like a weak man moved in with her? The first issue you will run into because you moved in with her, is the lack of respect and authority she will have for you as "the" so-called man of the house because it's not your house. You're just a guest. She will always know (as well as you) that nothing in the home is yours.

She is taking care of you. She will feel that she can talk to you any kind of way. She will because she can disrespect you at any time and because you are living "with" her, she will expect you not to respond or say anything back. Most times, men in this situation don't because they do not have anywhere else to go where they can live for free except maybe home to their parents. You think that she loves you and wants you for sex, but she wants you and is with you because she can control you and rule you. In your first argument, she will let you know how much authority you have when she says to you, "You don't run anything here. You didn't buy anything here either. You moved in with me. I am running this household." Then she will tell you because she knows you're a poor excuse for a man, "What you need to do is be a man and..."

When you hear this, of course, you will catch an attitude and try with very little success, to defend yourself when you can't because what she has said is true. Remember, you created this dysfunctional relationship and stripped your authority when you decided to move in with her. It never dawns on you why she allows you to stay with her. Let me tell you how and why she picked you out and is allowing you to live with her. It is because she knew and saw you were weak and took advantage of you. Your "weak" behind let her do it because you wanted to be the weaker one. You're doing it because you don't want the responsibilities that come along with being a leader. She knows you will never raise your voice to her or act out because to her you are weak, a disgrace and a poor excuse for a so-called man. You think you're the man when you're actually the woman, and you don't even know it.

The messed-up thing about this situation is she picked you out, figured out you were weak and had low self-esteem and learned over time, if she put her foot down on your neck, you would become depressed, angry and frustrated and want to leave but won't because you're not a leader. Now you're standing there looking and feeling like most women in this situation feel, foolish and used, not knowing what to do about it. You tell yourself this is love, not understanding loving someone is never a free pass to hurt someone that you care for in your relationship.

To understand this better, you need to reread or read the story of Jacob and Rachel in **Genesis 29:1-35, 30:1-43, 31:1-55**, (KJV). Here you are shown an excellent example of a man's love for a woman. In the story, Jacob loved Rachel and wanted her so much that he made a deal with her father to work for him for seven years for her hand in marriage. After seven years, he was prepared to marry the woman he loved and wanted, but unfortunately, after getting drunk on his wedding night, he was tricked by the father into marrying her older sister. He didn't find out until the next day. When he did, he was so determined to marry Rachel that he made yet another deal with her father to work another seven years for Rachel's hand in marriage, crazy, right? Not when you love and want someone badly enough.

Sure enough, seven years later, he got the woman he wanted. Now I bring this story to your attention because I want you to understand that Jacob waited 14 years for this woman without so much as a kiss from her or anything else at all. Compared to men's behavior today, it shows how sad we are. Men today, expect to sleep with a woman once they purchase them a meal, buy them something or give them money. This is because most women have made it so easy for us to do so. You'll notice his waiting had nothing to with sex but for her love. He was willing, ready, and able to put in the work, and "wait" to marry her. He had shown her he could "provide" many times over, so this aspect was not in question.

Do you think if Rachel were to have slept with Jacob before he married her that he would have married her anyway? I don't think so. He would have done what most men do today. He would have tried to convince her that they have a good thing going on and say, "Marriage can wait. Besides, it's just a piece of paper. We will get married when we can afford it." Now I know there are a lot of women out there today who are cool with this arrangement and the men they are with are not going to object either, but there are also many Christian women that men are running this game on who will not allow you to do this with them. I know you know what I am saying.

It is just what men do, but we need to stop it. I mean stop giving them future promises while trying to get sex today. Believe me when I say your women remember just about 99.99% of all the promises you make and tell them you're going to do IF they allow you in their lives. Women may forget the words you say to them, but they never forget how the words said, made them feel.

They will recall when they need to, everything said at the drop of a dime and will repeat your own words back almost word for word to prove her point because YOU told her. It says in **James 1:22**, (KJV), and men need to take heed to it "But be ye doers of the word, and not hearers only, deceiving your own selves." In other words, keep your word and do the things for her, you promised. If you cannot do all you've told her, tell her what you can do, and stop lying to her and yourself. If you are one of those kinds of guys who loses girlfriend after girlfriend, job-hopping, find it hard to hold on to money, and you're blaming everyone else except yourself for the reasons why things aren't going right for you, there is a reason for this.

Does anyone remember seeing the 1994 movie, **Groundhog Day**, starring Bill Murray? In the film, because he was unable to appreciate all that he had, Bill Murray's character relives the same day repeatedly until he gets himself together. When he finally realized and made the changes needed, he broke out of the cycle and lived his life better because he realized his old self wasn't living right. I mention this because, in his quest to get what and where he wanted, he encounters a slight detour. Being on this detour helped him understand what he had to do to get himself back on the path towards his destiny. Inside of two hours, he figured this out. In real life, it sometimes takes a little longer.

Many of the detours taken on our way to our destiny make us sometimes feel we are never going to understand the changes needed in trying to get it right. According to the Bible, it says it took Moses and his followers 40 years to get their correct understanding before they reached the Promised Land. Abraham's journey took 25 years, and Paul's (Saul) trip took three years. As you read in **Chapter 37 in Genesis** starting in the first chapter, it was through his dreams he learned he was destined for something. It was also clear he wasn't mature enough at that moment to be put straight into his destiny. His faith was tested (as was his faith in God) all along his way through his many detours to finally reach his 'destiny,' which was in Egypt. I am sharing this with you because I don't want it to take 40 years before many of you "get it" and turn your life around.

An excellent example of this is when a person loses their job for whatever reason, and they go through a variety of emotions. They point the finger at many others as the reason why this has happened to them while never blaming themselves. Asking God, "Why have you allowed this to happen to me?" Not realizing he is in this position for several reasons. He doesn't know, see or feel what he is going through is temporary and has no idea things will get better.

When this happens to you, you must understand "why" God allows things to happen to us. We must understand "why" He felt it necessary for us to go through it to reach the destiny He has set for us. Understand, it is during our "detour" that He addresses our character. It is through our "test" (detours) and "process" that He sees our growth, our change and our understanding of what needs to be corrected for us to move forward. God wants you to reach your destiny, and if He has to set us down, set us back and allow time to pass for us to realize this, then it will take as long as it needs to. We must understand that any detours we experience on our way to our destiny are His way of measuring where we are in our lives while on our way to reaching what God has for us.

Listen, my time is up but before I go, let me say this, I know God loves and accepts us for who we are and I feel this is true, but I hope those hearing this know He never leaves you the way he finds us. I want to ask a favor of you if you're married or looking to get married if you can do this for me. I hear people who want to talk about things say that they are "waiting for the right time." I say in cases such as this, "Make the time right" to get done what is important to you and your relationship. Sit down with your mate and make sure you laugh, read, study and pray together daily and apply His words to your life to find peace. Remember for a woman to know, believe, follow you willingly, trust, and feel she can rely and count on you; you must "Listen to her intently, reassure her gently, and love her generously."

As leaders, providers and heads of households, we must remember that "True leaders don't look for followers. Followers find them." In your relationship, your job is that you are expected to *lead* with responsibility and understanding and to listen to your spouse because God equipped her with all she has for you!

As I leave you this evening, remember that no matter who or where you are and what has happened in your life, "What has happened in your past relationships cannot be changed or undone, but what you remember of your past and how you remember it and what you do with it can be. Always know, our past failures are nothing more than opportunities to "train" ourselves to do a better job next time. When talking about your past, know it is not for you to tell of a different past, but to tell your past history differently." I hope what I have shared helps more than it hurts. We all deserve someone to love, and we all deserve a second chance to find true love. Thank you and goodnight.

Session Six

Love doesn't pay the bills!

It is Friday morning, November 08, 2019. I am on my way to work to do my show. It is a beautiful day in Atlanta this morning. When I got to work, I checked my email, and I was surprised to see emails still coming in from those who attended the **Men's Ministry** three weeks ago, telling me they enjoyed my message and that what I said needed to be said. During the day, I emailed a lot of people back and thanked them for the kind words. I reminded them I would be speaking at **For Sisters Only** in a few weeks in New Orleans at the Mercedes Benz Stadium and that they should attend. I had a few minutes before I went on air, so, I took a moment to text my wife.

KingDray
I said a prayer for you today, I asked
God if He would touch you with His
healing hand and give you the comfort and
peace you need to get through your day.
Love You, Sweetie!

Sexywife69
Thank you. Have a great show,
love you too.

Mr. Pearson is speaking: Good morning, everyone! I want to welcome our listeners to the show, **Why does love hurt so Good?** I am Ondray Pearson, and for the next two hours, I will be taking your calls and answering your relationship questions, issues and concerns about things going on in your love life. Listen, if you are unable to get your questions on the air today, feel free to email me directly at ***pearsonondray@gmail.com***. I will respond as soon as I can. We will give you additional information after the show, but for now, the lines are open, and the number here is 1-800-877-K103. After the break, we will take our first caller of the day. I am Ondray Pearson here on K103, we will be right back.

We are back. Karen who's on the line?

Karen is speaking: We have Karlie from Marietta on the line.

Mr. Pearson is speaking: Good morning, Karlie. How are you doing, and what is your question?

Karlie is speaking: Good morning to you. I am doing fine. Well, I am a Senior Accountant at IBM. I am 36 years old, single, successful and very independent. I am in a good place in my life right now. I am ready to meet, settle down, marry and have children with the right man. I am not looking for a hookup or a one-night stand. I prefer to meet a single unattached Christian man with Christian values who is ready to settle down.

Mr. Pearson is speaking: Okay.

Karlie is speaking: The problems I have encountered on the few dates I've been on have been the way men react to my responses to their questions concerning what I do for a living. Not so much my job but the fact that I am able to take care of myself without a man's help. Men are always telling me where they work, their title and how much money they make. When they ask me what I do and I tell them and add that I can and do take care of myself, they look at me as if I'm crazy, as if I'm asking them to pay my rent or something. I guess they thought I was a "thirsty" woman looking for a free meal and for them to "take care of me." They have asked me, once I told them about myself, "What kind of man are you looking for?" I tell them, "I am looking for a man who can take care of all my needs." Maybe it is my fault because I didn't explain what I meant by the words "every need" and they tend to think I am only talking about my financial needs? Often they reply by asking, "So, when you say 'every need' are you saying you want a man to pay your bills and buy you things?

It is then I realize I should have explained myself better on what I meant. Selfish men hear and think, "She wants me for my money." I knew he wasn't the one because he said, "You said you were "independent." Why do you need someone to take care of you? Women are always talking about how they want equal rights and equal pay but insist on men funding their financial needs in the relationship. What's that all about?" Now, as you can imagine, the date was over at this point. To be honest with you, this has happened so often that I was beginning to wonder, am I choosing the wrong men to date? Are my standards in men too low because it seems I am attracted to good looking men who think like this? Maybe if I seem a little more impressed by what they do and have, maybe they would act a little better?

I can't help that they are offended by me being able to take care of myself. I didn't feel the need to stroke a man's ego that way to have a conversation with him. He needed to be a little more patient and realize he needed to impress me not manage me. Maybe what I say comes off a bit aggressive, as if I don't need a man, but I believe in being honest and upfront on what I bring to the relationship and my expectations for my man. I know I can and will add to the relationship and not just take from it. A real man hearing this will understand and admire this in his woman not run from it.

I feel this is the reason why I haven't had many second dates. I am not going to apologize or deal with foolishness to be in a relationship with a man. I am a real woman with standards and expectations, and I am looking for the friendship of a Christian man with confidence, someone who can handle an intelligent black woman. I let them know I am dating with a purpose which is to get married. I am willing to put in the time to build a solid friendship, but one thing is clear. I don't want to waste my time with someone who doesn't want what I want.

Mr. Pearson is speaking: That makes sense.

Karlie is speaking: I was talking with one of my girlfriends, Zoe, one night over drinks about my dating problems. I told her every time a man asks me what I am looking for in my man, and I tell them, they get offended. She asked, "What are you saying?" I told her, "I want a man who can take care of my every need." She asked, "Did you define and explain what you meant?" I said, "No, why should I have to explain this? Every man should know what I am saying." Listen, if I have learned one thing about most men it is that you have to explain many things to them because they hear words differently than we do. When you said, "take care of my every need," most of them understood, "She is trying to get my money." It is a shame so many men get caught up in their feelings when a woman says this to them. If they were confused, they should ask to get clarification to make sure there are no misunderstandings on their part.

I understand they get played and burnt by scandalous women, but they shouldn't assume all women are the same. There are some good women out there looking for good men. A real man would realize and know that God has equipped us with skills that can enhance any relationship and the man we're with, to make them a better man with us. It is a shame these men are so hard to find. I don't feel comfortable, nor will I dummy down my success to make a man feel important. I will adjust and work with my man who is working with me, but I will not degrade myself to make a man feel like a man to be with me. I know too many women who have dummied down themselves for men who didn't appreciate them. They end up being mistreated and disrespected. They called what they had with them love, that's not me. I know how I am sounding comes off a little crazy, but I am not angry, just disappointed in the men who are not stepping it up and being the man God created them to be with a woman.

So, I have two questions for you one, "Why are so many men afraid of an 'independent' career-minded woman?" Secondly, "How do I filter through the foolishness of boys pretending to be men and find a man ready to seriously commit?"

Mr. Pearson is speaking: These are two excellent and interesting questions that I get asked a lot by successful smart career-minded women like you. The answer to the first question on why men are intimidated by independent women is this, in my opinion:

For a lot of men when they hear women say, "I want someone to take care of me," it translates to "they want someone to take care of them financially." Many think and believe women only want them for all they get from them and not a relationship built on trust and building a future together. Most of these men who think this way have come across those women who were taught and raised more on how to survive then how to love a man or themselves, making it harder to invest in anyone for long term. Their immediate goals are to get all they can get before the man gets what he wants from them and move on to the next man — treating most men as a means to an end who transport them from one place in life to the next.

Those words make most men cringe and think if they do get with them, they will bring to the relationship little to nothing to the table except drama, bills, problems, emotional and financial baggage, additional debt and most of the time more mouths to feed. They use them for their resources and add nothing to their lives. At the same time, women are reacting to the fact that very few, if any, men are faithful or loyal and many use fear to rule them instead of loving them.

Many career women have often found themselves dating "pretenders." These are the guys who use pickup lines from the 1980s thinking that all they need to do to "get with" a woman is spend a little money. These are the ones who forget they're living in 2020 where many women have their own and don't need other men to take care of them financially. Real women want more than sex and a smile. They want a commitment from a man. They want a man with goals, vision and a plan to get there. Real men understand and know women have more to bring to the table than just their bodies. They don't make promises. They make commitments. Now for many "thirsty" women, these old lines and lies work flawlessly every day of the week and twice on Sunday because they are looking for "trinkets" from whoever they can get it from and are more than willing to exchange sex for them.

Many of these views of both men and women come from thinking in the mindset of "worldly" desires and not the "biblical" attractions as they relate to marriage. Christian men and women who know the Bible, understand that "communication" and "understanding" is a primary key to having a successful marriage, not trinkets. Now, for those listening who are not familiar with the term "thirsty," it has many meanings but in this situation, a thirsty woman is a person who will willingly exchange sex for the "things & stuff" men promise them. Real women who know their worth would not consider this as an option. Their dignity and respect mean more than trinkets given to them from a man.

Karlie is speaking: Yes, you get where I am coming from, and you understand what I am saying. Men today need to stop thinking women are stupid because we are not. Real women are not impressed with trinkets because they know there is more to a relationship than just trinkets. Just because I can afford my own doesn't make me wrong. Selfish men never share and only think about themselves.

Mr. Pearson is speaking: You are correct. These pretenders believe those old lines, "If you were with me, I would buy you a new car, a house, expensive clothes and take you on expensive trips, etc…" not realizing these lines from the 80s and 90s are losing their face value if they still have any at all. Women today can say proudly, "I already have a new car. I have a home. I've got name brand clothes, and I go on trips twice a year. What else can you do for me?"

Karlie is speaking: Why do you feel it is so hard for men to deal with successful women?

Mr. Pearson is speaking: Yes, it is hard. With the changes in the world today, many men are finding it very difficult to accept the fact that women are on the come up. They no longer have to rely or depend on men for their survival. The world's view and position of men today has changed drastically. A lot of men have become comfortable with the role reversal in their relationship and have no problem with the woman being the "leader" in the home. So many so-called Christian men and other men, in general, seem to be comfortable living off of women than ever before. Many men have given up their right to be taken seriously by women and are looking at women like they are crazy because they are refusing to take care of grown men financially in the relationship.

The days of the man bringing home the bacon and their woman cooking it has flipped dramatically. These changes have happened primarily because weak men have put women in a "do for you" position by abandoning them and their male responsibilities. These women in these positions have no choice but to be both "the mother and father" of their household. They have been forced to figure out ways to survive and provide for their families. Meaning, they have to make money, bring home the groceries and cook it up because they have children depending on them like you used to rely on him. He let her down but she can't let her kids down.

Men have put women in tough situations financially, when they leave the family dynamic, creating broken families. They've made it necessary for the woman to assume their role as the "breadwinner" of their household. Then, they catch an attitude with them because they no longer depend on them for the things they want, need or feel they deserve. These weak boys pretending to be men overreact because they are in their feelings. They are unable to retain their title or be seen in most women's eyes as someone that can lead a relationship. This makes them feel useless, thus, making them upset and mad at the woman's success because they are jealous. All this because the titles that were once men's exclusively, now apply to women as well.

Gone are the days where women depended on a man for their survival, wants and needs, allowing the man to feel in control of the relationship. Men feeling like this will keep that woman with them are mistaken. Those days are gone, but many weak and silly men don't know it yet.

Karlie is speaking: These Neanderthal thinking boys pretending to be men are wasting women's time and are standing in the way of the serious and responsible men who are looking for us. They need to find those women who are looking for them. They are not hard to find.

Mr. Pearson is speaking: This is true. A reason for some of their bad behavior is because of the changes in the world. A lot of men are having a hard time figuring out where they fit in. Many have no idea how to be useful or how to make themselves seem valuable to most women, so, most have stopped trying. They revert to what they feel they know, games and foolishness, to attract women. Their egos and pride conclude that if the woman makes more money than they do, they will lose control of the relationship. They feel she will act out (as many in this situation do) and voice their position to control and disrespect them. They fear that they will be made to feel useless and less than a man in the relationship (as most men do to them). This is not the woman's fault who has educated herself in order to have a better life. The man needs to step up and match her and work together to build their relationship.

Let's be clear. A woman does not need a man. She wants a man. Sure, she can do it all herself, but many prefer sharing their journey with someone. It's hard for most men, when they meet these women, to understand the pressure they are under to compete and stay in their positions. These are women who are bosses at their day jobs and who are willing, although it is hard, to come home and allow her man to be the boss in their home *IF* their man has earned this in the relationship. Most married couples of a household are very much equal but have different duties, and they are defined explicitly in the Bible, if you follow the Bible. With God first in your lives, everything else will fall in line. There is nothing wrong with having expectations for your mate. You have to be careful how you declare your wants and needs, so you don't come off as offensive and bossy. Try not to bring work home, if you can help it because if there is a problem between the two of you, you need to be able to stay respectful to maintain a happy environment in the home. We must relay it in a way that it doesn't lead to the wrong assumptions or create misunderstandings of what we want in our mate.

Karlie is speaking: I don't mean to interrupt, but I don't have the time, nor will I waste my time, playing games with men. I can tone down my expectations a little and how I deliver them, but I will not put up with him lying to me. I am not that woman. I am not a weak woman looking for a handout. James Brown said it best when he said, "I don't want nobody to give me anything. Open up the door, and I'll get it myself." No man is going to make me feel sorry for working hard to have the things I do have. Don't get me wrong. I don't mind sharing and allowing my man to take the lead, if he has shown me that he is worthy of it, but so many men expect women to hand them the crown and key to the kingdom when they haven't even earned it.

Too many men feel that when they give you something or do something for you, you owe them something in return. Trust me, I will show my man that I appreciate him taking care of me, but I am not going to kiss the ground he walks on just because he bought me a meal. I can do that myself. There has to be more to a relationship than just "trinkets," and that's what I am looking for in a real man. When I get married, I know my views will change. I will willingly adjust because I would feel and understand that my Christian husband got me fully 100%. I will view things differently because it is His way for the wife. But for now, and until He presents the right man for me, I will never feel sorry for doing well for myself.

Mr. Pearson is speaking: I agree. Before I continue, let me say this, "A man treats a woman as he sees her. He learns how to treat her by watching how she treats herself." Meaning, if a woman carries herself respectfully, a real man will have no choice but to approach and treat her the same way IF he wants to have a conversation with her. Too many women today play themselves short because they are and often seem "desperate" in their attempt to be with someone. The desperation often gets them used quicker than most. Many of these women living this way have said, "It is better to have half a man than no man." It is this kind of thinking that makes it harder for many women to get the respect they deserve.

Listen, I tell women this all the time. If you dress like a hooker and carry yourself like a hooker, you will attract a pimp. He will see how desperate you are to be loved and wanted. He will put you to work and make you think he is doing it for your benefit. I agree with you, a successful woman should never feel ashamed for doing well. A weak-minded man who is unable to relate to a strong, educated and successful woman like yourself is not the man for you.

The problem and the reason this cycle keeps happening is not the fact men don't know or understand their role in their relationship. It's that they are taking advantage of a loophole women have left open. Men understand their role. They just don't want the responsibilities of that role. They have found a loophole that many women aren't willing to close up to make their relationship better with their man. Women need to understand what that loophole is and close it quickly or continue to suffer in silence. Boyfriends today have got it made because of the low expectations of women. They all get free benefits without investing hardly anything. Don't be fooled. A lot of men understand the definition of marriage but "act" confused at times because they don't want to "commit" to you legally.

Women in relationships also play a "major" role in the blame. Too many women are giving themselves to their boyfriends and not to their husband. Women who give themselves to a man who is not their husband before they hear "I do," are gambling their entire youth away. They're "hoping" that he will see them as a good wife and marry them. Many may say that they see, think and feel you could be their wives but very few, if any, will make you their wife. It should be a red flag when the guy doesn't push marriage. It makes sense from his perspective. He doesn't benefit from getting married as he sees it. He is already getting the sex, having the kids and everything else a married man would get, all without a legal paper to bind them in case they decide to leave. They can go without any consequences, and women are allowing this because they don't want to be alone.

A lot of men will use a woman's "youth" up and then move to someone much younger and start all over again, using them and filling their heads with future lies for sex today. Women with low expectations make it harder for successful women to enforce on a man "standards or expectations" because they know if she doesn't "act right" they can move on and find a woman who will, quickly. Many of them sleep with the "boyfriend" early in their friendship when the man has put in no work or earned the right to them, making one-night stands the norm. To most men sex is sex. Most of the time, it doesn't matter what woman gives it to them.

Karlie is speaking: I understand what you're saying, but men need to realize that not all women want or need to be saved by them. "To take care of them" can mean things other than just money but because they think so small-mindedly, they are unable to see and process that a good woman can bring equally if not more to a good relationship. God has equipped us with many talents to enhance our men if they can get out of the way and allow us to do what we're capable of doing for and with them.

Mr. Pearson is speaking: This is true. Another problem men have with some successful women is that they have great expectations of them but none of themselves. Many expect perfection when they aren't themselves. They can tell men what they expect from them but will never tell him what he can expect from them or stick to it. Men cannot have too many expectations for them because women don't want to have things that they are expected to do, they want to have the option to do things or not. Most want their way in the relationship. Many men have said, "As long as you do what the woman says and give her what she wants, you're a good man. However, don't have an option that differs from her own. She will see that as you are going against her."

A lot of women promote themselves in a prostitute-like manner, giving off vibes to the man that they can have them for a price. These are those "thirsty" women we spoke about earlier. If you notice, I didn't mention the word love in this scenario. I didn't because this kind of behavior has nothing to do with love. It is merely an exchange of goods for money. It is no secret all men worldwide will forever pay in some form or fashion for sex. Let's not kid ourselves. It doesn't matter if they take you out to dinner, to a movie, to a club, buy you drinks, etc., they are paying for the opportunity to sleep with you when the time comes. It is a horrible game to play because so many things can go wrong. People who feel used will react in many ways. Some will walk away, and some will cause harm.

I am mentioning this because women dating today know the difference between a "friend" gift, and "I am trying to get with you" gift. Many play the games and get all they can get from him, knowing that he is trying to get with them and then say, "I didn't ask you to get these things for me, you volunteered." Now a nice guy will walk away hurt but walk away. Some not so nice men will get violent and could damage the woman for playing games with them knowing they were serious. I suggest if you're not interested, don't take "anything" from a man.

Karlie is speaking: I understand, and I agree. Other than flowers, I will not lead him on if I am not interested. If I see him as a potential mate, I will tell him upfront before he feels whatever he has done is deserving of me giving him something else, you feel me?

Mr. Pearson is speaking: Again, I agree with you. No man will respect you if you don't respect yourself. Too many women wear signs that they are for sale.

Karlie is speaking: What do you mean women wear signs?

Mr. Pearson is speaking: Many women like to advertise or show off their bodies in such a way that men see sex, not love and not a relationship. They want to smash them. I know these kinds of games will continue to go on, but I want those playing to know, especially women, you can lose and get hurt. Winning isn't all it's cracked up to be if you're still alone.

Karlie is speaking: Why do so many men feel they must disrespect women to get with them?

Mr. Pearson is speaking: Women allow them to do this. Mutual respect must be established from your first meeting or conversation that you two have. Men who have problems with successful women need to find themselves someone else. It is not fun for women who are good to lower their standards so low that they are a good woman playing a bad one to attract a man. They will never respect themselves, nor will the man know how you came into it.

Karlie is speaking: Do you feel men are that shallow or are women so needy that they need to be someone's "thot"?

Mr. Pearson is speaking: Both. No woman needs to trade sex for men's money. Men need not allow their ego to get in the way of meeting a strong woman who brings more than just her body to the relationship. They should welcome them because marriage is a "partnership" not a solo act with a sidekick. Don't get me wrong. Yes, some women have unrealistic expectations and may need to rethink them. However, by no means should they lower them to the point they have none because men are unable to step up to the plate and be men. Listen, there are two kinds of men in this world that you are going to meet, "men who want to spend on you and those who want to invest in you."

Karlie is speaking: I have met the man who wants to spend on me. It is time to meet the man wants to invest in me. How do I find him?

Mr. Pearson is speaking: The man who is looking to "invest" in you will take his time to get to know and understand who you are. He will not feel threatened by your status or the money you make. He will ask you what you feel you need to grow and give it to you with no questions asked. He will see the great potential in you and know that what he is investing in, is worth it. In other words, he is investing in something he feels will add value to his life, that has and will return GREAT dividends. Any good investor knows, "The better you know what you're investing in, the lower the risk of you losing your investment."

Karlie is speaking: Now that is the kind of man I am looking for, but it is so hard because most men will say these things but never follow through. It is hard trying not to waste your time on them.

Mr. Pearson is speaking: This is true, but if you are patient and you watch to see if his actions match his words, you will be able to see and know if he is in it for a short term or the long run to be able to move forward with him. Don't measure your love for him on the things he offers and gives you, base it on how he makes you feel and if you can see a future with him.

Karlie is speaking: I understand. The more information with clarity is better than less information and being confused.

Mr. Pearson is speaking: Your second question was, "How do you get through the boys pretending to be men to meet that serious, responsible man ready to settle down?" This one is a little trickier to answer, but I will try. The subject of love and finding true love has been the most challenging thing to do throughout the centuries. Love will always be timeless, misunderstood, a mystery, hard to control, sometimes joyful (when you have it in your life), sometimes painful and something we as people will always want and feel we need in our lives to be happier. It is such a mystery that for years, psychologists have yet to find ways to explain it. Books on the subject have yet to come up with adequate words to describe it and people who have been in a relationship "feel and think" they know all there is to know about it when they really don't.

It is no secret. We all want someone to love and to be loved. One of the issues we struggle with and sometimes are frustrated by when trying to find love is our inability and understanding of "how" to get, keep and maintain it once we have it in our lives with someone. I feel the frustrations come from the fact that we have yet to understand that love is more of a choice than an emotion. Love is not something we can manufacture, buy, sit on a shelf or pick up when we want it. It's nothing we can hold in our hands or control, and for most people, that can be a little unnerving.

Yes, there are many ways to find your true love, and an excellent place to start is with you knowing some of the things you want in YOUR man and recognizing them when you see them in someone you feel has potential. This process itself takes some time. I believe that when God believes you're ready, He will "present" someone in your life to you. He will not "quote on quote" pick them out for you because that is not what He does. God will present someone He feels would be right for you and the rest of the "getting to know" part is on you. You see, loving someone as I see it is about giving of ourselves and hope without knowing what we have given out will be returned. Doing this sometimes scares us. Don't worry though; I feel even with these concerns, unconditional love with someone who wants the same with you is possible!

Karlie is speaking: To be honest with you, I would like my potential mate to show me more than tell me because it lets me know he has good intentions towards me. It's not about his money or the things he could get or give me. For me, it's about chemistry and being compatible, talking and doing what we say we're going to do to be husband and wife and not selling me a pipe dream. Like I stated earlier, I am a Christian woman and my man needs to be Christian. He needs to think and walk in Christ for me to submit and follow him the way the Bible says I should.

Therefore, until I meet my future husband, I will continue to date, work and handle my own life. I don't, nor will I ever, rely on a "boyfriend" to determine if I live well or not. As a Christian woman, my submission comes with and belongs to my husband who follows Christ. I feel my husband will treat and see me as equal in our relationship though our "functions" are different. I know if he loves me, he will not diminish or see my role as less important even if I do make more money.

Mr. Pearson is speaking: A man who doesn't put in the effort to get to know you, who lies and plays games, is not worth your time. A few weeks ago, at the **Men's Ministry**, I told those men who attended a woman needs a man with "a vision and a plan." Someone who knows and sees the future of the relationship and is more than willing to explain and make sure you understand the steps being taken to get there. Someone who can communicate with their woman the road he feels will be best to get them there. Someone who isn't afraid to seek advice from his woman and someone able to make a few adjustments if need be to ensure they both get where "they" plan to be together.

Karlie is speaking: Amen brother. I feel you. We are on the same page.

Mr. Pearson is speaking: Trust me, when I was looking for my wife, (and I am glad I found her,) I wanted her to know that I wasn't looking for someone to live with. I was looking for someone I couldn't live without. Unfortunately, for every one woman willing to wait for the right man, many aren't ready to wait at all. These are your women who jump in too quickly, get hurt, then claim, "All men are dogs." I know what they mean is that the men they have allowed into their world and dated weren't any good. When they continue this kind of behavior, they will often say, "There are no good men out here today." What they are saying is that they are not willing to trust in God and wait for Him to send them the right man. As you know, anything worth having doesn't happen overnight. It takes time to develop.

Karlie is speaking: I agree. I am willing to wait because I want my man to know me, understand me, love me, be there for me, encourage me, have my back, pick me up when I am down, listen to me when I want to vent, make me feel that "I" matter to him and I am first in his life behind God.

Mr. Pearson is speaking: You're looking for a man ready to make a great investment in you. If marriage is what you seek with the right man, you're on the right track. You're doing it the way God intended. The road you are traveling isn't going to be easy, and at times you will feel like giving up and giving in to the very next man who says he likes you. When you feel this way, ask God for His help and stand strong, okay?

Karlie is speaking: Okay! My concern right now is the fear of being rejected. I don't want to be too vulnerable with someone who I am not sure likes me that way and end up getting hurt. Maybe that is why the men I have met thus far have been a little less forthcoming and upset with me. I have been very cautious with opening myself up to them before I know where we are going, if we're going anywhere at all. I want to feel and understand my man is with me for me and not for my body. Is that too much to ask?

Mr. Pearson is speaking: Not at all. Let me say this. The author, C.S. Lewis, explains love this way, "To love at all is to be vulnerable." I agree with him, and I take this to mean, "Love unexpressed is pointless." Unfortunately, with love comes both pain and pleasure. They are inseparable, and to be loved, we must open ourselves up to the idea happening to us. It is tough to love someone without being vulnerable simply because it is the way we show how much we care for someone. The only way to try and avoid being hurt is to not engage in loving someone. Is being unloved something you want for yourself?

Karlie is speaking: No, not at all. Is there a way to have more pleasure than pain?

Mr. Pearson is speaking: Honestly, there is no sure way to avoid pain in a relationship, but you experience less of it if you start building "trust" in your relationship from your friendship. Understand this, "trust" is not a right; it is a privilege you earn by proving you are trustworthy. Easier said than done I know because women often hear men say, "Trust me, I got you" when you hardly know them. Those asking this have no real idea what they are asking of you or how difficult that is for you to do when they have not earned it. It is an unfair thing to ask you when he has not shown or proved he deserves to be trusted at all.

Christ's standard for trust in **John 14:11**, (KJV), says, "...believe me for the very works sake." Meaning you believe in what you have seen me do. Men need to understand, "If they don't put in work on your job, you will get fired." In short, they need to invest in you and not try and buy you because your love is not for sale. The Bible tells them you're worth more than money, and if they believe in Christ, they understand what this is saying.

Karlie is speaking: I agree with you. A man's conversation, his ability to communicate and his subject matter are deciding factors on whether I am willing to trust him. Another problem I have with men is the use of the words "I love you." It seems they say it only because they believe women need to hear it. Men think that once we hear those words, they have control over us, and we will then sleep with them. It is hard to believe them when the same words are used to describe other things they claim to love as well.

Mr. Pearson is speaking: You are right. Too many men use the words "I love you" as their means of "sealing the deal," which is to sleep with you. In other words, many men believe those words guarantee them control over you, and with this control, you will do anything for them. Yes, you're right, if said too often for too many things, it loses its value and meaning. It seems to me you've heard this a few times and for the moment, it seems to have lost its "value" or true meaning when it is said to you. Therefore, you have your defenses up, and this is a valid reason for women feeling this way to do.

Karlie is speaking: This is what bothers me the most. I am an emotional woman when it comes to loving someone. I know it is much easier for me to allow my man into my heart, then it is for him to let me in his. This scares me because for me if he hurts me, my pain goes deeper than just physical.

Mr. Pearson is speaking: This is true, and I understand what you are saying. The kind of pain you are describing is much worse than any physical pain. It often shakes us to the core of our identity, hopes, and dreams of what we thought we knew about loving the person we've chosen to love. I understand loving someone isn't easy, and it is hard to say who is and who isn't going to hurt us. Knowing yourself as you do and having a strong relationship with Him can help you as you go through your search. I have always said, loving someone is like riding a roller-coaster; we get on board willingly, and we know we are about to go for a ride. We don't know at the end of the ride how we will feel about what we just experienced. We're scared, we're excited or it could make us wish we never got on it in the first place. Either way, to experience these kinds of emotions, we must first "willingly" get on board."

We've got to take a break, but when we come back, I will continue this conversation.

Okay. We are back. Karlie, are you still there?

Karlie is speaking: Yes, I am here.

Mr. Pearson is speaking: Okay, as I was saying. *True love* in a relationship deepens with communication and understanding and with this, your love for one another goes beyond the passion of the romance. Don't get me wrong. I know intimacy in your relationship, having your needs met and security is essential to you in the relationship. The most important thing to remember though, is the more we know about each other, the less we feel vulnerable with one another.

Remember, it is during the dating stage that we do our best to show we are loveable. Trying to play it cool enough that we're somewhat interested but not so much that we look thirsty and somewhat desperate. Our desperation to be loved by someone shows in our search, and it shows who we are and what we have become, and it worsens if our hearts have been broken. So, we should know ourselves enough to ask questions for information while keeping the conversation going.

Karlie is speaking: You said our desperation shows? How?

Mr. Pearson is speaking: Well, it shows a side of us of things we've said and done that we could never have imagined we would do. Inevitably during this process, we feel worthless or undeserving of love from anyone because we are unable to find that right person. The harder we try, the more desperate we seem.

Karlie is speaking: This is something I fear.

Mr. Pearson is speaking: I am not saying you're desperate by the way; I am just pointing out our world's perspective. People tend to think something's wrong with a person who is unmarried and over a certain age when there isn't. When it is right for you, is the right time, not when others think it is.

Karlie is speaking: I agree.

Mr. Pearson is speaking: I would say, in your situation, to take your time and allow God to guide your feelings for the person you see as having potential. As a Christian woman, you know, God uses our feelings to draw us closer to Him. When dealing with life, love and relationships, our feelings alert us to danger and provide us with insight into various situations, both good and bad. Even though our feelings can trick and confuse us when we care for someone, we must "test" our feelings.

Karlie is speaking: I don't want to get hurt.

Mr. Pearson is speaking: It's not uncommon when you start to like someone that old feelings start to creep in and give you doubt or make you doubt yourself. It reminds you of yesterday and in some cases, makes us feel hopeless, not good enough, not worthy, unlovable and helpless to a point where you tell yourself, "Why try again, to be hurt again?" Let me be clear. Your feelings do not define you. You're defined by what God says about you. Meaning this, we need to trust and believe in God to "present" the person He feels will best love us for who we are.

Now to be fair and realistic, there are reasons why some of us are unable to find or obtain the "unconditional" love we've heard so much about growing up. I know in our quest for finding true love it can be complicated, and that complication comes mainly from us. Our self-interest sometimes can complicate our dreams of finding and sharing unconditional love with someone. We are and can be our worst enemy. We can mess up the gifts and blessings that God gives us sometimes but not always on purpose. It is caused sometimes because we tend to protect our hearts and often promote ourselves. With this kind of thought process, we often wonder and ask ourselves in our relationship, "What am I getting out of this relationship?"

Karlie is speaking: I must admit I have done that a time or two.

Mr. Pearson is speaking: Janet Jackson asked the question many women often ask men they're dating, "What have you done for me lately?" Gwen Guthrie told men directly in her song, "You've got to have a J-O-B if you want to be with me." but, Syleena Johnson said it best in her song **Guess What**. She told men "what it takes" to keep a good woman when they've found one, and all men worldwide need to listen to the song because it makes perfect sense. Listen need to listen carefully too, if they want to be with a good woman. Who knowingly wants to waste their time on the wrong person? No one wants to willingly be someone's bus stop until they can transfer to someone else. No one wants to invest time in grooming you into something better than you were when they met you, only to hand you off to someone else.

Karlie is speaking: I know that's right.

Mr. Pearson is speaking: I told my wife when we were dating, that I wanted both love and sex at the same time. I saw a future with her, and I was willing to wait and marry her to prove it. I saw and still see value in her that could improve me as a man. I understood anything worth having was truly worth waiting for, and she is and has been worth it ever since.

In **Ephesians 5:6**, (KJV), it says, "Let no man deceive you with vain words: for because of these things cometh the wrath of God upon the children of disobedience." In other words, a good man will see "value" in you, be truthful to you about everything, and give you what you need... love. A "simple" man aka someone playing games cannot see beyond his wants and needs, thus making him useless to any woman. Listen to what it says in **Philippians 1:9-10**, (KJV), it says, **9-** "And this I pray, that your love may abound yet more and more in knowledge in all judgement;" and **10** says, "That ye may approve things that are excellent; that ye may be sincere and without offence till the day of Christ;" It is fitting, and if you continue to allow Him to help you, your true love will appear when He feels you're ready. I hope I was able to provide adequate answers to your questions today, Karlie.

Karlie is speaking: You did more than that, and I appreciate it.

Mr. Pearson is speaking: Well if you come across a man who says he is a Christian, then ask him if he is familiar with **Galatians 6:7**, (KJV). "Be not deceived; God is not mocked: for whatsoever a man soweth, that shall he also reap." I say this because He sees everything and knows what men are doing to women so they may get away with their foolishness toward you right now. At some point though, what goes around will come right back around again on them twice as hard. Thank you for your call, Karlie.

When we come back from break, we will take more calls. We'll be right back.

We're back. Karen, who do we have on the line?

Karen is speaking: We have Tierra on the line.

Mr. Pearson is speaking: Good morning, Tierra, how are you doing this morning?

Tierra is speaking: I am doing well.

Mr. Pearson is speaking: What is your question?

Tierra is speaking: Well, my husband and I have been married for six years. In our fourth year of marriage, I found out that he cheated on me. It hurt me so that I nearly for a while thought of checking out of the marriage. We didn't divorce, but we did separate for a while. I wasn't sure if I wanted to work things out or leave. I had invested four years of my life with him and our marriage, and as a Christian woman, I found it hard to let it all go. During our separation, I needed to feel wanted and desired, so I began going out with my girlfriends to clear my head. One night, while we were out, I met someone. His name was Will. We started talking and meeting up for lunch and dinner for a while and soon became close. I told him I was separated, and I wasn't sure if I was going to return to the marriage or not. I didn't want to mislead him if I changed my mind, his wanting to get to know me and be my friend, and he said it was okay, we can be friends.

When he said this, I was a little relieved and felt I could just be me and get through what I was going through. He said all the right things and all I, in my situation, needed to hear. Strangely enough, I started to enjoy his company very much so that one night, while having dinner at his home, we crossed that line and became intimate. I knew it was wrong to do as a Christian woman, but it had been so long since anyone had made me feel wanted or seen me as a desirable woman. Crazy or not, I let myself go and enjoyed the moment. Strangely enough afterward though I knew what I did was wrong, I felt relieved. Now I know I should have seen it coming and stopped it, but I was relieved because I felt attractive and wanted again. I haven't felt that way in the months since my husband and I separated. As I drove home, I knew I had cheated, and I wondered if I had done it because he had done it to me or because I wanted to for me. Either way, I knew I couldn't tell him because if I did, the first thing he would do is say I did it on purpose to hurt him because he had cheated on me. Even if what he is saying is true and I somehow did do it to get even, and I am not saying it is, how could he be mad at me when he cheated on me first?

Now I know two wrongs don't make it right, and there is more to the story, and I have questions. For the moment, let me say and ask, "We both cheated, does this mean our infidelities cancel each other out? Does this mean we can start with a clean slate?"

Mr. Pearson is speaking: Well, this is a tricky situation to be in and one many today find themselves a part of and no clear answer to resolve it. Before I answer your questions, you said there was more to the story?

Tierra is speaking: Yes, I feel with the lying and cheating he has done and then, me cheating and not telling him, I am not sure if he knew, he would want to stay in the marriage. I know not telling him is just as bad as lying but right now, where we are in our marriage, being separated and all, I know it will not help matters. I know it sounds crazy, but I do love him, and I feel he loves me. I am not ready to leave the marriage. I know I have to tell him at some point about what I have done, but how do I? The other thing is with all his lying, he does make it hard for me to trust and believe him sometimes.

Mr. Pearson is speaking: Has he always lied? Are the lies bad or harmful lies? Is this a deal-breaker for you?

Tierra is speaking: Yes, he has always told harmful lies. I noticed when we first got together, he was trying to impress me or sound like a big shot, and he would stretch the truth a little. I would know he was lying when he would end what he said, with "if I am lying, I am dying." Since he cheated, I have noticed he has started to lie about the simplest things and questions I would ask him about us and household things, and I am not sure why. When he talks, he will omit words. He'll keep me in the dark, tell me half-truths, and he thinks there is nothing wrong with it. I do not believe he is cheating or anything like that, but I am concerned about what may have brought this behavior on that he finds it necessary to lie to me for no reason.

Mr. Pearson is speaking: Your question has many layers, and one that has left many women in similar situations scratching their heads. Let me address the two questions I hear you asking which are "Because you both cheated does it make you both even and should you be able to start clean from there" and "Why do men lie for no reason, right?"

Tierra is speaking: Yes!

Mr. Pearson is speaking: As far as why most men lie when they don't have to, that is easy. They lie because they can, like most people. For most, they want to see if they can fool you into believing whatever they are telling you. Until you catch them, they will go with it and think nothing about it. FYI: Men who lie a lot believe you will never catch them because they are that believable. Now because I hear his issues from your side only, I will keep my answer a little broad because this is really about a person's behavior.

Tierra is speaking: Okay.

Mr. Pearson is speaking: I have learned over the years that people have their motivation for the lies they tell. A few potential reasons are: They don't want to hurt your feelings. They don't want the drama from a difference of options. They don't believe that most women can handle the truth. They simply don't always see the upside of telling you the truth. They are trying to impress you. They are trying to make themselves look more valuable or desirable to you. They just could be immature, insecure and selfish, who knows? For most, it comes down to 3 primary reasons why a person would lie instead of telling the truth, and they are:

(1) They are hiding something from you.

(2) The person could be trying to hurt you.

(3) They are doing so to make themselves look and seem as if they are on top of the world, all to impress you.

I say this because not everyone is "wired" the same. With the way people are these days, it's hard enough to navigate your way through, and even more complicated when things in your relationship don't go according to plan. Now, I am by no means making excuses for him because I know when this happens, we experience all kinds of emotions, doubts and insecurities. If we allow them to grow and fester, they will overwhelm us into doubting ourselves and our relationship. Our fears and worries compel us so, and it doesn't matter if it is real or imaginary, they will keep us from enjoying our relationship, and lead us to crave validation and confirmation elsewhere in order to feel part of something.

Now, I can't say why he may have cheated in the first place, only he knows why he did. I do know this though, "women need a reason to cheat, and men just need a location." His lying seems to me to be more about validation and confirmation from someone else. I say this because you said it yourself, "He wants to look like a big shot to people." In your case, you have been married for over 6 years. You know him pretty well and had become immune to his harmful lies and antics because to you, they were just something he did. I can say this, in most cases, it takes something the man did or said and hasn't delivered on to make their woman "think" and consider getting it from someone else. Many men never figure this out or think about this fact until it is too late.

Tierra is speaking: Well, that makes sense because he doesn't need to lie to me. I have heard him lie to his friends. They don't call him out. They all laugh because they know his tell-tale sign and phrase when he is stretching the truth, "If I am lying, I am dying" and realize he is just trying to be the center of attention. Now, lying to your friends to look like a big man is no reason to lie to me and cheat.

Mr. Pearson is speaking: I agree with you. It's like the author, Arthur Conan Doyle said, "When you have eliminated the impossible, whatever remains, however improbable, must be the truth." And in your case you're right, his behavior of lying to you, even after the fact, shows he didn't value your marriage enough to talk to you first to see if the two of you could have worked things out before he decided to cheat.

I honestly don't feel most men want to lie all the time, but many will to avoid hurting you and drama. Many do this without thinking about the consequences of their actions. For most men, they feel women ask them questions, expecting them to lie. I know it "sounds" crazy. Most women, regardless of what they say, who claim they want a man to tell them the truth, can't handle the truth and for most, they don't want the truth. For most men hearing what they perceive to be a loaded question with no real right answer, they will run through, in their head, millions of scenarios because they're always thinking in a mindset of wins and losses, victories and defeats. Meaning, they're searching for "an" answer that will both satisfy you and still get them what they want … peace. Is this right to do to someone you love? Probably not, but now keep in mind women do the same thing because they aren't looking to hurt their mate either.

Tierra is speaking: I understand that, but the truth is not our enemy. Knowing what I have done and being a Christian woman, I feel we should be able to be open and honest with one another, right? Growing up, my mother would always say that we should be real with the person you claim you love. I am trying to be with him. I don't mind him lying to his friends to look like the man, but he needs to keep it 100% with me. I am more than his friend. I am his wife.

Mr. Pearson is speaking: That sounds good because you answered one of your questions, "Should you tell him?" Based on what you're saying, you're going to tell him and let the chips fall where they may, right?

Tierra is speaking: Well, I guess so, but how wrong am I if I keep my secret and wait until he catches me as I did him? He would have never told me about what he had done I feel, if I hadn't found out for myself.

Mr. Pearson is speaking: You could do that, but honestly, as a church woman is that Godly-like to you? Are you telling me you have been from day one 100% honest with him when you've spoken to him? I doubt it, and it is not always a bad thing. Some lies are necessary. We are human, and it is in our nature to "protect" those we love. Yes, even though sometimes we mishandle these things in our efforts to do so, our intentions are good and our hearts are in the right place. If we're honest, no one in a relationship will ever have a drama-free relationship. Many of us will have less drama than most, but we cannot avoid any simply because we don't all think alike. We don't all agree or believe in the same things always nor are we always willing to go along with them to be with someone. Don't misunderstand. By no means am I advocating a behavior of lying, but I will not sit here and lie to myself and think everyone is always going to tell me the truth. Honestly, to keep it real with you, I sometimes may not want to hear the truth. Most people's mental state at that time may not want or be able to handle it.

Tierra is speaking: I understand, but now I am in an odd position because I have now done what he has done and I foolishly still want to stay in the marriage. I don't want to continue to live a lie and call it a relationship.

Mr. Pearson is speaking: I hear you, and I agree with you. Relationships are built on trust, and breaking that trust in your marriage is not good, but you can rescue it IF both parties are willing to forgive and move forward. As strange as it may sound, men cheating on you doesn't mean they are unhappy with you. It's just that some want more sex or attention. Whereas like I mentioned a few minutes ago, for many women, it is just not about sex it is more about them looking to fill an emotional void. Women who have cheated have said their reasoning for doing so was because they were lonely. They didn't feel emotionally connected to their mates anymore, and at times, in the relationship, felt taken for granted. Many men don't understand what women may sometimes want most is to *feel an emotional connection* to them daily.

Now, I am not saying this is a good reason for women to cheat in their marriage. I am just pointing out reasons why some women feel the need to do so. Some people believe "infidelity" for most is simply a need to spread their seed to as many women as they can. Even though it has been happening since the dawn of time, there is no excuse for this behavior in a marriage.

Tierra is speaking: I agree.

Mr. Pearson is speaking: Listen, most women cheating with someone (as do most men) for a long period are looking to "transition" out to that new relationship to get out of a bad situation. They see this as their escape route or way out. You have to be careful because sometimes people wanting out of the relationship will create problems on purpose and use it as a reason to leave when in fact there was no real problem. They just wanted out. I don't feel though, this was something either of you set out to do. I'm just stating that it is possible. People who want to salvage their relationship, who are grappling with infidelity, will seek help before doing so because they value their relationship.

Tierra is speaking: I do value my marriage, but you are right. I was looking for something I felt I was missing in my marriage. Now that I have done it, I feel bad that I did and wish I could take it back. I know two wrongs don't make a right and as a Christian, it was wrong. I just need to figure out the best way to tell my husband that during our separation, I met and slept with someone. I need him to understand I didn't just find someone, nor did it just happen. It took me a long time to warm up to the idea, and go through with it. I need him to understand that it wasn't done to get back at him. Even though I realized the risk of losing my marriage, it was something I felt I needed to do for me.

Mr. Pearson is speaking: You're right, but he also should have thought through the risks and consequences of losing you as well, but he didn't, and that makes him just as guilty. Now you're at a point, where your love for one another is truly going to be tested. If, when you tell him what you've done, he still wants to work it out, just maybe biblically, you both can repent and start rebuilding your trust, communicate more and be faithful going forward. As far as those harmful lies he tells, that's another story.

Tierra is speaking: He acts selfish and immature sometimes, which makes me feel he doesn't want me to know the truth. Why do you think that is?

Mr. Pearson is speaking: Selfish and immature, how old is your husband?

Tierra is speaking: He is 36 years old.

Mr. Pearson is speaking: Okay, that helps me to help you understand what I am about to share concerning men in relationships at a certain age. It is crucial in their development to coexist in a real one-on-one situation with their mate. With true maturity in some men, they learn and display an understanding that honesty may not always get you the best immediate results, but it is best to have a successful relationship. This kind of insight helps certain men at certain ages to realize lies and especially lies to your wife aren't worth it. They understand from the wisdom they have acquired that to keep the peace sometimes, we as men must take the blame for things even in most cases, even when it is not our fault.

Now, this can be and would be noticeable in the man's behavior. I am not saying he will not lie in situations to protect you because it is in most real men's DNA to protect and be protectors of those they love without explanation. It is something most men will gamble on to keep you and their family safe. Yes, some men do overcompensate for their shortcomings and lie, but if they are serious about the relationship they have with you, they will overcome them over time. With you loving him and showing him love through their insecurities, they will eventually not feel the need to lie about certain things. Remember when you were growing up, your mother told you, "Women mature faster than boys?" I believe and agree with this.

Tierra is speaking: What about if he is insecure and not yet matured, what do I do if this is the case?

Mr. Pearson is speaking: Well, from what you've described, he seems as if he is more mature than not. So you will know, insecure men can be unstable, and this could lead them to tell unnecessary lies. In cases where he is selfish as well, he will care less and overlook any damage his lies cause because he is looking out for himself only. These are characteristics only found in the kind of men who only care about themselves.

If you both read your scriptures, it will give you a little more information about marriage areas like this. It says in **Ephesians 5:33**, (KJV), "Nevertheless let every one of you in particular so love his wife even as himself, and the wife see that she reverence her husband." In other words, the Bible says a man should love his wife, and his wife should reverence (respect) her husband. He is supposed to love you, and you are supposed to respect him, and cheating doesn't show this.

As one flesh, it only seems right to share and be truthful with one another. I only bring this up because God told the man in **Colossians 3:19**, (KJV), "Husbands, love [your] wives, and be not bitter against them." and in **1 Peter 3:7**, (KJV), "Likewise, ye husbands, dwell with [them] according to knowledge, giving honour unto the wife, as unto the weaker vessel, and as being heirs together of the grace of life; that your prayers be not hindered." Which means there is no room for foolishness, infidelity or lies if you are to be like Christ. In this situation, if you both believe in God, then it's time for you both to ask for forgiveness. Do as it says in **Galatians 6:2** (KJV), "Bear ye one another's burdens, and so fulfill the law of Christ."

You both should sit and have a serious talk and you should talk to him because it is hard for you to follow him as a man of the Most High when he has done wrong, also. He cannot tell you from **1 Corinthians 14:35** (KJV) if they wanted to know something concerning the word of God go to their husband, "And if they will learn anything, let them ask their husbands at home: for it is a shame for women to speak in the church." or **1 Peter 3:5,** (KJV) "For after this manner in the old time the holy women also, who trusted in God, adorned themselves, being in subjection unto their own husbands:" or bring up **Ephesians 5:24**, (KJV), "Therefore as the church is subject unto Christ, so let the wives be to their own husbands in everything." Listen, it is his job to put his house and marriage back in alignment, and make things right between you both.

I shared with men in a Bible Study that telling lies to your wife is just as bad as treating her wrong. I showed them in **Colossians 3:19**, (KJV), where it says "to love their wives and not to be mean to her, "Husbands, love your wives, and be not bitter against them.", **Ephesians 5:25**, (KJV), "Husbands, love your wives, even as Christ also loved the church, and gave himself for it;" And in **Ephesians 5:28**, (KJV), "So ought men to love their wives as their bodies. He that loveth his wife loveth himself." Because lying to your wife only makes her feel alone in the marriage. Even though you've had your setback, he cannot fault you when he has done the same thing. He should realize he set the example that you ended up following. Women mirror what their husband does. I am not saying this gets you off the hook, but it does explain how you may have gotten where you are in your marriage.

Tierra is speaking: Alone is how I felt. It's as if he is afraid to talk and share himself with me. I want to reach him and nip this in the bud before it gets worse.

Mr. Pearson is speaking: This makes perfect sense. With all that we've said, remember this: most Christian men will do right by their woman and never give her a reason to lie or cheat on them. They will show them and give them whatever they desire to feel emotionally connected to them and to keep them. For women, men aren't that hard to understand. Most men require three things. They are (1) Acceptance, (2) Appreciation, and (3) Approval. Give a man these things and ask for the world, and you will get it every time.

Tierra is speaking: I can see that.

Mr. Pearson is speaking: My Uncle Wayne, who has been married for many years, told me this: "If you ever have a problem with one another, solve it inside your house not outside because you cannot fix *inside* problems *outside*. Don't get to a point where you're telling everyone, like your "in-laws" your problems because when you two make up, if you do, you will now look like a fool for going back to a person you just dogged out and said didn't love you. You were thinking when you were telling them how you felt that they would keep your conversation between the two of you. However, what you did was give them something to gossip about, (which was you and your business). Remember, people love drama and especially if it is someone else's. Keep your home business in your home because if not, you will make matters worse and harder for you to fix your issues once things calm down.

Tierra is speaking: How?

Mr. Pearson is speaking: Well, because your in-laws as I understood it, could quickly become out-laws if you're not careful. Meaning this, when you two are going through a few issues you tend to tell your friends or family, thinking it will make you feel good afterward, but it won't. All it has done is given them some gossip about what's going on in your household. Both men and women do this saying, "I needed someone to talk to since I couldn't talk to you." Here's what happens when you involve others in your business.

You run over to your friends' or family's house and tell them all your problems because YOU need an ear to hear, but instead of them being your confidante, they take the information and spread it throughout the family that you two are having issues. They may go so far as to say you two are about to get a divorce, spreading rumors. You did it because you were mad and you hoped you would get some sympathy, but all you did was spread your in-house problems throughout other people's homes. They are not rooting for you to reconcile. They want you to fail so they can say, "I told you you shouldn't have married him/her." How does that fix your issues at home? It doesn't. It just makes matters worse because now everyone knows you're having problems.

Tierra is speaking: I know that now. What you're saying is accurate because it just happened a few days ago to me and has caused me additional problems. I told my sister about my husband's lying and asked her not to tell anyone, but she did. Now my family thinks my husband is nothing more than a liar. Now I've got to try and fix this with them to get them to understand that my husband does lie sometimes, but it's not as bad as it sounds.

Mr. Pearson is speaking: Good luck with that! Listen, I know we have touched on a lot of "what ifs, what could be's and maybe's" and the fact of the matter is that honesty is the best policy but not always the most practical one in every situation. Infidelity is wrong, period. Worldly and biblically. God never told you to cheat on your mate. He asked you to love him. I am not saying people need to lie, but I do feel as I said earlier, *some* lies are necessary in certain situations. I know it may sound like a cliché, but honesty goes both ways. Both men and women must eliminate contributing temptations that cause us to consider lying before telling the truth. We should all try and create a pleasant environment where you both speak openly.

I hope I was able to give some behavior aspects to determine with your husband where he is mentally, emotionally and spiritually as it applies to the lies and being unfaithful. I believe if he rereads his Bible and asks God to give him the understanding of his actions, he will see the damage of lying and being unfaithful in the marriage. It will help him to repair and restore you both to where God intended you to be in your marriage. If he did this and was honest with himself, he would see and realize when you're talking and asking questions, you are being nosy per se, but more than that, you are concerned because you love him and respect him enough to speak with him about your concerns. I think like I said, he is old enough and this phase you both have experienced if prayed on, you will both be able to put it in the past if you seriously mean what you say when you repent to God.

377

Tierra is speaking: I believe so too after speaking with you. Thank you so much for all your help.

Mr. Pearson is speaking: Great. Have a great day, okay? Who is our next caller Karen?

Karen is speaking: We have Matthew Ray from Marietta on the line.

Mr. Pearson is speaking: Hello Matthew, how are you today? What is your question?

Matthew is speaking: Good afternoon, sir. Thanks for asking, but I am not doing so well.

Mr. Pearson is speaking: Talk to me, I am listening.

Matthew is speaking: Well, Mr. Pearson, my question is, "How can I communicate more effectively with my wife?" Let me explain what I am saying. When I first met my wife, we had a lot in common and got along great. We got along so well that I asked her to marry me after just a few months of dating. It has now been four years, and even though we are still making our mistakes as we grow in love, we are doing okay.

Mr. Pearson is speaking: It sounds like you've found the perfect woman for you. At the same time, you seem to have something else more on your mind that you want to talk about, what's going on?

Matthew is speaking: Well, you are right. I have a lot on my mind. Lately, something in my wife has changed, or it may have always been there, and I chose not to see at the time we were dating. My beautiful, thoughtful angel who used to encourage me daily has turned into a nag and is complaining about everything I do or say daily. There is not a day that goes by that she doesn't accuse me of something. I feel I am defending myself every day for things I didn't do. It is always something she thinks I did or will do.

She always attacks me saying hurtful things (or things she thinks hurt me when they don't). She pushes me to the point that I also say hurtful things to get her off me. By the end of the night, she expects me to apologize to her for HER attacking me. Most times I do it because I love her. Whenever she doesn't get "her way," she disrespects me by attacking my manhood. She often tells me, I am not a real man. She tells me I don't know what marriage is all about, and I should have stayed single and never married.

Mr. Pearson is speaking: I hear you. It could be she has more going on with her internally than you are unaware of, and that is what is making her act out and come at you with guns blazing. Did something change in your life recently?

Matthew is speaking: Okay. Like I said, we met, dated for about seven months and decided to get married. In the beginning, she was sweet, considerate, loving, understanding and all that. I was on a natural high, just thinking about coming home to her every day. Our friends and family felt seven months wasn't enough time for us to really get to know one another. At first, I disagreed, but lately, after damn near four years, I feel they may have been right. I am not going to lie. The thought did cross my mind, but I guess my feelings for her at the time overtook my reasoning. Then I overheard her telling her cousin, "He (meaning me) needed to get a second job because as his wife, I will want things, and he needs to be able to get them for me." I should have paid more attention.

Mr. Pearson is speaking: It sounds from that comment that she wasn't thinking of the both of you but more about herself and her needs in the marriage. Did you two, before getting married, talk about finances and how it was going to work as a married couple? I am asking because a lot of marriages fail because they do not talk about their debt with their partners. It's necessary to do so because no one wants to walk into the marriage and find out later that they have now taken on your debt as well as their own.

If you two had bills with the same companies such as your cell phone, car insurance, etc. you could combine them and save money, but that depends on whether the other person trusts you enough. I have seen married couples not do this because they don't trust each other like that yet. A lot of women are afraid of doing this because they think if he gets mad at her, he would have the power to shut off her phone. Due to this lack of trust, she doesn't want him to know who she is calling or talking to either.

Her idea of your role as "head of the household" is reduced to just paying bills and giving her what she wants, not running the family. If you didn't give her money to spend, she would make sure you didn't have anything extra after paying the household bills because she would make it her business to increase the household bills knowing you would have to pay them. This leaves you with very little money to spend, which makes her feel she is controlling you even if she doesn't get the money in her hand.

As a wife, this is a silly and selfish plan to have because the more you spend on bills, the less you can and will spend on her. Sure, she has her own money from her check, but her goal is to get and control your paycheck also. All this comes from past trust issues she developed from a prior marriage or relationship, and she has carried it over into yours. I say this because a lot of women today don't always marry for love but more for a place to stay. They're with a man for his status and resources. It's using someone at the highest level.

Matthew is speaking: No, we didn't talk about finances beforehand, but I see your point. Don't get me wrong. I wasn't worried about the money or paying bills if I felt loved and appreciated by her, but at times I couldn't even get that. I love my wife, and I would do anything to protect her for the rest of our lives together. Regardless though, I was prepared for any increase and to support my wife's needs. You're right though, something did happen, and that is when the changes in her occurred.

Mr. Pearson is speaking: So when did she start to change as you stated earlier?

Matthew is speaking: Thinking back, I remember she began to change when I got laid off from work. I had told her months before I wasn't sure what with the problems that my manager and I were having that I would be there much longer. Sure enough, they let me go. When it happened, I came home and told my wife. She was upset and blamed me for it happening. She had nothing positive to say to me, nor did she try and encourage me at all.

Her attitude and tone were as if I had done something wrong, when I hadn't. She attacked me by asking, "What did you do?" When I told her I didn't do anything, it went just as I said it would months ago, she replied, "Well you had to have done something. A job just doesn't lay people off for no reason. I'll bet it was your mouth. You couldn't keep it shut. You're always trying to be right. You probably pissed her off by talking back. Now what are you going to do and how are you going to pay these bills without a job?

Mr. Pearson is speaking: Wow! That doesn't sound like a woman who had trust in her husband, had your back or that she believed in you at all. She said it like you couldn't turn things around. She seemed like a woman looking for an excuse to bounce. I have never heard of any Christian women bailing or acting to their husband like this over the loss of a job. It says in **Hebrews 12:15** (KJV), "Looking diligently lest any man fail of the grace of God; lest any root of bitterness springing up trouble you, and thereby many be defiled;" and in **James 3:14** (KJV) "But if ye have bitter envying and strife in your hearts, glory not, and lie not against the truth." In other words, it sounds as if she is looking for a way out. If she had these thoughts, she should have repented. No real woman who loves her man would attack him this way, knowing he just lost his job.

A real Christian woman in this situation would have stood by her man and said encouraging words not attack him. You probably didn't feel all that good losing your job even though you knew it was possible. She does not have the right, nor is it right to attack you like that. It seems as if she forgot your vows where it states, "for better or worse." Kicking you while you're down is not what a loving Christian woman does to her Christian man.

It seemed as if she took the loss of the job worse than you did. I can only imagine you coming home to this kind of hell. It says in **Proverbs 21:19** (KJV), "It is better to dwell in the wilderness, than with a contentious and an angry woman." And in **Proverbs 27:15** (KJV), "A continual dropping in a very rainy day and a contentious woman are alike." In other words, she seemed angry, not supportive in YOUR time of need. Complaining and being irritable toward you is not a sign of a virtuous wife. When she said "I do," she married you for better or worse not just for better and better, and it is clear that she has forgotten this. How did you feel when she said these things to you?

Matthew is speaking: Honestly, I felt surprised and hurt. I didn't think me losing a job would bring me this much stress in such a short time. I thought and hoped she would be a little more understanding and supportive, but I was wrong. The way she responded you would have thought I would never work again. I asked myself, "Where was the Christian woman now? Where was the woman who claimed when she met me, she loved my drive? Why was my Christian wife who I had taken care of all this time now feeling I wasn't going to figure this out and fix it?

I was disappointed because this didn't seem like the so-called Christian woman who told me she was ready to submit to her husband who loved and took care of her. It sounded like something Satan's child would say. She has deceived me, and I fell for it by marrying and giving her my love. I thought she would be there for me when I needed her to be. You would have thought my Christian wife would have known the situation we were in was just temporary, but she didn't see it that way. It seemed as if she was gearing up to leave me because I lost my job. I wondered then who had I married?

Mr. Pearson is speaking: You are correct the Bible says in **Proverbs 12:4**, (KJV), "A virtuous woman is a crown to her husband: but she that maketh ashamed is as rottenness in his bones." In other words, your wife should have been the first person to make you feel good knowing it bothered you as well. She should have been providing encouraging words even if she was concerned. She should feel that you would make things right, not show doubt in you. It is part of her wifely duties to get you back on your feet. If she had faith in you this would have all been done without you having to say a word to her. She would have known what was needed.

She should have said something like, "We are going to be alright. I remember you had spoken to me about the problems you were having with your manager and the fact she was trying to get rid of you, months ago. I know you told me to prepare for the possibility of you leaving, so this isn't a surprise to either one of us. Things happen for a reason. It is their loss because you are a good man. You will find something soon that's even better. Regardless, we'll get through this together. With you getting your unemployment, we're going to be okay. We will work it out until you get something else. I know you will find something sooner rather than later because you are a good man, and a company would do themselves a favor by hiring you. What I am saying sweetheart, is there is no need to worry, we will be okay. We've got each other."

Hearing this would have made you feel that even if the world isn't on your side, you knew she was. She would have helped you find something new or better and not just tell you as a selfish woman would, to take any job. What you needed most was to feel you had that "ride or die chick" on your side, and she was down with you no matter what. A seasoned woman would have done this, no questions asked. She would have known that part of her job as the wife would have been to "encourage her husband not discourage him." Your wife wasn't thinking about the two of you. She was thinking about herself.

Matthew is speaking: You're right, and I agree. Hearing that would have made me feel much better. I wouldn't have felt so much like a failure for losing my job. Her attitude did shift, and she did come across as if it was over. I saw it, but I dismissed it because I didn't think my wife would consider leaving me because I lost my job, but she did.

Mr. Pearson is speaking: You do understand what I've said shows how much a woman loves and respects her husband. How your wife acted is not a sign of a loving, supportive wife. It is a sign of a selfish woman thinking and looking out for herself. In some situations, the woman will use this moment to cheat. A woman thinking like this will not see her marriage as honorable, but the situation as more of a way to cheat. I apologize if what I am saying offends you, but I have to keep it real with you because you seem like a good guy.

A supportive Christian woman, knowing her husband, would have understood the situation and would have known it was "temporary" not "permanent." She would have known as it says in **1 Corinthians 7:10** (KJV), 10- "And unto the married I command, yet not I, but the Lord, Let not the wife depart from her husband:" and work with you as you get myself back on track. She would have known financially what you were bringing in, what you were paying and figured out how she could help during this time as it says in **Proverbs 31:16** (KJV), "She considereth a field, and buyeth it: with the fruit of her hands she planteth a vineyard." In other words, standing by your side would have included her giving the option up to you if you wanted her to take any old job to help make ends meet (this would depend on how much savings you two had put away) not push you into anything so she wouldn't have to help.

There are many reasons why she would blow up. One of the reasons would be because she wasn't thinking about the two of you. She is thinking selfishly about herself. Her thought process at the time seemed to have been the longer you are out of work, the more she might have to help financially, and that wasn't what she signed up for when you two got married. She feels, regardless of the situation, it is still your job to figure things out without her involvement financially.

She knew, if you told her what you brought in from your unemployment, that it was not enough to cover all your household bills. She figured out at some point, that you were going to ask her to help financially, and she was afraid of that. My question with you being out of work and looking, why would your Christian wife sit back and purposely watch her husband struggle by himself? To watch him stress himself out and borrow money from friends and family to help take care of you both, this is not a real Christian woman. You say she left, when and for how long?

Matthew is speaking: She used this opportunity to act out and leave the relationship. She started making frequent trips to go and supposedly see and spend time with her mother, but I had my doubts that this was what she was doing. I felt Susan was looking for someone who could take care of her. She left me for a while and stayed gone while I was out of work, and I told her she needed to come back home. She removed herself while I struggled with the bills and was looking for another job.

As a Christian man, I thought about **Jeremiah 3:1** (KJV), where it says, "They say, If a man put away his wife, and she go from him, and become another man's, shall he return unto her again? shall not that land be greatly polluted? but thou hast played the harlot with many lovers; yet return again to me, saith the LORD." I didn't think she would cheat on me over me losing my job. I held close to the scripture in **Matthew 19:6** (KJV), where it says, "Wherefore they are no more twain, but one flesh. What therefore God hath joined together, let not man put asunder." Hoping that she too would remember we are married.

It was two months before I found something else, but in those two months I saw a side of my wife I had never seen, and I didn't like it. When I told her because she was working that I needed her to help me with the bills she refused at first but then paid them with an attitude. It was the same for buying us food. I figured if I paid the bills without a job, she would at least buy us food. She eventually did, but I had to fuss about it first. When she did buy food, she would purchase a lot of items she enjoyed knowing I wouldn't eat them.

At first, I thought she got what she got after thinking about us both, but I was wrong. I later found out she did this on purpose, brought all the things she liked first than whatever money was left, and as an afterthought, she would grab a few things I wanted. She would go to the most expensive stores and purchase the most costly items for herself, knowing we couldn't afford it, saying, "She needed the things she got." She didn't look for any place for us to cut corners or save money. She just kept on spending her money as if to say, "I am working, and it's my money, why shouldn't I spend it the way I want." She looked at me as if the bills were "my bills" and not ours. She showed no signs that she even cared "how" the bills got paid, knowing I wasn't working.

At the time she was working, and I wasn't, she felt my new job was to cook and clean the house. I would sometimes because I had the time in between searching for a job, but she made it seem it "was my job." Since she was working, she now felt my job was to be a house husband. When I returned to work, things got worse. She developed an attitude and said to me, "Now you think you are all that because you are back at work." I felt damn if I did and damned if I didn't. All that had happened made me question if my wife was with me for my love or her security and someone to take care of her. I leaned towards she was with me to be "taken care of."

Mr. Pearson is speaking: Like how?

Matthew is speaking: She became bossier than ever. She would talk to me in a tone as if she was upset with me all the time. She would order me around, put more demands on me, act like what I was doing as her husband wasn't enough and was meaningless. I couldn't help but think she was doing all this to distance herself from me in the hope that *I* would divorce her and according to the Bible, remarry with no consequences for not saving her marriage. She would try and treat me as if I was her child instead of her husband. She even said because she couldn't control me, "Why don't you do what I want you to?" For some reason, she thought to handle me this way was the best way to get control over me or prevent me from running her.

I wondered where this all came from, and then I recalled a conversation I had overheard between her and her mother in her mother's kitchen one day we were over. They were talking about how they both had been taken advantage of by men in their past relationships. Telling one another they weren't going to allow it to happen again. They said, "No man was going to rule or run them anymore." I learned from family members how my wife had done this same thing to her last husband, who the family thought was a nice man to her.

She got in his face so much that he eventually started slapping and pushing her around. I heard because he didn't want to catch a case he left. She told me she walked away from the marriage because he wouldn't do as she asked. I felt terrible to hear she had been hit and abused but honestly from what her family says, they said she pushed this good guy to his edge to the point where he reacted, maybe in the wrong way but he responded to being bullied by his wife, and she didn't expect him to do so.

Now I wasn't that way but hearing this did explain a lot for me and why she felt confident about getting in a man's face. I didn't plan on abusing her or mistreating her, but this duck and run attitude she has had to stop because if all she did was get married to be taken care of, she was going to have to do more than act out with me.

Their exes must have, and because it seemed they both were looking for free rides from their men, I guess part of getting the so-called "free ride," (living for free) was to take a lot of verbal abuse. Like I said "they" both claimed they left the men because of this, but it sounded to me as if it was the other way around. This made them feel used. I couldn't help but feel this mess that happened to my wife had carried over to me. I felt her acting out was her way of making sure I didn't verbally abuse her. Defending herself and getting off the first hurtful things was nothing more than a cry for help, but I didn't know what or how to help her with this.

I kept thinking this woman said she was a Christian woman, and she follows the scriptures. For the life of me, I couldn't understand "what" Bible she was following because I didn't recall reading anywhere in the scriptures where the Christian women act this way — and leave at the first sign of financial trouble, who does that?

Mr. Pearson is speaking: This could be an issue. Women hurt that bad usually, but not always are relieving their past as it is present and you're the old problem with a new face. Women like this inadvertently blame the current man for the past man's problems thinking all men are the same when they are not. From what you've heard so far, it sounds as if you are on to something by thinking she is lashing out at you because of her past. It triggered her when you were out of work, and it brought back bad feelings the moment you asked (but she heard "told") to help financially.

She felt during that time by you making her help that this was a form of ruling her and running her, and she didn't appreciate it. Now she wouldn't have felt that way if she were following the Bible and knowing the situation would not have refused to help when she knew you just lost your job. Now her venting to her mother as she did was nothing more than her preparing herself for battle with you (but it could have been any man, to her all of them are the same).

You were a man, and at some point, you in her mind were going to try and do the same thing her ex had done, and she was merely getting ready for battle. When I see people like this, I say, "Here comes trouble without a cause," because they are so prepared for battle and used to losing so often, they never know when they have won. Meaning, she had a good man going through something and to her your situation wasn't going to change, and you would take it out on her. Your wife didn't like how it made her feel and this was why now it seems she was locked and loaded for battle with you when she was not getting things done her way.

As the wife, she felt whatever you had done for "girlfriends" you've dated before her, then she should receive much more because she was your wife. Her job as your wife seems to be in her mind, to "BE" the wife and anything else she may have "felt" like doing for you extra was a bonus, and you should be appreciative that she even thought about doing it. The fact is you being out of work upset her, but when you returned to work it scared her.

When you were out of work and reality kicked in that she "had" to help. She thought her helping was doing you a favor not helping her family. Couples, as I understand, know when one falls the other falls as well. Her mind wasn't processing the situation as a "couple." She was processing as a single-minded person. Single-minded married people think and have escape plans, ways out if and when things don't seem to be going right. They're always thinking about options. These people come into situations planning and preparing to leave before they even get started.

What she was concerned the most with it seems, is that if you didn't have money to pay bills, you would ask her. Before you do, however, she got up and left temporarily in order to force you to "figure" things out, and she would return afterward. Acting like this is by no means a Christian woman you've married. She may go to church and read her Bible, but she doesn't seem to apply any of what she has learned. Again, I ask, what real Christian woman thinks or acts this way in a marriage?

Matthew is speaking: In this situation or any one for that matter, I would have no problem stepping in and doing whatever we could to help her family if that was what she thought was needed. She knew I wasn't a lazy husband nor was I trying to flip our roles in the marriage. It was a brief unavoidable situation that happened to me. Sadly, yes, she did panic and acted out of character of that of a Christian wife, but I still loved her. All of this was in the first few weeks I was out of work.

Mr. Pearson is speaking: Do you think she acted out of character or could this have been who she was, but you never saw this side of her because you've been taking care of her all this time? You see from day one, you did everything it seems for her. You allowed her to do whatever she felt she wanted because you were working. You thought and knew it was your job as the provider. She showed no gratitude for all you were doing because to her "you were supposed to do all that."

Matthew is speaking: I never looked at it like that. However, now that you mention it that would explain a lot of things she has been going through. Her behavior has not changed, and it seems to come and go. I wondered what she meant when she said to me the day I returned to work, "You think you're all that because you're back to work." She made it sound like a bad thing. First, she complains I wasn't working, and now she feels a certain way when I return to work, I'm confused.

It seems she wakes up looking for reasons now to argue with me. I know it sounds silly, but it's like fussing is her way of getting attention from me. She spends most of her time trying to catch me doing something wrong. She always thinks I am up to something when I want to do things by myself. She still thinks when I pick up my cell phone, get on the computer or I'm watching television that I prefer to do that than spend time with her. I mean I would love spending time with my wife, but I don't want her to be fussing about nothing the whole time.

I get tired of hearing how great other men who were with her were and how much better they treated her. It makes me ask her, "Why in the hell are you here with me? Why didn't you marry one of them and stay with them?" What woman gets mad when her man isn't a dog, isn't doing her wrong, isn't cheating on her, isn't always lying to her who is trying to love her and treat her right? It says in **Proverbs 26:25** (KJV) where it says, "When he speaketh fair, believe him not: for there are seven abominations in his heart." I love my wife and would never do anything intentionally to hurt her.

It's like she needs me to mess up and do something wrong, so she can say, "I got you. I told you so, or I knew it." "You're just like all the rest." I can't help but think she is waiting for the clock to strike midnight assuming I will revert to a man that looks more recognizable. You know, the guy who cheats, mistreats, uses, verbally abuses her, lies to her and dumps her for someone else. I am not that kind of man, but she doesn't see that, and that's disappointing.

From time to time, she will get up out of the blue and run and spend a weekend with her mother (or someone's house because she never tells me where she is going). I am not sure if she is doing this to make me jealous, to get away from me or to relax but whatever it is, I am not feeling it. Now if I were not a Christian man, I would think she was cheating on me. At this point, I wouldn't put anything past her. No matter what I do, she finds something wrong. The more I give and do for her, the more she wants me to give and do for her. I know she feels she deserves whatever. Coming at me as if I was the one who prevented her from having anything and that I am supposed to get it for her when she is acting like this is just crazy. Is what I am saying making sense?

Mr. Pearson is speaking: Yes, it seems she still has flashbacks of the hurt from her last relationship, and you're paying the cost of it. Because she hasn't fully dealt with her issues, she brings them to you and says, "Deal with it, it is who I am. If you want to be with me, this is how it is going to be." Instead of saying, "I have past issues I am still dealing with, and I need your help. She instead forces herself into a situation and makes you deal with it not knowing it could destroy your marriage. You can help her move forward, but you cannot go back in time and correct something an ex of hers has done to her. She knows this, and she knows she must admit there is a problem before she can move forward.

All of the anger comes from her not dealing with her past hurts. Vowing herself not to allow this to happen again without dealing with what has happened to her, while married to you, is not going to help your relationship. It is going to affect and possibly hurt it if she doesn't address it. Seeking a professional is a possibility.

It is a tough situation to be in, and it will take some time to fix. Until there is a change, you are the enemy. She will always feel you're trying to "get over" on her. You're trying to trick her or use her because that is what her ex did. To her, right now, married or not, you are someone who could hurt her, and until she feels she can trust and be vulnerable with you, she will occasionally drift back into her past state of mind and direct her anger toward you when things don't go as she has planned in her mind. By the way, I agree with you and believe there is a good chance she married you for security, not love.

She needed this because it seems that she is unable to live alone. Sure, she may have been on her own when you met her, but I would bet she was living very basically in all her living needs. She saw you as a way for a better life. Marrying you was the best ticket because as your "wife" she was entitled to be provided for. She knew what her plan was when you thought it was for love. I am not going to say she married you to use you because I haven't heard both sides, but I feel she had an agenda and marriage and controlling her husband was THE plan.

Matthew is speaking: Well, how do I deal with it because I am trying to love her, and she is fighting me and making it hard to show her love?

Mr. Pearson is speaking: Well, this is a tough situation and it depends on how bad she is, whether she knows she needs help and would be willing to get it in order to have a happy life with you. I can tell you this. She will keep on using whatever she has learned about you and your past against you forever. That is all she has to use to hurt or defend herself against you hurting her. Yes, men will do the same thing as well but using past personal information as a weapon to hurt your partner is never the best way to create the trust or build a solid foundation for loving one another. It is a recipe for failure or divorce.

Matthew is speaking: There are times when she will just come out of left field and start an argument so that she can fuss about other things on her chest. Jumping around all up in my face like a rabbit, yelling about how I am not going to train her to do what I want her to and saying over and over again that I am not going to do it, not going to do it. When I ask her, what she is referring to she doesn't have an answer. She keeps repeating how I'm not going to run her or make her feel like she could not be herself. Saying, "If I push her, she will push back."

To this day, I still don't know why she does this daily as if she gets paid for it, but she does this religiously. I looked on the internet to see if I could find something to explain her outbursts and this behavior and what I saw fit all her symptoms was the actions of a person who is Bipolar. Now I am no doctor, but when I read the signs, more than 70% fit her mood swings and behavior.

Mr. Pearson is speaking: I think I can explain this in a way you can understand, but it doesn't mean you are wrong in what you're thinking. Before you two got married, your wife felt you as her husband would fall into her idea of what a husband was and would do. She saw you as her wind-up toy that she could bring out to entertain herself when she was bored. For a while, you stepped in and did as she thought and felt you should, and you had no problems and saw no issues to be concerned with because you were doing all she thought you should and would do as the husband.

Somewhere along the line, probably when you got laid off, her view of what you had been doing changed. You expected her while you were out to step up and find where she could contribute and do so as your wife. That wasn't her plan, nor did she see that in her future. You felt it would not be long before you found something else and there was no need, with you having savings, to panic. Her view, attitude and behavior saw it differently. She didn't nor was she concerned about you being out of work, she expected you and you alone to continue to make things happen as the husband without her involvement.

She didn't see when you asked her to contribute as her "helping," she saw it as you trying to get her to do your job. All the fussing, arguing and acting out was nothing more than her saying she didn't like this new arrangement, and she wasn't going to do it. Even when you went back to work and returned to handling the household, she felt, by then, violated because she asked and you made her help. You put her in a "have to" situation, and it bothered her when, as your wife, she should have felt it was what a wife was supposed to do, but instead it reminded her of her ex.

When it happened, it triggered her flashbacks of her ex ruling and running her like she was accusing you of doing, and she wasn't going to stand for it. That's why she fights you on anything. She doesn't feel like the wife, she should do. Can you see now why she is still acting out towards you? It has nothing to do with you really. It was the situation that triggered this "selfishness attitude" within her again. You had no way of knowing that asking your wife to help in a time of need would make her act out like this.

She naturally suppressed these feelings for years and had not yet dealt with them. Even if you wanted to "fix her" as she thinks you should, it would nearly be impossible for you alone. Her issues have been with her for a long time, and she hasn't addressed them because she doesn't feel she has a problem. One of the symptoms is her thinking and feeling nothing she does in the relationship is her fault. She will tell you whatever she does or has done is because of you and it's your fault because you did it first. She will say, "I am following your lead." Pointing the finger is her way of avoiding her part in the matter we're discussing. She uses this as her "out" to act out. Until she admits and takes responsibility for her actions, your life will be a living hell. She is nothing more than a time bomb waiting to go off. She seems to be willing to destroy your marriage if she doesn't get her way rather than talk out the issues you both are having and fixing it. A Christian woman would look for more ways to "save" her marriage, than "destroy" it.

Matthew is speaking: Now that you put it that way, I can see it now. Here is something else she does. When I get home, I don't hear, "Hello, honey, how was your day?" I hear, "Why didn't you take out the trash?" "Why didn't you make the bed up the right way when you got out of it?" "I am hungry, what are you cooking?" "Why are you getting home so late?" "Why didn't you call me and tell me you left work?" "Why didn't you text me today to say hello and ask me how my day was going?" … and this is every day. I am her husband, not her servant. I am not put here on earth to wait on her hand and foot, sleep with her and to work and pay bills. I plan to live my life, not just exist in it. I don't feel like her husband. Her opinion is not always my opinion.

She doesn't get it. Just because I don't always agree with her doesn't mean I don't love her, but that is how she sees it. As the husband, I am the leader, not the one to be led. I listen to her, and if what she suggests helps us and does not hurt us, I am all in. All the yelling at me, trying to put me down, saying hurtful things to cut me because she knows what buttons to push, disrespecting, belittling me, attacking me and saying I am less than a man when she doesn't get her way or because I will not allow myself to be controlled by her is stupid.

I am a very patient man. Some would say a foolish man for putting up with her acting. I guess it is the reason I allow her to do what she does. I do my best not to say hurtful things, but she pushes me to the point where I feel the need to respond and get her off me.

Mr. Pearson is speaking: Yes, you are a patient man. Most men would have divorced her by now, but you seem to care for her. To her, she is asking a simple question, but the tone used doesn't suggest it is a simple question. It suggests she is looking for something more. It sounds in a way, that this is her way of "protecting" herself BEFORE you hurt her. I believe she is afraid of getting hurt and this is the reason she is saying the hurtful things she does when they aren't necessary. Understand that something or someone, probably an uncle or male family member has told her NOT to show or acknowledge you when you show her affection because it makes her seem weak. So, she will like what you're doing but respond as if you are irritating her with what you're doing. Understand that this is a game most men play with women.

Women liked to be flattered and told they are beautiful often, and those men they are dating will refuse to acknowledge them and often "make" them beg for their attention. She is doing the same thing, but it isn't working the way she thought it would, and she doesn't know what to do to make YOU do as she wants you to. She is as my Aunt Lula used to say, "She is so smart she is stupid." I think "she is so heavenly bound; she is no earthly good." I say this because she is using scripture that favors HER agenda, not how God intended it to be and feels she is following the Bible when she is not.

I can almost bet she comes across the same with strangers she meets. I would also say she has very little if any friends and I doubt she is close to any of them. Those friends she has understand her "standoffish" ways and only reach out when they are in the mood to deal with her. I bet she has a hard time holding a real conversation because she isn't sure if someone is trying to play her or not. She always seems to be looking for a fight even if there isn't one. If anyone were to tell her she comes off this negatively, she will get upset and defend her behavior. If you got deep into her past, I bet you would find men who she's dated who have left the relationship because of her, not because they didn't care or love her but because of her inability to communicate.

I know this because I dated a woman who felt the world revolved around her and thought that everyone should do and "give" to her while she "accepts" from everyone. I hate to say this, but your woman may have started coming off sweet and loveable in the beginning, but unfortunately, you married the representative and not the real her. If you hadn't gotten married so quickly, you might have seen this coming and possibly not married her until her issues were worked out. However, you're married now and you're dealing with it as you go along.

Now you see the real damaged, hurt, low self-esteemed, paranoiac and how scared she is not getting what she believes she deserves. You see how hard it is for her when she cannot be in control of everything and everyone around her, how afraid she is to let her guard down fearing she might receive something from someone for real that she has never had…love. A lot of this is happening because she doesn't know, really, "how" to communicate with you or people without coming off so angry. She comes off mad because she needs to protect herself from anyone trying to hurt her first, and this is why she sounds, looks and acts angry all the time.

I bet her friends can see it in the way she walks, the way she talks, the way she stands with her arms folded, etc. because these are signs of a person trying to get you before you get them. Again, this is not how a Christian married woman feels or loves her husband or trys to show her love. Listen, the one thing people forget when they get married, is they give up their independence. You marry for love, and you trust your partner, if not your marriage fails. Married people must think and act as one unit if you expect it to grow and last. Christian men and women should know this before they get married.

It says in **1 Peter 3:1 and 7**, (KJV), **1-** "Likewise, ye wives, be in subjection to your own husbands; that, if any obey not the word, they also may without the word be won by the conversation of the wives;" and **7-** "Likewise, ye husbands, dwell with them according to knowledge, giving honour unto the wife, as unto the weaker vessel, and as being heirs together of the grace of life; that your prayers be not hindered." In other words, this behavior she's displaying in your marriage isn't what married people who believe and follow the Word do. This situation is a clear sign your union is out of alignment.

Matthew is speaking: I have told her many times that she isn't going to disrespect me as her husband and head of the household and receive all that she feels a husband should provide. She tells me she feels I'm always trying to take away things she is supposed to receive as the wife. She is one who does not like to hear the word "no".

When she feels she isn't winning the argument or getting things her way, she reaches for the Bible and tries to find scriptures to make her pointless point stronger when all it does is make her look foolish. She tries to point out how I, as a married man, should act. She forgets what the Bible says about how a wife should behave in the marriage and feels her outburst is not unwarranted.

Mr. Pearson is speaking: Listen, I can hear you're frustrated, but you need to remember as a follower of Christ what it says in **1 Timothy 5:8**, (KJV), it says "But if any provide not for his own, and especially for those of his own house, he hath denied the faith, and is worse than an infidel." In other words, regardless of what she is going through, you must continue to do right by her, perform your husbandly duties, and provide for her. I can see you have an uphill battle and it is a hard one, but the good news is that it is a battle you can win. You stated you questioned her love for you. You say you love her, and because of how you're feeling right now, you doubt she loves you at all, but she does strangely enough. What you're going through needs time to work itself out.

Matthew is speaking: I understand what you're saying, and I also know we both need to find a middle ground to strengthen our relationship, and that could take months if not years. I am willing to put in the work. Listen, sir, when I said, "I do," I didn't agree to be her personal "yes" man nor did I ever say she wouldn't hear the word "no" sometimes. I never said I would "BE" what she envisioned her husband would be and give up my own identity in the marriage, and I never said she would ALWAYS have her way.

What I said and thought and agreed to was that I would love her, respect her, protect her, take care of her, learn her wants and needs and fulfill them to the best of my abilities, always be there for her, encourage and build her up and be the kind of man she would feel was worthy of her love. I knew when we were dating, and I had made it a point to "meet her in her mind first instead of the bed." I wanted to be with her, and I told her I wanted both sex and love at the same time with her. I have never claimed to be perfect, but I am doing my best to fulfill my role as her husband, according to the Bible. I expected her to know and perform her role as well. This fighting and arguing about so much of nothing to get some attention is getting old for me.

Mr. Pearson is speaking: You're right. It shouldn't be like this all the time. It is almost like you two need to get a divorce, but as we both know God doesn't like divorce. Here is what I suggest if you want to be with this woman. You two need to have a serious conversation and think about getting her professional help.

Matthew is speaking: I know she would be happier if I played the role and agreed to all she tells me and wants me to do, but I can't do that. It is not who I am, and she knows this. It was never like this before. We used to talk. We agreed to disagree and left it alone, but now she must win the argument and be right all the time.

Mr. Pearson is speaking: Are you listening and acknowledging her when she speaks?

Matthew is speaking: Yes! Believe me, when she expresses what she is feeling about something or makes suggestions, I acknowledge her. I let her know I have heard what she has said, and I understood. Once she is done speaking, I speak and share my thoughts. She doesn't want to listen to what I have to say, and she often cuts me off and shows very little interest. If my thoughts are not the same, she says to me, "Why don't you just agree with me?" When I ask her, why are you yelling, acting out and responding like this? She replies, "I am defending myself!"

Mr. Pearson is speaking: What is she defending herself from?

Matthew is speaking: Remember I said earlier that she and her mother were talking. She thinks I am trying to control, and she is fighting me on any and everything not to be controlled by me. Why? I don't know. I have never tried to control her at all.

Mr. Pearson is speaking: It sounds as if she has some serious "insecurities" within her.

Matthew is speaking: Well, I am not trying to control her. I am trying to work and build a future with her, but she is fighting me.

Mr. Pearson is speaking: Well, this is where you need to have patience with her.

Matthew is speaking: If she has a problem, I need her to talk to me and not at me. I am not a mind-reader, nor can I tell every day when she isn't feeling like herself. She must help me somehow to help her. I cannot apologize or help turn what she is feeling around if she doesn't talk to me instead of blaming me for any and everything. I am tired of defending myself on things I have not done nor plan to do. When I make a mistake, then she has cause to be upset not before. We can't grow a relationship doing things this way.

Mr. Pearson is speaking: You are right, but I encourage you to readjust or change "how" you listen and acknowledge her. Listen and see if this sounds familiar to you. When you ask her, "Honey are you okay?" and she replies, "I'm okay, or I am fine" you have to read between the lines what she is really saying to you. What she is really saying when she says "I am okay" is, please ask me more questions to find out what is really going on with me. When you do this, you need to be sympathetic to her issues. When she speaks, you need to "listen" to what it is she says is bothering her but more importantly, let her know whatever is bothering her bothers you as well.

Matthew is speaking: Really? I am supposed to figure all this out from her saying, "I am fine or I am okay?" That means she needs me to ask more questions? I am sorry, but this is a little stressful with my already stressful day.

Mr. Pearson is speaking: Yes! If you want her to stop feeling as if she must defend herself, help her to trust you, stop her from feeling controlled in the relationship. It will also stop the yelling she does, this is a must, and it will go a long way if you do it. You see when you disagree with her (even if you feel you're right to do so) she feels she is alone because what she hears you saying to her is "You are wrong in the way you think about things."

When she says, she is "defending" herself, she means defending her opinion and the way she thinks and feels about something vital to her. I sometimes think (not always) when women come across upset, it is not because they can't have an opinion, it is their way of saying they want you to "acknowledge" and "see" their point of view of the situation. You need to seem interested in whatever she is saying. Now the tricky part for you is to not come across so condescending in your views or opinions when you don't agree with her because it makes her feel you are not trying to understand her.

Matthew is speaking: What do you mean?

Mr. Pearson is speaking: What I mean is "how" you disagree and being able to explain YOUR point of view is critical. If what she suggested isn't the best solution to the current situation, tell her calmly. Don't make her feel her suggestion or idea was a bad one. To accomplish this, you must be open and objective to what really would work for the situation. In times of differences of opinion agree to disagree on things. Married people can do this from time to time and it's okay.

Matthew is speaking: Okay, I am with you so far.

Mr. Pearson is speaking: For men, these days a woman's way of communicating seems like overkill sometimes. They need so much information for them to understand you. Most women feel the amount of information men provide isn't enough for them to understand.

"Details" for most women, helps them see the whole picture, and it gives them a better understanding of what it is you're saying. So, when the conversation is over, they can walk away knowing all that happened from an event from the names of those involved, what was said, etc.

Men want "Headlines," meaning give me the facts. When two men are talking about sports, all they want to know is who won. Maybe later, they will come back around to how the game was played but for now, who won will do. Two women talking, they both layout the whole scene from where it happens, who it happens to, what happened afterward, who all was involved to what they would have done if it was them. To prove what I am saying think about when the two of you watch a program on television. If you were to ask afterward about the show you both just watched you will get two different perspectives and both would be right according to "their" understanding of what "they" believe. Yes, couples can disagree and be okay. You are bound to have some differences. It is what brought you both together in the first place.

Matthew is speaking: Although I have the title, Head of Household, she wants to run me and tell me "how" to run it as if I am the puppet and she is the puppet master.

Mr. Pearson is speaking: I understand. It is times like these when you need to remember what it says about your wife in **Proverbs 18:22**, (KJV) "Whoso findeth a wife findeth a good thing and obtaineth favor of the Lord." **Proverbs19:14**, (KJV), "House and riches are the inheritance of fathers: and a prudent wife is from the Lord." **Proverbs 31:10-12**, (KJV) **10**- "Who can find a virtuous woman? for her price is far above rubies." **11**- "The heart of her husband doth safely trust in her so that he shall have no need of spoil." **12**- "She will do him good and not evil all the days of her life."

In other words, you have a good woman, but right now, you do not bring out the best in her. You have yet to tap into her attributes and the skills God equipped her with. Remember everything starts with you, and when you come correctly and explain to her through your examples that this is according to scripture how you're going to handle and work in your marriage, just maybe she will respond to you differently because she sees in you a Christian man running his home in a Christ-like manner.

Matthew is speaking: I can do this.

Mr. Pearson is speaking: I stated earlier that you have an uphill battle in which you can still win if you apply a few principles and adjust your way of thinking. As a Christian man, you know Christ is the head of the man, and man is the head of the woman, meaning everyone is under someone. Her following you faithfully comes from this and through this, she will believe in you or believe in her heart you have her best interests at heart. What may seem to you as nagging is nothing more than your wife saying, "Help me understand where "WE" are going so I can feel comfortable on our way there."

For it helps her feel secure knowing the direction you're taking her in the relationship. I can't fault her for asking for information because if you have no clue where you are going, and you are not following Christ, why would she support you. As a Christian man, it is your job to put her mind, heart and soul at ease. No Christian woman wants to follow her husband if he is not following Christ. Something as simple as you understanding things from her perspective could stop her from feeling as if she must defend herself every time you talk.

Matthew is speaking: Okay, that makes sense. I understand, and yes, maybe I need to be a little more expressive in the things I am thinking and doing. What about the part about her disrespecting me, any suggestions? Coming home, hearing all of what I should have done and did not do isn't something I want to listen to every day. I often ask her to, "Give me a moment to settle down BEFORE telling me everything I didn't or should have done. I have explained to her often, "My job is stressful enough. I don't want to come home and be more stressed out. At least at work, I get paid to be stressed out, at home, I pay to be stressed. That is not what a man should come home to.

There is nowhere in the Bible where it says her job as my wife is to stress me out, find ways to add additional bills to my already long list or make "my home" feel and be a battlefield. It should be a place where I come to rest, relax and recuperate from the world. Lately, it has not been that. If I knew this was the basis of being married that I would have to deal with, I would have stayed single and just dated her. It seems that sometimes she knows I love her unconditionally, but for her to love me, it appears to be conditionally based on the things I provide for her, how is that fair to me to feel this way?

Mr. Pearson is speaking: What are you saying you want her to do?

Matthew is speaking: I am not asking her to be the breadwinner. I got that. What I am asking of her is to start by respecting my position as the man of the house. Stop coming at me daily as if I am not doing enough. Stop accusing me of doing things I haven't done and stop fighting me on everything I do as the provider in our best interest. I agree with you, and I will go forward and include her in any new plans or any changes that come up, but she needs to understand that HER way is not the only way. If I go with another option, it does not reflect that I don't love or respect her.

I am trying to show my wife love, and I have read **Ephesians 5:33**, (KJV), where it says, "Nevertheless let every one of you in particular so love his wife even as himself; and the wife see that she reverence her husband." and in **1 Corinthians 7:3**, (KJV), where it says, "Let the husband render unto the wife due benevolence: and likewise, also the wife unto the husband."

All I am asking for her to do is go back to what she had done before, which was to encourage me and say helpful things. Don't go by the fact that the Bible says I am to be a provider for you as the right to act a fool and be disrespectful. Occasionally say some encouraging words, appreciate me for me, talk to me like I am her husband and not her child, give me space, and acknowledge me as the "provider." She could get a whole lot more out of and from me with words such as "please and thank you." Ordering me around and acting a fool with me will get her nothing.

Mr. Pearson is speaking: It seems you have given this some thought.

Matthew is speaking: Yes, I have. Listening to you, I can and will say these changes could and may be partly my fault for not keeping her informed on everything I am doing all the time. I have given her no reason to doubt me, no reason to doubt that I cannot and would not provide for us. I am and should be more to her than just a "paycheck," her personal "ATM" or someone who is with her to take care of her and pay bills. I may be the provider, but she can help "bridge" the gap when a situation like me being out of work happens and not panic and act out. She can do more than have her hand out all the time. Honestly, I would like for her to treat me sometimes and make me feel she appreciates me for holding it down as I sometimes do, is that too much to ask?

Mr. Pearson is speaking: I feel you, and no, that is not a lot to ask of your wife.

Matthew is speaking: I am not rich. My check varies, but I make a good living to support us. I never told her we couldn't and wouldn't do extraordinary things. What I have said and still say is that there may be times when I would have to save for it beforehand. When I told her this, she replied, "It doesn't matter, and I do not care what you make, when I want something, I want it. I don't care how you do it. You need to do it."

Mr. Pearson is speaking: All the things that are happening in your household are the result of your household being out of alignment.

Matthew is speaking: What do you mean because I heard you mention *out of alignment* earlier?

Mr. Pearson is speaking: What seem to be daily matters and petty things are signs of your marriage being *out of alignment* with God's rules of marriage.

Matthew is speaking: Could you break that down, please.

Mr. Pearson is speaking: Yes, the Bible explains in full detail both parties' roles as it pertains to marriage. In a nutshell, the Bible says a woman is equal to her man in "being" but not in "function." In other words, you both are considered equal partners in the relationship, but your "roles" are not the same. It says in **Ephesians 5:22-24**, (KJV). Now, as you said, you are walking in a Christ-like manner, and it is your wife who is not, right? It is your job to help get her back in alignment to enjoy your marriage.

Matthew is speaking: I understand, but how?

Mr. Pearson is speaking: Listen to me and write this down because it is essential to understand why being out of alignment is not what God wants for you. Marriages that are out of alignment make it easier for the devil to create problems between you both, creating the opposite of what He wants for you. The devil knows it is God's plan for those who are married to be happy, and the devil also knows by you doing this, it brings you closer to Him. So, any opportunity he (the devil) has to create a division between you two, he will.

The devil loves those "pretend" Christians, who say they follow and know God's laws, but they are not. It makes his job more manageable. They have switched their roles, they are confused, mixed up and taken out of context the laws and understanding of marriage. Many people, who read the scriptures, only apply the ones they feel comfortable with. They dismiss the ones they think do not apply to them, meaning their everyday agenda. God's words don't describe marriage like that in **Ephesians 5:22-24**, (KJV).

Matthew is speaking: I remember reading that.

Mr. Pearson is speaking: Understand this, God covers Christ; Christ covers man and man covers woman. It is a man's job to make Him look good and the woman's job to make the man look good. Now, I understand your wife is rebelling right now, but I need for you to remember what is said in **1 Timothy 2:13**, (KJV), "For Adam was first formed, then Eve." And therefore, you must be the first one to say I am sorry. You must take the high road and fix what He has asked you to do. In other words, you must understand God blames you when your household is out of alignment, not her.

You see this in **1 Corinthians 11:8**, (KJV), "For the man is not of the woman; but the woman of the man." Meaning, issues and problems though they may not be your fault are your responsibility to fix and correct them and put them back in line with what He has created for marriage. He expects you to help her get back in alignment (as well as keep yourself in alignment). I know it's hard, but to fight the creation that God created for us is the same as fighting the creator who created it and you know you cannot win that fight, why try? He knew what He was doing when He created marriage.

Matthew is speaking: I understand, and I will do all I can.

Mr. Pearson is speaking: A Christian woman under the authority and in alignment sees and hears things from God's angel that will help you on your behalf. A rebellious wife out of alignment and refusing to come under authority will never receive any help from the angel He has assigned to help her. Meaning this, you both will miss out on your blessings.

I understand what you're saying because early on in our marriage, my wife and I had similar issues, questions and concerns. We learned it was common among married couples. We realized most couples have in their relationship conversations, "me and you" time, difficulties and stressful moments, as well as good physical and intimate moments which is the way God intended marriage to be between two people.

We sat and talked and shared our concerns with our pastor, Pastor James. He gave great advice. Like most people think and do, when we sat down our first time, it was clear we blamed one another for the problems we were having without understanding our underlying problem which was that we both caused our issues. He first spoke with us together and then, individually, to get a clear understanding of what we thought the problem was and to understand our views on what we each thought could be done to correct it. He reiterated that when done correctly, communication was the foundation stone of any healthy relationship, but like everything, it could also be misused if done incorrectly.

Our problem wasn't that we didn't communicate. It was the *way* we talked. My wife wanted to know everything I was thinking all the time but didn't feel she should do the same for me. I communicated, but I was selective of what I said and when I said it because there were some things she didn't need to know. Pastor James told us having some secrets are okay sometimes, but we shouldn't practice keeping them from our spouses on a regular basis because some secrets can cause a lot of damage if found out and taken out of context. He gave us this example and asked this question, "How surprising would a surprise party be if you knew about it?" In this case, not knowing shows your mate when she found out how much you thought and care you put into something for her. If he had told her what he had planned, it wouldn't have been such a "surprise" birthday party.

He gave advice, and I share this same advice with those couples I know who are having problems and issues to help them see things

409

can get better if you put forth the effort to make things better. He mentioned that when couples are having issues, they need to keep it within the home. Well, this causes a slight problem because until the couples "talk" to each other about their issues, who are they supposed to talk to if they want to vent and rant? He said first tell our Pastor and if our pastor is not available to speak to our best friend but no one else.

Of course, I asked why and he said, "I suggested your pastor or best friend because usually when couples are upset with one another, they tend to go to family members and vent. Although the family will listen, they are listening for dirt and something to gossip about to the other members of the family. The main mistakes many couples in situations like this do is take their anger out and say hurtful things about one another, not because they don't care about one another but because they are still mad at each other.

The information you put out there is like putting something on the internet. It is out there forever, once it is said. It is hard to be upset and angry at someone and keep most of what you dislike about them to yourself when you're hurting but we should. One of the things I've learned in my marriage is that you've got to be careful who you tell your business to. Everyone doesn't need to know everything about you or your business. You don't realize that those you're telling your business to are people who may want to help you but not before they report it to the world first. As the neighborhood report, they only gossip "your" news to anyone who will listen as if it is their responsibility to do so, with no regard to the damage it can cause you or your relationship. At the same time, giving you one-sided jaded advice, agreeing that you are the victim in the story, but in actuality, they are just trying to get more details from you that they can tell, thinking they are helping you. It is your fault because you brought them into a situation they should never have been a part of at all.

He made it clear. You cannot fix your "inside" issues, meaning *in* your home, "outside" your home. If your marriage isn't strong enough to withstand outside interference, it could create more problems between the two of you then what your original issues were. The only way to prevent this from happening is to know and follow what God has told you to do according to His Word. Remember and understand, God intended marriage to be a loving, monogamous relationship between one man and one woman exclusively. Though it is hard to do, you must "talk" and try and resolve your issues, concerns and problems within first before seeking outside professional help. Do not rely on friends and family to solve your problems.

By the end of our talks, we realized we needed to reevaluate the way "we" communicate in order to understand one another better, and it worked.

Matthew is speaking: Husbands, love your wives, even as Christ also loved the church, and give himself for it;" in **Ephesians 5:25**, (KJV), it is something I understand and am doing my best to do.

Mr. Pearson is speaking: That's great. As the "Head of Household" whether you are doing wrong or not, if she "feels" there is a problem, then to her there is. It is your job and responsibility to understand what is making her feel the way she does, help her work through it, and your responsibility to get her back in alignment with God and you.

Remember you can tell her anything, but if you include her, she will understand and feel she also has an investment in the relationship. If done correctly, she will stop yelling, stop acting out and stop coming at you with guns blazing. She will feel more secure with where you are leading her, that you are following the steps of a Christian man, and that you have her best interests at heart. I know we've talked a lot, but I hope all that was said was helpful.

Matthew is speaking: Yes, the information was beneficial. Mr. Pearson, I love my wife, and I will get our marriage back in alignment with what God wants us to do. Thank you for your help. I appreciate it all.

Mr. Pearson is speaking: Have a great day, Matthew. When we come back in our **Real Talk** segment, I have an email that I feel will help those out there going through a divorce. It is entitled, *"How do I deal with Divorce when I still love him?"*

I'm Ondray Pearson on K103! We are back. I got this email from a listener, and when I read it, I felt it was something worth sharing with others who are going through and feeling like there is no way out.

Dear Mr. Pearson:

My name is Evelyn. I was married to my husband, Chris, for 11 years. We have three children together. I have felt for years my husband and I were happy in our relationship, but something happened that confused me. Let me start at the beginning. My husband of 11 years came to me and said, out of the blue, he wanted a divorce. He gave no explanation and no reason why he wanted it. He just said he wanted out of the marriage. When he said this, I was shocked and at a loss for words. I didn't see it coming at all. I had no idea he had been thinking about this. My heart sank, and I broke down and cried. I didn't know what to say or do. I went through a list of emotions. I was hurt, upset, mad and confused. I couldn't believe it was happening. I asked him if it was something I had done and did this mean he didn't love me anymore? For some strange reason at that moment, I wanted to know how long he has felt this way. I felt whatever it was we could fix it. I wasn't ready to lose my husband of 11 years. I wanted to understand what was going on.

As he packed his things, he told me he had been unhappy for a while, but he had stayed as long as he did because of the children. He asked me, hadn't I noticed how he wasn't home as much? How we didn't spend time together or sleep together or talk like we used to? Chris said he knew by the way we interacted that something was wrong. So now he just needed to leave. He wasn't happy anymore and did not want to pretend anymore. I asked him, what about me, what am I supposed to do? I have been a stay-at-home mother throughout our marriage, and I have no money to support our children. He told me, "I still care for you. I will make sure you and the children are well taken care of. You will get a fair settlement. I am prepared to pay child support and alimony. You can keep the house and the rental property, and everything else we can work out later." When he left that first night, I lay in bed and just cried. I had no clue he was unhappy with me or that his love for me had changed. It hurt me to tell the kids their dad was leaving.

Anyway, it has been some ten months now, and I haven't spoken to him since I signed my divorce papers. I am still having a hard time wrapping my head around the fact that I am no longer married. I never thought I would get a divorce. I thought I would be married forever and that we would grow old together. I know it sounds crazy, but I am here today because I still have feelings for him, and I miss him sometimes. I know it has been ten months, but I am not over him yet. I still consider him, my friend.

We had not yet figured how to get along or coexist with being parents to our children. He calls every so often to check on the children. He seems to have moved on with his life. He doesn't even acknowledge or talk about it when we are around. I do not expect him, when he is around, to bring up what we shared, but it would be nice to know he enjoyed our time together.

I had always wondered "why" he had insisted on leaving so quickly that night and "why" he had no problem just packing and moving, but I found out my answer a year later. During one of our conversations about our children, he slipped up and said he had a child. He was a father again. He didn't tell me the age of the child. I just assumed he had only recently had a child. It wasn't something I wanted to hear. I surely didn't want to know he had a child with another. It had only been a year since our divorce. I asked my kids whether their dad had mentioned a new child to them and had they met the child. The kids said they met Jennifer, dad's girlfriend and their little brother, Devin. He was two years old and walking pretty good.

When they said two years old and walking pretty well, I started to think, "How could this child be two years old? Our divorce was just a year ago." The only way this could have happened is if he had cheated on me during our marriage. I couldn't believe what I was hearing. My heart sank once again if this was true. I thought I was over him, and listening to this made me mad. I fell back into a depression. It was bad enough going through the divorce and the fact we were no longer married anymore. Now I learned he cheated on me during our marriage. It was just too much for me to handle.

Ondray Pearson

I comforted him, and he told me the truth, surprisingly. He was supporting both of us at the same time. It was clear now Jennifer must have insisted he leave me because she was having his baby, and he did it with no regard as to how it would hurt me. He had the nerve to tell me Jennifer reminded him a little of me. He said we would get along great and could possibly be friends once we met. Hearing this mess coming from a man who had slept with another woman, had a child with her while we were still married, spending "our" money on another woman and lying to me the whole time, I just wanted to beat his....

I felt foolish for loving this man and giving him 11 years of my life. I feel blessed for the children we had, the only good thing, it turns out. He hurt me emotionally to my core. I felt so betrayed. Mr. Pearson, I need your advice and help to deal with this. I need to know what I should do to get past the feelings of betrayal, and I need to get my life back on track. I don't know what to do, where to turn or how to deal with all the emotions I am feeling right now. It has been a year, and it hurts even worse now hearing he cheated on me during our marriage. Can you help me, please?

Signed,
Hurt and Confused

Dear Hurt and Confused,

I felt your pain as I read your letter. I sympathize and understand what you have gone through. It is never an easy thing to deal with divorce. It is one of the most painful things our heart can experience. The process can seem overwhelming at times. During this time, you feel as if your world has turned upside down. It affects your daily routine and makes it very difficult to get through your workday and stay productive. Listen, I know my words can only help a little but know this, you are not alone. Many women (and some men) have gone through what you've been through or are going through it right now and regardless of the circumstances of who was right or wrong, divorce still hurts.

I know the pain you're feeling seems as if it will never go away, but things will change, and with time, you will be your old self again. It is normal at this time to feel sadness. Although it hurts, and you think your life has ended, it hasn't. It only means it is time for you to start a new chapter in your life. There is no quick fix for what you're going through, but there are a few things you can do to get through the difficult adjustment period.

During this time, you will experience and go through seven stages of emotions on your way back to rejoin the world. You mentioned you had experienced a few of them, but I would like to walk you through them, so you will recognize for yourself where you are right now with your emotions. They are Denial, Anger, Bargaining, Depression, Acceptance, Hope and Fulfillment. These are stages psychologists agree are part of the healing process. Let's explore them in a little more detail. Grab a pen because you will need to write them down, so you can review later.

1. Denial - This is the stage where you do your best to ignore or minimize what has happened, hoping it was all a dream or that it never happened at all.

2. Anger - This is the stage where you experience your most intense emotions. You will question and feel anxious about your future because venturing into the unknown can be frightening. To you, feeling sad, angry, confusion, useless, exhaustion and frustration at this time, is normal. In your situation, it is "normal" to experience these kinds of emotions.

3. Bargaining - This is the stage where after you feel the mixed emotions aren't solving the problems or the feelings of abandonment you're experiencing. You start looking for other solutions, and you're willing to compromise to put things back the way it was to end the pain you're feeling.

4. Depression - This is the stage where when holidays, an anniversary or birthdays come around and you start to see and feel what was, just isn't any more. Like we all do when someone we care for isn't there anymore, we begin to rerun old "good times" we used to have to make us feel good, but it hurts us more because we remember so much. It hurts worse when you're lying in bed alone and can't sleep.

5. Acceptance - This is the stage where you see the light at the end of the tunnel. You start giving yourself permission to feel and function again. At this stage, you believe, understand and know you can recover.

6. Hope - This is the stage when it is "evident" things are changing for you. You start to understand that you do not have to go through this alone. You're now taking care of yourself emotionally and physically. You're not making any major life decisions or changes. You're easing yourself back into the world. You're talking to more family and friends. You're thinking about and feeling you're ready to love again or at least that it is possible.

7. Fulfillment - This is the stage where you have moved on. You have pulled yourself together, got your life back on track. You're no longer thinking or living in the past.

With this information and your trust in God through your journey, you're able to come through and look back with no regrets or bad feelings toward your ex-husband. I know you feel down now as most people would, but you must understand that putting your life on hold will never allow you to live and grow. I suggest you keep the faith and believe in God, and you will recover from this sooner than later.

Do not try and do this by yourself. Ask Him for His help, and allow Him to help you. Remember what He said, "…. Behold, I make all things new" (**Revelation 21:5**, (KJV), and know He hears you, and He will help you. In other words, as He gives you a new future, you must refuse to trade it for the pain of your past. I hope my words help you through your situation. I know it is not easy, but you will get through this because you are not alone. He is always with those who believe in Him.

When we come back, I will give you your **Inspirational Vitamin**. We are back.

Your **Inspirational Vitamin** today is entitled **"Don't complain, be thankful!"**

Many of us do this often, knowing it changes nothing. People in society today complain about so many things like, what they don't have, what others have that they want or how life isn't fair for them when what they should be doing is thanking God for allowing them to wake up each morning to HAVE an opportunity to have anything. When things are right in our lives, those who believe in Him, thank Him, but when things go wrong, we question why God allowed this to happen to us. Why do we blame Him, and never blame Satan for our misfortunes or at least believe he could have been responsible? Why do we just blame Him first? It is because as humans with a minimal perspective on the things that happen to us in our lives, we need to blame someone and not ourselves.

We tend to forget sometimes that He will never give us more than we can handle. Just because we can't see His face, we need to know and feel His presence. Whatever we go through, He already knows. When unsettling things happen to us, this point often disappears from our minds. When the reason or purpose is done, that unclear moment becomes clearer and passes. My mother always told me, "When you think you got it bad, someone else is worse off than you." I didn't understand this until I read the story of Job in the Bible. Once you have read all he experienced, it will put whatever is going on with you in a new perspective quickly.

In the story of Job, he was known as a righteous man with good character. He was revered as the "greatest of all men of the east." He had it all, wealth, family and high status in his community. Through a challenge brought to Him from Satan, Job's faith in Him was put to the test. Satan said basically, "Only because you have done this for him, does he serves you." Implying that if He took the things Job had obtained from him, he would distrust, lose faith, curse Him to his face and renounce him.

Satan told Him Job didn't obey, fear or worship Him out of love and appreciation alone. Job served Him but out of his own selfish motives. He suggested to God testing his theory. The events to follow were a series of events that would "test" Job's faith in Him. Job during this process lost everything, his wealth, his children, his friends and even his health. In all this, Job sinned not, nor charged Him foolishly (**Job 1:22**, (KJV) nor in all this did Job sin, not even with his lips (**Job 2:10**, (KJV). Nevertheless, despite all that had happened to him, he remained faithful to Him. Job's wife's words in **Job 2:9**, (KJV), translated to him that he should "Curse God and die." His friends "insisted" what was happening to him was the result of his sins. Job insisted he had done nothing wrong, and there had to be a reason for this to happen to him.

To make a long story short, Satan tried everything he could to break Job's faith and trust in God. Even though Job questioned Him, he never broke or stopped believing at some point God would help him. Satan's plan had backfired. Instead of Job losing faith in Him, he only got closer and believed in him more. By the end of the story, you learn and see Job's reward for his faith and belief. God completely turned his life around. His health returned. He started a new family. His wealth returned, and he received more than he had before. Job ends up living a long and blessed life. It is a great example and situation where Job was what seemed down and out, and he didn't complain but remained faithful to God. Instead of complaining about what we don't have, we need to be grateful and give thanks to Him for what we do have. We should try to encourage others in similar situations and not focus on our problems.

It says in **1 Thessalonians 2:5**, (KJV), "For neither at any time used we flattering words, as ye know, nor a cloak of covetousness; God is witness:" In other words, even when we do not give thanks to Him by our words, we should have a grateful sense of His goodness in our hearts. He knows full well all our aims and purposes, as well as our actions and desires. It is from this He tests our hearts that we must receive our rewards. So, we must balance our criticisms of others with patience and praise.

Life has its ups and downs, and things don't always go our way. It is in these times that we need to learn to let go of things. We need not focus on our failures but more on our successes. We need not obsess on stuff we can't change but more on what we can influence in our own lives as well as others. When you feel the weight of the world is too much to carry or that you cannot do things alone or you're feeling you are losing control, turn to God. Ask Him for His help and allow Him to take control. You will see things work themselves out.

I heard it said, and I believe it, that there is power in prayer. We must pray on all occasions "good and bad," and understand complaining is nothing more than wasted energy. Praying to God allows Him the opportunity to energize our lives where we can live and not just exist while we're on this earth.

With that said, this was your **Inspirational Vitamin**.

My time is up for today. I hope the conversations today helped inspire you. Listen, our setbacks and failures in our lives are temporary. We should all view them as an opportunity to rebound to get it right. As you go through your day, remember, "If you set your eyes and heart on your destiny, you will not be in any danger of your history affecting your path. Be very aware that whatever you're investing yourself in, that is where your passion is." I will leave you today with a song by **Israel & New Breed**, *New Season*. Remember your past is not what your future holds. Anytime you put Him first in your life and allow Him to guide your steps, you will never go wrong. I am Ondray Pearson. Have a great rest of your day from me and those at K103!

Thanks to those who were inspirational in me getting this done:

I want to thank those people who made an impact on my life. First, let me thank my God in heaven for all that He has provided me. I know it is all because of Him I have been able to do the things I have done and continue to do. Thanks, **Tonya** - It has been a rough road for us both, and yet I wouldn't change it for anything in the world. I cannot thank you enough and tell you how much I appreciate how you took on my issues with cancer as a new wife and helped me through it when you didn't have to. I am glad you did. Thank you to my mother, **Joy Pearson** - What can I say? You have been a "Super Mom" to me ALL MY LIFE. I know growing up and still to this day, at times, I work your last nerve from all the mess I've gotten myself into, but despite whatever it has been, you have been there for me. The reason I've been able to grow and learn to be who I am today is because of your advice, guidance and love. I know I don't say it often as maybe I should, but I appreciate you praying for me, protecting me, loving me for who I am and believing in me when I had doubts in myself. In short, "I love you," and I know you love me.

To my little brother, **Danny Pearson** AKA "DP"/POP" - What can I say? At times, it seems you're the older brother, and I'm the younger one as much as you have helped me overcome situations I have been in and through all this time. You have always given me good advice and have been there for me. I can never pay you back for all you've done for me. I appreciate the fact that I can always count on you when I need you the most, and I hope you know you can count on me as well. Despite my craziness, you love me anyway, not because you have to but because you do. I love you too! **Martina** - You have raised our two beautiful and smart women known as our children. You've guided them and groomed them to be the intelligent, independent women they have become. For this, I applaud you and tell you that you've done a great job! You have been and always will be my friend. To **Chris** - Thank you for stepping in and doing your part with the girls, it's what real men do! To **Deja** (aka Deja boo), & **Nicole** (aka my twin, aka Nikki) - Nothing you two have accomplished thus far in your lives has surprised me at all, simply because I always knew you both would go far. You both continue to set the bar high and surpass it. I am glad to call you both my babies. As sisters, you both are great examples of what sisterhood should be. I know you both will continue to be successful in all you do. I love you both, and I hope both of you know this forever.

To my **Aunt Sherry** - You've always been more like a big sister than an aunt. You have often given me good advice when we've talked, and I love you for it. To my **Aunt Lula** - What can I say? You have always shown me love and looked out for me over the years. I want to say thank you, and I love you. Keep your business going and know I am here to do whatever I can for you. Family members I've not mentioned, I love you too! To **Yolanda Jones** - You know we have seen and been through a lot over the years in the "Pink House." We may have been apart for a while, but as a family does, we found our way back to each other. You have said many times that I was your hero for beating cancer, but honestly, you are and always have been my hero just for being yourself. For all you have been through to be where you are now, I am proud of you and glad to be a part of your life.

To **Joe T.** - Man, you have been like a brother to me for a long time. I value our friendship. Who could forget the "Chill Crew"? I'm glad you are a part of my life. Love you, man. **Linda and the Family** - You've been more like another aunt than my friend. You know I appreciate you. I thank you for all your support during my time of need. To **Gordon and Jackie** - You are the sweetest and funniest people to be around. You both brighten up a room whenever you set foot in it. I'm glad I can call you both my friends. **Gordon** - The Falcons need help. Possibly, if they played by themselves, they might win. Let's hope they get back to the Super Bowl and win it this time. We don't need another 25-point meltdown.

Cedric - (Go Ravens!) You have been a true friend to me since we first met at AT&T. You've helped me out when I needed the most help. So I say, "Thank you." You're much appreciated. I'm glad you're my friend. FYI: No more chasing big booty women. Settle down and be happy. You deserve it. **Erik/Anna -** (Go Giants!) Erik, you have been a good friend to me since we met and worked together at PNC Bank. **Adrienne -** I will always remember our time together. We had some good times. You know where you stand with me *(smile)*. I appreciate you pushing for me to go to the doctor. You saved my life, and I will forever be grateful. **Lacey Seabrook -** "My friend" (and we should have been more *(smile)*. You are still someone I can hang out with in Detroit. **Prema -** You know you're like a little sister to me from the day we first met. I hope I have been a good big brother to you. I value your friendship, and I am glad we met. **Rodney -** (Go Steelers!) Man, you have continued to be a good friend to me. Remember I'm here to help you with your business ventures when you need it. **Tia Sheffield -** I admire your business skills. Don't forget. When you become a millionaire, I need a job! To my friend, **Tonsie -** We can only wonder what could have been, but regardless I'm glad you're my friend.

To all my **Westover family -** (Go Wolverines!) **James Caldwell -** I always knew you would do something in music. Keep up the good work, and remember Price forever! **Michael King -** Still the best damn drummer on the planet. **Reggie Pelt -** It's time for us to record our next project. **Trina Butts -** You are the one woman that got away. **Jeff Phillips IV** and **Danny Simmons -** When is our upcoming tour? **Nancy France -** Still fine! You know I always wanted to get with you. **Taurus Martemus -** It's time for a Chill Crew reunion. **Yolanda Katrina Heath -** What a great time we shared! Wherever you are, please know I will never forget our years together. I love you still, and **Melvin Payne -** Rappers today have nothing on you. You're still the best. To those not mentioned, I didn't forget you, I just ran out of space. Let's all keep staying in touch on Facebook, okay? **Alisa Head -** Who would have ever thought we would live so close together? **Stacey Fulcher -** How is your Pink Panther doing without me *(smile)*.

Anastasia - What a first date! I will never forget it. **Kelvin McNeill** aka the "Mack man" - It is time for you and Pop to do a new show. Fayetteville State University is waiting! **Reginald Pearson** - What's up! **Paula Ridgeway** - We left something special on the table. I wish I could have gotten you out of Saint Louis. Man, what we could have been together. **R.I.P. to Craig, Diana, Jerome, and James Brannon**.

To my **SunTrust family - Narinder** - You have always been kind to me from day one. You're a good person, and I am glad to call you my friend. I am trying to put in 20 plus years like you, girl. **Carlan Burke** - Listen, I need a credit card machine. Man, you are the *coolest* person I know. We must hang out more. **Maria** - You helped me a lot when I came on to the job. I appreciate that. **Jessica** - I am glad we had a little time to work together. I enjoyed working with you. **Alyssa** - It is time to get you your million-dollar position. When I hit it big, you got a job with me, okay? **Hansanee** - You're free! Thank Goodness! **Reena** - When I get my millions, I need you and **Richard** to invest it well for me, okay? **Humberto** - It is time to take your business bigger. **Angela** - You are one of the most helpful people to have as a friend. **Ghada** - You have shown me nothing but love and kindness without judging me from the day I started working with you. You are a good person, for real. I hope the final version of the book is better than the drafts you thoughtfully read for me. I see you more as family than just my friend. I thank you. You are my biggest fan! **Rihanna** - Girl you need to come back to the platform, you can sell! **Sharif** - You are like my little brother. **Khurram** - You are a good person and friend. **Z** - It's time to get a new job. The one you want. **Joann** - Thank you for getting me back in the game, I miss you! Andrew, it is time to invest and make me millions. **Michael** - Please help **Andrew**. **Kevin** - I need a beautiful but affordable home, okay? With no down payment *(smile)*. Thank you for all your help after I left. I appreciate it more than you know. Oh, I have not forgotten I owe you lunch. **Rick**, **Melissa**, and **Scott** - (my trainers) You were there showing me what I needed to do to be successful in this business. It is because of you that I have succeeded, thank you!

Jennifer, Jolly and **Patricia** aka Doc *(smile)* - Thank you, ladies, so much for listening to me ramble about this book. Your feedback and understanding helped me see what I thought I knew differently. It helped me a lot. You have and will always be good friends of mine. **Tyrone Pryor** and **Trabien Shivers** - You guys are like my younger brothers, and we will always be those guys singing our hearts out as "Revilo" out of Greenville, North Carolina. Yes, I still have my copy of "Smile." A reunion and do-over is in order soon! To all my family I haven't mentioned - You know I love you all! To friends and family, for those, I haven't listed, I didn't forget you. I just ran out of space, but I love you all.

To my **PASDAC family** (Pennsylvania Avenue Seventh Day Adventist Church) - You all have made me feel like family from the first day I attended. You've shown me nothing but kindness and love, thank you. A special thanks goes out to **Pastor James, Sr.**- Thank you for taking the time to listen to my wife and me about our concerns. Your advice helped a lot. I appreciate it. To **Ms. Virginia Logan** - You have been like my other mother. You've treated me like a son of yours. You have always had nothing but kind words to say when we talk. I value your friendship, and I hope I am worthy of yours. Your kind words helped me in my time of need. **Greg Logan** - You are like the Uncle I never had. A good person from day one. I thank you for attending our wedding and being there for me (and my wife) during my surgery. You are a true friend. For the rest of my **PASDAC family (not listed)** you are all special to me, and I love you all. I appreciate you and wouldn't want to be anywhere else. To **Pastor Quinn**, at **The Breath of Life** church, thank you for preaching and sharing real information.

****All scriptures used where indicated were taken from the King James Bible and the Apocrypha.** ***All information used, the advice provided, comments, and responses on various subjects and situations talked about are the creation of the author for educational and entertainment purposes.

Printed in the United States
By Bookmasters